THE SILENT DEAD

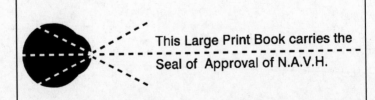

This Large Print Book carries the
Seal of Approval of N.A.V.H.

THE SILENT DEAD

TETSUYA HONDA

Translated by Giles Murray

THORNDIKE PRESS
A part of Gale, Cengage Learning

GALE
CENGAGE Learning·

Farmington Hills, Mich • San Francisco • New York • Waterville, Maine
Meriden, Conn • Mason, Ohio • Chicago

GALE
CENGAGE Learning®

Copyright © 2006 by Tetsuya Honda.
Thorndike Press, a part of Gale, Cengage Learning.

LIBRARY OF CONGRESS CATALOGING-IN-PUBLICATION DATA

Names: Honda, Tetsuya, 1969– author.
Title: The silent dead / by Tetsuya Honda.
Other titles: Sutoroberī naito. English
Description: Waterville, Maine : Thorndike Press, 2016. | Series: Thorndike Press large print mystery
Identifiers: LCCN 2016036937| ISBN 9781410495099 (hardcover) | ISBN 1410495094 (hardcover)
Subjects: LCSH: Women detectives—Japan—Fiction. | Murder—Investigation—Fiction. | Large type books. | GSAFD: Mystery fiction.
Classification: LCC PL871.O64 S8813 2016b | DDC 895.63/6—dc23
LC record available at https://lccn.loc.gov/2016036937

Published in 2016 by arrangement with St. Martin's Press, LLC

Printed in Mexico
1 2 3 4 5 6 7 20 19 18 17 16

JAN 1 7 2017

CAST OF CHARACTERS

TMPD, Unit 10:

Reiko Himekawa — Lieutenant and squad leader, Homicide Division, Tokyo Metropolitan Police Department

Tamotsu Ishikura — Sergeant, Himekawa's squad

Kazuo Kikuta — Sergeant, Himekawa's squad

Junji Otsuka — Officer, Himekawa's squad

Kohei Yuda — Officer, Himekawa's squad

Mamoru Kusaka — Lieutenant and squad leader

Haruo Imaizumi — Captain, head of Unit 10

Hiromitsu Ioka — Senior Officer, Kameari precinct

Kensaku Katsumata — Lieutenant and squad leader, Unit 5, Homicide Division,

Tokyo Metropolitan Police Department

Noboru Kitami — Lieutenant, fast-track trainee, assigned to the Kameari precinct

Hashizume — Director, Homicide Division, Tokyo Metropolitan Police Department

Wada — Chief of Homicide Tokyo Metropolitan Police Department

Komine — Lieutenant, Criminal Identification Bureau, Forensics

Sadanosuke Kunioku — coroner, Tokyo Medical Examiner's Office

NOTE

100,000 yen is approximately equal to 850 US dollars or 750 Euros

Carlsbad City Library

Georgina Cole Library
1250 Carlsbad Village Drive
Carlsbad, CA 92008
Phone: (760) 602-2019
www.carlsbadlibrary.org

Checked Out Items 10/4/2018 14:47
XXXXXXXXXX9344

em Title	Due Date
1245008209953	10/25/2018
tar wars, the Cestus deception : a Clone Vars novel	
1245011157660	10/25/2018
he silent dead	
1245008672069	10/25/2018
lalo : contact harvest	

Amount Outstanding: $1.00

eceipt required for lost item refund within
  months.
Monday - Thursday: 9 - 9 pm
riday and Saturday: 9 am to 5 pm
Sunday: 1 pm to 5 pm

PART I

A putrid rain was falling, turning the whole world gray.

I knew what was really out there in front of my eyes. The passing taxi that was sending up a curtain of muddy water from the potholed street was green. The umbrella that the little school kid was holding was red. I looked down at my shoulder. I could see that my navy blue school blazer had turned black in the rain. My mind recognized the colors — but my heart couldn't *feel* them.

My perception is monochrome. Not like a black-and-white photo, though. It's got none of those soft edges, or depth, or sense of reality. It's more like a crappy watercolor, a meaningless shadowy blur. Spilt ink on a sheet of white paper — that's the gray universe where I live.

The flimsy prefab house was old and its walls rain-blackened. The front door was unlocked. I pushed it open in silence. Straightaway a sour stink invaded my body. I'm not imagining things. The house itself was sick, rotten.

Leaking sewage. A rank, animal odor. A thick, musty atmosphere. Mold on every surface — the floor, the walls, the ceiling. Living in that vile place was enough to destroy anyone's sense of smell. Sadly, mine still worked. And the stink was rotting me from the inside out.

"That you?"

The voice gurgled like sludge oozing from a drainpipe. It came from the dimly lit living room at the end of the passage. It was about as welcome as a cockroach burrowing into my brain. I covered my ears. I did not reply.

"I'm talking to you, shit-for-brains."

A shadow reared up and blocked the living room doorway.

He'd gotten dressed in my honor. He wore a sleeveless running shirt. It looked gray to me; in reality it was probably brown. Otherwise he was naked. Everything in this place was foul. Dirt and ugliness was my world.

"Didn't you fucking hear me?"

Enjoying yourself, are you? Is bullying me really so much fun? Just because you're my dad, you think you've got the right to make my life hell. You've been kicked out of your gang and hightailed it back here with a load of drugs you probably stole. You may think it's fun to see which will hold out longer — your decaying body or the supply of drugs you're stuffing it with. But it's got nothing to do with me. Nothing.

"Get over here," he growled.

He grabbed me by the hair, same as always, and dragged me into the room. My mom, covered in sores, was sprawled on the ripped-up couch with the sticking-out springs.

Her eyes swiveled toward me. She recognized me but didn't lift a finger. I didn't want or expect her help. Still, it'd be nice if she could at least manage to *look* a teeny bit upset. Her scrawny arms were black and pitted with track marks. *Come on, Mom, I'm being abused here. Can't you manage a teeny-weeny frown?*

"This one's for you."

His thick palm smacked the bridge of my nose. It knocked me off my feet and onto the floor.

"Yee-haw."

He straddled me, panting and laughing like a maniac.

That again?

I wondered where he got the strength. A

washed-up two-bit gangster, he'd never even tried to support his family. He was so busy being perverted, most of the time he forgot to eat. The guy was sinking in a swamp of drugs and filth, but he was still as strong as a horse.

My uniform tore. Probably where I'd sewn it up the day before yesterday. Tomorrow I'd have to go to school in my tracksuit.

None of my classmates would speak to me. Same with the teachers. They all kept their distance. Because I stank; I stank bad enough to make them gag. Still, I was grateful that the school let me in at all. It was somewhere to escape to in the daytime at least.

My seat was right at the back of the classroom. They'd made a space for me by shifting a locker full of cleaning stuff out of the corner a little way. I sat wedged in between the locker and the window. During lessons I could only see half the blackboard, and the teachers never asked me any questions. At school I was alone all day. I didn't care. It was nothing compared to the hell I went through at home.

Every day was the same. My clothes were ripped, and I was punched and kicked. I was throttled and my face shoved into the floorboards.

And with every passing day, I was losing my ability to see color, my ability to taste food, even my ability to speak. The only thing I never lost was the ability to smell the foul stink of it all. My father wasn't the only one sinking into the swamp. I was the same. I was going down with him. I knew he could kill me at any time. I don't know why, but it never occurred to me to take my own life.

Someday my life is going to change.

I was sure of that. I didn't know how. I just knew that someday something would change.

Today was that day.

On the floor, right in front of me, I noticed something that looked like a squashed pen. It was plastic, pretty, baby-pink. The tip was silver, and the other end was white. It loomed up toward me like something from a 3D movie. The cheap box cutter that had slipped out of my breast pocket.

"What the fu— !"

He looked down at me in bewilderment. He had no idea what had happened. He was clutching at his throat. From between his fingers, red blood was pumping out, spraying all around the room. Red — that brilliant, vibrant red — poured all over me and drenched me like glorious Technicolor rain.

Perhaps the world is not gray after all!

He grunted and groaned as he rolled on the floor. He looked like he was about to burst into tears.

That's funny. I always assumed he wanted *to die.*

I looked at the box cutter in my hand.

That was a whole lot easier than I thought it would be.

"He-he . . . help me!"

Fixing me with a look of terror, he dragged himself to the far side of the room. *Duh, you think the wall's gonna save your life?* He finally made his way to the couch where Mom was sprawling. He grabbed one of her feet and gave it a shake.

"He-he . . . help me, please."

He looked back at me from time to time as he tugged at her. Mom just gawped dreamily down at her own feet. Didn't move a muscle to help him. Minutes passed. His pleas for help became incoherent. The eyes, which looked at me with terror, gradually became as dim and bleary as my mom's.

"Beautiful," I murmured.

Everything was red now. The blood had transformed my dreary gray life into a place of brilliant, vivid color. My dark, stinking nothingness was a brave new world.

Freedom.

The word just popped into my head.

My mom — my putrid, grungy mom — had been spray-painted a beautiful scarlet. I just stared at her. Then the color slowly started to fade. Blood blackens as it dries.

Oh God, I don't want everything to go back to gray again!

In a momentary panic, I slashed the box cutter across my mother's throat.

The pigsty of a house was burning. A red redder even than blood came billowing out the windows. Thick and surly black smoke hung heavily over the scene, as if a dark cloud had swallowed the whole neighborhood. Through the haze, I caught a glimpse of a streetlight like a full moon beneath a veil of cloud.

The firefighters came and tried to put out the fire. Clouds of white smoke shot up every time they trained their hoses at the house. I was watching from behind a hedge in the park a little way away. I couldn't be certain, but it looked like they weren't putting much of a dent in the fire. It was burning as fiercely as ever, despite all their efforts. I liked that.

A fire that fierce was sure to reduce both bodies to ashes. It wouldn't be too hard for the police to find out that the man had been

17

an addict. They'd probably conclude that he'd gone crazy and killed himself and his wife. It was perfect. I was free from that bastard. I had sidestepped my destruction at his hands.

"I've got to go now . . . I want you to forget what happened today. No, strike that. I want you to forget *everything* that's happened in your life so far. Let it go. Make a fresh start."

I nodded. That was what I planned to do. It didn't make saying good-bye any easier.

"Can't we see each other?"

"Better not."

"Never?"

"Not never, but for a while . . ."

Am I going to be alone again?

Black smoke. White smoke. Bright streetlights. The pitch-black park. I could feel myself slipping back, down into my old gray world.

1

Tuesday, August 12
Otsuka, Bunkyo Ward, Tokyo

Reiko Himekawa was in a restaurant not far from the Tokyo Medical Examiner's Office, having lunch with the coroner, Sadanosuke Kunioku.

"Burning a dead body until it's completely carbonized isn't such an easy thing to do, is it?"

Reiko was having tempura with her chilled noodles. Kunioku had gone for the more basic option. She felt a bit guilty, knowing that today was Kunioku's turn to pay. Still, it wouldn't make sense to come here and not try the tempura. That was what this place was famous for.

Kunioku slurped appreciatively as he tipped broth from his bowl into his mouth.

"No, it's not. When an amateur tries to get rid of a body by burning it, the body usually ends up in the boxer stance."

19

Reiko had heard of the boxer stance. Some people called it the pugilistic posture. It was a phenomenon caused by the flexor muscles and protractor muscles contracting at different rates due to heat. The back rounded out, and all four limbs pulled tight to the body.

Plenty of killers tried to dispose of their victims by burning the bodies. However, fully carbonizing a human body without a large furnace was all but impossible. If they tried burning a body on a patch of empty ground, the body rigidifying into the boxer stance was actually the best possible outcome. In the worst-case scenario, the body actually expanded in the heat. The heat of the fire also served to harden internal tissue structures, resulting in less overall postmortem change. Whichever way you sliced it, it wasn't a very smart way to dispose of a corpse.

Passing off a murder victim as the unfortunate result of an accidental fire wasn't easy either. Since dead people didn't breathe, they didn't ingest any smoke; the resulting absence of soot in the windpipe was something an autopsy could easily uncover. At that point, it became clear that the victim was dead before the fire started, whether murdered or from natural causes.

Burning the body of someone who had died from natural causes was an infringement of Article 190 of the law. "Destruction of a corpse" was a criminal offense.

"I recently worked on a fully carbonized body," continued Kunioku. "It was actually a tragic case — a child who'd fallen into an incinerator. It wasn't easy, but I managed to establish that the kid was still alive when he went into the flames. I wasn't able to determine whether it was an accident or not, though I heard that the local police decided to call it an accidental death in the end."

Reiko and Kunioku lunched together once or twice a month. They went to all sorts of places — fancy French restaurants, back-street grilled-chicken joints, ramen noodle bars — but the topic of conversation was the same whatever the venue: bizarre deaths.

Their last get-together had been at a smart Indian restaurant. Kuniko had talked about *Naegleria fowleri,* a parasitic amoeba that bred in bodies of fresh water during the summer months. The amoeba went directly into the brain via the nasal cavity, where it propagated, consuming the brain and reducing it to mush. Japan's second-ever death connected to *Naegleria fowleri* had recently been recorded in Tokyo.

21

That particular case had been an accidental death resulting from infection, but Reiko and Kunioku had discussed the feasibility of using the amoeba for murder. Kunioku had mentioned something about testing the water quality of the lakes and ponds in Tokyo. Reiko wondered how that turned out.

Kunioku poured a little more broth into his bowl.

"It was just too awful. The parents were young and half out of their minds from grief. To make things even worse, we discovered that the kid had fallen into the incinerator because of his old grandfather's carelessness."

Reiko nodded. She glanced up at the mop of tousled gray hair that made Kunioku look so much older than he actually was. There was something inherently comical in his referring to anyone else as an "old grandfather."

Still, Reiko always enjoyed her dates with the old man. He had vast experience as a coroner.

Coroners were experts in unnatural death. They dealt on a daily basis with whatever fell into the gray area between death while receiving medical treatment and straightforward homicide — accidental death, sudden death, death from sickness at home, suicide, murder tricked out as suicide, and murder tricked out as natural death. For a detective like Reiko, everything that Kunioku talked about was fascinating.

He turned on her with a mischievous glint in his eye.

"Got yourself a man yet, sweetheart?"

She almost choked on her noodles.

"Oh no. Not you too."

"Me too? What do you mean?"

Reiko snorted, her mouth a tight, straight line of scorn. "I mean you plus my father, my mother, and my aunt. My aunt's the worst of the lot. *You're already thirty, Reiko. You can't keep playing cops and robbers forever, you know.* I'll be thirty next year — that's a fact — but that 'cops and robbers' stuff is going too far. She's even started setting me up on dates with prospective husbands on my days off. *Pushy* isn't the word for the damn woman."

Kuniko chuckled gleefully. "So? How did the dates go?"

Reiko grinned back. "So far this year, I stood two of them up and left one in the lurch when I got called to a crime scene mid-date."

They both laughed loudly. When the hot soba broth was served, Reiko poured a generous amount into her bowl. It was perfect timing. The air conditioning in the restaurant was a little strong. It felt good when she came in off the street, but now she was feeling chilly.

"Hey, doctor," she began, putting her bowl back down. "Why do you invite me out to lunch like this?"

Kunioku put his bowl down too.

"I get to have lunch with my angel. I enjoy being with you."

"Like being with a grandchild?"

"Ouch! No, like being with a girlfriend."

"My turn to say 'ouch.' "

Kunioku pulled a weepy face.

"You're going to break my heart. . . . Anyway, one-sided love is good enough for me at my age."

"How about your job? You've been doing postmortems on unnatural deaths for decades. Do you still enjoy it?"

"Absolutely. Even now, I still learn something new every day. Forensic pathology isn't like clinical medicine. It doesn't advance by leaps and bounds. We don't have miraculous breakthrough drugs and amazing medical devices. All we have is the data we accumulate through performing countless autopsies, and the instincts and perceptiveness that come with experience. Experience isn't something that can be acquired overnight. That keeps all the ambitious youngsters below me at bay. The job's a perfect fit for an old lazybones like me."

Kunioku picked up his bowl again. The back of his hand was mottled with liver spots of different sizes. "The pay's not great. That's the only fly in the ointment. After all, I'm an employee of the Tokyo municipal government. If I had my own practice, I'd probably be able to live a little better. Frankly, though, I'm more than content with this life of mine, plying my scalpel to communicate with the silent dead — and having lunch with you from time to time."

Reiko secretly saw Kunioku as the grandfather — no, that wasn't fair — as the uncle she'd never had. She liked the way he was prepared to come out and say that he enjoyed a job that would have most people running for the hills.

As a cop, she wanted to be like that, too.

She'd made lieutenant at the unusually young age of twenty-seven, despite not being on the management fast track. Soon after that, she'd been tapped by the Tokyo Metropolitan Police Department and was made a squad leader in the Homicide Division.

A young woman lieutenant — younger

than many of her subordinates — working Homicide got tongues wagging. Inside the department, there were plenty of people ready to grumble about her being a "little miss" who "just knew how to ace tests." Whenever she messed up, her colleagues judged her far more harshly than they did her male counterparts. Everyone talked pointedly about "the unbridgeable gap between exams and real-life experience." Within earshot, naturally.

The working environment was hardly comfortable, but it never even crossed Reiko's mind to put in for a transfer. She was proud to be a detective and couldn't conceive of doing anything else. Like Dr. Kunioku, she wanted to be able to say, hand on heart, that she enjoyed her work. Luckily, she got on well with the men in her squad. That was largely thanks to her direct boss, Captain Haruo Imaizumi, head of Unit 10, who was responsible for bringing Reiko into Homicide in the first place. She had a superior officer and subordinates she could trust. That made her one of the lucky ones.

With all the grief her family gave her for not being married, these days she had more stress to deal with outside of her job. Next year she'd hit thirty. Still living at home, she would graduate from a "singleton" to an "over-the-hill." The time was coming when she wouldn't be able to laugh off their criticisms any longer.

After working on a stalker homicide case in Itabashi, she'd spent the three days' leave she'd wangled at the family home in Minami-Urawa. Not a relaxing time. Now she was on standby at the Tokyo Metropolitan Police Department HQ in central Tokyo, waiting to be called in on a case. If nothing came in today, it would be her sixth day just cooling her heels. No murders was good news for society at large but bad news for Reiko, who ended up spending more time stuck at home with her parents. If nothing came up, she'd have to traipse back to Minami-Urawa again tonight. Maybe it was because her neuralgia was acting up, but recently her mum seemed to be more hostile than ever.

Please, God, give me something to do!

No, God wasn't in the business of doling out work to homicide detectives. Murderers were the people who sent jobs her way.

"Hey, darling, anyone home?" No sooner were the words out of Kunioku's mouth than the cell phone in Reiko's breast pocket started to vibrate. She pulled it out with glee. It was the TMPD.

"Himekawa speaking."

"It's me. Where are you?"

It was Captain Imaizumi of Unit 10.

"I'm having lunch with a friend."

"With Dr. Kunioku? You available?"

"Yes."

"Good. Kusaka's been rushed to hospital with acute appendicitis."

Mamoru Kusaka, like her, was a lieutenant in the Tenth with a squad under his command. He was also Reiko's second least–favorite person in the universe. There was no love lost between their squads. The news of his appendicitis actually brought a smile to her lips.

"You mean we get to step in?"

"That's right. I may need to bring in Katsumata too. We'll see how things go."

Lieutenant Kensaku Katsumata was a squad leader from Fifth. In the department, though, his nickname was Stubby. Everyone referred to his team, which was made up of intel experts, as Homicide's Public Security Bureau. Joining forces with them would be bad news for Reiko. They'd suck up any leads that she and her boys dug up and give them nothing in return. That's how they operated. Even with a head start, Reiko's team would need to be careful not to have a march stolen on them.

28

"I understand. We'll try to work fast."

"The crime scene's in Kanamachi. The local police station is Kameari. Here's the address."

Reiko jotted down the details in her notebook and consulted her watch. She'd need just under an hour to get to the place.

"I'll be there before three."

"Good. I'm heading over there now myself."

She clapped her cell phone shut. Kunioku was smiling at her.

"You look like the cat who got the cream."

Did she? Macabre though it was, nothing gave her as much pleasure as heading out to a crime scene.

"No, it's just — I'm just thinking that this case saves me from having to go home to my misery-guts parents' place."

She wasn't ready to go all out and admit to being happy.

2

Tuesday, August 12, 2:37 P.M.

Reiko got off the train at Kanamachi station and hopped on a bus heading north. She checked the address of the crime scene and saw that the body had been found very close to Mizumoto Park. The park was next to a flood control basin.

Smothering heat enveloped her the instant she got off the bus and momentarily stopped her in her tracks. Something cold and nauseous welled up inside her. She hated summer. It brought back memories of that awful night. That summer when she was seventeen.

It's okay. You're not in high school anymore.

Reiko forced the demons down. That was her old self. Just memories. She was weaker then. It had gotten easier over the years. She was more able to keep those memories at bay, particularly since making lieutenant. That she was a police officer, and the pride she felt in her rank helped her stay in control.

These damn freckles I get in the summer are a much more serious problem now.

She gave a toss of her chin and held her handkerchief over her eyes like a sun visor. The gesture was of little practical use, but it made her feel better. Although this neighborhood was within the twenty-three wards that made up Tokyo, there were fewer tall buildings this far out. That meant less shade — and more sweltering heat.

She crossed the main thoroughfare and caught a glimpse of water — it looked like a river — through the railings. That had to be the inner reservoir. It was nothing more than a triangular fishing pond ringed with concrete. Twenty or so rowboats — probably for fishing — were moored along the bank, the paint peeling on all of them. No one was actually fishing.

Normal enough on a weekday afternoon.

As she walked along the pond, she spotted the police on the far side. Why weren't there any police cars? Had they all parked somewhere else? She walked over to the scene.

METROPOLITAN POLICE. KEEP OUT.

The familiar yellow tape blocked her path. The uniformed officer on guard gave her a skeptical look as if to ask, *Who's this damn woman?*

"Afternoon, Lieutenant."

Officer Yuda, one of her subordinates, hailed her from over the uniformed officer's shoulder. "Lieutenant! Over here!"

"Yuda? You got here quickly."

The uniform now realized he had a lieutenant from the Metropolitan Police on his hands. The condescending look vanished. Suddenly he was all respect. The change was almost too obvious.

Reiko took her time as she ducked under the tape he was holding up for her.

That's what I love about an organization with a tight chain of command.

The police force, like the army, had a strict hierarchy. It had nine levels, and from the bottom up, they were officer, sergeant, lieutenant, captain, superintendent, senior superintendent, chief superintendent, superintendent supervisor, and superintendent general. A local police commander was the equal of a division head at the National Police Agency, while the director of any major department at the Metropolitan Police outranked the chief of any of the smaller prefectural headquarters. This system made it clear who had seniority and enabled the rapid establishment of a chain

32

of command. In this case, the Kameari precinct, which was the local police station, and the Metropolitan Police, the citywide police force in Tokyo, were going to set up a joint task force, and it would run like clockwork.

The badge on the left side of his chest indicated that the officer was two ranks below her. Age, gender, looks, experience, character — none of that mattered. Reiko outranked the man. That was that. She loved the sheer certainty of it.

Once you made lieutenant, the police force became an almost agreeable place to work. Reiko had to work twice as hard to get there, but her efforts paid off when she made lieutenant at only twenty-seven. She had no qualms about pulling rank. She'd earned her place, owed nothing to connections, and there was no reason to hold back.

Following Yuda, she strode over to the crime scene. She guessed that the plainclothes officers standing around were from the Kameari Precinct Major Crimes Squad. She didn't recognize any of them. She was getting some stares, but she decided to ignore them. Introductions could wait.

"Where's everyone?" Reiko asked Yuda, without turning her head.

"Everyone" meant her squad, which was

part of Unit 10. Four men worked for Reiko: the forty-seven-year-old Sergeant Tamotsu Ishikura; Sergeant Kazuo Kikuta, thirty-two; Officer Junji Otsuka, twenty-seven; and, last but not least, Officer Kohei Yuda, twenty-six.

"Ishikura and Kikuta are making the rounds with the Mobile Unit. As for Otsuka . . ."

Yuda gestured.

Otsuka was standing at the edge of the pond about twenty yards up the lane. A blue tarp, strung between the railings on the left and a utility pole on the right, blocked the way.

So that's where the body was found.

At this stage, the forensics team from the Met was probably still inside the makeshift tent. Officer Otsuka came over to them, running down the walkway.

"Good to see you, Lieutenant," he panted, nodding at Reiko.

"How's it looking?"

"They'll be done any minute now."

"Which team is it?"

"Komine's crew."

Lieutenant Komine, of the Criminal Identification Bureau, rubbed Reiko the wrong way, but he was experienced and good at his job.

"What's the state of the body?"

"Well, that's . . ." Otsuka shot a glance at Yuda, then turned back to Reiko.

"It'd be quicker if you had a look for yourself, Lieutenant."

"Really? Then let me do just that."

Reiko walked over and down a pathway marked out in yellow tape. Her men followed. On either side, forensic investigators from the local precinct and the Met were down on their haunches, hunting for the tiniest piece of evidence. The investigators from the Metropolitan Police all nodded at her. The blank and leery stares she got were all from the local police.

They stopped in front of the blue tarp.

"Lieutenant Komine, this is Reiko Himekawa from Homicide. Can we come in?"

A pause.

"I guess so," replied a low and sluggish voice from inside.

Reiko parted the tarp and peered inside.

At first glance, it looked as if it was empty except for the forensics team. She couldn't see a body. Taking a more careful look, she spotted a bundle wrapped in blue plastic sheeting about the size of an average adult.

She stepped into the tent, looking over at the blue bundle.

"Is that our body?"

"Yup."

"Why is it wrapped up with sheeting?"

"Search me. Only the perp knows that."

"Sorry?"

"Only the killer knows why he bothered to giftwrap the victim."

"The body was in this condition when it was dumped here?"

"Not exactly. It was tied tight with plastic cord — at either end, then around the neck, the elbows, the waist, and the knee area. Other than that, yes, it was like this."

A young investigator was holding up the cord, plastic and white, that Komine was talking about. They'd cut it off and rolled it into a ball.

Reiko took a step forward. "Could I have a look?"

"Be my guest." Sullenly, Komine peeled back the sheet to reveal the corpse. The body was a welter of different colors, a camouflage pattern of white, red, brown, black, and purple blotches against the blue of the tent.

Reiko grimaced involuntarily.

"That's quite something," she said.

"Yeah, and take a whiff of it. He's pretty ripe."

Reiko took a closer look at the body. It was completely naked; clearly male.

36

Midthirties, around five feet six, medium build. Innumerable small lacerations on the face and the upper body. The blood from the cuts had dried, caking the whole body in a reddish-black crust. There were multiple contusions and abrasions, and several of the cuts had something glittering embedded in them. None of them, however, appeared to be fatal. The fatal wound was probably the one to the throat — the left carotid artery was sliced open, the incision made by a sharp blade.

The weirdest cut, though, was the long broad one that went from the solar plexus to the hip. The wound appeared to have been inflicted after death, and, unlike the incision at the throat, the edges of the wound were not puckered. The corpse's lower body was almost wholly uninjured. It was high summer, and the wounds were all in a state of advanced decay.

Komine cleared his throat. "Reckon he's been dead a couple of days."

"And the cause of death . . . blood loss?"

"Most likely. This was the fatal wound," Komine said, pointing briefly at the throat. He then directed Reiko's attention to the abdomen.

"This cut here was inflicted postmortem. . . . But you probably already noticed that, given your fetish for corpses."

A corpse fetish? Me?

Reiko refused to let her annoyance show and went on with her questions.

"What's the shiny stuff?"

"Glass fragments. I'll need to get the lab to take a look, but my guess is it's just ordinary window glass. It's not going to be easy to trace. The sheeting and the plastic string probably won't help us much either."

That type of blue sheeting could be found on any construction site, and anyone could get their hands on it. The homeless frequently used discarded pieces to rig up shelters. If they were lucky, this particular variety would have been made by a small manufacturer. If it was from a larger firm, though, it would be hard to trace. All Reiko could get from the choice of the sheeting and the cord was that the killer was careful.

Reiko gazed into the victim's face, moving in close enough to touch him.

"Oh, here we go," spat Komine.

This was how Reiko always communed with the murder victims. She couldn't avoid it. It was a ritual she had to observe.

You can tell me. What was the last thing you saw? Tell me.

The man's face was expressionless despite rigor mortis having worn off. His cloudy, half-open eyes gazed at a single fixed point in space. In her experience, corpses sometimes expressed emotions like terror and resentment. How about this man? Was he regretful? Sad? Scared? Angry?

Didn't you feel anything at all?

The body in front of her remained silent. What would Kunioku be able to learn from it? The man had been murdered — that much was obvious — and as such his body would be sent to the forensic pathology laboratory for examination, rather than to the coroner's office. But there was nothing she could do about it. Kunioku, she was sure, would have been able to get the corpse to speak to him.

Legwork was the first stage in any investigation and often the most crucial. That meant canvassing the neighborhood, knocking on the door of every house in the area.

Sergeant Kikuta called out to all the investigators scattered around the crime scene.

"Everyone, fall in."

In Reiko's squad, Kikuta was in charge of giving orders. Soon after her promotion, Reiko had humiliated herself when she'd tried to bark an order only to have her voice crack and go shrill. Ever since, Kikuta made it a point to give orders for her. He was little bit older than she was, honest, and always willing to help. He was her number two, her most reliable subordinate, as well as the biggest of them physically.

"I want Homicide and the Mobile Unit in the front row. Everyone else, line up behind them. On the double."

Reiko waited in silence for the men to form up. The next step would be to assign two-person teams, each with one officer from the Met and another from the local precinct, to canvass a specific area. Reiko did a headcount: four investigators from Homicide, six from the Mobile Unit, and from the local precinct —

"— eleven from Kameari," Reiko reported to Captain Imaizumi, who had just arrived.

"Okay, add yourself to the group then."

"Yes, sir." Reiko walked over to the one local officer who did not yet have a partner. She gasped when she saw who it was.

Kikuta, who was standing next to her, looked over. "Oh. My. God. *You?*"

The officer smirked, mumbled something incoherent, then stuck his tongue between his teeth. "Yeah . . . um . . . me."

It was Senior Officer Hiromitsu Ioka. They had worked on a homicide together in Setagaya last year. Ioka was an odd-looking fellow — bug eyes, buckteeth, and jug ears. Ioka was a year or two older than Reiko. His title of senior officer wasn't even official. He was at the same level as an ordinary patrolman.

"Aren't you based in Setagaya?"

Ioka scratched his head. "Yeah, well, I got transferred to Oji in April, then was moved here last month."

"What's with all the transfers?"

"Everyone wants a piece of my investigative talents?"

"Doubtful. You probably just piss people off everywhere you go."

"That's enough of that," Captain Imaizumi called out to her, squaring his shoulders impatiently.

"Sorry, sir." She got a grip on herself and took her proper position in the lineup. Ioka snickered and winked at her.

That's Ioka for you, thought Reiko. Despite his rank, the man didn't just make off-color remarks, he even flirted with her. He wasn't a bad guy — just not cut out for the police.

"Himekawa, you take the first sector. Houses one through eight in Block 40."

"Understood."

"Understood," Ioka chimed in, stretching out the last syllable of the word.

The man was hopeless! He constantly

played the fool. It was infuriating. Last year, Kikuta almost punched him a few times. Now Reiko was worried about how this investigation was going to go.

Once all the sectors were allocated, the eleven groups dispersed for the door-to-door. As he was leaving, Kikuta directed a scowl at Ioka.

"Shall we get going, Lieutenant Reiko?"

"That's Lieutenant Himekawa to you."

"Come on. It's not like we don't know each other."

"Watch what you say. I don't want people getting the wrong impression."

"That's so harsh."

"Why don't you just stay here and go fishing instead?"

As if taking Reiko's sarcasm at face value, Ioka swung around and mimed casting a line into the pond.

He was such an idiot, you almost had to admire him.

In a door-to-door canvass, the closer your allotted sector was to the crime scene, the better it was for you. It meant more information and a higher likelihood of finding clues. As a lieutenant, Reiko was guaranteed the pick of the bunch.

Just as with individuals, some departments

outranked others in the police. Since Homicide, as the name implied, specialized in murder cases, they automatically took the lead here, with the Mobile Unit slotting in under them. The allotted sectors for the door-to-door got further away from the crime scene the further they went down the ranks of Homicide, and then the Mobile Unit. A local precinct officer like Ioka was very fortunate to be paired up with Reiko, a lieutenant in Homicide.

"I can't believe that fate has brought us back together, Lieutenant."

Ioka's tone was familiar. Inappropriately familiar. The investigation had barely begun, but Reiko felt suddenly drained at the thought of all she was going to have to put up with.

"We'll start by talking to the person who found the body," sighed Reiko, shaking her head and turning away from Ioka.

She pushed her way through the right-hand wall of the crime-scene tent and emerged onto a road. Another yellow walkway had been laid on this side; again the forensics guys were hard at work all around it. Beyond them, she could see all the parked police vehicles. There was a sidewalk and a narrow watercourse off to one side of the road. Reiko wondered if the watercourse

43

connected to the flood basin in the park.

The person who found the body was a housewife whose home directly overlooked the crime scene. Reiko pressed the intercom on a gatepost with a nameplate saying "Hirata." A short, plump, middle-aged woman stuck her head out the door.

"Good afternoon. I'm from the Metropolitan Police Department."

Reiko showed her badge. The woman frowned, bristling disapprovingly. "I know why you're here. I've already told everything I know to the officer from the local precinct."

The woman's tone made it clear that the last thing she wanted to do was to go through the whole thing for a second time. Reiko detected a note of powerful personal dislike in Mrs. Hirata's eyes. She seemed to be sizing up Reiko and thinking, "You're young, stuck-up, tall — and a woman!"

Reiko had to make an effort to keep her face blank.

"Yes, madam, I'm aware of that. I know it's a bore, but we'd like you to repeat to us the details of how you discovered the body. We have some additional questions as well."

Mrs. Hirata sighed. Looking disgruntled, she opened the garden gate and ushered them in.

"Thank you."

The shady little garden was pleasantly cool. Reiko wondered if it had been watered recently. While the exterior of the house was far from new, the inside was clean and tidy.

"This way."

The moment Mrs. Hirata showed them into the air-conditioned comfort of the living room, Ioka raised his hand.

"I shouldn't, Mrs. Hirata, but could I trouble you for a glass of something cold? I'm so thirsty."

Reiko tapped him on the waist.

Stop that right now!

"Okay. Why don't you sit down?" Mrs. Hirata gestured toward the sofa, then vanished into the kitchen.

"What the hell do you think you're doing?" hissed Reiko, jabbing Ioka with her elbow.

"I need a drink."

The woman was angry enough about them being there in the first place. What the hell was Ioka thinking, pestering her for a cold drink the minute they got inside? They didn't need her any more hostile than she already was.

Mrs. Hirata reappeared. Unexpectedly, she was all smiles. She brought in a tray with a pitcher and glasses, then handed one to each of them. "I imagine you'd probably like nothing better than a nice cold beer, but seeing as you're working, well . . ."

"Thanks. I'm going to enjoy this just as much."

Ioka downed his glass of barley tea in one gulp. Mrs. Hirata began to pour him a second. Why was she looking so pleased all of a sudden?

Things got worse when Mrs. Hirata decided to chitchat a bit.

"It must be very hot outside?"

"Hot's not the word," Ioka replied. "More like unbearable."

"Summer weather must make your job even tougher."

"Too right. Why can't the criminals just take a break till it cools down a bit, eh?"

"That sounds unlikely."

"You reckon?" Ioka laughed uproariously. *Is the man a complete moron?*

Reiko cleared her throat and broke in. "Sorry to push things along, but I'd like to start by asking you to list the members of your family."

The moment Reiko opened her mouth, the look of annoyance returned to Mrs. Hirata's face.

"Of course," she said, after a short pause. "There's my husband, who's got a regular

46

office job. Then my son. He's a university student. Plus there's my father-in-law. He's over at the senior center right now. And me."

"Your son, is he . . . ?"

"He's not at home right now."

"No, what I meant is, is he on his own?"

Mrs. Hirata looked nonplussed.

"Of course he is. He's a student. He's hardly likely to be married."

Reiko realized she'd phrased her question badly.

"That's not what I meant. Is he your only child?"

The woman's eyes widened. "Oh, I am sorry," she said, grinning at Ioka. "No, I have two sons. The eldest one has already finished university and lives in a company dorm for unmarried employees. He's up in Utsunomiya. Not that far, really. The least he could do is to come back and see his mom for the Obon summer holidays."

"Couldn't agree more," said Ioka, smirking.

Was it the Obon holiday this week?

When you had a job that was completely out of sync with everybody else's, important dates like that slipped your mind all too easily. Reiko guessed that the rest of this week would be a holiday — at least for those companies that believed in giving their staff time off. She wondered what was normal. Five days off from tomorrow was probably standard.

"Is your husband at work?"

"Yes. He works for a foreign company, so he doesn't get to take Japanese public holidays off."

Reiko nodded.

"Thank you for this," she murmured before picking up her glass. Rather than gulp the tea down like Ioka, she restricted herself to one modest sip. Any liquid she took in would only come back out as sweat, and the only thing people disliked more than a dirty, sweaty man was a dirty, sweaty woman. Reiko was especially careful when doing house-to-house inquiries.

She got Ioka to write down the names of everyone in the family and turned back to Mrs. Hirata.

"I want to ask you about how you found the body. It was this morning? Is that correct?"

"Yes, that's right. The bedroom — I mean, our bedroom, since it's mine and my husband's — is directly above this room, with a window that looks over that way. First thing in the morning, I opened the curtains."

"What sort of time was that?"

"Six on the dot. That was when I first

48

noticed it."

"In the hedge?"

"Yes. At first, I just thought it was a piece of trash. We've had a lot of that — what's it called? — illegal dumping in the little wooded area by the shrine over there. I just thought, 'Oh no, are people dumping stuff in the hedge now too!' "

Illegal dumping? Reiko wondered if the forensics team had explored that angle.

"You didn't phone it in then, though?"

"No. I'm rushed off my feet first thing in the morning. I pack my husband off to work, get my father-in-law and my son out of bed, make breakfast, put the rubbish out — the proper rubbish, that is — turn on the washing machine . . ."

"You actually contacted us at eleven thirty a.m. Why that time specifically?"

"That's because . . . let me see . . . my father-in-law wanted to go to the senior center, and I took him as far as the bus stop. On my way there, I thought, 'I do wish people wouldn't dump garbage around here.' Then, when I took another look at the thing on my way home, I suddenly felt frightened . . . I realized it was shaped like a body."

"So you called us."

"Yes. I figured that even if it turned out

not to be . . . what I thought it was, the police wouldn't be angry at my reporting such an outsized piece of trash."

"You made the right decision."

"I did, didn't I? Yes, I . . . I think I did."

Reiko couldn't quite follow the woman's thought process from anxiety to relief. In any case, Mrs. Hirata was clearly a well-intentioned bystander. Having originally thought the body in its blue sheeting was bulky waste, she'd called it in the minute the shape of it worried her. Her story was plausible and consistent.

"What was the latest time yesterday that you saw the hedge without that thing in it?"

"Without that thing?"

"All I'm trying to do here is to get an idea — just as far as you yourself are aware, Mrs. Hirata — of when the body was put there. Your answer will help me establish a time-frame."

A look of relief washed over Mrs. Hirata's face.

"Well, I'm pretty sure it wasn't there yesterday. Certainly not when I got back from doing the shopping."

"Which would be what time?"

"Around four thirty or five."

"I see. And roughly what time did you close the curtains in your bedroom?"

"Just before turning in. Around midnight, I'd say."

"You didn't see it then?"

"It was dark. I wouldn't have been able to see it even if it was there."

That made sense.

"Did you hear anything suspicious? See any suspicious-looking vehicles?"

"The car they used to bring that thing here, you mean?"

"Yes."

"There is a road — a small one — running in front of the house. There's not much in the way of traffic, but I don't actually notice every time a car goes by."

"I see. Let's move on, then. Now, roughly when did the other members of your family get home yesterday?"

"My husband got back about eight o'clock. My son at eleven thirty, give or take. My father-in-law didn't go out all day yesterday."

"Did your husband or son say anything about the hedge?"

"Nothing. Even in the dark, anyone walking that way would have noticed it. I'm pretty sure they'd have said something if they'd seen it. . . . On second thought, perhaps my son wouldn't. No, I doubt he'd mention it."

That was strange . . .

No, thought Reiko, it wasn't Mrs. Hirata who was strange. What was strange was to dispose of a body in a place like that.

A hedge beside a fishing pond might be discreet enough in the night, but the local residents would notice the body as soon as day broke — which was exactly what had happened. There was a lot of pedestrian traffic as well. Things like that wouldn't have been difficult for the perpetrator to figure out. It simply wasn't a good place to dump a corpse. Reiko had seen a digital photo of the body when it was still tied up with the PVC string. The rope work had been very professional. Reiko could not reconcile that meticulousness with the sloppiness of the choice of where to dump the body. At the moment it was just a vague, niggling feeling — she couldn't yet explain it.

Reiko nodded briskly, then bowed. "Thank you very much, Mrs. Hirata. We may ask you to come down to the station tomorrow to go through all this again. I know it's a pain, but we'd really appreciate your help. And if anyone in the family, particularly your son, remembers anything, please let us know. Anything at all."

Reiko scribbled the phone number of the Kameari police station onto the back of her business card before she handed it over. Mrs. Hirata took the card with both hands in the formal manner, scrutinized it, then looked up, as if to compare the card with its owner.

What is it now? You're thinking, "So that's a lieutenant, is it?"

The real question was whether Mrs. Hirata even understood what lieutenant actually meant. With Reiko's luck, the woman probably thought that sergeant was a higher rank. But what could you expect? Ordinary civilians knew next to nothing about the police.

Or are you insinuating that I don't look like a lieutenant should?

As these thoughts were running through Reiko's mind, she noticed for the first time how neatly made up Mrs. Hirata was. She was startled. Had she been like that when they first arrived? Or had the woman secretly done her face while she was in the kitchen fixing the barley tea?

Damn! Maybe I'm the one who looks like shit!

Reiko began to worry that she was the one with makeup problems.

After shutting the garden gate behind them, Reiko and Ioka turned for another look at the Hiratas' house. Bathed in the strong afternoon sunlight, the house gave the impression of being just right for the family that lived in it.

"That barley tea was delicious."

Ioka mopped at his forehead. It was already damp with sweat.

"Yeah —"

Reiko's cell phone began to vibrate. As she pulled it out, Ioka craned to see the display.

"Call from the parents, eh?"

The caller ID was "Himekawa Home." It had to be Reiko's mother. Her father was at work so couldn't be calling from home at this time.

The phone continued pulsating gently. She knew what her mom would say: something trite like "Make sure to be back in time for dinner," "When's your next day off?" or "Don't forget to call your auntie in Yokohama."

Reiko pressed the decline button.

"There's no need to do that."

"Forget about it. Let's go to the next house."

Reiko followed Ioka to the house next door. The nameplate said "Matsumiya." Reiko pressed the doorbell.

Oh damn. That's what happens when you

54

get stupid phone calls from people!

She had completely forgotten to retouch her makeup.

3

Tuesday, August 12, 7:30 P.M.

A piece of paper reading "Mizumoto Park Dumped Body Task Force HQ" was taped to the door of the largest meeting room in Kameari police station.

The body had actually been found just outside the park, thought Reiko to herself. Or was she just being pedantic? She sat down in the middle of the front row.

"Right, let's get started. Everyone, stand to attention! Bow!"

The thirty or so people involved in the case were present, including the forensics guys. The investigators were all there too. That meant they'd had enough time to complete their door-to-door inquiries.

The commander of Kameari police station, Chief of Homicide Wada, and Captain Imaizumi, the head of Unit 10, were sitting at the front of the room facing everyone else. Director Hashizume from Homicide was running the meeting.

"I want to start with the autopsy report," he began. "The victim was male, midthirties, one hundred seventy-one centimeters tall, around seventy kilograms. Blood type B. Cause of death was hemorrhagic shock, the result of massive blood loss from a cut wound in the neck area. Estimated time of death is between seven p.m. and ten p.m. the day before yesterday. The cut runs in a straight line from below the mandible on the left to the upper larynx. The depth of the incision is between two and five millimeters. The length, twenty centimeters. Enough to sever the left carotid artery."

Hashizume made a throat-cutting gesture.

"The murder weapon had a thin blade — something like a razor blade or a box cutter. From the way force was applied, we're assuming that the victim was cut from behind with a circular motion around the neck. Questions so far?"

No hands went up.

"Next are the numerous cut wounds visible on the torso. Putting the big and small cuts together, there were ninety-four in total. All were shallow. While bleeding did occur, it wasn't the cause of death. Fragments of glass of varying sizes were found in fifty-two of the cuts. There was also bruising with signs of vital reaction around eleven of the deeper cut wounds. No broken bones. All the above leads us to conclude that the victim was lying faceup with a sheet of glass on top of him and was beaten with downward thrusts of a blunt instrument about the size of a fist. Like this . . ."

For a second time, Hashizume acted out the scene, raining blows down on an imaginary body stretched out in front of him.

"Wonder if it was a magic trick that went wrong?" Ioka whispered.

Highly unlikely, thought Reiko.

Her first idea was that it was some kind of group torture. They had started out by placing a sheet of glass on the victim's torso and beating him through that, then switched to something else when the time came to finish him off. The hallmarks of a torture scenario were there. A voice from behind her said, "Wonder if it was a torture kind of thing?" Someone else seemed to have reached the same conclusion.

The big question was *why* the victim had been tortured. And had he been killed because the beating through the glass got him to talk? Or had whatever he confessed to been something that his torturers weren't prepared to let him get away with? Either way, Reiko knew that making up her mind too early was never healthy. Preconceptions usually ended up hindering rather than helping an investigation.

"If there aren't any questions, I'll move on. The last cut wound to be inflicted was made after death. It extends from the solar plexus down to the hip region. It's nine and a half centimeters deep and thirty-six centimeters long. This cut was made by a blade of a certain thickness, such as a jack-knife, possibly a broad-bladed carving knife. The knife was thrust deep into the solar plexus, then slowly pulled down at a uniform depth toward the hip, slicing the victim open. The damage inside the wound is quite messy, suggesting that whoever did it used both hands and brought all their strength to bear to open up the abdomen the full thirty-six centimeters. Any questions?"

Reiko's hand shot up. Hashizume signaled for her to go ahead.

"This slicing open of the abdomen — was that all it was?"

Hashizume looked puzzled. "What are you getting at?"

"I'm wondering whether the victim might have had something concealed inside his stomach — something that the perpetrator wanted. As a result of the torture, the victim didn't just get his throat cut, he also had his stomach sliced open. Given that, my guess is that the perpetrator rummaged around inside the wound after opening him up."

Hashizume scanned the sheaf of documents in his hand. On the other side of the room, a young detective clapped his hands to his mouth. An attack of nausea brought on by an over-vivid imagination? Officer Otsuka, who was sitting beside him, patted the youngster sympathetically on the back.

"I can't see any such findings in the report. If anything like that had happened, you can be sure it would have been mentioned. No, if it's not here in black and white, then that's not how it went down."

Hashizume was probably right. If anyone had rummaged around inside the victim after slicing him open, it would definitely have made it into the autopsy report.

"Thank you, sir."

Reiko sat back down. Hashizume turned to the next page of the report.

"Next up are the contusions and abrasions on the wrists. A minute quantity of adhesive residue was detected on the skin of the wrists. It's not yet one hundred percent certain, but we suspect that his wrists were held in place using packaging tape. We're guessing that the tape got all bunched up, either because the victim struggled or because he tried to tear it off. That caused bruises and abrasions roughly one centimeter wide on the backs of both wrists. From this we can conclude that the victim's wrists were tied and that he was completely immobilized as he was beaten through a sheet of glass, before his throat was cut from behind. . . . That brings the autopsy results to an end. Any more questions?"

No hands went up.

"Good. Next is Forensics. Let's start with the representative of the Metropolitan Police."

Someone from Forensics seated behind Reiko rose to his feet. It was Lieutenant Komine.

"Thank you, sir. I'll start with the blue vinyl sheeting in which the body was wrapped. It's sheeting of a kind that's frequently used on construction sites; the manufacturer is a firm called Moniwa Building Materials Ltd. We've tracked them down to Kawasaki. There are seven different sets of fingerprints on the sheeting: one belongs to the victim; none of the other six are on record. Then there's the plastic string. We're still trying to track down the manufacturer."

Komine paused a moment. "Unfortunately, we haven't yet been able to identify the victim. There are signs he'd had work done on his teeth, so we've sent in a search request. The results should be forthcoming in the next day or two. . . . Let's move on to the crime scene and its immediate environs."

Komine and the top forensics guy from the local precinct reported their findings. Apparently, they hadn't discovered any significant evidence. Several items they'd found had been forwarded to the forensics lab, and data was expected either tomorrow or the day after. With that, the interim forensics report was out of the way.

"Next is the house-to-house. Sector 1."

"Yes, sir."

Reiko got to her feet. She would have liked a microphone but was going to have to make do with her natural voice.

"We made house-to-house inquiries in the immediate vicinity of the crime scene. The person who discovered the body was a Mrs. Yasuko Hirata, a housewife. Her house directly overlooks the crime scene. At six o'clock this morning, from her bedroom on the second floor, Mrs. Hirata noticed the blue vinyl sheeting in which the body was wrapped. At the time, she erroneously assumed that it was illegally dumped garbage and didn't bother to phone it in. The next time it caught her eye was a little after eleven o'clock when she accompanied her father-in-law to the Mizumoto Park bus stop. On her way home, she noticed that the bundle was human shaped and called the police at eleven thirty. Her account tallies with the report of Sergeant Arai, who was first on the scene.

"Mrs. Hirata didn't notice the bundle yesterday; nor did she notice any suspicious noises or vehicles in the course of last night. I just got off the phone with her now. Both her husband, Mikio, who's now home from work, and Yasujiro, her father-in-law, stated that they noticed the bundle this morning, but had nothing further to add to that fact. The other member of the Hirata household is Masayuki, the second son, a university student who lives at home. He's still out, and I haven't been able to talk to him yet. I intend to pay the Hiratas another visit in the near future."

Reiko went on to report on the other houses in her sector. Her testimony was pretty much identical for all of them. And it wasn't just her; the reports from all the other house-to-house teams were equally disappointing.

None of the local residents heard anything

or saw any suspicious vehicles during the night. And while many of them had noticed the blue bundle in the morning, they'd all walked past it without an inkling that there was a body inside.

It was strange. Dumping a body in a place where the local residents were guaranteed to notice it simply didn't make any sense. Why did the perpetrator wrap up the body so carefully only to leave it in such a half-assed location? Did he *want* it to be found? That was something they couldn't really know until the body had been identified. It seemed pretty certain that the victim wasn't a local resident. No one had gone missing since Sunday night; at least, no one from the houses they'd visited so far. Could the victim have some other sort of connection to the neighborhood? At this stage all they could do was cross their fingers and hope the victim had gotten his dental work done somewhere in Tokyo.

They were almost done. For the first meeting on a case, it had been on the short side. That was largely due to the lack of any worthwhile physical evidence or testimony.

Wada, the chief of Homicide, took the microphone to bring the meeting to an end.

"At the moment we don't have a clear idea about anything — the victim's identity, the purpose of the crime, or the perpetrator's motive. But given the premeditated and bizarre method of this killing, it's reasonable to assume that the perpetrator could commit a similar crime for a second, even a third time. Preventing that is the minimum we can do. Starting tomorrow, I want all of you to work together as a close-knit team so we can solve this case fast. Every day, every minute, every second counts. . . . Okay, that's it for today."

Director Hashizume gave the order, "Attention! Bow! Dismissed."

The meeting was officially over.

Reiko was gathering up her stuff when Kikuta called to her from one row back.

"How 'bout a quick drink, boss?"

"Nice idea. Why not?"

Reiko caught the eye of Captain Imaizumi at the front of the room and mimed tipping a glass. Imaizumi frowned and waved her suggestion away.

What can you expect from a man who's recovering from a stomach ulcer?

Reiko gave a crisp little bow and turned from Imaizumi to Ishikura.

"Hey, Tamotsu, you should come out with us every once in a while."

Three of the four men in Himekawa's

squad were young. Tamotsu Ishikura was the exception. Despite the fact that he was pushing fifty, he was a valuable member of the team. His age and his experience made him slightly harder to manage than Otsuka or Yuda but were also the reasons Reiko wanted to go out drinking with him. At the end of the day, he was on her team too. She wanted the chance to speak to him frankly, exactly like she did with the young members of her team.

"I'd like to. Today's a bit difficult, though. This place is pretty close to where I live. It's an opportunity for me to get home early for a change."

The flesh on Tamotsu's burly back bulged as he bent forward in an apologetic bow.

"No problem, Tamotsu. You live in Ishikawa, don't you?"

Reiko knew that Tamotsu had a daughter at university and a son in middle school. She also knew that the son had a truancy problem and that the daughter was getting antsy about landing a job after graduation. Reiko would have preferred to have learned all this from Ishikura himself, rather than from Kikuta, who was her source, but at least she had an idea of the man's family situation. She certainly didn't intend to put any extra pressure on him.

"All right then, see you tomorrow. Good night." Ishikura bowed several times, bundled his jacket under his arm, and dashed out of the room.

"In the circumstances," blurted out Ioka, "I'll be happy to take Ishikura's place."

"Hey hey hey, Ioka. This way."

Otsuka grabbed one of Ioka's arms from behind.

"I don't remember inviting you two to join us!" Ioka looked at Otsuka and Yuda superciliously.

Yuda followed Otsuka's lead and grabbed hold of Ioka's other arm. "We've got other plans."

"Other plans? Why?"

Yuda and Otsuka ignored Reiko's question.

"But I want to go out with my sweet Reiko —"

Kikuta's eyebrows shot up.

Otsuka put his other arm around Ioka's shoulders. "Don't be so unfriendly, Ioka. We're buddies. Didn't we all get soaked together on that rainy stakeout in Setagaya?"

"It's not like I *wanted* to get wet with you."

"Otsuka's right, Ioka. The three of us really ought to go for a drink," said Yuda, playing his part in the double act.

67

"What's going on here?" stammered Ioka.

"Don't you worry. Come on, let's go," Otsuka said.

"Just a minute," protested Ioka.

"It's okay, I'll bring your bag for you," Yuda added.

"That's not what I meant."

Neither Kikuta nor Reiko said a word.

One on either side, Yuda and Otsuka frog-marched Ioka backward out of the room. Going down the stairs like that could be risky, thought Reiko.

"Maybe I'll . . . come with you." Kikuta was visibly tense. Reiko wasn't stupid. She knew a setup when it was staring her in the face. Was this Otsuka and Yuda's scheme, or were Ishikura and Captain Imaizumi in on it too?

"Great. Shall we go then? It's just the two of us," said Reiko, looking Kikuta in the eye. He swallowed nervously. She could have sworn that there was the hint of a blush on his cheeks.

They finally agreed to go to a local chain bar and restaurant. "Cheers."

"Cheers."

They downed the first round of beers like contestants in a drinking competition. After a while, a few small food dishes appeared on the table, along with a second set of beers.

"By the way, that date you got set up on — how did it go?" asked Kikuta, carefully avoiding eye contact.

Reiko's mouth turned down at the corners. She glared at him.

"Are you going to give me a hard time about that too? What is it with you all? Why's everyone in such a hurry to marry me off?"

"What's this 'you too' business?"

Reiko didn't bother to reply. She just scowled at Kikuta as he squeezed edamame out of the pod.

"Ah," he murmured. "Is Dr. Kunioku putting pressure on you?"

Kikuta's square jaw crushed the beans and his cheeks bulged with the seaweed salad — which Reiko had ordered. His thick neck with its prominent Adam's apple seemed able to swallow limitless quantities of whatever he poured down it. Reiko was used to Kikuta's heroic appetites; normally she'd have admired his way of eating as a sign of manly vigor. Now, though, it looked more like cowardice: he was shoving stuff into his mouth to avoid having to say anything.

What are you trying to tell me?

Reiko wasn't a child and she wasn't a fool.

She could tell what a clumsy, down-to-earth fellow like Kikuta was feeling, even if he didn't say it out loud. Still, she didn't want him using her ability to intuit his feelings as an excuse for not putting them into words. Some women might be okay with that; Reiko definitely was not. She wanted him to make the effort to articulate what he felt. The way he projected a vague sense of *wanting* to say something only to take refuge in food, beer, and, finally, shoptalk, drove her crazy.

What do you really want?

Reiko had no problem with people being uncommunicative at work. God knows, she could be uncommunicative herself! But for Kikuta to invite her for a drink *after* work only to wolf down everything on the table without even trying to tell her that he liked her — it was unforgivable! Well, maybe "unforgivable" was a bit on the arrogant side. She could see why he was behaving the way he was, but it still raised the question of why he'd arranged for them to go out alone together in the first place.

This wasn't the first time, but it was always the same. Kikuta would invite her out right after she'd been on one of those meet-a-potential-husband dates. If he didn't like her going on them, why didn't he come out and say so? If he liked her, he should damn well show her that he liked her. If he'd just say the word, then . . .

Reiko waggled her empty beer tankard at a passing waiter. As if responding to a signal, Kikuta muttered, "The guy must have been tortured."

There it was: the same old pattern. Maybe she was partly to blame: she knew what he was doing but still played along. The instant Kikuta began talking about work, her irritation at his lack of candor slipped away like sand through her fingers. In her mind's eye, she'd already summoned up a full diagram of the corpse. The new data from the evening meeting floated alongside it like the annotations on a slide.

"I wonder . . ." she replied thoughtfully, her brow furrowed and her lips moving without her willing them to do so. "Until we've identified the victim, there's no point in debating the whole torture-or-not question. The thing that really bothers me is that thirty-centimeter-long cut in the abdomen. I can't figure out what it means."

"Yeah. You brought that up in the meeting."

Kikuta polished off his fourth mug of beer.

"The phrase you used was so gross. What was it? 'Rooting around in the wound'?"

"Not true. I said 'rummaging around.' "

Reiko finished her third beer.

"Pretty graphic either way. That kid who almost puked — you know who he is?"

"The kid who's partnered up with Otsuka? Uh-uh. No idea."

"Heard his dad's the director of Tokyo's Third District."

The Third District Headquarters administered three wards — Shibuya, Meguro, and Setagaya. A district director had the rank of chief superintendent, which placed him close to the top of the police bureaucracy. His son would have all sorts of advantages.

"Kid's on the management fast track then?"

"You betcha. Graduated from the National Police Academy. Must be doing his on-the-job training here."

Kikuta broke into one of his trademark wry grins. Reiko tilted her head thoughtfully. "It's a bit weird, though. I mean, why drop a fast-track glory boy right into the thick of it? He's only going to stick around here for three months or so. All trainees have to do is to rotate through a certain number of departments."

"I know the answer to that one. Kid was babbling about it being 'valuable experience.' "

"What crap! Anyway, if dry heaving in meetings is the best he can do, he's a no-hoper."

"Yeah! I hear you."

Reiko suddenly realized that Kikuta was looking straight at her. Typical! The man had no trouble making eye contact when they were talking about work. His eyes had been swimming all over the place when he asked her about her recent date, but now he was staring at Reiko intently enough to knock her backward. That was the look she wanted him to have when he came out and told her he liked her. With that level of intensity, she'd have no trouble telling him that she liked him too. . . .

Unfortunately, the chances of Kikuta picking up on how she felt were less than zero.

"That fast-track program's really something, y'know. A young kid like that, and he's already a lieutenant."

Reiko was so frustrated that she wanted to sweep all the dishes Kikuta had eaten his way through onto the floor.

Look at how much you've eaten! Don't tell me you expect me to go halves on this!

The night was getting late. Outside all was quiet in Kanamachi.

4

After having the overall thrust of the investigation laid out at the morning meeting, Reiko caught a taxi in front of the Kameari police station. She reached the crime scene at 9:30. She was just getting ready to resume the house-to-house inquiries when her cell phone buzzed. The order was short and sweet: get back to task force HQ urgently.

She smiled sardonically as she returned her phone to her pocket. "We've got to turn round and go straight back."

"Don't know why we bothered coming in the first place!" Ioka snorted.

"They've identified the body. Amazing what you can do with dental work."

Ioka pumped his fist in triumph. "Amen to that. Not sorry to kiss this neighborhood canvass good-bye. It's going nowhere."

"Come on. You know this sort of legwork

can generate valuable leads."

Despite her chiding of Ioka, Reiko felt like punching the air too.

She was fairly sure in this particular case that canvassing the neighborhood was a waste of time. The careful planning of the crime hinted at more than the usual complexity. Wada, the chief of Homicide, had described it as "bizarre," but Reiko detected an intensity of purpose that went well beyond bizarre. She could see it in the meticulous way the body was wrapped in the plastic sheeting and in the fact that no one who lived nearby had heard or seen anything suspicious. Reiko was certain that they could keep canvassing the neighborhood till the cows came home, but ultimately they weren't going to make any discoveries here. Reiko had no qualms about throwing in the towel. It was round one to the perpetrator.

Interviewing people who knew the victim and the results of the forensic tests seemed more likely to generate meaningful results. She was happy to have a new angle from which to approach the case.

There is one thing I can't figure out. . . .

They were walking down the lane beside the pond to get back to the main thoroughfare when Reiko abruptly swung around for a second look at the spot where the body had been dumped. A narrow patch of green right by the pond and a hedge with small, dark, and densely packed leaves. Why had the perpetrator put the body there specifically?

The sky was cloudy. The surface of the pond was a thick inky black.

"I've called this meeting because a call just came in from a dentist in Nakano. He has a patient whose dental work is a match. The patient is Taiichi Kanebara, thirty-one years old. Works at an outfit called Okura Trading, an office equipment leasing company. His current address is Apartment 707, Grand Heights Heiwadai, Nerima ward. He's married with no children. His wife filed a missing persons report at the local station last night. . . . Himekawa and Otsuka, I want you to get to Nakano to double check our X-rays against the dentist's records. After that, go to the office of Okura Trading and start asking some questions. Ishikura and Kikuta, you go and check out the victim's apartment. And take the crime scene techs with you. Yuda, you stay here on standby. The Mobile Unit can take over the neighborhood canvass. Ikegami, you take sectors one and two. Hagio, you do three and four. Sectors five and six can be handled by . . ."

Although the meeting was not yet over, Reiko got up and made a beeline to the front left corner of the room, where the desk sergeant was handling the case documentation. She was handed a brown folder containing the dental X-rays of the corpse, a printout of Taiichi Kanebara's personal data, and a handwritten note with the addresses of the dentist and Kanebara's company.

Reiko headed for the door. Ioka and Otsuka were right behind her, followed by Lieutenant Kitami, the "fast-track glory boy" Kikuta had spoken about the night before. Reiko was under no obligation to pay him any special attention, and she wasn't interested in making a good impression. All she wanted was for him to stay out of their way. She hadn't reckoned on having an extra investigator on her team and had to suppress the urge to tell him not to slow them down.

"How was last night, Lieutenant?" asked Otsuka as they hurried down the stairs. He lowered his voice to be discreet.

"How was *what*?"

"Oh . . . er, nothing. Sorry."

Reiko hadn't meant to be quite so sharp,

but it had the desired effect. Otsuka slowed down and fell in step with Kitami at the back.

Damn Kikuta! Making me go halves with him like that. Reiko blew air impatiently through her nose.

Ioka slipped in beside her.

"Should start getting busy now."

"As long as we're making progress, I'm happy."

"We'll need to change trains twice to get to Nakano."

"Thanks for telling me. I was planning on taking a taxi, but with the traffic I guess it could take a long time."

They took the Joban line to Kitasenju, then switched to the Chiyoda line as far as Otemachi, then transferred again, to the To-zai line to Nakano. Reiko checked her watch as they passed through the turnstile at Nakano. It was exactly 11:00 a.m.

Their first port of call was the victim's dentist. The Nakano Dental Clinic was three minutes' walk from the station on the fourth floor of a slightly dilapidated build-ing. The clinic itself was bright and clean inside.

Someone at the task force HQ had called ahead to say they would swing by, so all the relevant documentation was waiting for them.

They talked to the clinic director's son, who looked after the bulk of the patients.

"I knew who it was when your fax arrived first thing this morning. There's something unusual about the alignment of Mr. Kanebara's wisdom teeth. Plus he's got cavities, as you can see. I told him that he should take the plunge and have them out, but he was too frightened. Your X-rays show that the cavities have grown much bigger since I last examined him."

Comparing the X-rays of the corpse with those on file in the clinic proved beyond a doubt that Kanebara was their man. They got word to the task force HQ, and Captain Imaizumi immediately ordered the forensics team, who were on standby near Kanebara's apartment, to go in and dust for fingerprints.

The investigation was finally developing some momentum.

The task force HQ had also contacted Okura Trading to let them know a couple of detectives were on their way. Like the dental clinic, the company was based in Nakano, in its own ten-story office building. The woman at reception was well briefed. Reiko only had to flash her badge for her to spring to her feet.

"Mr. Asada from Sales is waiting for you in meeting room three on the sixth floor. Please go down this hall and take the left-hand elevator."

A man in a suit was waiting for them as the elevator doors slid open.

"Good morning."

He was tall, around forty years old, with thinning hair.

"Hi, I'm Reiko Himekawa from the Metropolitan Police."

"Hello," replied the man gruffly. "My name's Asada. I'm head of Sales. I was Kanebara's boss. Why don't you come in here so we can talk?"

They must have heard he was murdered. All the higher-ups — seven or eight of them, from the CEO on down — were assembled in one room with anxious expressions plastered on their faces. Asada started to introduce them one by one with their fancy job titles. Reiko refused to go down that road. She interrupted him midflow.

"Sorry, but due to the nature of the case, there are limits on what we can tell you. At the moment, all I'm at liberty to say is that someone we believe to be Taiichi Kanebara was murdered. It's a little inconvenient, but we're going to have to talk to all of you one at a time. Either you can vacate this room for us, or we can move to another, smaller room. Which shall it be?"

The man who had been introduced as the CEO instructed Asada to get another room ready, then turned to face Reiko.

"You said your name's Himekawa?"

"That's right. Himekawa from Tokyo Metropolitan Police Department, Homicide Division."

"Would I be correct in assuming that you're the person in charge of this investigation?"

"That's correct."

Asada returned to let her know that the new room was ready. Reiko told Otsuka and Kitami to keep an eye on the executives and stop them from talking to each other about the victim. Reiko would call whomever she needed into the other room for a one-on-one. She didn't expect the top managers to be of much use; the people she wanted to talk to were the ones who'd worked with Kanebara every day.

Reiko could feel someone's eyes on her. *Which of them is it?* Glancing around the room with feigned casualness, she realized it was the CEO. *That guy creeps me out,* she thought to herself.

As she left the room, she treated him to a curt little bow.

The new room was a meeting room big enough to accommodate ten people. It felt hot and humid. The air conditioning must have just been switched on.

The first person Reiko interviewed was Asada, Kanebara's direct boss. Asada said he'd been at home the Sunday night Kanebara was thought to have been murdered. His family were the only people who could back up his alibi, but he didn't strike Reiko as suspicious.

According to Asada, Kanebara's wife had called him Monday morning, looking for her missing husband. When he checked, he found that Kanebara was a no-show. Kanebara's wife had asked whether she should call the police and report him missing. He told her to sit tight for a while. The wife eventually filed a missing persons report at Nerima police station on Tuesday evening.

"Kanebara was a serious fellow, but he wasn't stiff or stuffy. He was very good with people, easy to get along with. The bulk of his work was making sales calls. He was smart, so I also put him in charge of handling all the trade shows and events we took part in." Asada paused. "You're quite sure it was Kanebara who was murdered?"

From his manner, Asada was having trouble accepting that Taiichi Kanebara had been killed. If he was putting on an act, he was an amazing performer.

"Did you notice anything suspicious in his recent behavior?"

"No," said Asada, cocking his head. "I don't think so."

"Was there anything different about him? Had he started doing anything new? It could be anything — maybe someone new he'd met."

Asada hesitated. "I'm sorry, nothing comes to mind. I really can't think of anything."

"Could he have done something to make enemies?"

"Enemies? Oh no, he'd never do anything like that. He wasn't that sort of person."

"You seem very sure. How come?"

"How come? He was a good family man. He worked twice as hard as anyone else on the team."

"So no friction or conflict connected to his job?"

"Look, we're in sales here. Sometimes we might poach a client from a competitor, but that's hardly the end of the world. I mean, heck, if my sales guys got killed every time they won an account from another company, there'd be no one left on the team."

"Okay, how about internally? Was there anyone inside the firm he didn't get along with?"

"Absolutely not. Kanebara was popular with everyone. His bosses, his teammates, his subordinates — we all liked him."

"Was there anyone he was especially close to?"

"Someone he was close to?" Asada thought for a moment. "I can't think of anyone in particular. I know I'm repeating myself, but I just want to stress that Kanebara didn't have any enemies and wasn't a loner or anything like that. With regard to close friends, well, as far as I know, there wasn't anyone here. . . . To be honest, the man never really opened up to me. Maybe that's just the way he was. I don't mean to speak ill of the dead, but our relationship was superficial. It sounds coldhearted, but yes, *superficial* would be the word."

Asada didn't have the faintest idea what went on in Kanebara's mind.

In the business world, when people paint their colleagues in glowing colors it's usually because it helps the corporate wheels run smoother and it's good for the collective. When they paint one of their number as black, it usually comes down to a direct conflict of interest at the individual level. With people as people, rather than as employees, relationships fall into more of a gray, ambiguous area.

Her interest in Asada was waning fast.

"I see. Did Kanebara have people working under him?"

"He did, yes. He headed a team of six."

"Men?"

"Yes, all men."

"Which of them was closest to him, or had known him longest?"

"The answer to both of those questions is Ozawa. Ozawa's about five or six years Kanebara's junior. The two of them worked at the same branch office before coming to the head office here. The sales guys usually look after their own client accounts, but for a while in the branch office Kanebara took Ozawa with him for on-the-job training. I think Ozawa was his favorite."

"Could you send him in to see me?"

A grave-faced Asada left the room. A minute or two later, a somewhat younger man came in, his face also taut with worry.

"Was Mr. Kanebara really murdered?" were the first words out of his mouth.

85

Ozawa was speaking too loudly. At this rate, everything he said would be audible in the corridor outside.

"I'm afraid so."

"But why? Why Mr. Kanebara? Where did it happen? Who did it?"

"To start with, I need you to sit down."

Ozawa didn't move. The boy was obviously going to be a handful, and the first order of business was to get him to calm down. Reiko crossed her arms and looked up at him.

"Listen, Mr. Ozawa, we want to catch whoever killed your boss. Right now we're busy gathering information. What I'd like you to do is tell me everything that you know about Mr. Kanebara, leaving nothing out."

"But how was he killed?"

Someone needs to teach this kid to listen!

"I'm not at liberty to tell you that."

"What about . . . when was he killed?"

"Around eight on Sunday evening. Where were you at that time?"

Ozawa gasped and gave her a poisonous stare. Did she suspect him? It took him a second to realize that the police are obliged to ask everyone connected to the victim to provide an alibi. Ozawa exhaled heavily and sank into a chair.

"I was at a friend's place in the country from Friday evening to Sunday evening. We were stuck in traffic on the way home all Sunday evening. There was an accident that caused a huge traffic jam on the express-way."

"Who was driving?"

"My friend with the house."

"Have you got your toll receipts?"

"Guess my buddy should have them, provided he's not thrown them away."

"I'll need his name and phone number."

Ozawa had left his cell phone at home that morning and his address book was in his desk. Reiko told him to go and fetch it, sending Ioka with him to make sure he didn't phone or text his friend. When Ozawa returned, she jotted down his friend's contact information and resumed her questioning.

"What sort of man was Mr. Kanebara?"

"He was very serious. He worked hard, played hard; he was a good husband too. He always called to let his wife know when he'd be home late, and he often bought her little presents."

"Had he done anything likely to make him enemies?"

Ozawa hesitated so briefly it was almost imperceptible.

"Make enemies? No, that's not Kanebara."

Ioka, who was sitting beside Reiko, inhaled loudly through his nose. Reiko took this as a signal telling her to pile more pressure. She ignored Ioka and tried a new angle instead.

"Did you notice anything different about Kanebara recently?"

"Different? What do you mean?"

"Think about the people he knew, bars or restaurants he frequented, his general behavior, his appearance — it could be anything. Did you notice any change?"

Ozawa was at a loss.

Ioka discreetly snapped his notebook shut. Another one of his "Let's press this guy harder" signals.

Ioka's right. Let's push this up a notch. Reiko refolded her arms, rested them on the table, and leaned forward. She deliberately changed her tone.

"Listen, Mr. Ozawa. I can't go into much detail, but Kanebara's murder was . . . let's say . . . unusually gruesome. Certainly not normal."

"Not like a random street stabbing or anything?" asked Ozawa.

Reiko just shook her head.

"For the moment, we really don't know

what sort of information we're looking for, what could constitute a clue. See what I'm saying? So think again. Was there anything different about Kanebara recently? There must be something you can give us — why somebody might have a grudge against him, anything."

"He wasn't the kind of person to make enemies." Ozawa sighed heavily and slumped in his chair.

Reiko could see there was something on his mind, but he couldn't decide whether to share it with them. He was probably worried about soiling Kanebara's reputation or upsetting the bereaved family.

After a pause to order his thoughts, Ozawa began to speak timidly. "This is just my own personal opinion, but, to be perfectly honest, I found Kanebara so gung-ho and intense that just being with him wore me out. I'm not saying he used to give the rest of us lectures about pulling up our socks and working harder. He didn't need to; the way he carried on himself sent a loud and clear message. That was how he put pressure on us. Starting . . . I don't know, maybe early spring this year, he was especially bad . . ."

Ioka's discreetly tapped his fingertips on the table. The phrase "early spring" had caught Reiko's attention too.

"I'm not sure quite how to say this. He just seemed to be, like, trying too hard. The difference between branch- and head-office sales is that here at the HQ nearly all our clients are large corporations. Mostly firms with over a thousand employees. We lease or sell them everything they need — not just copiers, faxes, and phones but desks, lockers, shelves, stationery, you name it. We each handle several of these big accounts. You can lose a client in a heartbeat, especially when the leasing contracts come up for renegotiation. If you don't get in there with your proposal well ahead of the competition, they can sneak in and grab the account from under your nose. What I'm trying to say is that in this job we work our asses off just to hang on to our existing clients. Our bosses don't expect us to be bringing in new business. But starting sometime this year . . . I can't say exactly when . . . Kanebara really threw himself into trying to win new clients. And I'm not talking about just any old company here." Ozawa paused. "He was trying to get something going with East Tokyo Bank."

East Tokyo Bank? That's one of the top five banks in Japan.

"You're talking about a blanket lease deal

for East Tokyo Bank?"

"No. A comprehensive agreement to supply their national branch network would be about as big it gets in our business. At the moment, East Tokyo spreads its business around. They lease a lot from an office equipment leasing company in which they own a big stake, as well as from the subsidiaries of that firm. They also deal directly with an office equipment manufacturer that's a major client for their banking services. To win away all that business in one go is just a pipe dream, a fantasy. There's no way on earth it's going to happen. Still, even a fraction of it coming our way would mean a massive revenue boost. It would be a major coup for us."

"Worth being hated for?"

Ozawa laughed listlessly.

"I don't think so. Because in the end, Kanebara couldn't pull it off. He didn't win the contract, so no one had any reason to hate him. Frankly, if you were serious about winning a contract of that size from ETB, you'd need to pull together a twenty-person project team just to initiate the negotiations. That's the way the business works. One man launching himself at them all by himself isn't such a smart move. If you had personal connections, it might be a different story —

but Kanebara didn't."

"So you guys, his colleagues, just sat there and watched him bust his balls for six months?"

Ozawa's brow creased. Reiko's choice of words was hardly tactful.

"Like I said, our business is mostly about holding on to existing clients. Kanebara was doing a magnificent job at that. None of us had any complaints on that score. As I said, I'm not here to badmouth the guy. He was a real nice guy — amazing, really. There was just this one aspect of his personality that made him . . . a bit exhausting to be around. I'm ashamed to say that I kind of wanted to keep my distance. I'm being totally honest with you here."

"Thank you," said Reiko, and she brought the interview to an end. As Ozawa shuffled out of the room, his retreating figure looked somehow diminished. Was he having second thoughts about having said too much?

Ozawa, and Asada before him, struck her as harmless. Her goal right now was to eliminate any grounds for suspicion, cross the person off her list, and move on.

"The way Kanebara snuffed it — that was going a bit far even for someone who prided himself on being hardcore," Ioka said, as he threw himself back in his chair and stretched.

Reiko consulted her watch. It was already ten to one.

They gobbled down a bento box lunch from the local convenience store. Asada offered to provide a catered lunch for them, but it was against regulations, and Reiko turned him down. The only thing they accepted was green tea. It was served to them by a female office clerk.

The afternoon kicked off with an interview with a Mr. Nukui from Kanebara's sales team. Unfortunately, the rest of the members of the team were out calling on clients. Reiko would have to postpone their interviews to the next day. Instead, they interviewed two of Kanebara's female colleagues, a man from another division who'd been part of the same graduate intake as Kanebara, and a couple of HR people. By the end of the day they had completed eight interviews.

Wednesday, August 13, 9:00 P.M.
Evening Meeting of the Task Force

The Mobile Unit, which had taken over responsibility for the neighborhood canvass from Reiko's team, had nothing new or interesting to report. Reiko felt sorry for them. After all, it was hardly their fault.

Next on the agenda were the interviews with the victim's family and other known associates. Homicide was in charge of this line of inquiry, and Reiko was the first to speak. She summarized what she had learned from the first set of interviews at Okura Trading.

"Everyone who worked closely with Kanebara had the same impression of him, as a serious, hardworking man. Within this group, however, a couple of his direct subordinates, Ozawa and Nukui, told me that they found it hard to keep up with him. Kanebara never said anything explicit, but his approach to work was enough to pile indirect pressure on them. Ozawa was very specific about that having started in early spring this year. I'll be interviewing the other three members of Kanebara's sales team tomorrow morning. I also got the names and job titles of the people at the East Tokyo Bank Kanebara was dealing with. I plan to see them in the afternoon. That's everything."

"Anyone got any questions?"

Since Director Hashizume was not there, Captain Imaizumi was running the meeting this evening. No one raised a hand.

"Okay, let's move on to the victim's family."

"Yes, sir." Kikuta, who was sitting in the row immediately behind Reiko, got to his feet. "We went to the victim's residence to speak to his wife today. She informed us that her husband went out to meet someone in connection with work on the night of his murder. She doesn't know the identity of the other party. Kanebara left the house a little after six thirty p.m. He has a car, but he didn't use it. He must have gone by train, taxi, or bus."

Train, taxi, or bus. That doesn't exactly narrow the field! Checking them all would require a ton of manpower.

"His wife saw nothing unusual in Kanebara going out drinking for his work. It was something he often did. What did strike her as strange was that he hadn't contacted her by one or two a.m. When she tried calling his cell, she couldn't get through. When he was still not back by morning, she called his office and found out that he'd not showed up to work either. She checked in with the company again around lunchtime. When she learned he was still a no-show, she discussed the situation with her husband's boss, a Mr. Asada. Asada advised her to hang on a little longer before filing a missing persons report, which is what she did. She waited a day, then filed a report at Nerima police station at seven p.m. last night."

Kikuta's information tallied with everything Reiko had heard directly from Asada.

"Kanebara and his wife went to the same university. He was a year ahead of her. They went out together as students and got married seven years ago. They don't have any children, but the marriage was a happy one. From spring this year, however, Kanebara started to go out once every month on a weekend evening. He gave a different explanation every time. It took Mrs. Kanebara a while to realize that something was going on. After six months, she began to get suspicious. She's not sure about the dates up until June, but she's confident that in July, he went out on the thirteenth, the second Sunday in the month. August tenth — the day Kanebara was murdered — was also a second Sunday. In other words, her husband was killed just after she'd realized that something wasn't quite right."

They'd been going out since university. They'd been together for over ten years. I think we all know what that means. . . .

"I asked Mrs. Kanebara about the possibility of another woman. She couldn't rule it out completely, but she thought it unlikely. She couldn't explain why she was so sure, so we'll just have to chalk that one up to women's intuition. Ultimately, her husband was just leaving the house at around six on a Sunday evening and coming back around eleven. He didn't have the time to get up to much mischief even if he wanted to. I also asked Mrs. Kanebara about the sort of man her husband was. . . ."

As Kikuta delivered his report, Reiko sank deeper into her own reflections. *Who was Kanebara meeting on the evening of the second Sunday of the month?*

Her first guess was someone from the East Tokyo Bank for some corporate wining and dining. The trouble with that theory was that — if Ozawa was right — the job was simply too big for him to handle without some kind of inside track. The man worked for a medium-sized office equipment leasing company and wasn't even an executive. Could he close a deal with a megabank single-handedly? No. It didn't matter how much Kanebara spent on corporate entertaining. The man lacked the authority to make the required decisions. It was way above his pay grade.

Reiko wondered about other angles. Although it went against everything people had told her of the man's character, perhaps she should explore the idea of him spying on or harassing competitors whose business he wanted to hijack. That might help explain the flow of events that led to his death by a thousand cuts. Every second Sunday he went out to do a little corporate espionage. Someone found out, and he was tortured and killed as punishment. Reiko dismissed the idea. Normal companies would never go that far in a squabble over client business. What was he doing on the second Sunday of the month?

This is a mystery wrapped in an enigma. Reiko pushed her thoughts to one side and looked up, returning her attention to the briefing.

"Ishikura will now tell you what he learned from the victim's neighbors," announced Kikuta, handing the baton to his older colleague.

"All right, Ishikura, it's over to you," said Imaizumi encouragingly. Ishikura rose stolidly to his feet.

"Let me start with how Kanebara's neighbors regarded him. . . ."

The meeting lasted until 10:30.

Over the next couple of days Reiko and Ioka were busy interviewing people who knew Kanebara. No matter how deep they probed, nothing came up that suggested that anyone hated the man enough to kill him. On the surface at least, everyone was singing from the same solemn hymnal. He was a "serious man" and a "hard worker." They had "lost someone very special."

Their inquiries at the East Tokyo Bank — the target of Kanebara's quixotic one-man sales campaign — didn't yield any significant clues. All they learned was that Kanebara had tried to win the bank's business not by a full-frontal assault on the head office but by building up multiple individual relationships at branch level.

"Kanebara was a hard worker. I can't tell

99

you how many times he visited this branch. At the start, I turned him down flat. We can't hand over the responsibility for all our computers to a new supplier just like that. Things aren't that simple. Same story with copiers and faxes. Head office makes all those big decisions. . . . But the guy simply wouldn't take no for an answer. He comes back at me with, 'Look, you need office supplies, don't you?' and he said he was happy to supply us with paper, ballpoint pens, erasers, business cards, binders — stationery, basically. He didn't care how it started, he just wanted to establish a commercial relationship with us."

It sounded plausible. Reiko imagined that Kanebara was one of those "journey of a thousand miles starts with a single step" types.

"To be frank, Kanebara put me in an awkward position. We are free to make some of our purchasing decisions at the branch level. But even in these areas, we tend to use suppliers with whom we have long-standing relationships." He paused a moment. "It's not the nicest way to put it, but this dime-store haggling went on for six months. Eventually I just thought I should do something for the guy, you know, throw him a bone. And then this. It's so tragic. . . .

I have trouble believing he's dead. We didn't yet have a full-fledged business relationship, but I'm sure this will be a blow for Okura Trading. Kanebara was quite a salesman. We'd have been happy to have him working for us."

That was what the deputy manager of the Nakano branch of the East Tokyo Bank had to say about Kanebara. Kanebara was also supplying other branches of the bank, albeit on the same modest scale. More for background than anything else, Reiko visited some of the other similar-sized leasing companies that dealt with East Tokyo Bank. None of them were involved in a tooth-and-claw battle with Okura Trading over the bank's business. No one had any reason to resent Kanebara.

"This whole line of inquiry looks like a dead end."

Reiko and Ioka were riding a train back to the Kameari police station. Dangling by both hands from the straps, Ioka looked uncannily like a monkey to Reiko.

"I agree," she replied. "Things might have been different in his private life, though. There are people who undergo a complete personality change when they're away from work."

Reiko grinned ruefully. The men on her

squad were champions of that sort of work-life imbalance. The private lives of Kikuta and Ishikura were a morass of poisonous relationships. Still, right now all that really mattered was for her guys to close the case. They had to find the perpetrator before the Mobile Unit did. It was a status thing.

"Not Kanebara, though. Remember what the wife was telling us? It might be different if theirs was an arranged marriage, but those two were college sweethearts who married for love. If the guy had a secret side to his personality, his wife would have told us."

"How can you be so sure?"

"What, you think the guy had a double identity that he managed to conceal from her for an entire decade?"

"Hell, you make it sound like he was moonlighting as a ninja assassin. I think it's possible he was concealing something from her, even if you don't."

"Oh yeah? Well, it's an idea, I suppose."

The conversation tapered off. Discussing a case in any depth on the train was never easy. Since anyone could listen in, you had to lower your voice and pussyfoot around the subject.

"Those ramen noodles we had for lunch were fabulous."

"I really wanted to get a side-order of

gyoza dumplings, but they make your breath stink of garlic."

"Shall we go to the same place tomorrow? We could reschedule our interviews at the Sugamo branch of the bank for around lunchtime."

"Not interested. Tomorrow it's my turn to choose, and I've already set up the schedule for the day. Which should let us eat lunch in a nice new Italian place in Koishikawa."

They exited at Kanamachi station. Reiko checked her watch. It was seven thirty. The setting sun still gave off a pale glimmer of light. The sky behind the dancing neon signs on the rooftops was pale purple. The asphalt still smoldered with the daytime heat. Just standing there, Reiko began to perspire.

God, I hate these summer nights.

The thought came and went. That's not who I am anymore, Reiko told herself firmly, willing the toxic thoughts of her gloomy past out of her mind. Summer nights were hot, humid, and enervating. Hardly pleasant, but that was as far as it went. Besides, she had her workmates now. They had all gone out for a drink together yesterday. With an effort, Reiko dragged herself firmly back into the present.

She noticed the bar she and Kikuta had gone to on the first day of investigation. She

103

realized with a start that they hadn't had time for a private word since. Since then, whenever they went out in the evenings, Otsuka and Yuda came along; last night even Ioka had joined them. Ioka was bunking down in the dorm at the Kameari station set aside for officers on standby, while the boys from her squad were making do with futons on the floor of the gym.

Poor things. They're having a hard time. The air conditioning is turned up too high, and it's freezing.

Reiko herself was staying near the railway station in one of those cheap, nondescript hotels for business travelers. The station commander had offered her a vacant room in the policewomen's dorm. For whatever reason, she found hotels less awkward, plus she loved the feel of freshly laundered sheets. The hotel was close enough for someone to walk her back every day. Living at home on a lieutenant's salary, she had money to burn; besides, the room didn't cost that much. Of course, if the investigation ended up dragging on for months, it would be a different story.

At the bus stop, Reiko pulled out her cell phone to double check that the ringer was on silent. She was pretty sure she'd set it before getting the train earlier.

Oh, that reminds me, someone called me from my parents' place earlier.

As a matter of principle, Reiko didn't answer calls from her parents when she was out in the field. Nor did she bother calling back later. She was pretty certain it would just be more nagging about meeting prospective husbands. She just didn't have the time to waste on nonsense like that.

Since she had the phone in her hand, Reiko took the opportunity to delete the recent call record.

When she looked up, she spotted the bus that went to the local bus depot via Mizumoto Park. She'd ridden it once, on the first day of this investigation. After that, she'd moved on to interviewing the victim's work colleagues and hadn't been back to the place where his body was found. She had yet to see the crime scene in the dark.

Maybe it would be helpful to revisit the scene.

Ioka was about to board another bus when Reiko called him over.

"What've you got in mind?"

Judging by the grin on Ioka's face, he'd gotten the wrong idea.

"Let's go take another look at the crime scene in the park."

"Huh? Why?"

"Just get a move on. It's that bus there, the one that's pulling out."

"We'll be late for the evening meeting."

"Big deal. First order of business will be the door-to-door. It's hardly urgent. If anything important comes up, they'll contact us."

"If you say so, Lieutenant. To the ends of earth will I follow you."

In the heat of the moment, Reiko squeezed Ioka's hand. She was excited.

It was dark by the time they disembarked.

They crossed the thoroughfare at the crosswalk, then walked up the lane that ran alongside the pond. The expanse of water behind the fence to their left was black and silent. They couldn't see the fishing boats although they had to be moored out there somewhere. Apart from the occasional resident heading home, the place was every bit as dark and lonely as Reiko had imagined.

"Lieutenant?" said Ioka behind her.

Reiko blanked him out.

It must have been just like this the night the body was dumped here. A bit later, though. By the time Kanebara was brought here, the locals had probably all put out their lights and gone to bed.

Reiko pushed on toward the place where the body was found. The lane was getting darker with every step, but Reiko found herself inexplicably unafraid of the summer night.

"Lieutenant, why are you bringing me somewhere so dark?"

The body must have been brought here by car. Which road did they use?

"The moment I saw you for the first time, I . . ."

They had to use this lane or the road that runs through the park, the one where the forensics guys parked their vans that day. They dumped the body at the junction of the two roads. Which one did they use? . . . Shit, I just don't know.

". . . thought to myself, 'The woman's beautiful, gorgeous.' "

The place is conspicuous in daylight, but at night, especially later, when it's even darker, it's actually pretty well hidden. Let's see. We've got a T-junction. . . . We've got a body, a T-junction, a hedge, a fence, and a pond.

". . . I can hardly believe it, Reiko. Don't tell me you're as crazy about me as . . ."

Ah! I feel it coming. I'm almost there. It'll come. I just need to stay here a bit longer, then the memory will surface.

". . . Do you remember? I was so

thrilled . . ."

Goddammit, won't that Ioka guy ever shut up? — What the heck is it? The thing about the body that bugged me?

". . . Perhaps we were just meant to be. How about a pinkie promise?"

That was it! The big incision. The big incision in the belly. The shallow cuts from the glass were about inflicting pain. The cut to the throat was to finish him off. So what about the abdomen? What the hell was that incision for?

". . . Our fates are joined by a crimson thread. . . . No, it's more like yarn. . . . No, no, it's got to be thicker and sturdier. More like a rope . . ."

What were they planning to do after slicing open the abdomen and dumping the body here? What if she flipped her viewpoint 180 degrees? What difference would it have made if they'd dumped the body here without slicing it open?

". . . You felt it too? That destiny brought us together at the end of last year? They transferred me not once, but twice. Still we met again, right here. It was meant to be . . ."

Why inflict further injury on the body after death? What was the point?

". . . You're trying to tell me that we should be together?"

Postmortem injury. Why the postmortem injury?

"Reiko, darling."

Postmortem injury. Why the postmortem injury?

"You feel the same about me, Reiko."

Postmortem injury. Postmortem injury. Postmortem injury. WHY THE POSTMORTEM INJURY?

"Reiko, kiss me."

Got it! Way to go, girl!

"Kiss me now."

"Will you shut your stupid mouth!" Reiko gave Ioka a mighty slap on the cheek. "What have you been burbling about all this time?"

Ioka's knees gave way. He sank to the ground.

"*Burbling?* That's horrible. Look, I can understand if my telling you how I feel embarrasses you."

"Believe me, I couldn't care less. I've figured this thing out. Now I know."

"You mean how deeply I love you?" Ioka bit his thumb nervously.

"That's something I'm happy never to find out about. No, what I've figured out is why they sliced open the abdomen and dumped the body here."

"Reiko baby, don't tell me that's what you were thinking about all this time?"

She smacked him on the top of his head. "Don't you 'baby' me, you smart-ass. What the heck else should I be thinking about when I'm on the job?"

"Your future with me?"

She smacked him again. "Stop it. We need to get going. We're late for the evening meeting as it is."

Reiko turned round and set off. Ioka dashed after her.

She was on the dark lane beside the pond. This time, the fence was on her right. She noticed a break in it. It led to walkway above the pond, like a jetty but running parallel with the shoreline. Perhaps it's for fishing, thought Reiko.

She wandered absentmindedly onto the jetty. It looked about a meter and a half wide. Certainly big enough for the fishermen to put out their chairs with enough room left over for people to walk behind them. It was a good thirty meters from end to end.

"What's this? It says something about bait . . ."

It was some sort of notice board. Reiko took a flashlight from her purse for a better look. Judging by its location, it had to be for the fishermen. There was a notice from the local district office about putting any leftover bait in the recycling box to be turned into high-grade fertilizer. Reiko's eye, however, was caught by something else.

It was a notice that said "Swimming Prohibited" in large red letters, and below that, "Danger: the water here is not suitable for swimming." It was dated August 10. The issuing authority was the Municipality of Tokyo Environmental Department.

"What is it, Lieutenant?"

Ioka was standing next to her, peering at the noticeboard.

"Tell me, Ioka," said Reiko. "Is this the kind of place you'd like to go swimming?"

"No way. It's far too dirty. Of course, if it came with the chance to see you in a swimsuit, Lieutenant, I might be persuaded."

"So you don't need a 'Swimming Prohibited' notice not to swim here."

"Here? No way."

"So why have they gone to the trouble of putting up this warning, then? And look who issued it. The Tokyo Municipal Government. Do you think there was an accident of some sort?"

Ioka thought for a few seconds, then smacked his fist into his palm. "It's . . . uhm . . . that . . . uhm . . . that . . . you know . . . When they test the water and find

111

bacteria or whatever, they forbid people to swim. That's it, a no-swim advisory."

"Bacteria or whatever?" Could it be — ?

Two nodes in Reiko's brain suddenly connected. The resulting short circuit set off a shower of sparks. A vague shadowy shape was visible in the flickering light.

It can't be. It can't be. It can't be. It can't be. It can't be. It can't be.

Reiko grabbed her cell and called the Tokyo Medical Examiner's Office.

"Tokyo Medical Examiner's Office here. How can we help you?"

"Hi, this is Reiko Himekawa of TMPD Homicide here. Is Dr. Kunioku there?"

"Yes, he is. Shall I patch you through?"

"Please."

She waited a moment, then Kunioku came on the line. "Hey, darling, is that you? What's up?"

"Actually, doctor, there's something I need to ask you. Remember the time before last when we had lunch, you told me about that bacteria — what was it called? — something like negligee? Can you give me the name of the person it killed?"

"Oh, you mean *Naegleria fowleri*? Strictly speaking, it's a parasitic amoeba, not a bacteria. The person who died from it? Just give me a minute."

Kunioku put the receiver down to go and consult his records.

"Uh-huh, here we go. The man who died was Yasuyuki Fukazawa, twenty-one years old, a resident of Adachi ward. Why do you need to know?"

"You also mentioned something about plans for water-quality tests at several locations in Tokyo. Did they manage to pinpoint where exactly Fukazawa picked up his negli-whatever?"

"*Naegleria fowleri*. They did the tests, but they couldn't peg his infection to one specific body of water. I remember something about them finding the parasite in a fishing pond in Katsushika ward. It was the only place in Tokyo they found it. Problem was, fishing wasn't one of Fukazawa's hobbies."

"Was it the pond at the entrance to Mizumoto Park?"

"I really don't know. Water testing's not my responsibility."

"Who was in charge of it?"

"In charge? The Environmental Guidance Section of the Department of the Environment and the Environmental Hygiene Research Center of Teito University did it together."

"Could you provide me with a copy of

their report ASAP?"

"I'm not sure . . ."

"I'm begging you, Dr. K. It's for an investigation I'm working on. There isn't time to go through official channels."

"Okay, I'll get it to you right away."

"Thanks so much. Can you also send over any information on the Fukazawa guy — whatever you've got there will be fine. Address it to the Task Force HQ at Kameari police station."

"No problem. I'll fax it over right now."

Reiko bowed into her phone and ended the call.

"What is it, Lieutenant? What's going on?"

"You'll find out soon enough. Come on. We need to get to that meeting."

6

When their taxi pulled up at the Kameari police station, Reiko and Ioka piled out and dashed up the front stairs. The uniformed officer on guard outside saluted them as they went through the automatic doors and into the lobby. The elevator showed no sign of coming, so they took the stairs to the third floor at a run. They charged down the corridor, shouldered open the door, and barged straight into the evening meeting.

"Director!" Reiko planted herself in front of the table at the head of the room where the top brass were sitting.

There had to be more than twenty people present, nearly all the investigators assigned to the case. All eyes were on Reiko. Kitami, the management-track kid with the family connections, looked especially disapproving. Oh, of course an elite brat would never be late, she sneered to herself.

"Why all the drama?" Hashizume asked.

His tone was grumpy, but at least he was giving her the chance to speak.

"Thank you, Director. There's something I urgently need to tell you. Can you call a timeout on the meeting?"

Captain Imaizumi, who was sitting beside Hashizume, scowled at her. "What's this about, Himekawa? I mean, you come bursting in —"

"Boss, I'm sorry. But if my hunch is right, this is no ordinary case we're dealing with. You'll need to have an emergency executive council meeting to revise the basic parameters of the investigation."

"What is it you want to tell us? Spit it out."

Reiko turned back to Hashizume. "As I said, sir, I'm happy to tell you in the proper forum. First, you've got to suspend this meeting."

The rest of the top brass — the station commander, his deputy, and the precinct chief of detectives — stared up at her dumbfounded. Reiko would never have tried anything like this if Wada, the chief of Homicide, had been there. With these guys, though, she felt she could push her luck.

"Director, please."

The higher-ups looked at one another. The chief of detectives' guy glanced at the head of Major Crimes. He in turn looked at

Lieutenant Kitami. Apparently he didn't like what he saw.

"You're quite sure this is going to be worth our while?" Captain Imaizumi's serious tone told her that he was ready to let her argue her case.

"One hundred percent, sir."

Hashizume, whose arms were crossed tightly on his chest, just groaned. "Listen, Himekawa, if you're going to do your usual thing of kicking up a ruckus based on nothing more than a hunch or your gut feeling or whatever, maybe you need to take a step back. Think about the bigger picture: this time it's not just about you. You could get Captain Imaizumi into trouble."

Reiko's eyes darted away from Hashizume to Imaizumi in the seat beside him. The captain gave her a discreet nod.

She couldn't help feeling guilty. She knew that Imaizumi's life would be a great deal easier if she was more like Kusaka, the other lieutenant in Unit 10. Kusaka always built his cases painstakingly and methodically, using physical evidence to bolster any testimony he had secured before sending the whole neat package up to the public prosecutor's office. Imaizumi, however, kept telling Reiko to do things "her way." She was just taking him at his word.

Did she jump to conclusions? Perhaps she did. She liked to think of herself as someone who could instinctively sense the overall contours of a case. It was the only way she knew to prove herself and to earn the respect of her colleagues. If she approached her cases the same way as everybody else, she'd never get the same recognition they did. She'd heard that Imaizumi had been the same when he was a detective: a risk-taker who went with his gut. That was why he had tapped Reiko for Homicide soon after he'd been promoted to a desk job.

"I think we should listen to what Hime-kawa has to say, Director," Imaizumi said with a sigh and a deferential bob of the head.

"If you say so, I'm okay with it."

"Thank you, sir." Reiko bowed at Hashi-zume, though the real focus of her gratitude was Imaizumi.

I'll get the guy, Captain. I swear I will.

Hashizume stood up to announce the temporary suspension of the meeting and to order everyone to stand by until it was resumed.

The top brass moved to a smaller room for the meeting of the executive council. Seven people took part. There was the commander, the deputy commander, and the chief of detectives from Kameari police station. From the TMPD, there was Director Hashizume, Captain Imaizumi, and Reiko. The seventh person was Ioka. He stood behind Reiko, brazenly passing himself off as a TMPD officer.

"Enlighten us, then," said Hashizume, digging a finger into his ear and not bothering to look at her. "What's your latest flash of inspiration?"

Hashizume's cynicism was understandable. Neither she nor her squad had closed a case for months. Given her recent track record, she was prepared to put up with a few sarcastic jibes when she interrupted a meeting with demands to be heard.

Reiko stood up. She was now standing shoulder to shoulder with Ioka. "Thank you, sir. I found that I couldn't stop thinking about the postmortem incision in the victim's abdomen. I kept asking myself what was the point of it. The perpetrator bashed glass into the victim before severing his carotid artery to kill him. Why bother to make a vertical slit in the abdomen after all that?"

"You think you've got the answer?" growled Hashizume, scratching his forehead.

Reiko gave an emphatic nod. "Usually, when a perpetrator inflicts postmortem injury on a body, it's about making the body disappear. Chopping up or burning a body are examples of what I mean. I think we're looking at the same thing here."

"Except that making a slit in the abdomen isn't much of a vanishing trick."

"You're right. Slicing the abdomen is just the preliminary stage. Like prepping the body for disposal."

The men exchanged startled looks. Reiko could see they had no idea where she was going with this.

"What I'm about to suggest to you is just my own personal hypothesis." She paused. "I am guessing that the perpetrator intended to dump Kanebara's body into the pond."

The five men shifted uneasily in their seats. Behind her, Ioka swallowed audibly.

"You all know that gases accumulate inside dead bodies as they decompose. What does that mean? Dump them in the water and all they do is float right back up to the surface. There was a case where a body that had been crammed into a refrigerator and chucked into a lake floated back up to the surface, refrigerator and all. The buoyancy of these decomposition gases is amazing. The gas accumulates in the intestines, inflating them like a balloon. Now, what would happen if you took the precaution of pre-puncturing that balloon? It's obvious. The intestines wouldn't inflate, and your body wouldn't come up to the surface. That, I believe, is the purpose of the incision in the abdomen."

Hashizume raised a hand to object. "In that case, why didn't the perpetrator dump the victim in the pond? There's nothing to be gained by leaving him sitting on top of the hedge."

The question was a valid one.

"I agree. Clearly, the body being left out like that wasn't good for the perpetrator. I believe the perpetrator meant for the body to be dumped in the pond, but it wasn't. My hypothesis is that there were two people involved: one person to transport the body to the pond, and another to dump it in the pond. For some reason, however, the person responsible for dumping the body in the pond failed to do his job. He never even showed up. I am guessing that's be-cause . . ." Again, she paused. "The person who was meant to dump the body in the pond was already dead."

"What grounds have you got for this hypothesis of yours?" broke in Imaizumi.

"Let me explain, sir."

Hashizume sighed ostentatiously and his shoulders sagged.

"This is a photocopy of the autopsy report of a man who died in suspicious circumstances one month ago. His name was Yasuyuki Fukazawa and he was twenty-one years old. He was infected with a parasitic amoeba called *Naegleria fowleri*. It's very rare, but is found in freshwater lakes and ponds during the summer months. The amoeba consumed his brain and killed him. The early symptoms of *Naegleria fowleri* are similar to meningitis, so your average doctor isn't likely to make the correct diagnosis. Fukazawa died on July 20. In the report, the coroner estimates that he was infected about one week earlier — so roughly July the thirteenth. That was the second Sunday in the month — the same day Kanebara made one of his mysterious disappearances. And the next second Sunday in the month is when he left his home for the last time."

Reiko put the autopsy report down on the table.

"The next question we have to ask is where Yasuyuki Fukazawa got infected with *Naegleria fowleri*. It's not one hundred percent, but it looks almost certain to have been the fishing pond near Mizumoto Park. The Tokyo municipal authorities conducted checks on water quality throughout the city. The Mizumoto pond was the only place where they detected *Naegleria fowleri.* What does that suggest to you? And by the way, I should mention that Fukazawa was on parole and was forbidden to leave Tokyo without special permission. Of course, he could have violated parole and gotten infected somewhere else entirely, but Tokyo seems a whole lot more likely to me. Which all leads me to conclude that on or around July 13, Yasuyuki Fukazawa must have either accidentally fallen into, or deliberately gone swimming in, the fishing pond."

Reiko picked up the water-quality test report from the table and opened it to the page about the Mizumoto pond. She then held it up for everyone to see.

"You've all seen the pond. You know it's not a place where people swim in the summer — or any other time of the year, for that matter. With a sluice gate on one side, two sides banked up with concrete, and on the fourth, a verandalike jetty thing for people to fish from, the place is clearly not designed for swimming. Despite all that, Fukazawa went swimming there. He went into the water and was infected with *Naegleria fowleri* around July the thirteenth. Which means —"

Captain Imaizumi sat in silence with his eyes closed. The top three guys from Kameari police station looked disgusted, as if they had bitten into a lemon. The only sound Reiko could hear was the breath going in and out of Ioka's nose.

"— Which means what?" Hashizume said, crossing his arms on his chest and throwing himself back in his chair.

"Which means that . . . there are probably more victims who were killed prior to Kanebara sitting at the bottom of that pond."

The top brass stared at her flabbergasted.

It was exactly what she had been looking forward to.

Reiko savored the moment.

■ ■ ■ ■

PART II

■ ■ ■ ■

My life was gray. The same as it always was.

I never settled into the orphanage they put me in after I lost my parents. And I never felt comfortable in the hospital they sent me to from time to time. I never felt like I was properly *alive*.

It was like I was still trapped in that house. That house that was supposed to have burned down and disappeared off the face of the earth. For years that feeling of being trapped had made my life hell: the stink, the yelling, the cursing, the beatings, the insanity, the self-destructiveness.

"I wish you'd never been born." That was always his favorite warm-up line. "Just fuckin' die, will ya? Life. It just goes around and around and around. You eat, you take a dump, and then you eat some more. Your mom, she squatted down and shat you out. You're a lump of shit. No, 'scuse my manners. You are one fine little piece of excrement."

Excrement?

Maybe he'd been right.

My life meant nothing. I had no control. There was someone to take me to the orphanage. When I made trouble, there was someone else to take me to the mental hospital. When they decided I was "better," they took me back to the orphanage. Then the next time I lost it, it was back to the hospital again. Like an endless loop: orphanage, hospital, orphanage, hospital, orphanage, hospital — eating me up and shitting me out, over and over and over again. My parents weren't the only ones to think I was shit; I was shit in the eyes of the whole goddamn world. That was the one thing I knew for sure.

Funnily enough, I didn't want to die. I guess I was looking for something. What, I don't know. My place in the world? That something that would make me feel alive? The ability to feel, to desire? Your guess is as good as mine. Whatever I was after, I started to wander the streets looking for it.

Shibuya was too flashy for me; Roppongi and Harajuku even worse. Ikebukuro was getting there, but it was Shinjuku that hit the spot. Shinjuku was perfect.

Incredibly filthy, incredibly noisy, incredibly crowded. As chaotic as the inside of my own head. At night, Kabukicho, the red light district in Shinjuku, was a blaze of neon, while its back alleys were sunk in darkness. There was light and there was dark. Plenty of both. Kabukicho was stark black and bright white, never gray. Nice and clear cut, how I liked it.

The district was crawling with yakuza. That gave me a buzz. My favorite place was this big park, because of the sense of hidden danger. It was crawling with homeless people. Occasionally I came across one like me there — standing at the roadside, yelling their heart out at the world. Shinjuku was the place where I could connect with my pain.

Even in that shithole — maybe *because* it was a shithole — I found people prepared to be nice to me. Like the old homeless guy.

"Look at you, kid, you're filthy. Why not try this on for size? I picked it up, but it's way too small for me. No point in chucking it. If you want it, go on, have it."

The old fellow handed me a black leather bodysuit, the kind that motorcyclists wear. I was grateful because the weather was just turning cold. I've worn it ever since.

Experiences like that were few and far

between. One cold morning the old man was cold and dead, and the cops came to the underpass and cleared away the whole cardboard village. I had to leave. That's when I decided to try my luck in Kabukicho. I was so filthy, everyone steered clear of me. It was straight back to feeling like a piece of shit again. The feeling got stronger, and before I knew it I must have done something, because I came to in some hospital. I quickly snuck out and headed back to Shinjuku. I changed out of my hospital clothes and back into the biker suit in a train station bathroom.

It was around then that I met Mako.

I was squatting on the curb, minding my own business, when she came up to me and hugged my head to her chest. "The world's a harsh place," she cooed. "It just ain't fair. But I understand you, I know how you feel." Mako had beautiful long platinum blonde hair and beautiful bright eyes. I put my head on her lap and cried my eyes out.

"It's awful. You need to be homeless, out on the street, to feel just a little bit alive. It's the same for me. I understand. Go on, cry. Cry your little heart out. It's not your fault. You haven't done anything wrong. I know. I understand." She paused, then said, "Come with me. I'll introduce you to some friends of mine."

Her friends were a group of kids about her age. They called themselves the Gang. Shinjuku was their stomping ground. They fought turf wars with other gangs and even clashed with the yakuza and the cops. They were involved in a lot of heavy shit, but they weren't going anywhere.

Mako was the one I liked. The others I didn't care for much. Like Mako's elder brother. His nickname was Toki, and he was the leader, because he knew how to fight. I didn't like the way he looked at me. It reminded me of the class monitor at school. What do I know? He let me stay, so maybe he was a good guy after all. He fed me the same as everyone else and must've patched up my cuts and bruises a hundred times. Maybe he only eyed me like that because I stuck so close to Mako. She was beautiful. No wonder Toki worried about her.

The Gang was good to me, so I fought hard for them. Nothing frightened me. I was willing to kill anyone, including yakuza or cops. Those guys bleed the same as the rest of us, right? They act all high and mighty, but the blood in their veins is the same as mine — and the same as my burnt-to-a-cinder daddy.

Look at the blood coming out of this cut

in my leg. It looks black on my black body-suit, but stick your finger in it, and look, it's a lovely rich red. Your blood's the same, see? Red. Hardly gonna be blue, I guess! Which is the nicer red, yours or mine? Hey, I'm just kidding. They're the same color. That's how it should be. It soothes me. My blood is this beautiful red color, just the same as everyone else's. My blood, your blood — there's no difference between them. I like that.

But Mako cried all the time. Whenever she saw me drenched in beautiful red blood, she would go crazy. Her brother had to grab her and hold her until she calmed down. I know why she made such a scene. She told me she was worried about me getting hurt. I felt so guilty whenever I ended up all bandaged up after a rumble.

I really got off on listening to the rest of the boys telling me what a kick-ass street fighter I was. I started thinking that maybe I'd found my place, that maybe this was what I'd been looking for, that maybe life was worth living after all. I could tell that the others guys respected me. It had been years, but I felt that a little color was seep-ing into my miserable gray life. I loved to look at Mako's long blonde hair.

Everyone in the Gang had a nickname,

the shorter the better: Mako, Toki, Kusu, L, Mochi, Taji. Mako wanted to give me one too. I never spoke, so I had to scratch my name into the dirt with a stick for her. "Great," said Mako. "We'll call you F from now on." It sounded nothing like my real name. I liked that. Felt like I'd changed into someone else.

I was always in the thick of any fight. I wasn't the strongest member of our gang, but I was relentless. No matter how bad I was hurting, I just fought on till the other guy begged me to stop. I got some nasty injuries, but I never, ever admitted I was beat. Perhaps I didn't know how. In the end it was always the other guy who ended up pleading for his life.

Just like my dear old dead dad, I suppose.

Word about me spread among the other youth gangs. They'd give me a wide berth when they saw me coming. It was quite nice, though it meant less fighting. Less fighting meant my world fading back to gray again. That I didn't like.

Then Mako was murdered.

Some guy from another gang found her body and brought us the news. She was stark naked and dead in a road tunnel near the Imperial Palace. It was harsh. It was ugly.

"The fucking bastards," said Mochi, his voice breaking. "They gang-raped her, and then they killed her."

Taji moaned and cursed as he pummeled the asphalt with his fists.

We were all slumped on the road, bawling. The guy who'd led us to the tunnel wasn't even part of our gang, and even he was crying his eyes out. The motorists were honking their horns at us, sounded like hundreds of them. We didn't budge. We just sat and cried around Toki and his dead sister.

"I'll deal with this," I stammered. "Just tell me who did it."

My gang-mates were utterly astonished. They couldn't figure out who had spoken. None of them had heard me speak before, not a word. The guy who'd taken us to the tunnel warned me it was better not to tangle with the guys who did it. Then we heard police sirens. They were getting closer. We split up and ran. We had no choice. We left Mako alone in that tunnel.

The next day, I started looking for the guys who'd killed Mako. I'd never heard of them, but it seemed like everyone else had. I walked the streets, listening to what people were saying, sometimes following them. As

I followed them, I pushed the blade of my faithful box cutter in and out in my pocket. *Clickety-click. Clickety-click.*

It took me three days to find the killers. There were three of them. They looked like university students. Maybe they were hipper new-look yakuza. Who cares? In this world, there are two types of people: winners and losers. And we all have the same color blood: red. Lovely, luscious red.

"It was him. He made us do it. We went too far. You hear me? I know we crossed the line, but he's the one who should pay."

"That's not what happened."

"Don't try and wriggle out of it. You got carried away and did all kinds of crazy shit to her. You were the one who strangled her."

"You were happy to watch."

"Yeah, I watched. I didn't join in."

"That's what you say. *Now.*"

I'd had enough. I didn't want to hear any more. I wanted to see some blood.

A gurgling shriek.

"What the fuck!"

It was a fountain, a beautiful bright red fountain. Everything in my vision was monochrome — everything except where the red blood was spraying into the air. I was back to glorious Technicolor. The sliver of sky between the rooftops was violet. The wall on one side of me was dark green, the other beige. The handle of my box cutter was baby pink.

"You're out of your fucking mind!"

One of the gang made a run for it. I let him go. I just gazed up at the night sky, drinking it in. God, it felt good. I remembered how it felt when I killed my dad. I remembered my mother. I remembered the cozy cardboard shelter of my old homeless friend. And I remembered Mako — her smile, her voice, her beautiful blonde hair, and most of all, her kindness.

At my feet lay a still-twitching body, its face red like a gigantic ripe strawberry. One of the three was dead, one had fled, but for some reason one of them stayed behind with me.

1

Saturday, August 16

First thing in the morning, a fleet of police vehicles swept into Mizumoto Park and parked around the fishing pond. The atmosphere was tense.

Everyone was there. Chief of Homicide Wada, Director Hashizume, and Captain Imaizumi from the Task Force HQ; the commander, deputy commander, and chief of detectives from the Kameari precinct; all the investigators from Unit 10, including Reiko's squad and their partners, plus a bunch of crime scene techs — making twenty in all. The Mobile Unit had dispatched a team of two commanders along with six divers from Water Rescue. Finally, around twenty uniformed officers from the Kameari precinct's Community Affairs Division were there to direct traffic and keep the rubberneckers at bay.

Rubberneckers were a royal pain in the

ass. Unluckily, today was a Sunday. On a weekday, the local residents and random passersby would have been bad enough, but today there was a crowd that included a contingent of rod-toting geezers who'd come for a quiet day's fishing.

"You'll be in big trouble if we don't find anything."

Hashizume made the same observation every time he surveyed the scene.

"Just because we've got a full house doesn't mean that we're putting on a show here," countered Reiko, turning to inspect the pond.

"Whatever. . . . But we were lucky that this park's located in Tokyo's Seventh District. The Water Rescue Team's based here too. We'd probably wouldn't have gotten anywhere with a mobilization request across jurisdictions."

"Yes, sir," Reiko replied half heartedly. She wasn't interested in the ins and outs of district politics.

"I've got no problem with you sticking your neck out, Himekawa, but you need to remember that there are twenty or thirty people out there who are after your job."

"Yes, sir."

Yes, sir, no, sir, three bags full, sir. You seriously think I don't know that?

The police department did its personnel evaluations by deducting marks for errors. The system expected you to do your job right — that was the baseline. Make a single slip up, and there was hell to pay. The higher your rank, the worse it got. It was a crazy system. The upshot of it was that useless jerks who made no mistakes because they did nothing scored higher than officers who worked their butts off but made the odd mistake en route.

Why do I get the feeling that seeing me demoted to local traffic duties wouldn't break your heart?

Reiko knew that at the end of the day Hashizume was a lot less worried about her being kicked a few rungs down the ladder than having his leadership put under the microscope.

Still, Reiko had a strong track record. So far at least, her hunches had usually panned out. After dragging his feet a little, Hashizume had finally called in Water Rescue. It was only when confronted with the sight of the divers doing their stuff and the huge crowd of gawkers that he began to lose his nerve. The sheer scale of it had driven him out of his comfort zone. Chief of Homicide Wada turning up at the morning meeting — something he almost never did — hadn't helped. Wada had questioned the need for an underwater search, and Hashizume had looked a fool when he could not explain his reasons properly.

It's risky, but someone's got to grab the bull by the horns, or else the case will go nowhere. Hey, no one ever said police work was supposed to be easy.

Reiko stared at the part of the pond where the divers had gone down. The glare of the reflected sunlight was too strong to look for long. She glanced at her watch. 10:30 a.m. The thought of the search possibly dragging on into the afternoon depressed her. Her thin blouse was already almost transparent with sweat. Half an hour before, Ioka had proudly announced that he could see her bra strap. Her answer was a deft knee in the groin. That had, briefly, shut him up.

The man who rented out boats and sold fishing tackle informed Reiko that the pond was three meters deep at its deepest point, which was smack in the middle of its roughly triangular shape. She needn't have asked, really. Of course it was deepest in the middle. Whoever disposed of the bodies had probably guessed as much, so the divers started their search there.

Four buoys floating on the surface of the pond marked the boundaries of the current search area. Each five-by-five-meter square took the divers between five and ten minutes to check. Then they moved the buoys and searched the next area. Reiko uttered a silent prayer every time the six divers came up for air. As the cycle of hope and disappointment was repeated, even the onlookers were starting to lose heart.

Are you searching properly, guys? Come on, I really need this. Reiko had no proof that there were bodies in the pond. It was just a hunch, so naturally she was on edge. All she could do was wait — and hope.

Around the sixth or seventh block, the divers had only been down for a couple of minutes when one of them broke the surface.

"I've found something. Hand me the camera."

Someone handed the diver a waterproof flash camera, and he dived back down.

Something?

What was it? Reiko was struggling — she'd been desperate to pee for a while already. Why couldn't the man just tell them what the damn thing was?

Three minutes. Five minutes. A diver, this one with no camera, came up and swam toward the bank.

"There's definitely something down there."

Chief of Homicide Wada squatted down and peered into the water.

"It's upright and the right height for a body."

The right height for a body!

"We've cleaned the slime and gunk off it. Whatever it is, it's wrapped in blue plastic sheeting."

Blue plastic sheeting!

Reiko broke out in goose bumps.

The diver with the camera surfaced. Pulling a bag of tools after him, he swam over to talk to his commander and Komine from Forensics.

"Is it okay if we cut it?"

Komine scratched his head dubiously.

"It'd be better if you can bring it up exactly as it is."

"I don't think that's possible. Even with all of us pulling, the thing didn't budge."

The Water Rescue commander tried to broker a compromise. "We can try and do what you want, but there's a real risk of serious damage to the 'package' if we pull it up by force. I'd recommend cutting it."

"I understand." Komine crossed his arms on his chest. "In that case, do what you think's best."

The commander nodded and gestured at the diver. "Okay then, cut it."

"Yes, sir." The diver went back down.

Some time passed, then all the divers resurfaced. This time, though, there were seven, rather than six heads. Six of them were black, and one was blue. The blue one floated up, gradually revealing its full length, like a surfacing submarine.

There was a commotion in the crowd, which now straggled around the entire pond. Here and there screams were heard.

Captain Imaizumi patted Reiko on her sweaty shoulder.

"Nice work."

"Thank you, sir. To be honest, it's a weight off my shoulders."

Reiko exhaled a mass of air from her chest. She felt as if she'd been holding her breath for hours.

They lifted the bundle onto the shore and unwrapped it right away.

A murmur of disgust rose from all sides.

The corpse was naked. Male again. The face was in so-called Beelzebub bloat — angry and swollen to about one and a half times normal size. There was something creepy about the big purple head stuck on top of the pallid, bloodless body.

Just as with Kanebara, there was an incision at the throat slicing through the carotid artery, as well as numerous lacerations on the torso — though how they had been made was not immediately clear. The abdomen too was a gaping hole. The putrefied intestines had partially dissolved, and puffy white lumps of flesh dotted the tarpaulin. All the cuts had puffy and swollen edges. They would have had a hard time recognizing the wounds for what they were, had they had not seen Kanebara's corpse first.

It was probably only because the body had been wrapped so tightly in the plastic sheet that so much flesh remained. Normally, hungry fish and the motion of the water would have worked together to skeletonize the corpse. Although the hands and feet were swollen and resembled monstrous mittens and socks, the flesh had not become detached from the bone. If the forensics guys could still get prints, it would make identifying the victim that much easier.

The divers' debate about cutting referred to the rope that had been keeping the body in place. The bundle had been tied to a cement block. With no trapped gases to push the body upward, a single weight was enough to do the job.

A temporary halt to the search was called

as the body was taken away to the forensics lab. The divers stayed behind to continue the search. There was no guarantee that the pond contained only that single body.

The investigators were ordered back to Kameari police station. The overall thrust of the investigation would need a rethink now that another body had been added to the equation.

Everyone was waiting in the big meeting room by 1:00 p.m. The Water Rescue team would need a little more time to develop their photographs of the underwater crime scene and to complete their report. Those investigators who had missed out on the discovery of the bodies were asking their colleagues how it had played out, while those who'd been in the park were skimming newspapers, drinking barley tea, and smoking cigarettes, all with a glazed look in their eyes. Other people were rereading files from the piles on the desk sergeant's desk. *There are a hundred ways to kill time,* thought Reiko as she looked around the room.

Suddenly there was a loud thump, and the door was thrown violently open. Reiko turned and saw a group of five men standing in the doorway in identical charcoal gray suits. They looked as if they were posing for a fashion shoot.

Stubby! Reiko whispered silently to herself.

Stubby was the nickname of Kensaku Katsumata, a lieutenant in TMPD Homicide, Unit 5. Because his guys were all intel experts, everyone referred to his squad as Homicide's Public Security Bureau. It was more than a mere joke. Most of his team were intel experts who had experience dealing with national security issues firsthand.

Damn. I'd completely forgotten about him.

Captain Imaizumi had warned Reiko that Katsumata was next in line to be assigned to the case if it showed any sign of dragging on. But the investigation had only just started and certainly wasn't on the rocks. Reiko guessed that the discovery of a second body had prompted the bosses to boost the number of investigators. Katsumata was just next on the roster.

The five men made a beeline for Reiko.

"You should think twice about swimming in ponds when you've got your period, princess."

Katsumata's booming voice filled the room. Kikuta sprang to his feet, his fists clenched and his face flushed with anger. Reiko pushed him back into his seat as she got to her feet.

"That shouldn't be a problem. I wasn't doing the diving myself."

"I know that, you hick. Anyway, your level 2 English certificate and your driver's license wouldn't do you much good underwater."

Katsumata's jibes were right on target. Aside from her college degree, those were her only two official qualifications. She had never dived in her life, and although her period hadn't started, it was about to.

The follow-up comment about the driver's license and the English qualification were clearly designed to take his attack one level past plain sexual harassment. Katsumata was sending her a message: *I know everything about you that there is to know.* He was more like a stalker than an ex–Public Security Bureau agent.

"Terribly sorry to disturb you while you're kicking back, Himekawa. I need to talk to you for a minute."

The four members of Katsumata's squad slipped in front of him and formed a circle around Reiko. First Kikuta, then Otsuka, Yuda, and Ioka got to their feet. Only Ishikura remained seated, reading his newspaper.

"What's the problem, guys? I need Himekawa, not her fan club."

Katsumata scowled at Kikuta. Unintimidated, Kikuta scowled right back. Katsumata was being deliberately provocative. If she didn't calm this situation down, it would soon get out of hand. Reiko decided to play ball.

"Okay," she replied, pushing Kikuta back into his seat for a second time. "I'll talk to you."

"You're a smart girl. Though I can't give you ten out of ten till you train your gorillas better. Now, let's go somewhere we can talk in private, without your little fan club hanging around."

Kikuta bunched his fists. Ioka and Otsuka restrained him.

Katsumata walked out into the hall, and Reiko followed him. At the door, she turned round and looked back at her squad. Kikuta looked as bereft as a kid abandoned by its mother. Reiko jerked her chin at him.

Katsumata took Reiko down the corridor to the empty meeting room. One of his men pushed the door shut behind them.

"Sit." Katsumata gestured at the nearest chair.

"I'm fine as I am."

"You're no spring chicken. Pushing thirty, I hear."

The bastard! But she had survived worse.

"What is it you wanted to discuss?"

"I just asked to see you for a minute, Himekawa. I didn't say anything about discussing anything with you."

"Well, what's this about then?"

"Sit down and I'll tell you."

When Reiko refused, Katsumata grabbed a chair and flung himself into it. He looked up and examined her with his beady little insect eyes. The man was short and stocky but extraordinarily light on his feet. He'd joined the force at the same time as Captain Imaizumi, meaning he had to be fifty or so. There was plenty of gray on his close-cropped head. Probably not from worrying about etiquette, thought Reiko to herself.

Reiko resigned herself and sat down. With their eyes on the same level, Katsumata's insectlike stare seemed slightly less intense.

"What can I do for you?"

Katsumata grunted and sprang to his feet. "To cut to the chase, I want you to share all your information with me. Everything. Don't keep anything back. I'm coming late to this case. That's a handicap."

Her eyes followed Katsumata as he moved around the room until one of his men interposed himself. She suddenly realized that the four of them had encircled her again. She'd have felt seriously threatened if they were not detectives like her.

"If you want to know how the investigation is progressing, Lieutenant Katsumata, I think that consulting the case file would be the best thing to do. All the reports and records are in there."

Katsumata shoved his grimacing face at her from between the shoulders of two of his men. "Don't try and bullshit me. I've worn out the documentation, reading and rereading it. There's one thing I can't find anywhere: an explanation of how you linked the incision in the abdomen of one guy to another guy who'd been killed a month earlier and was lying at the bottom of a pond. Your drivel about 'intuition' may be enough to get Captain Zoomzoom to dance to the beat of your drum, but it doesn't wash with me. How'd you figure out there were two perps — one to dump the body in the hedge and another to stick it in the water? How'd you know that Fukazawa was responsible for that? How could you be so sure there was a second victim in the pond, when nothing in the investigation pointed to that? How —"

Reiko's temper got the better of her. She bounced to her feet and shoved Katsumata's goons aside. *Who's calling who a bullshitter here?*

"I've got *nothing* to hide. Whatever you want to know, just ask, and I'll damn well tell you. So stop dancing around. What do you want to know?"

Katsumata's shoulders juddered with laughter.

"Full and uninhibited cooperation. Way to go, princess. Here's question one, then. How did you make the link between the incision in the abdomen and the bodies being dumped in the pond?"

Reiko emitted a snort that was half contempt, half irritation. "Because it didn't make any sense. Why was such a carefully wrapped and tied body left in such a half-assed location? That was an immediate disconnect. I started thinking about the three different kinds of cut wounds, and it occurred to me that the deep postmortem incision might have been made to help dispose of the body. The hedge was right beside a pond, so I put two and two together."

"How about the idea that two people were involved, one to wrap and transport the corpse, and one to get rid of it?"

"Having two people was the only way the theory about the bodies being dumped in the pond makes sense. Plus the hedge where the body was left was at a T-junction. It was difficult to see at night, but for someone with instructions to look for a body on the hedge at an intersection, it would be easy enough to find."

"How about the guy who died in suspicious circumstances a month ago? Was it your coroner chum who tipped you off about that one?"

"That's right. Doctor Kunioku mentioned an unusual autopsy he'd dealt with. That was before the Kanebara case had even started. Then I noticed the 'Swimming Prohibited' notice at the pond. Seemed weird to put up a sign like that where no one was going to go swimming in the first place. My unconscious just joined the dots."

It was Katsumata's turn to sneer. "That's not much of an explanation in my book. Anyway, here's the $64,000 question. You ready? You tagged this Fukazawa guy as the guy responsible for dumping the bodies in the water. Fine — but didn't it occur to you to ask why the actual killer — or whoever was responsible for wrapping and transporting the body — delivered it to the pond despite Fukazawa having died three weeks earlier?"

Katsumata jabbed a thick finger at Reiko.

"The other guy — his buddy — had been dead for *three whole weeks*. How could the guy who transported the body not know that? Just because Fukazawa was dead didn't mean they lacked options. They could've gotten someone new to do the job, or the guy who brought the body could have taken care of it himself. But that's not what happened. The perpetrator or whoever just went right on expecting Fukazawa — who was dead — to take care of the body. How come? Admit it, it's a question worth asking. Didn't it bother you?"

Dumbfounded, Reiko groped for a reply.

"Uhming and ahing's not good enough. I need a proper answer."

"Maybe there was a communication failure." Reiko tilted her head doubtfully. ". . . Or something."

"Or something? Is that the best you can do?"

"I'm saying that it's a possibility."

"Un-fucking-believable. You requested the Water Rescue team without clearing that point up first?"

"I suppose so."

"*You suppose so.* I give up. I see you've got balls, but I'm more worried about what kind of brains you've got."

"Is that another of your questions?"

Katsumata spread his hands, palms outward, in a gesture of defeat.

Reiko had chosen to go with the idea that the mixup was due to a banal failure of communication. Why the need for elaborate theorizing? Maybe Katsumata was justified in dismissing her explanation. In the end, though, they were talking about human beings. Why did every single thing the killers did have to make sense? Criminals could be careless. Where did he get off giving her such a hard time?

"Let me tell you something, Himekawa," said Katsumata, rounding on her with a scowl. "The way your mind works — it's downright dangerous."

"Dangerous for whom?"

"Dangerous for you, you stupid hick."

"I am having trouble grasping your meaning."

"Try grasping a bit harder, moron."

You're not my boss. You've no right to call me a hick and a moron.

"Very good. I'll think about it very carefully. Now, if you'll excuse me."

Using both hands, Reiko shoved two of Katsumata's minions out of the way and made for the door. When she opened it, she found the four members of her squad plus Ioka standing anxiously outside. Katsumata unleashed a parting shot.

"Hey, Himekawa, are you still afraid . . ."

Reiko had already shut the door halfway. Now she gave it an almighty kick.

". . . of hot summer nights?"

The noise of the slamming door shook the walls and echoed down the corridor, all but drowning out Katsumata's parting words. But she knew what they were. "Hot summer nights." That was what he'd said: "Are you still afraid of hot summer nights?"

No, he can't know. He can't know about what happened to me.

"Lieutenant, are you okay?"

Kikuta reached toward her. His hands seemed to recede into the distance as she reached out to grab them.

A black mist spread across her eyes.

2

Sunday, August 17, 11:00 A.M.

Reiko and Ioka were visiting Nishiarai police station. Yasuyuki Fukazawa's apartment was in the Nishiarai precinct.

"How could I forget? That liquefied-brains case was a shocker," Captain Ito said.

Captain Ito was the head of Community Affairs. "If I remember right, we decided there was nothing to investigate. Has something new come up?"

An uneasy shadow flitted across Ito's face. He had reason to be leery when Homicide began poking into a case that the Medical Examiner's Office had already ruled to be death due to infectious disease. If Homicide turned up something suspicious, the precinct's handling of the matter might come in for criticism or even a sanction of some kind. His worries were groundless.

"We accept the official diagnosis on Fukazawa's death. We suspect, however, that he may have been involved in another case entirely. It's something that's just come up. That's what we're here to talk to you about."

Ito grunted awkwardly.

"Your men discovered Fukazawa's body in his apartment in Kohoku. Is that right?"

"Yes, I believe so."

"Of course, they inspected the premises thoroughly."

"That's right. A thorough inspection was made."

"Could we see the report?"

"Ye-yes, I'll dig it out for you right away. Hey, Furuta!"

A young policeman got up, took a file down from a shelf, and brought it over to the captain. The captain flicked through it until he found the report form on the inspection of Fukazawa's apartment, which he handed to them.

Reiko skimmed through it. She wanted to check the floor plan of the apartment and also see whether Fukazawa shared the place with anyone else. The hand-sketched map showed a small entranceway leading to two adjoining rooms. The first room was six tatami mats in size and included a kitchen, while the second was four and a half tatami mats. It was on the second story of a cheap wood-built block of flats, and it had no bath.

Someone had written the name "Yukari" in the cohabitant box on the form.

"So he was sharing with someone?"

"Yes, his sister. She's three years younger."

"That's this Yukari here?"

"Correct."

"Is Yukari now living there alone?"

"No, I think she gave the place up. I'm pretty sure she was in the hospital when Fukazawa died. The girl has a history of mental instability."

"Do you know which hospital she's in?"

"Yes. Just a minute." Captain Ito got up and grabbed the phone on a nearby desk. "Hi, Ito here. Glad to find you in. Listen, you remember that Yasuyuki Fukazawa guy? . . . The brain meltdown guy? Yeah, that's him. Which hospital is his sister in? You went to see her, right? Which hospital was it? . . . Oh, really? Well, the TMPD is looking into the brother. . . . No, it's not like that. You've nothing to worry about. . . . Okay, Central Medical College Hospital. . . . No, I don't think that's important. . . . Yeah, got it. Okay, thanks. So she's at Central Medical College Hospital? Is she in the psychiatric ward?"

Ito sat back down behind his own desk.

"Who were you talking to?"

"That? Senior Officer Todoroki. He visited

the hospital, but the doctor wouldn't let him see Yukari. Said she wasn't up to it."

"I see."

Reiko went on reading the report.

The body had been found by the manager of the building, together with one of Fukazawa's workmates. Fukazawa, who worked for a local security company, called in sick and missed three days of work. His colleagues got worried when he stopped answering his phone, and one of them came round to check up on him.

"This is where he works?" asked Ioka, pointing to the address of the security firm.

"Oh, by the way," pitched in Reiko. "We heard that Fukazawa was on parole. What had he done?"

"Oh, that . . ." An expression of sympathy appeared on Ito's face. "Basically, he set fire to his house while his parents were still inside. He didn't murder them, though. They were already dead when he started the fire."

"His parents!"

Reiko returned her attention to the report. Fukazawa was seventeen at the time. Apparently he had poured gasoline over his parents' bodies, which were in the living room, and burned the house to the ground, before handing himself in three days later.

The statement he had given at the time was in the file.

My parents were dead when I got back home. I guess they overdosed. They were both addicts, very violent. Their deaths came as a relief to me. Still, they were my parents, so I couldn't help feeling sorry for them. I knew no one would bother giving a proper funeral to a couple of drug addicts like them, so I decided to take charge of the cremation myself. And I wanted to destroy that house where so many horrible things had happened.

Not the most pleasant family background.
"Some people working the case took the view that the parents hadn't overdosed, but they were so badly burned that it was impossible to prove an alternative cause of death. In the end, Fukazawa got three years in juvenile detention. Pretty harsh in light of the facts. I mean, the guy had his reasons. I guess they just wrote him off as bad lot because of the time he'd already spent in juvie and in reform school.

"He began working his security company job and moved into that apartment as soon as he got out. The boss there also works as a juvenile probation officer. He couldn't

160

speak highly enough of Fukazawa. 'Well on his way to becoming a model citizen' was how he described him. Hell, it's so damn ironic. Next thing you know, the poor guy's drunk some dirty water or something and his brain turns to gunk. It's frightening."

But Reiko's attention had moved elsewhere. "It says here that he had 730,000 yen in cash."

The local police had searched the apartment looking for clues to shed light on Fukazawa's activities prior to his death. The list of impounded items did not include a diary, but there were receipts, magazines, photographs, and a single-use camera. Among those personal effects was an envelope containing ¥730,000 in seventy-three used ten-thousand-yen notes. The envelope itself was a dog-eared manila envelope rather than a logo-emblazoned one like those the banks provide customers when they withdraw large sums. It had a definite whiff of criminality.

"We never figured out where the money had come from," Ito said with an anxious frown. "Fukazawa's boss insisted he couldn't have saved that much on the salary he was paying him. Was Fukazawa working a second job? No, he didn't have the time for that. Okay then, was he earning it through criminal activity of some kind? To a man, his buddies say no. Apparently he lived very frugally and never seemed to have cash to spare."

The furrows in Reiko's brow deepened. *Was the money Fukazawa's reward for helping dispose of the bodies?*

It was a lot of money for a job like that. Or, rather, it was too much for simply dumping two bodies in the pond, but too little if he'd committed the murders as well. Anyway, Fukazawa had died before he'd been able to dump Kanebara's body. Could he have been paid the full ¥730,000 for dealing with the body they'd dredged up yesterday? No way. It was far too much for that — and it was an odd sum of money in the first place.

Are more bodies down there?!

The Water Rescue team had kept searching until yesterday evening without finding more bodies.

"Is something bugging you?"

Ito was obviously desperate to hear what Fukazawa was mixed up in. Someone brought them tea. The captain put out repeated feelers as they drank it. Reiko brushed him off every time.

"Thanks for making the time to see us."

"Not at all. Hope I was some use."

Ito probably felt he'd been left hanging, but that wasn't Reiko's problem. The investigation was confidential, and there was no compelling reason for her to open up to him about it.

"Bye. If there's anything else I can do, feel free to call," Ito said as he walked them to the lobby to see them off.

The poor man was obviously desperate to find out what was going on.

When they emerged from the Nishiarai police station, it was as hot as ever outside. The weather appeared to be getting worse, and the sky was a lowering mass of heavy gray clouds. Since it was a Sunday, instead of the weekday snarl of semis and construction vehicles, only the occasional passenger car whizzed along the road directly in front of the station. By three or four that afternoon, there'd probably be a traffic jam due to all the cars coming off the expressway at the Kahei Interchange. For now, though, the road was relatively quiet.

The sight of the broad empty road suddenly transported Reiko back to Minami Urawa, the site of the family home. She was back in her past. Back in that horrible summer. That black summer when she was seventeen years old.

"Are you still afraid . . . of hot summer nights?"

Reiko gasped and sucked in a deep breath.

Her chest felt tense, brittle.

The terror. She was supposed to have conquered it.

These days the only thing that brought the fear back was the sight of that bastard Kusaka. She thought she'd gotten used to his face. Her heart was beating painfully fast. There was a high-pitched whine inside her head. *I can't breathe, can't breathe, can't breathe. . . .*

"Lieutenant? Lieutenant?"

Next thing she knew, Ioka was standing in front of her, holding her by the shoulders. He was shaking her, shouting. It took her a while to catch on.

I'm a lieutenant. I'm not a high school kid anymore.

In her mind, Reiko did a rapid review of her life since the incident. *The court case. Entrance exams. University. Graduation. Joining the force. Training period. First job assignment. Working. Taking an exam. Working. Taking another exam. Working. Yet another exam. Getting into Homicide, my dream job.*

Running through the chronology of her life was one way she could push the fear back into the past where it belonged. That whole episode was over and done with. She'd put it behind her. She no longer had any reason to be afraid.

"Are you all right, Lieutenant?"

Ioka pressed one hand into her armpit to hold her upright as he bent down to pick up her handbag with the other. Reiko wasn't even aware of having dropped the thing. She tried yoga breathing. It was a technique she'd picked up in the bad old days, when she was willing to experiment with anything that might help. Gradually her breathing slowed and her pulse rate normalized. She suddenly became aware that the plainclothes cop on guard duty outside the station was strolling over to check on her.

She and Ioka were not yet close enough for her to tell him about her past. Now she felt strong enough to put on an indifferent front.

"I'm fine. Don't worry about me."

In the end, that was all she came up with. Her main worry was why Katsumata had chosen to bring the matter up at all.

What's that old buzzard trying to do to me?

"Okay, Ioka, let's go."

Reiko grabbed her handbag from him, slung it over her shoulder, and stalked off. Her mouth was clamped shut, her lips a tight line.

■ ■ ■ ■

Sansho Security Ltd. specialized in managing vehicular traffic to and from construction sites and in monitoring parking lots. The office was a three-story building. The president lived on the top floor; the middle floor was a dormitory for employees; and the ground floor contained a garage and the actual offices. That was where they met Mr. Kishikawa, the president.

"You want to know about Fukazawa? He was serious — a good man."

The majority of Kishikawa's employees were young men who had been in reform school or juvenile detention. Everyone currently living in the dorm upstairs, he explained, was on parole.

"I know what I'm doing. I can make something of people that society's written off as bad apples. But Fukazawa wasn't like that. Yes, I was tough with the boy; I had to teach him how to behave properly, how to be polite, stuff like that. At bottom, though, he wasn't a lost cause. He didn't say much, but I know he doted on his sister. I always liked Fukazawa."

Kishikawa was wearing traditional Japanese costume and — despite being indoors

— a pair of sunglasses wrapped around his gleaming bald head. The man's fashion sense was certainly . . . distinctive. It was a look you occasionally came across in the higher ranks of the yakuza. For a normal company boss, it was highly unusual.

"Why do you think Fukazawa rented a place of his own rather than living here in the dorm?"

Kishikawa pursed his lips. "He rented a place so his sister would have somewhere to go when she got out of the hospital. Thing is, there was no way he could afford to pay his sister's hospital bills *and* his rent, even if he skimped on meals. That's why I said to him, 'You're eating breakfast and dinner here with the boys in the dormitory.' I twisted his arm. He still had to pony up for lunch when he was on site, not to mention weekends. My wife was worried he might be doing without."

"Except that a large amount of cash was found in Fukazawa's apartment. Did you know that?"

"Yes, the Nishiarai police told me about it. My best guess is that he got the money from some stash of his father's in the family home before the place went up in flames. He worked for me for less than a year all told. How much was it? Seven hundred grand? No way on earth he could save that much with me."

Meaning what? That Fukazawa covered his sister's hospital fees and the rent by helping dump dead bodies?

"Do you think Fukazawa got into anything sketchy to earn that money?"

Kishikawa closed his eyes behind his sunglasses and slowly shook his head.

"I don't think so. At least, as far I could tell. Like I said, he worked here less than a year, so it's not like I knew all his ins and outs. Still, going by impressions — and that's all it is, my personal impression — I don't think so. That kid — I can't imagine him doing anything criminal just to get cash to fool around with. Did you know he was in reform school before he got packed off to juvenile detention? It was for nothing — a brawl or something stupid. If his parents had bothered to fetch him from the station and promised to keep an eye on him, he'd have been let off with a warning."

Kishikawa paused for a moment and looked out of the window. "I still haven't taken on board what happened to him, the way he died. . . . It's too damn sad. Hell, the sister never even made it to his apartment in the end. Not once. She's in her late teens, you know. He wanted to buy her a

168

vanity desk and a bed — you know what girls that age are like — so I lent him some money. He was paying it back a little every month. He wasn't sure what sort of place would be best for them: one room with a bath, or two rooms without one. What with her being a teenager, he thought she'd need her own room . . . and she never made it. . . . It was a struggle for him to pay the rent *and* repay me what he'd borrowed, but that's the kind of straight-up guy he was."

Kishikawa's tone was measured and dispassionate. He showed no sign of tearing up. Oddly, Reiko found that all the more affecting.

"I think I've got the picture. We'd like to have a word with Fukazawa's coworker, the one who found his body."

"Sure. That's Togashi. Afraid he's out on a job right now. He's just tending a parking lot, so why not go and talk to him there? Can't imagine he's rushed off his feet."

It was the parking lot of a university hospital in Arakawa ward. Reiko and Ioka thanked Kishikawa, left the office, and climbed into a taxi.

Ioka didn't broach any personal topics during the journey, and a taxi wasn't the best place to discuss the progress of the investigation. The silence was long and a little awkward, but Reiko welcomed it.

"At the end of the day, Lieutenant, you are my boss. I know that," volunteered Ioka, after a while.

Reiko turned and looked at the side of his face. She didn't reply. She was unable to.

How well do you really know me, Ioka?

What was Ioka trying to tell her?

No. It couldn't be that.

Having the rank of lieutenant meant everything to Reiko. It was the thing that sustained her. Perhaps Ioka had somehow sensed that and tried to boost her morale by stressing that she was very much his boss.

If so, then Ioka is frighteningly perceptive.

He was a caring and compassionate man. That much had come across.

Silence was indeed golden. Reiko took the opportunity to briefly shut her eyes.

Togashi's testimony tallied with what Kishikawa had told them. Togashi, however, was far less amenable, at least at first. When they approached him in the attendant's booth inside the parking lot, he yelled at them to piss off. Fair enough, thought Reiko. For a guy with his background, especially one who was serious about rehabilitation, few things were more unwelcome than cops showing up at his workplace.

170

When they kept their cool, Togashi gradually opened up about Fukazawa. Mainly, he just said what "a great guy" he was over and over again. He was adamant about not knowing where the money had come from and even joked that if Fukazawa was so loaded, he really should have sent some of it his way.

"Sometimes I think that if I'd met the guy earlier — you know, like when I was a kid — maybe my whole life would have turned out different. I never met Fukazawa's sister, but the way he looked out for her, stuff like that, it made me realize what a mess I'd made of my life. It's thanks to him that I'm starting to get my shit together now. May not look like much, I know but . . . Don't go pissing on his grave, please."

They tried to get more out of him about the sister, but Togashi clammed up and refused to say another word. He didn't even look up to watch them leave when they turned away from the little prefab booth.

Although Reiko's watch indicated that it was after six, there was still light in the gray sky.

"Shall we go catch a train?"

Ioka nodded, and Reiko started walking.

3

Sunday, August 17, 2:00 P.M.
Katsumata was on his way to Central Medical College Hospital.

He'd spent the morning at family court and the local district attorney's office looking into Fukazawa's past. What had he done to be sent to reform school and juvie? How many stints had he done? What had the family court said about him in its judgment? How had he behaved inside?

Like all the other detectives, Katsumata always got saddled with a partner from the local precinct when he was on a case. Giving them the slip — usually while on a train — was a point of pride with him. Although they made useful enough street guides on their own turf, they were dead weight as soon as they were out of their own precinct. He moved faster when he was alone. If he needed help, he could just call on the guys from his squad, who always got rid of their local partners too.

In the reports Katsumata filed, he never criticized his local partner for having lost track of him, preferring to drop a discreet word in their ear, "Better get your shit together, man." The next couple of days, the local man would desperately try to stick with him. They never stood a chance. By day four, there was usually a tacit agreement for both sides to do their own thing.

That was how Katsumata liked it. In the end, a homicide detective has got to be a lone wolf. He wanted to trust the guys in his own squad, but you never knew when they might try to steal the credit for closing a case. That was the good thing — the one good thing — about his days in the Public Security Bureau. They always kept the same guys in the squad, and the squad operated as a single tight unit.

Maybe old age was catching up with him. He'd started thinking that being appointed captain and riding a desk like Imaizumi wouldn't be such an awful fate. His problem was, he was too old to cram for the test. No, on second thought, if the choice was between studying and staying on as a lieutenant, then being out on the street was the better option. People who aren't prepared to hit the books go nowhere, and he was no match for the bookworms.

Bookworms like Reiko Himekawa, he thought. *That broad . . .*

Katsumata disliked Himekawa. The thing he most disliked about her — could not, in fact, stand — was her demure and all-too-perfect looks. *That face of hers. She's good-looking, and she damn well knows it.* As far as he was concerned, however Reiko behaved — chatty, silent, angry, or weepy — in her heart of hearts she was always thinking, "I've always got my looks to fall back on." That was why he'd been driven to say what he said.

Her fainting was a surprise. I certainly put a dent in her confidence. Uppity broad.

When Katsumata was transferred to Homicide, he'd made a point of going through the files of everyone in the department to find out when they'd joined the force, where they'd been posted, which cases they'd helped close, and who'd pulled the strings to get them the holy grail of a Homicide job. He hadn't made an exception for Reiko Himekawa. If anything, the fact that she was a woman only made her more interesting. He'd even checked up on her history from before she joined the force.

Her family lived in Minami Urawa in Saitama. She attended a four-year women's college in Tokyo and joined the police as part of the regular graduate intake. After a stint at the Police Academy, she had been assigned to Shinagawa police station. There she started out in Traffic — the classic fallback for female cops — but was soon moved to Criminal Investigation. It took her two runs at the test to make sergeant, but she passed the exam for lieutenant the first time, at the age of twenty-seven. Since most people make sergeant at around thirty, Reiko Himekawa was making rapid progress up the greasy pole, especially for someone not on the management fast track. As a new lieutenant, she headed up an investigation unit in the Traffic Division until Imaizumi tapped her for Homicide. Which was where she was now.

Her story from before joining the force was much more intriguing. Something happened when she was in high school. Himekawa was the victim of a crime. The case culminated in the death of a detective sergeant, and Himekawa ended up on the witness stand.

She was seventeen at the time. Afterward, she had a truancy problem and was even sent to a local psychiatrist for a while. She nonetheless managed to graduate high school without repeating a year, albeit by the skin of her teeth.

You're pretty damn cocky given your history. It doesn't compute. I'd expect you to be a whole lot less sure of yourself.

That was what drove Katsumata crazy: Himekawa's attitude. Just because they were the same rank, she seemed to think that his age counted for nothing. Just because she was a looker, she thought she had the right to disrespect him. Shit, the broad wasn't even a real looker in the first place. She was tall with a baby face, and that tricked people into *thinking* she was cute. It was an optical illusion. A mirage. That posse of fanboys who wet their pants at the sight of her were all fools. Especially Kikuta. He was the worst of the bunch. He was completely under her thumb. A pussywhipped zombie.

That wasn't all. The woman lacked even the most basic grasp of how investigations were meant to be conducted. An investigation was like a game of checkers. The goal was to get your pieces safely to the other side of the board, something you did by slowly and steadily moving *all* of them forward. Himekawa, though, preferred bold moves, leaping over multiple squares to capture her opponent's pieces, without bothering to occupy the center of the board first. And she had no doubts about the effectiveness of her method. She might as well have jumped up and down, flashed her panties, and chanted, "I solved the case. I solved the case." But Himekawa was just a woman — and a damn stupid one. As for Imaizumi, who'd mobilized the Water Rescue team on her behalf, well, what could you expect? Hashizume, who had let the mobilization request go through, was the biggest fool of the lot.

Director Hashizume, you seriously think I don't know? About that toupee you wear?

Despite approaching her cases ass-backward, Himekawa got results. Katsumata had to respect that. This year she seemed to be slightly off her game, but last year she'd closed a multiple street stabbing case in three days and needed just half a day to solve a robbery-with-murder. She hadn't relied on testimony or physical evidence to find the perpetrator. It had been a matter of intuition. One look at the guy was enough for her. "He's a killer. I can see it in his eyes." Based on some such bullshit reason, she would pick out her prime suspect, then do all the necessary legwork to get an arrest.

She seemed to be following the same playbook with the current case. She made an inspired guess about the bodies being dumped in a pond, then managed to link that to Yasuyuki Fukazawa's suspicious death. The woman had something — something well beyond normal detective instincts. He was sure of that.

Don't tell me that she's a frigging psychic. . . .

It was time to forget about her. Katsumata was on the case, and he was going to tackle it his way. His direct boss, the captain in charge of Unit 5, was a moron. The man wouldn't give him any trouble, though.

Director Toupee, Captain Zoomzoom, and Little Miss Uppity, all working the case together. It's a recipe for disaster.

Things could get even worse if Kusaka's squad, which was also part of Unit 10, was brought in. Kusaka was a tough bastard. His acute appendicitis would probably only keep him out of a circulation for a week, max.

Fuck Kusaka too. I'm gonna be the one who cracks this case. End of story.

The automatic doors of Central Medical College Hospital slid open. Katsumata strode in.

The slut at reception had on way too much makeup, and her dyed brown hair didn't suit her.

"Hi, I'm from the Tokyo Metropolitan Police Department. Need to see my badge?"

The girl looked up with a deer-in-the-headlights look on her face.

"Excuse me?"

"I asked if you needed to see my police ID, dumbo."

"Wha-what do you mean?"

She wasn't getting it. He had no choice.

Katsumata whipped his ID out of his jacket pocket, swung it open, and shoved it in her face.

"The name's Katsumata, Tokyo Metropolitan Police Department, Homicide Division. I need to see Dr. Omuro of Psychiatry, now."

Everyone — the in-patients who were ambling aimlessly around the lobby, the emergency cases and outpatients who were sitting around waiting their turn — turned to stare at them. The penny finally dropped. The girl now realized why Katsumata had asked her if she really wanted to see his ID.

"If you could wait a moment, sir."

She abandoned the reception desk and dashed into a room behind. Probably the administrative offices, thought Katsumata. The girl couldn't be bothered to shut the door properly, and it was wide open when she began jabbering. "The police are here.

What should I do? Has something happened?"

None of your business, bitch.

A man in a suit, obviously higher in the pecking order than she was, came out and beckoned Katsumata to one corner of the reception desk.

Fuck, man. What does it matter where we talk?

It wasn't worth making a fuss about, so Katsumata strolled over to the corner. "I'm looking for Dr. Omuro?"

The man started writhing and squirming. He reminded Katsumata of those wimps you sometimes see at the public bath who contort themselves to hide their tiny little todgers. The man kept bowing at him, over and over again. He was a born fucking loser.

"I'm terribly sorry, Officer, but Dr. Omuro is currently in a meeting at the Medical Office —"

"Which ends when?"

"Uh, it should be over in an hour. No, sorry, in thirty minutes."

"Which, man? Spit it out."

"Uh, yes. I mean no . . ." Now the man was just babbling.

"That's enough. I'll wait. Where is the Medical Office?"

"Sorry?"

"You mentioned the Medical Office. If that's where the doctor's meeting, then I'll wait right outside."

"Oh-ah. It's on the sixth floor of the new wing. You turn right out of the elevator."

"Gotcha." Katsumata marched off. The hospital administrator looked like he had something more to say, but Katsumata didn't intend to hang around.

The hospital was a labyrinth. Despite the maps posted on the walls, it took Katsumata a long time to find the connecting passage to the new wing. Even then, he wasn't home and dry: there was only one elevator, and it was stuck on the fourth floor, showing no sign of coming down anytime soon.

This fucking hospital. Katsumata ground his teeth as he waited. Several people got in line behind him, including a few who were in wheelchairs. When the elevator finally arrived, he grudgingly let them on first. He made sure he was standing at the front so he could get off easily.

He looked around the elevator. *Damn sick people everywhere.*

Hospitals were one of the many things that Katsumata hated. His policy was to tough it out when he felt under the weather. The last time he'd been to the doctor had to have been four or five years ago. He'd been coming down with pneumonia and had gone to see his local physician. His symptoms immediately got a whole lot worse. It was the clinic and the other patients there — that's what had fucked him up.

The whole thing started with a cold I got from my wife. We were just about to get divorced. That damn woman — no, I'm not going to go that way.

Katsumata shook his head to drive away the anger that was building up inside him.

He was the only person to get off at the sixth floor.

The creep at reception had told him to turn right out of the elevator. He decided to take a peek at the floor guide. The neuropsychiatry ward covered the whole floor. Was neuropsychiatry the same as psychiatry? He had no idea.

Katsumata had visited a mental hospital once before. Ages ago. For an investigation in which a lobotomy patient was the prime suspect. This place was different. The patients being helped around by nurses didn't look like they had completely lost it. That meant people who were outwardly normal needed psychiatric treatment too. That was a sure sign of a sick society.

Well, as long as the medical profession can make a buck, eh?

Katsumata tapped a passing nurse on the shoulder. "Hi, I'm looking for the Medical Office. I've got to talk to Dr. Omuro." He pulled out his badge. "Can you fetch him for me?"

"I'm sorry, sir. He's in a meeting."

Her unruffled tone rubbed Katsumata the wrong way.

Oh, so his meeting's more important than my investigation, is it?

"Okay. Forget it."

Katsumata stalked off without much idea of where he was going. He found himself in a long corridor with two doors on the right and five on the left: the men's and women's toilets, an unmarked door, the door leading to the emergency stairs, and another unmarked door. . . . The Medical Office wasn't indicated anywhere. Not helpful.

They'll need a decent-sized room for a meeting.

Katsumata pushed open the last door on the right. It was a meeting room all right, but it was empty.

Goddammit, this hospital's driving me crazy.

Katsumata slammed the door shut and tried the next room. This was his last chance. If it was empty, he'd have to go back with his tail between his legs and ask the nurse a second time. He'd have to cheer himself up by giving the creep downstairs a good smacking later.

You aren't making my life easy.

Was this the Medical Office? It looked just like any other stupid office. There were three men and a woman, all in white coats, around a group of six desks. The oldest-looking of the men was standing, holding a file and fiddling with his glasses. He was about to say something, but Katsumata got in first.

"Is there a Dr. Omuro here?"

All eyes went to a man who looked about thirty. So that was Dr. Omuro, thought Katsumata. A typical posh little mommy's boy.

"I am he." The confident and authoritative tone was typical of his class. Katsumata decided to introduce himself properly. "My name's Lieutenant Kensaku Katsumata from the Homicide Division of the Tokyo Metropolitan Police Department. Could I have a word, please?"

Omuro glanced uncertainly over at the older man, who cocked his head, then nodded with evident reluctance. Omuro turned toward Katsumata without getting up.

"What do you want to talk to me about?"

Clearly, it was beneath the doctor's dignity to even stand.

"I need to ask you some questions about

Yukari Fukazawa."

Further looks were exchanged. There were frowns, questioning glances, headshakes. *Is this the psychiatry department or some kind of damn telepathy lab?*

Katsumata's patience snapped.

"I haven't got time for this. Here's what I'll do. If you're in the middle of things, I'll just park myself here and wait. Hurry up and finish your meeting, or reschedule it — it's up to you, but I need to talk to you soon."

Omuro tried to give him a disapproving scowl. The result was unconvincing. "I don't know who you think you are, bursting in on us like this. Just because you're the police, it doesn't give you the right —"

"Oh, put a sock in it. One month ago, an officer from Nishiarai police station came here with a request to interview Yukari Fukazawa. You turned him down. Believe it or not, cops don't visit psychiatric patients just for the fun of it. I'm here specifically to interview her. Whether this is a serious meeting or a circle jerk you're doing here, if you've got a grain of civic responsibility in your body, you'll bring it to an end and start giving me some serious cooperation on this investigation."

That seemed to do the trick. The doctor

pulled himself to his feet, nodded briskly to the old man, his boss, and walked heavily toward Katsumata.

I'm not asking you to run, but pick up the pace a little, Doc.

Katsumata opened the door and, in an effort at politeness, ushered Omuro out into the corridor.

The doctor led him to a consulting room. The decor was bland: a PC sat on a square table beneath the window at the far end, and a curved desk jutting out from the wall divided the room in two. Presumably the doctor delivered his "What seems to be the problem?" spiel from behind there.

Sure enough, Omuro plunked himself down on the far side of the desk. "What can I do for you, detective?" he said, in his best bedside manner.

"I told you already. I'm here to ask about Yukari Fukazawa."

Now what?

There was a frown of annoyance on Omuro's face. "I had to say no to the last detective who came, and I'm afraid —"

"Cut that out," broke in Katsumata, pounding his fist on the desk. "You damn well listen to me. First off, the last guy and me — we're two different people. You may

186

think all cops are the same, but if you think that turning down one cop's interview request means that the rest of us are all going to roll over and die, you've got another think coming. If you want to turn down my request, then go ahead and turn me down to my face, here and now. But you'd better come up with cast-iron reasons for doing so."

The doctor said nothing. Was the fellow finally going to stop giving him the runaround? That would be welcome. Sadly, it was not to be.

"From what you have said, I gather that you are aware of my having turned down another similar request one month ago. In other words, you were fully apprised of the situation before you came here."

You pompous little prick!

If there was one thing that Katsumata despised more than weaklings who gave him no pushback, it was uppity bastards who stood their ground.

"Listen, doc, don't make me repeat myself. The person you turned down last time wasn't me. This time I'm here in connection with a homicide investigation. Yukari's dead brother wasn't just a freak whose brains turned to gunk; there's a possibility he was involved in something else altogether. That's why I need you to tell me about his sister. You read me?"

Omuro sighed. Katsumata took it as a promising sign. Perhaps he was beginning to grind him down. Once people got tired of resisting, it was usually a short leap to the uncontrollable talking stage.

"This is a very difficult situation," said Omuro, treating Katsumata to a defiant stare. "You're obviously very serious, so let me explain the situation. First, I will need to see your badge or your business card. You introduced yourself as Kensaku Katsumata of the Tokyo Metropolitan Police Department, I believe. Forgive my ignorance, but the name doesn't ring a bell."

You pigheaded posh fucker.

Katsumata pulled out his card and slid it across the desk.

"You're a lieutenant?"

"Quit stalling and just tell me what you know. Let's start with Yukari Fukazawa's condition. What's she got?"

"I'm not at liberty to tell you that."

"You're playing the physician-patient privilege card?"

"You know about that? That should make both our lives easier."

"Easier?"

"Because you'll understand why I can't

188

tell you anything."

Katsumata was flabbergasted. The only people he knew who took that confidentiality crap seriously were those management fast-track types. Katsumata despised them all, those Little Lord Fauntleroys who turned up for their training in fancy suits, preening themselves like managers strutting around the factory floor. Bastards!

Come to think of it, one of those rich twits has been assigned to this case. . . . Noboru Kitami, the eldest son of Chief Superintendent Katsuyoshi Kitami, the director of Tokyo's Third District. Katsumata had noticed an almost feral sharpness in the boy's eyes. It was unusual for someone with his privileged background. Katsumata wondered whether he should make a few tactful inquiries about the boy.

He's not my top priority now, so bugger him.

Katsumata ran a hand over his close-cropped head and resumed the attack. "Are you really prepared to put medical confidentiality ahead of people's lives? Listen to me, doctor. People are dead. To be precise, two people have been murdered. Disorders of the psyche are a serious problem, but we're talking about people losing their lives. See? I'm not planning to publish the details of Yukari's mental condition in the media. I just need to know one thing: is the girl capable of talking to me? We can deal with everything else later — whether I can actually talk to her, or whether you'll show me her medical history so I can try to piece together an idea of her life. How about it? You don't need to tell me what's wrong with her, just tell me, is she or isn't she capable of talking to me?"

"I'm sorry." The doctor's voice quavered as he looked Katsumata right in the eye. "I cannot answer that."

The bimbo at reception, the incomprehensible layout — hell, this whole hospital is driving me nuts.

Katsumata glared back at the doctor. "Why, for fuck's sake? Why can't you even tell me if she's capable of talking?"

"Because whatever I tell you, I know you'll still insist on seeing her."

"That's crap. I won't see her if it's pointless."

Omuro's eyes had a pinkish tinge, and Katsumata thought he could even see a glint of moisture. *What the heck?* Had the doctor developed a soft spot for the girl? That would really throw a wrench in the works. Sometimes men in love were more bullheaded than yakuza who'd sworn oaths of loyalty.

"You've fallen for Yukari?"

"You can't be serious."

Omuro's face was postbox red. He rose to his feet and planted his fists on the top of the desk.

"That is the most ludicrous thing I have ever heard in my life."

Nice display of heartfelt sincerity, bro. But I know you're bullshitting me.

"Well, what are you sniveling for?"

Omuro thumped the table. The guy couldn't even take a little good-natured ribbing.

"I'm not crying, dammit. I am just trying to fulfill my responsibilities as a doctor by keeping an overbearing bully like you as far as possible from my patient. Coming into contact with a person like you makes patients regress. Fear creeps up on them and knocks their recovery off course. From what I've seen of you so far, I think it would have been better to let Officer Todoroki to speak to her. He had ten times the tact and delicacy."

Trying to play the old insensitivity card? You are so fucking naive. You seriously think that will work on me?

"I apologize for my lack of delicacy," sneered Katsumata. "It's just that I feel responsible for this case."

"And your eagerness to ride roughshod over my patient's rights is an expression of this noble sense of responsibility?"

"I'm not riding roughshod over anyone, my friend. If I wanted to do that, I could have got Yukari's room number from a nurse and interviewed her then and there."

"That's absurd. You must be out of your mind."

A psychiatrist calling me a nut job? That really takes the cherry. The fellow's insults just keep getting better.

Katsumata scrutinized the doctor's sorrowful face. The man was a mystery. Why was he so rabidly against the police interviewing a patient of his? Katsumata had to see the girl, though. He'd be up shit creek otherwise.

Yasuyuki Fukazawa had been sentenced to three years in juvenile detention without remission. Himekawa's squad was investigating his activities during the year between his release and his death. It was the plum assignment, with plenty of fresh and relevant information ripe for the plucking. As a latecomer to the case, Katsumata had been assigned two less-promising fields. He had one of the guys in his squad looking into the friendships Fukazawa had formed while in jail. He himself was left with the years before Fukazawa went to jail. The chances of finding any evidence that linked to the present case were low, but Katsumata was ready to give it a shot.

He had a nagging doubt about the verdict handed down by the court four years earlier. Katsumata refused to buy the idea that Fukazawa was only guilty of routine arson and the destruction of bodies. Heck, many of the investigators at the time had suspected him of far worse. Lack of evidence was all that stopped them from arraigning him for homicide.

Fukazawa killed his parents before *setting the house on fire. That much is clear.*

Whatever murders Fukazawa had committed in the past would probably have some connection to the present case. It was nothing more than a gut feeling. Katsumata had no intention of shouting from the rooftops that Yasuyuki Fukazawa had killed before based on a mere hunch. There was already one fool woman of a lieutenant doing enough of that. Katsumata's MO was different: establish the facts, gather supporting evidence, secure testimony, whittle down the possibilities. That was how investigations were supposed to work, and that was why securing Yukari Fukazawa's testimony was so crucial. Her knowledge of her brother's history made her a key witness.

All of sudden, Omuro began to speak. The words seemed to seep out of him, almost against his volition. "Panic disorder, depression, depersonalization, self-harming tendencies . . ."

"Huh?" Katsumata's emitted a mystified grunt. It was designed to elicit an explanation from the doctor. It didn't work.

This guy's a piece of work.

Katsumata understood the medical terminology — or he sort of did. Panic disorder and depression were straightforward enough. Self-harming tendencies was probably what the media referred to as "wrist-cutting syndrome." Depersonalization was the one that really had him flummoxed.

That's quite a list to lay on a man in one go.

"Yukari has all of those?"

"Yes. You can see that she's in an acute state of mental disorder."

"Well, can she speak to me?"

"The best answer I can give you is that sometimes she can and sometimes she can't. However, we have to be extremely cautious about exposing her to people she doesn't know. The problem isn't really whether she'll speak to them at the time. The problem is the very real risk of exacerbating her symptoms later on. That's what I need you to understand."

"Okay. Can you tell me how long she's been hospitalized?"

"She's been with us for a long time. She can leave when she is feeling better. She's returned to the orphanage on several occasions. Recently, though, she's been here all the time."

"I'll need to confirm that. Can I see her printed records?"

"That's not possible. If you had a warrant, it would be different. As it is, it's against the privacy laws."

Katsumata sighed. You came across people like this from time to time: people who saw themselves as justice personified and refused to compromise. Omuro was so focused on protecting his patients that he'd lost any sense of proportion. Katsumata didn't have the time to get a warrant. That's why he was here, talking to him man to man. For all the good it was doing him. And persuading a doctor to change his mind cost serious money. Anything less than a million yen was chicken feed to them. He might have had access to that kind of money back in Public Security, but in Homicide — no way.

"I see." Katsumata put his hands on the desk and hauled himself to his feet. "For today at least, I'm going to give up and go home. Next time you see me I'll have the warrants I need to secure your full co-operation. You'd better be prepared to tell me everything you know about Yukari Fukazawa — or else."

"Oh, now you're threatening me. That's a nice note to end on," said Omuro, biting his lip.

"Take it like that if you want." Katsumata went to the door, opened it, then turned around.

Omuro had lowered his forehead onto the desk, and his shoulders were quaking.

Is the fellow blubbering? What a creep.

Shaking away the disgust with a brisk jerk of his shoulders, Katsumata shut the door behind him. The nurse he'd bumped into earlier was just coming out of the bathroom opposite. Katsumata scrutinized her face. She was nicely made up. In fact, she looked exactly like the kind of woman who'd appreciate a bit of extra pocket money.

4

Monday, August 18, 8:30 A.M.

Captain Imaizumi had an important announcement to make at the morning meeting.

"Is everybody ready? We have figured out the identity of the body found in the Mizumoto Park pond, so that is where I want to start today. The victim is a Yukio Namekawa. He was thirty-eight years old, lived in Azabudai in Tokyo, and was married with two daughters. He worked for Hakodo, one of the country's two biggest ad agencies, as a so-called creative. Apparently he made quite a name for himself in the business. A couple of years ago he was in a car accident, a one-car incident in which no one but Namekawa himself was injured. We were able to identify him because we took his prints then, and they're a match with the body. A missing persons report for him was filed on the nineteenth of last month."

The captain moved briskly on to assigning that day's tasks. "Himekawa and Katsumata, I want you to talk to Namekawa's colleagues at the Hakodo office."

Reiko caught her breath. *Why's he pairing me with Stubby?* She looked past Ioka's shoulder at Katsumata. He was sitting on the far left at the front. He was busy taking notes from a file and his face was expressionless. Beside him sat an old, battle-scarred sergeant from precinct. Today she and Ioka would be working with those two.

The thought was enough to bring back the nausea of the day before. This time she managed to keep her breathing under control. Yesterday she'd been weak. She'd not been able to forget Katsumata's parting remark, and that, combined with the heat and the all-too-familiar-looking landscape outside Nishiarai police station, had triggered those memories of what had happened to her on that day when she was seventeen years old and had left the house.

I don't care what Katsumata says. There'll be no more fainting fits today.

Her face was a grim mask. When she reopened her eyes, she found Ioka anxiously inspecting her face. He smiled and nodded. "I'll take care of you, Lieutenant."

Reiko grinned back. "Thanks. I'm okay

now. I won't let him get to me."

I'm not the same person I was back then.

Reiko and Ioka left the room while the meeting was still running.

They went to Hakodo to interview people who knew Namekawa. Allowing for the differences in the two firms' businesses, perceptions of Namekawa at Hakodo were remarkably similar to those of Kanebara at Okura Trading.

Namekawa, everyone agreed, was a creative prodigy whose name inspired respect not just at Hakodo but in the broader world of advertising. When Reiko inquired about the nature of Namekawa's work, she was informed that he was an all-rounder who did everything from directing TV commercials for a cosmetics brand to designing the package for a popular brand of instant noodles. Most recently, he'd produced a music video for one of those prepackaged pop superstars.

In his private life, Namekawa was apparently quite the stud: his affairs ran the gamut, from a high school girl to a well-known actress. In addition, he had a steady, long-term mistress. According to his colleagues, his wife put up with his ostentatious philandering in silence. Either she had a generous and forgiving nature, or she was just too worn out to be jealous. Whichever it was, Reiko couldn't sympathize. She could never accept a partner who screwed around. Anyway, the wife wasn't her problem. Kikuta had been sent to interview Namekawa's family.

The Don Juan antics aside, Namekawa had more than a little in common with Kanebara, as the testimony of one of his subordinates showed.

"Namekawa won a major award for one of his TV commercials the year before last. He wasn't obsessed with awards, but he still seemed to lose his way after that. His mojo kind of deserted him. It stayed that way for most of last year. He was still Yukio Namekawa, though. Even in a downswing, he churned out plenty of top-notch work. The other production companies were left eating his dust. The thing is, I knew the guy. I could see what was really going on inside him. His ideas weren't as sharp as before. The creativity was still there, but he was treading water. He was playing defense rather than offense."

This is the stuff that people with artsy-fartsy jobs worry about?

"That all changed this year. He suddenly recovered his form. It was like he was a different person. Even more than before the award, he was hitting it out of the creative park every time. I was like, 'Wow! This guy's incredible, a genius.' At the same time, he seemed a bit out of control. None of us could begin to keep up with the pace he set. But he was always like, 'Feed me. Give me more work!' "

The bit about no one being able to keep up set off alarm bells in Reiko's head, but she didn't interrupt.

"I warned him that he'd kill himself if he kept working at that rate. You know what his comeback line was? 'You've got to live every day like it's your last, so you've got nothing to regret. Otherwise, what's the point?' He was quite angry. I know what he was getting at . . . I think. . . . Still, living every day without regret and actively fling-ing yourself into the arms of death are two different things, in my book. Namekawa looked like he was in the second category to me, so I wasn't so surprised to hear about his death. . . . How did he die? Was it a fight or something like that? How come no one found him for a month?"

Reiko decided that the notion of a grudge killing wasn't worth pursuing, at least for the time being. As a star in his profession, Namekawa was more likely to have enemies than Kanebara; at the end of the day, though, he too was just a hired hand, a salaried employee. It was hard to conceive of any work problem that would lead to murder, let alone such a bizarre one.

Nor was there any sign that Namekawa was connected to Kanebara in any way. There was no reason why the star creative talent at an advertising agency and a salesman from an office equipment leasing company should cross paths. To be certain, Reiko checked: Hakodo didn't lease its office equipment from Okura Trading.

The next person they interviewed was Namekawa's personal assistant. She had a good grasp of his schedule.

"Oh, you're right. He made me cancel an engagement I'd penciled in for the evening of July thirteenth. You're interested in the month before too? That would be . . . June eighth. No, he had no work engagements on the eighth either. The second Sunday before that would be May eleventh. He blocked out that evening too. Gosh, I never realized. What was Mr. Namekawa doing every second Sunday?"

That's what we're here to find out.

Working back through Namekawa's diary, they discovered that he'd been keeping the second Sunday of the month free since

December the previous year. When the PA had scheduled something for April, he simply failed to show up. Where was he? What was he doing there? His colleagues had no idea. Tellingly, the blocked-out Sunday evenings and his frenzied overperformance at work — what his subordinate referred to as his "comeback" — had both started at almost exactly the same time.

Perhaps Namekawa had some special experience on Sunday, December 8, last year. It was something that happened every second Sunday. What, though? Was he meeting someone? Was it an organized event, or some sort of natural phenomenon? A negotiation of some sort? What?

Whatever it was, it had inspired Namekawa to throw himself back into his work with manic energy. Then, roughly six months later, on July 13, he had suddenly disappeared. Reiko guessed that the missing person's report had not been filed until six days later because Namekawa — unlike Kanebara — didn't work the usual nine to five, Monday to Friday.

Something on the second Sunday of the month had affected both men the same way, motivating them to work harder. According to Mrs. Kanebara, her husband had started going out once a month in early spring, though she'd not been able to provide precise dates. Early spring was also when Kanebara had launched his one-man sales assault on the East Tokyo Bank. That was suggestive.

In the end, both Namekawa and Kanebara had been murdered on the second Sunday of the month. In truth, it wasn't certain that Namekawa had been murdered on July 13 — that was speculation on Reiko's part. The coroner had placed his death "sometime in mid-July" as the state of the body made greater precision impossible. Still, it made sense: Namekawa had gone missing after canceling an evening engagement for the thirteenth, and he had been killed in the same way as Kanebara.

From there it was a short step to imagining a whole series of victims: Kanebara in August, Namekawa in July, someone in June, someone in May, and so on. Namekawa's involvement with the second-Sunday business dated from December the year before. If that was true, then a nine-victim tally was the best-case scenario.

That also means that somebody else will be killed on the second Sunday next month, too.

What the hell was going on? What was this thing that got people so stoked about their jobs on the one hand, but came with the possibility of violent death on the other?

Reiko and Katsumata took a meeting room each at the advertising firm to conduct their interviews. Namekawa's immediate boss had drawn up a list of the employees who were closest to the victim, and they divvied it up between them.

Reiko and Ioka had done half of their scheduled interviews when Reiko consulted her watch. It was ten past twelve. She suggested breaking for lunch. Being hungry wasn't the point — she was eager to learn what the Katsumata team had found out.

The journey that morning to the Hakodo office had taken them almost an hour. Katsumata didn't say a word to Reiko either on the train or in the street. Once they arrived, he'd limited himself to suggesting that they divide up the interviews and drawing up a roster.

Just my luck, being paired up with that old stalker.

In fact, Katsumata's silence had been a boon to Reiko. Normally, every word he uttered was like a needle probing an open wound. She'd promised herself not to let him get to her, but that didn't stop her feeling apprehensive. His keeping his mouth shut meant she'd been able to give her full focus to the interviews this morning.

"I suppose we really ought to invite Lieutenant Katsumata to join us for lunch," Ioka ventured.

Reiko sighed. "I don't think we *have* to, but it would be unprofessional not to brief each other on what we've learned this morning. Pooling information now will help us get better results this afternoon."

Reiko started to feel uneasy before the words were even out of her mouth. Would Katsumata be willing to pass on what he'd found out? No, the man was a bastard, but surely not even he would refuse to share information from interviews they'd agreed to divide up between them. Besides, neither of them had the full picture; he needed her input as much as she needed his.

"Okay, let's go." She left the room, and Ioka followed her. They went down a gleaming, blue-carpeted corridor and into the open-plan space where the creative team was based. Reiko had no idea what people in ad agencies did all day, but the place looked like a war zone. Most offices quieted down during the official lunch break between 12:00 and 1:00, but here people were charging around every which way. Behind their shoulder-high partitions, all the desks were buried under heaped up files, product packages, mock-ups, and samples.

At the far end of the room, beyond the maze of partitions, there were three meeting rooms. Their walls were plate glass down to waist height. Katsumata had set up shop in the one on the far left. A yellow blind had been pulled down, blocking her view into the room. The same had been done with the room on the far right, though there the blind was green. Presumably pulling the blind down was to indicate that the room was in use. Reiko idly wondered what color the blind in the middle room was.

Reiko raised her hand to knock on the door of the meeting room on the left.

"Excuse me, miss," said a woman sitting nearby.

"Yes?"

"Your friends left around half an hour ago."

For a moment, Reiko was nonplussed.

"My friends? You mean the detectives who were using this room?"

"Yes."

Ioka pushed the door open. It was empty.

"What? Both of them?"

"Yes. In fact, they took Ms. Shiratori with them."

Ms. Shiratori . . . ? Damnation.

Kasumi Shiratori knew Namekawa better

than anyone. The woman had been his lover for years.

"I thought Ms. Shiratori wasn't due back until the afternoon?"

"I think the idea was it would be safer to schedule her interview in the afternoon. As it was, she got back to the office early, and your friends . . ."

Katsumata was a dirty operator.

When they divvied up the names, Kasumi Shiratori had been on Reiko's list. She was a key witness. Her name had come up repeatedly in the interviews she had done that morning. Their relationship was an open secret in the office. The woman had been Namekawa's lover since before his marriage. She knew all the ins and outs of his work and his personal life.

Damn that Stubby for a double-crossing bastard!

Snagging one of her interviewees was bad enough, but then to take her out of the office! What was the man thinking? There was no point in calling Katsumata's cell. He wouldn't pick up. She could try calling Shiratori directly, but Katsumata wouldn't let her slip through his fingers. If he let her go, it'd probably be after warning her to say as little as possible to anyone else.

He fucking played me.

Now Reiko realized why Katsumata had been so quiet that morning.

Kikuta went to visit Namekawa's family at their home.

The house and the wall around it were both made of brick. Kikuta's first impression was that the place was a grand old mansion; on closer inspection, however, Kikuta realized that the bricks were not the real thing, but modern siding treated to look like brick.

He pressed the button on the intercom on the front gate.

"Hello, who's there?" It was an upperclass woman's voice.

"Good morning. I'm from the Tokyo Metropolitan Police."

A pause.

"Wait there a moment."

A minute later, the front door opened. A woman in a moss-green dress emerged. Kikuta put her at the same age as Reiko, possibly a little younger. From the way she walked down to the gate — even her way of standing behind it — Kikuta could tell that she came from a good family. She was genteel. That was the word.

As soon as she had opened the gate and let him in, Kikuta bowed deeply at her.

209

"Mrs. Namekawa, allow me first to offer my condolences."

She bowed back at him, slowly and in silence, then motioned for him to go into the house, mumbling "This way" in a barely audible voice. Kikuta had the sense that her husband's death wasn't what was making her so glum. The woman didn't look like much of a live wire in the best of circumstances. He couldn't picture her strutting around, pounding on desks and yelling at people, like Reiko did.

Guess Reiko's more my type. . . .

Kikuta and his young partner from the precinct followed Mrs. Namekawa into the hallway. Several expensive-looking pieces of furniture immediately caught his eye. Although he wasn't equipped to judge the aesthetics, even he could tell that the stuff must have cost an arm and a leg. A big shot creative director at a top ad agency obviously pulled down a hefty salary.

"This way, please." The woman ushered them into a large living room. The floor was an expensive-looking parquet number made from exotic woods rather than your normal cheap flooring. A number of photographs in solid-looking frames sat in a bay window framed by lace curtains. Must be family pictures, thought Kikuta. Kikuta and his partner sank down into the deep, soft sofa she pointed them to.

Mrs. Namekawa served them some iced tea, then settled down in the chair opposite.

"We're very sorry to intrude at such a difficult time."

It was the standard thing to say in the circumstances. The wife gave a quiet little nod. She didn't seem unduly shaken up by her husband's death. Despite feeling quite unable to establish any sort of connection with the woman, Kikuta went ahead and asked her about her family.

The woman's name was Tomoyo. She was twenty-eight years old, ten years her husband's junior. She got a job in a trading company after graduating from a two-year junior college. It was there that she had met Namekawa, who was in and out of the place for business. They had gotten married six years ago, and their first child was born the year after. They now had two girls, ages five and three. She came from money, and her family had given them help to build this house.

Tell me about it. Your normal working stiff under forty could never afford to live in a palace like this.

Kikuta glanced at the bay window. "I need to ask you something that might be a little awkward. Try not to get upset."

"I see," she replied hesitantly. "Well, go ahead."

Her eyes were fixed on the coffee table.

"How was your relationship with your husband?"

"Our relationship was neither good nor bad," she replied with a wan smile. "Let me put this on the table right away: my husband and I weren't all that close. It's embarrassing for us as a family, but I might as well tell you. God knows, you'll find out soon enough if you ask around at Hakodo. My husband had a lover at work. Her name is Kasumi Shiratori, and they'd been going out since before our marriage."

Tomoyo's whole demeanor seemed strangely impassive given the circumstances. Kikuta couldn't be bothered to hide his distaste. "You were aware of that when you married him?"

She gave a heavy shake of the head. "No, I only found out after we'd gotten married. My husband came right out and told me when I was pregnant with our second girl. I'd sort of sensed it before. He was quite happy to come back home without washing off the telltale signs. I may not be the sharpest tool in the shed, but even I knew what was going on."

212

By telltale signs, Kikuta assumed she was talking about lipstick on the shirt collar, the smell of perfume, and so on.

"Lately I've begun to think that it was my fault. At least partly. Namekawa proposed, I said yes, and we got married. But you know how I felt? I was just like, 'Oh, so this is what marriage feels like. Big deal.' It was the same thing when I had my daughters and when we built this house. 'Is that it?' Listen, I'm a woman. Of course I was flattered when he asked me. The man worked twice as hard as anybody else. All my friends told me he was a great catch. I felt pretty smug, pretty pleased. . . . But somewhere in my subconscious I was, like, willing myself to be happy. What I'm trying to say is that I really didn't know what I felt."

The woman was looking down at the floor, and her head was wobbling gently from side to side. "My husband used to criticize that side of me. He'd say, 'So go on, tell me what you think.' When he took that tone, I completely lost my nerve. I honestly couldn't tell if I was happy or sad, how I felt about anything." She lapsed into silence. "I think that's why he told me upfront about his mistress. He said the same thing, 'Go on, tell me what you think about that.' . . . And you know what I thought? I

213

thought, 'Oh, you're having an affair? So what.' I guess I felt angry at being cheated on — angry and a bit worried about our future. But my main reaction was just, 'So this is what being cheated on feels like. Big deal.' " She paused. "Do you think there's something wrong with me?"

At a loss for words, Kikuta felt that a noncommittal grunt would be an inadequate reply. His best bet, he decided, was to change the subject.

"Very . . . uhm . . . interesting. Now, can you give me any pointers as to what your husband has been doing recently?"

"I'll try, though given the nature of our marriage, I may not be that well informed. My husband took his work very seriously and wasn't at home much, even on weekends. When he was, though, he was a wonderful dad, really sweet with the girls. I'd started to think, 'Hey, what we've got here is good enough.' He didn't hide any of his income from me. Everything he earned was for us, for the family. Who knows, perhaps for a married couple our relationship was on the good side." A brief silence. "I suppose people despise for me for allowing a third person into the marriage. For my part, I just felt, 'It is what it is.' "

Kikuta was getting increasingly annoyed.

The woman wasn't providing any useful information, while her whole attitude to relationships — no, her approach to life in general — was violently rubbing him the wrong way. She might as well be from a different planet. How had she been raised to turn out like this?

This interview's probably a write-off whatever angle I take. . . .

Kikuta decided to try asking the woman about her husband's friends.

Lieutenant Katsumata was sitting opposite Kasumi Shiratori in a swanky Italian restaurant. Of course, Kasumi had chosen the place. Katsumata's own tastes ran more to deep-fried pork cutlets.

The woman was definitely a looker. She caught his eye the instant she breezed into the office a little after eleven o'clock. At the time he'd been interviewing one of Namekawa's subordinates. With a leer, he'd asked, "Who's the babe?"

"Her? That's Kasumi Shiratori, Namekawa's mistress. I told you about her."

She was wearing white slacks and a black sleeveless blouse and had a bag and a white jacket slung over her shoulder. The jacket, Katsumata assumed, was for rooms where the air conditioning was cranked up too

215

high. He was struck by her eyes: they were big, like a Westerner's.

That is one tasty piece of ass!

Katsumata had only seen photographs of Namekawa. The guy looked like a player. The two of them must have made a great couple. His gut told him that the broad knew everything there was to know about Namekawa. According to the roster they'd drawn up, Himekawa would be interviewing Kasumi that afternoon — assuming, of course, he played by the rules. . . .

"Okay, that's enough. You can go," snapped Katsumata, bringing his interview with Namekawa's subordinate to an abrupt end.

"Matsuoka, it's time for us to skedaddle." He slapped his partner from the local precinct on the back. Yesterday his partner had been a young officer, but today he was paired up with a grizzled old sergeant. If the man had his own ideas about how things should be done, he had the sense to keep them to himself.

Katsumata paused to think at the door of the meeting room. According to the schedule, Himekawa was due to finish her first round of interviews at around twelve o'clock, but if she popped out for bathroom break or something she might notice that they'd already left. Katsumata figured a ten-minute head start would be enough to smuggle Kasumi safely out. To create the impression that the room was still occupied, he left the light on and lowered the disconcertingly bright yellow blind. Then he walked over to her desk.

"Hi. You're Kasumi Shiratori, right?"

Kasumi had only just sat down. She glanced suspiciously up at Katsumata, then nodded when she realized what it was about. He didn't even need to flash his badge.

"Is it my turn?"

The voice was husky and sensual. Everyone Katsumata spoke to described her as a combination of brains and beauty. They were right. The woman was a true stunner, not a dime-store Barbie like that hick Himekawa. Look at that bone structure! True class. Okay, the broad was fucking around, but at least she was doing it with a top creative director. This is how God wanted women to be!

Look at her. The broad's glowing. That's a woman at the top of her game. She was the kind of woman it was easy to fall for but about whom you should think twice before marrying. When you genuinely liked a woman, sometimes retaining distance in the relationship made sense, especially when the woman had a job. That was what Kasumi and Namekawa had done. Shagging was a whole lot more fun when you had some time apart. Not being together left you with some secrets and kept the lust alive and the sex enjoyable. There was nothing secret or sexy about taking your evening bath in a prearranged order and climbing together into an old futon in worn-out pajamas. When a man and a woman had no more secrets, it was all over.

I'm freshly divorced; I'm a man and in full working order!

Katsumata had slipped thirty thousand yen to Sergeant Matsuoka, his partner, to take himself out of the picture while he took Kasumi out to lunch. Small infusions of cash were very popular with sergeants of a certain age. You just told them, "Here's some pocket money. Now you go off and play," and they'd vanish as fast as a fart in the wind. Matsuoka fit the bill. And he wouldn't kick up a fuss about whatever Katsumata wrote in the report for the day, either.

"What was your take on Namekawa's disappearance?" asked Katsumata, as he sucked the spaghetti up from his plate. The stuff had some long and unpronounceable foreign name. He'd scoured the menu for Japanese-style seaweed spaghetti, but there was none on offer. By pretending he was having udon noodles with a stingy serving of broth, he could just about bring himself to eat them.

Whatever he was having, Kasumi had ordered it for him. He'd just asked her to get him the lightest thing on the menu. What was it called? "Pero-pero" or something like that. It was so light it was next to nonexistent. The only tastes he could pick up on were olive oil, garlic, and chili. Some key ingredient must have been left out by mistake. Seasoning might have helped, but there was neither soy sauce nor brown sauce on the table.

Kasumi put down her fork. "I had no idea what was going on. I mean, Namekawa was hardly the kind of person to miss a whole day of work. Even when he was working through a backlog of jobs, it never took him more than a few hours. I heard nothing for several days; after a week, I just had to accept that he was dead somewhere."

Her neck was white and slender. She was having the same dish as Katsumata. The spaghetti that she was sucking down left her scarlet lips glistening with olive oil. There was something obscene in the sight! She was everything a woman should be!

"That's quite a laid-back response to the death of your longtime lover."

Apparently, Kasumi liked her emotions like her spaghetti — light.

"You think that's wrong? Don't tell me you suspect me."

Katsumata let that pass.

"Aren't you broken up about it?"

"Of course I am. I want to bawl my eyes out."

"But you don't."

"No, not during work hours."

After the meal, they were given ludicrously strong coffee in ludicrously small cups. What the fuck was that about? Katsumata admired the way Kasumi tossed hers back. The broad certainly had style.

Get a grip on yourself, Katsumata! This is business, not pleasure.

Katsumata refocused and pushed on with his questions.

"Was there anything different about Namekawa before his disappearance?"

"Different? How do you mean?"

"Could be anything — though I'm most interested in what he was doing on the second Sunday of the month. . . ."

Kasumi's perfectly sculpted eyebrows twitched.

"The second Sunday? Did something happen . . . ?"

"That's what I'm asking you. Were you with him on the second Sunday of the month recently?"

She stared down into her empty coffee cup.

"I need you to tell me a bit more."

The woman really was a cool customer. She never spoke without weighing up the angles. Katsumata was the same. Don't give anything away without getting something in return, or you'll never catch yourself a big fish.

"Namekawa was going somewhere every second Sunday. Wherever it was, we don't think it had anything to do with his work. I want to know if it had anything to do with you."

Katsumata thought he'd been doing her a favor by speaking so frankly. He was flabbergasted when her face crumpled and she began to cry.

"I don't know," she whimpered. "When I asked him what he was doing, he wouldn't tell me. He was always hooking up with women — not just me and his wife — but he never tried to hide that. Whatever he was doing on those second Sundays, though, that was different. He came right out and said he had no intention of telling me what was going on. He got quite aggressive. I was afraid he'd found another woman and was going to dump me *and* his wife." She paused. "Now he's dead, and I still have no idea what was going on."

"You thought it was another woman?"

Kasumi gave a small shake of the head. "I don't know. When I pressed him about it, he'd totally fly off the handle. Then this sad, pained expression would come over his face. We'd been together ten years, but for the first time he was keeping secrets from me. Normally he'd tell me everything — about work, his family, everything. . . ."

"When did you notice the change?"

"The end of last year, I guess. Just when he rediscovered his passion for his work." Kasumi suddenly inhaled sharply. She looked up at Katsumata and said, "I've just remembered something. He said something weird when I was trying to get an answer out of him."

Okey-doke. Here comes your big fish. Reel it in carefully.

Masking his excitement, Katsumata looked flintily into Kasumi's eyes. "What did he say?"

"He starts off by asking me if I know anyone who's been in a war. My grandpa fought and died in World War II, while my dad was just a schoolboy at the time, so I said that no, I didn't. He goes all quiet for a while, then starts with this spiel about how people who make it back from war have a special kind of mental strength. He said he'd recently been able to experience that feeling firsthand, or something like it. He frightened me. It was like I didn't know him anymore."

Katsumata sat lost in thought for a while. *What the hell has war got to do with anything? If this is my big fish, it smells a bit rotten to me.*

The thought reminded him of Namekawa's putrid corpse.

5

Otsuka was in charge of interviewing Namekawa's friends.

There was an unspoken rule within the
police force: every officer had to stay strictly
within the parameters of their own investigation. If a promising lead came up when they
were doing a neighborhood canvass, they
couldn't follow it up outside their assigned
sector. They had to find out who was in
charge of the relevant sector, brief them,
and then pursue the lead with them.

For that reason, when Otsuka was assigned to investigate Namekawa's friends,
he had no right to interview Namekawa's
direct colleagues at the ad agency — Himekawa and Katsumata were handling that —
or his broader network of work connections,
which Ishikura and one of Katsumata's
squad were taking care of. Meanwhile Kikuta, Yuda, and another guy from Katsumata's team were looking into Namekawa's

family — friends of the wife, the parents of the daughters' playmates, people they'd met at the PTA.

What Otsuka was left with were Namekawa's friends from his college days. With almost nothing to go on, Otsuka decided to visit Namekawa's college, Haseda University. Namekawa had graduated from Haseda fifteen years ago. That was all that Otsuka knew about the victim's college days.

Universities are like an alien planet to me.

Otsuka had taken the Metropolitan Police entrance exam fresh out of high school. For his first job, he was assigned to the Koganei police station on Tokyo's outer fringes. A humble Community Affairs officer, he was passionate about becoming a detective. He knew that the reality of the job was nothing like the cop shows on TV. He wouldn't be spending his time firing his gun or punching smart-assed suspects. That didn't matter. If anything, the lack of glamor made him want it worse. While going about the daily grind of giving street directions, dealing with lost-and-found articles, and dropping in on local residents, he submitted multiple requests for a transfer to Criminal Investigation.

Opportunity came knocking sooner than he'd dared hope. A robbery-murder took place just a few hundred meters from his regular beat. A task force was established at the precinct, but the workload proved too much for the CI detectives. They decided to draft some cops from Community Affairs to lend them a hand. Otsuka was one of the lucky ones pulled off routine duties. All the CI detectives wanted Otsuka to do was to act as a neighborhood street guide. Otsuka didn't care. He was elated and flung himself into the investigation with gusto.

Several days later, the perpetrator was apprehended somewhere else entirely. Somewhere Otsuka had never even heard of. He'd canvassed the neighborhood until his legs had turned to lead, but his contribution to solving the case was a big fat zero. Nonetheless, his partner, a seasoned CI hand, had nothing but kind words for him.

At the party to celebrate the successful conclusion of the case and the winding down of the task force, the old detective clapped Otsuka on the back, grinned, and told him he was "one heck of a stubborn bastard." Clasping the man's hands, Otsuka bowed so deeply that his forehead almost touched his knees. He didn't want anyone to see the tears in his eyes.

Soon after, Otsuka's transfer request was approved, and he joined the larceny division of the Criminal Investigation Bureau. Only later did he discover that the old detective had put in a good word for him. Determined not to disappoint his secret patron, Otsuka applied himself doggedly to his job.

Otsuka was just made that way. He never unearthed key leads or directly contributed to closing important cases. What he specialized in was working his way through the list of initial suspects and flagging any who were obviously innocent.

Ultimately, every investigation was a process of elimination, and somebody had to do the eliminating. It was a tedious job but an important one. His colleagues noticed his contribution and valued it.

In the squad, Ishikura was the one who valued Otsuka's contribution the most, more than even Himekawa and Kikuta did. "Your tenacious approach really helps tighten the focus of an investigation. You're doing an important job."

That was how Otsuka ended up being saddled with Namekawa's university. Unfortunately, there were few places Otsuka felt less at home than on a college campus. He'd visited several for various investigations over the years, and they always made him feel like a fish out of water.

It had taken him a while to realize that at

university not all the students went to class when the bell signaled the start of classes. There were youngsters out on the lawn playing catch, youngsters in the dining room eating, drinking, and gossiping. Wasn't college supposed to be for studying? Instead, to Otsuka, universities looked more like vacation resorts that had been plunked down in the middle of the city; students were just spoiled brats who lived the life of Riley.

It was summer vacation, but despite there not being any classes, plenty of students were milling aimlessly around. There was a group sunbathing on blankets at the edge of the big sports field, and the sound of someone performing a drum solo came from one of the buildings. Mysteriously, a mud-stained rugby player was dragging an empty bicycle-drawn trolley after him. A criminally sexy girl greeted the rugby player with a wave.

"Hiya. Seen Komori anywhere?"

"He was in the library a minute ago. You want his notes, rights? He gave them to me."

"Are they in your locker?"

"No, they're in the rec room chest."

"Okay if I help myself?"

"Pick up mine too, will you?"

What are you two talking about? What is a

"wreck room" anyway?

The girl, in a fluffy top that made her look as though she was about to sprout wings, vanished into a gloomy-looking building. A cute young girl had no business in a dump like that.

At their age, Otsuka already had his nose to the grindstone. In the summer, he spent the day either at the station or doing the rounds on his police-issue white bicycle. When he was assigned to nights, he'd sit at his desk staring out at the dark street, darting out from time to time to give a rowdy drunk a talking to. In those days, he had mostly dealt with old people who lived alone, housewives, store owners, janitors, real estate agents, workers in local factories and workshops, elementary school kids who came to hand in coins they'd found on the sidewalk. University was a different planet.

Otsuka glanced over at Lieutenant Kitami. He was squinting up at the sky, looking thoroughly bored as he lit a cigarette. *I forgot. The guy's a rich kid who graduated from a top university.*

Kitami got into the National Police Agency without having to take the state examinations. The only way you could do that was by having a first-rate degree. He probably had a law degree from Tokyo

University. Having completed the three-month-long cadet course at the National Police Academy, Kitami was now in the field as a trainee.

Seems like a mellow enough guy, given his background.

Kitami was already a lieutenant as soon as he graduated from the academy. On his first day with the task force, he'd introduced himself to Otsuka with a deep and respectful bow. Since Otsuka was just a regular officer, he'd been taken by surprise. As there'd been plenty of other detectives around, Kitami could just have been playing to the gallery.

"I'm a total greenhorn, Officer Otsuka," he'd said. "I'm looking forward to you showing me the ropes."

Kitami was perfectly coiffed, and his features were handsome and regular. He wore trendy frameless glasses and a suit and tie that were obviously expensive. By contrast, Otsuka's hair was a tousled mess, his three-year-old suit was rumpled and shapeless, he'd picked up his tie cheap from a street vendor, and his looks were nothing to write home about. Despite being under no obligation to do so, Kitami had treated him with respect. It wouldn't be fair for him to be standoffish in return. Besides, word had come down from the top brass to go easy on the boy. Otsuka decided to err on the side of caution and ratchet up the deference.

"Do you think the administrative offices of universities are closed during the summer vacation, Lieutenant Kitami?" Otsuka asked solemnly. A little groveling couldn't do any harm.

Kitami gazed thoughtfully at a tall building on the far side of the playing field. "It's the middle of a recession. I would guess that the career center, where they help the students find jobs, is still open."

That made sense. Students needed jobs like everybody else.

With the economy in a rough patch, finding jobs was probably not easy for recent graduates — that much Otsuka could figure out for himself. But making the leap from there to figuring that the career center would be open over the vacation would never have occurred to him.

Otsuka decided to let Kitami take the lead in tracking down Namekawa's college buddies while he tried to avoid saying anything tactless and making an enemy of the young lieutenant.

"Why don't we start by finding out what

clubs or societies Namekawa belonged to when he was a student," Kitami suggested.

They explained what they were doing to one of the clerks in the career center. After setting up camp in one corner of the room, the clerk brought them the written records of the different clubs at the university.

"The clubs all submit annual accounts. The accounts include a list of the members for the relevant year," announced the clerk offhandedly. There were around three hundred clubs and societies at Haseda, so a single year's worth of accounts was enough to fill several thick binders. Kitami and Otsuka were going to have go through the accounts for all four years Namekawa had been a student. That meant an awful lot of checking.

In an effort to speed things up, Otsuka called Kikuta and got him to ask Namekawa's wife what clubs her husband belonged to as a student. She had no idea. He called Himekawa and asked her to do the same thing. She replied that asking that of the man's coworkers would be a complete waste of time, then hung up.

Something's pissed her off, thought Otsuka.

So much for shortcuts. Otsuka and Kitami began examining the accounts. Since

Namekawa had worked for an ad agency, they looked at the Advertising and Marketing Study Group first, but had no luck. Since he had been quite robustly built, their next ports of call were the rugby, American football, and soccer clubs. Another blank. They were going to have to grind their way through the whole lot.

It was half past four by the time Otsuka came across Namekawa's name. The students had mostly gone home, and they could feel the resentful glares of the office staff burning holes in their backs. "Here it is, Lieutenant Kitami," yelled Otsuka excitedly. "He was in the hiking club."

Perhaps Kitami wasn't cut out for this sort of simple, mechanical work. He looked exhausted and only managed an indifferent grunt. Identifying a group of potential interviewees in Namekawa's fellow hikers was only a small first step, and it was all they had to show for their day's work when they reported at the evening meeting.

The next morning they called Yuzuru Takeuchi, who had been the head of the hiking club when Namekawa was at university. Takeuchi had last seen Namekawa at a reunion in November the previous year, he said, but they had not really seen much of

233

each other since graduation. A guy by the name of Tashiro would be a much better bet, as he had stayed in close contact with Namekawa over the years.

Tomohiko Tashiro was thirty-nine years old and worked in sales for an electronics company. He was amenable when they called, and he made time to see them that evening.

They met in a café in a busy pedestrian street in Shibuya, not far from Tashiro's office. Otsuka and Kitami both got to their feet when he came in and bowed. "Sorry to call you out of the blue like this, sir."

"That's not a problem. . . . But is Namekawa really dead?"

The man came across as an archetypal "salaryman," earnest and rather dull.

"I'm afraid he is. We contacted you because we heard from Yuzuru Takeuchi that you and Namekawa were good friends."

"That's right. About once every three months — six at the most — we got together for a drink. It's a ritual we've kept up since graduation. There's no business relationship between our two companies; it was a purely personal thing. Namekawa always used to tease me, 'You guys should hire me to make a TV spot for that new product of yours.'" He sighed. "I can't believe he's dead. If you don't mind, how was he killed?"

"He was stabbed," Otsuka said. It wasn't the whole truth, but it kept things simple. There was no need to let Tashiro know that his friend's body had spent a month rotting at the bottom of a pond.

"When was the last time you two met?"

"Let's see. The end of April, I think. Yes. The Golden Week holiday was about to start, and I remember Namekawa saying he had a backlog of work to get through."

"Did you notice anything strange about him?"

"Strange? I don't think so." Tashiro tilted his head to one side. "Wait, let me rephrase that. There was something strange about him, but that was just how Namekawa was. I mean, he had multiple women on the go and was working his ass off, which was business as usual for him. There was one thing, though. Last year he told me he'd been in a creative slump."

Himekawa had mentioned Namekawa's creative loss of form at the meeting yesterday evening.

"You see, the year before last, the guy won a grand prix for this TV commercial he made. It was a really big deal, apparently. But when all the fuss died down, he lost all interest in his job and couldn't seem to get it back. When we met up this April, he was firing on all cylinders again. I thought, 'Great, he's back on track. . . .' I still can't believe he was murdered. . . ."

Tashiro's statement lined up with what they'd previously learned.

"Do you have any idea how Namekawa pulled himself out of his slump?"

"What snapped him out it? Not really. I didn't know much about the slump in the first place, let alone what got him out of it." Tashiro sank into silent thought for a moment or two. "No, it's no good. I don't recall anything."

As a matter of routine, they asked Tashiro where he'd been on July 13, the day they believed Namekawa was killed. He told them that he was in Osaka on business, which they later verified with his firm.

As they were wrapping up the interview, Tashiro asked Otsuka, "Was Namekawa murdered last month, then?"

"Uhm, well," Otsuka mumbled half heartedly, "I guess he was, yes. Anyway, we need to be getting going."

They left Tashiro in the café, sitting at the table alone.

It was eleven thirty when the evening meeting ended and they emerged from Kameari police station. Tonight followed the usual pattern. Rather than going out for dinner, Himekawa's squad headed straight to a bar near the railway station for a drink. The relationship between Himekawa, Kikuta, and Ioka had started getting interesting over the last few days. After a few drinks, of course.

Ioka was always pushy with her at the pub. Every second word was, "Lieutenant Reiko, I love you," and he frequently tried to sneak a kiss. Sometimes she would shove him away with a "No, thank you very much," other times she would give him a mighty slap in the face. She did her best to look angry, but she usually had the ghost of a smile.

All this provoked extravagant reactions from Kikuta. Yesterday he had seized Ioka by the lapels and bellowed at him, "No way in hell am I going to let you take Reiko away from me, you creep."

It was the booze speaking, of course, but for Kikuta, shouting about his feelings and referring to Reiko by her first name was quite a showy performance. The man was almost giving Ioka a run for his money.

Reiko's response was interesting in its own way too. With a face flushed scarlet from drink, she sat quite still, slumped forward over the table with her hands clamped tight around her napkin.

"Did you hear what I said, you jerk?" yelled Kikuta, pushing Ioka out of the way as he sat down heavily next to Reiko. Still clasping her napkin, Reiko gave a convulsive nod of her head, then another and another and another. It wasn't clear if Kikuta was responding to Reiko's nodding when he put an arm around her shoulders and dragged her forcefully toward him. Far from resisting, she leaned into him and kept right on nodding. With one arm wrapped around her and a tankard clutched in his other hand, Kikuta sat there and slowly drank his beer. Off to the side, Ioka sniveled about what an unfair place the world was, before falling asleep and starting to snore.

"God, what a bunch of misfits," said Yuda with a rueful grin. "Things could get interesting if any of them remember this tomorrow."

Never was a truer word spoken.

Today had been all too similar to yesterday. There'd been nothing worth calling a breakthrough in the investigation. They'd all completed their assigned interviews and dumped their not very helpful reports with the desk sergeant. Despite last night, Kikuta didn't seem to be any more intimate with Himekawa. Nor did Ioka, for his part, look ready to give up.

I'm looking forward to the sequel down the pub tonight, thought Otsuka. But he was in for a disappointment. His cell phone buzzed as they were about to board the bus to the railroad station. Pulling it out, he didn't recognize the caller's number.

"I'll catch up with you later," he said to the other four. (Unusually, Ishikura had agreed to come out tonight.) He knew he'd find them at the usual place. He moved away from the bus stop to take the call.

"Otsuka here."

"Hello, this is Tomohiko Tashiro. We met earlier. Sorry to call so late."

Otsuka had handed Tashiro a card with his cell phone number scribbled on it and told him to get in touch if he remembered anything.

"No problem. Did you remember something?"

Tashiro seemed to hesitate.

"It doesn't matter what it is. Trivial things can sometimes be important."

"Well, I was thinking about Namekawa. . . . I doubt it's important, though."

"You never know. Go ahead and tell me."

"Okay. When we met in April, Namekawa

kept going on and on about how he was feeling truly and fully alive. At the time I just thought he'd gone and got himself another hot girlfriend or work was going well, but . . ."

"But what?"

"Detective Otsuka, do you spend a lot of time online?"

"Some, not a lot. I mean, I've got a PC like everybody else."

"Have you heard of something called Strawberry Night?"

"Strawberry what?"

"Strawberry Night."

Just at that moment, Otsuka glanced back at the front door of the police station. Kitami, his partner, was just coming out, flanked by the station commander and the local chief of detectives. Otsuka slipped behind a police car for cover.

He had a feeling that the fewer people who knew about this phone call, the better.

6

The "Mizumoto Park Multiple Dumped Bodies Case" investigation had hit a wall.

Things had gotten off to a promising start when Reiko spotted the link between Taiichi Kanebara's sliced-open abdomen and Yasuyuki Fukazawa's death by *Naegleria fowleri,* and, as a result, they'd retrieved the body of a second victim, Yukio Namekawa, from the pond. Now, despite all their efforts, they couldn't find anything to connect the two victims. They had also failed to establish a link between Fukazawa, the man Reiko believed to be responsible for dumping the bodies in the water, and Kanebara or Namekawa.

It's weird. I expected smoother sailing than this.

The sum total of their knowledge could be expressed with a couple of bullet points. One: both Kanebara and Namekawa habitually went to an unknown destination on the evening of the second Sunday of the month. Two: both men had been throwing themselves into their work over the last few months.

Even then, there were inconsistencies in the chronology. With Kanebara the change had occurred in spring, whereas with Namekawa it was the start of the year. Why the discrepancy?

The neighborhood canvass produced no results. The victims' personal effects yielded no clues. Interviews with the families, friends, and colleagues produced nothing to connect the two victims, either to each other or to the person allegedly responsible for disposing of them. Fatigue was starting to show in the faces of the task force members, and the initial energy of the investigation was almost dissipated.

Thursday, August 21, was the tenth day since the discovery of Kanebara's body on the hedge. An announcement was made that the task force would get a day off on the twenty-second.

"The way things stand, we are still in the dark about many aspects of this case, including motive, method, and the original location where the crimes were committed. On the plus side, we now have a good idea of where we need to focus our efforts. Both victims had the same numerous small cuts on the torso, the same severed carotid artery, and the same deep incision in the abdomen. Both victims exhibited a similar pattern of behavior on the second Sunday of the month. We know where the blue plastic sheeting and the string used for bagging the bodies came from. There's no shortage of clues that could lead us back to the perpetrator. If we are methodical, there's no reason why we can't crack this case.

"You've all worked incredibly hard for the last ten days, and you're worn out. I can't tell you if we're eighty percent there, or if the solution to this case is quite literally around the corner. None of us knows how this is going to play out. At times like this, it's easy to start feeling edgy and lose focus. I want you all to take tomorrow off. Use the time to recharge, mentally and physically. I want to see you back here the day after tomorrow, bright-eyed, bushy-tailed, and totally committed to wrapping this thing up."

The more passionately Chief of Homicide Wada spoke, the more convinced Reiko became that what he really wanted to say was that they didn't deserve any time off.

His "take a day off the case" speeches are all the same anyway.

In fact, though, Reiko was emotionally worn out. In addition to the slow progress of the case, the stress of dealing with Katsumata in the office and in the field was getting to her. Their relationship had gone from bad to worse after the Kasumi Shiratori episode. She badly needed a break from the man, even if it was only a short one.

Why don't I spend my day off at home?

Unusually for her, Reiko didn't go out drinking that night. Instead she went directly back to her parents' house.

The journey home took just under an hour, about the same time as the commute from home to the Metropolitan Police Department headquarters in central Tokyo. The distance was quite doable, had she wanted to travel to Kameari police station from her parents' place on a daily basis.

When Reiko was working on a case, she always stayed in a hotel. It had nothing to do with distance or convenience; she simply didn't want to go home. Any excuses she made about the investigation being in trouble were lies she told herself as much as her parents.

It's the walk from the station I can't bear.

The fastest way home was through a residential district with a park, but Reiko had avoided that route for years. Although it took longer, she always walked along the main road and took care to drop by the video rental place and the convenience store on the way. It had nothing to do with getting a movie, something for dinner, or a magazine. She wanted to make sure that she was picked up on the shops' CCTV to prove that she was still alive and kicking at a specific time. She'd kept up the habit for years now, despite her doubts about its usefulness.

The family had moved into their house in Minami Urawa in Reiko's first year at junior high. She was thrilled to have her own room for the first time in her life and had fantasized about walking her dog in the nearby park. (Unfortunately, she'd never gotten around to getting a dog.)

She got home in twenty minutes. The place was unusually quiet. She looked at her watch. It was still only twenty past ten. Her father was probably still slaving away at the office. Her mother, who was a night owl, never went to bed before he got home. Strange. It was way too early for the porch light to be off like that. What was going on?

The best thing for me would be if Mom's out.

Reiko took the key from her handbag and opened the wooden front door with its coat of peeling paint.

There was something funny about the interior of the house too. The living room to the left of the passage was in darkness, and a light was on in her sister's room upstairs. Her sister had moved out a couple of years ago when she got married, and her room was no longer in use.

As Reiko locked the door behind her, a voice came from the top of the stairs. "Reiko?"

It was Tamaki, her baby sister.

"I didn't know you were visiting."

Reiko put her handbag, which was swollen with a change of clothes for tomorrow, down on the hallway step.

Tamaki came down the stairs. She had her sleeping newborn baby daughter in her arms. Reiko's first-ever niece, Haruka.

"I'm not *visiting.*"

Tamaki's face was contorted with rage.

"What's with the death-ray stare?"

Reiko went into the living room, switched on the lights, and began hunting for the remote control for the air conditioning. The house was unusually humid and stuffy. She was barely moving and the sweat was pouring off her.

"Remote, remote, where are you hiding?" she murmured, pulling up the sofa cushions.

246

There was nothing there.

"What have you been doing?" said Ta-maki, gently rocking her baby as she came into the living room.

"Me? Working, of course."

What an idiotic question! Ignoring her sister, Reiko went on with her search.

"Working where, exactly?"

Reiko didn't like her sister's condescending tone.

"What does it matter where? Since when do I have to account for everything I do to you? I'm tired, so give me some space, okay? And where's Mom?"

Tamaki's eyes widened. "You're not here because of my message?" she asked, with open annoyance.

"What message?"

Where the hell was that remote control?

"I called your cell at lunchtime."

Lunchtime? Oh yeah, come to think of it, someone did call me.

"Did you call me from the home phone?"

"Yes."

"Sorry, but when I'm working, I don't answer calls from here."

The expression on Tamaki's face was a welter of conflicting emotions: amazement, scorn, distress, and tearfulness.

"So what Mom told me is true."

"Why should I pick up? She'll just nag."

"And you've no idea where that nagging mother of yours is right now?"

"No. That's why I asked."

Tamaki's face momentarily softened and she stopped rocking her baby.

"She's in the hospital."

"Huh?" said Reiko, not understanding.

"Mom's been hospitalized."

"Hospitalized?"

"How many times do I have to say it? Mom's in the hospital."

"When?"

"This morning. She saw Dad off to work, when she suddenly got this pain in her chest. She called the ambulance herself. She also called you, though she knew you wouldn't pick up."

Chest pains? Hospital? Reiko felt as though someone had emptied a bucket of ice-cold water on her head. A chill spread through her body.

"How . . . how's she doing?" There was a quaver in her voice that she could not control.

"The heart attack could have killed her, if she hadn't called the ambulance so fast. She's stable and out of any immediate danger as long as she rests. They are doing some tests. She may have to have bypass surgery. It depends on the results."

There was a history of heart problems on her mother's side of the family. Narrow coronary arteries. It was a genetic thing.

"Why didn't you pick up?"

"I was working on a case," she stammered. "I couldn't."

"Couldn't . . . or *wouldn't*?"

Tamaki's voice was loud and bitter. The baby opened its eyes in alarm. Tamaki ignored it.

"You think 'couldn't pick up' is any sort of excuse? I want to give you a piece of my mind. Dad called me this morning to give me the news. I called my mother-in-law and asked her to take care of the house. Then, lugging my baby and bags, I took God knows how many trains to get here from all the way across Tokyo. When I finally made it, I tried calling you while I was getting together the stuff Mom will need while she's in hospital. I didn't just call you once or twice, but hundreds of times. When I got to the hospital, I found Dad waiting out in the corridor. He was trembling, and his fists were clenched tight. He'd wanted to call you too, but he didn't know your number. I didn't know it either. I called you from here because your cell phone number is pre-programmed into the home phone."

The baby had started wailing. Tamaki broke off to comfort her. "It's all right, little one," she said softly. "There, there. Come on." The baby kept on crying.

Reiko bowed deeply to her sister. "I'm sorry, truly sorry."

Tamaki glared at her. "I'm not the one you should be apologizing to."

"I know . . . but still, sorry."

Reiko couldn't remember the last time anyone in her family had given her such a roasting — or that she had said sorry. She had nothing to say in her defense. The idea that her mother might be ill had never even crossed her mind.

"Your not answering the phone had nothing to do with being busy." Tamaki spoke as if she could see right through her. Tamaki snorted contemptuously when Reiko stayed silent. "I heard that you blew off three dates with prospective husbands."

"It was two, not three."

"You may not count taking a call mid-date before rushing off to catch a murderer as blowing someone off, but I do."

Reiko was again at a loss for words.

"I'm sorry," she said after a pained silence.

"Whose fault do you think it is Mom collapsed today?"

The back of Reiko's neck went suddenly

cold, ice cold.

Was Tamaki going to blame her for her mother's condition? She certainly wasn't guiltless. She had torpedoed those three marriage dates. That was a fact. But was that really what had triggered her mom's heart attack?

"It's our auntie in Yokohama."

Reiko was relieved that Tamaki was pinning the blame on someone else.

"Auntie was always criticizing Mom. You know why? She says that it's because Mom was out that day that you can't find yourself a husband, that what happened to you happened because Mom wasn't here. It wasn't like she only made the claim once or twice. Oh no. Every time you blew off another date, it gave her a pretext to lay into Mom. You had no idea, did you? Mom called me in tears I don't know how many times. She actually believed that what happened to you was her fault. On top of that, her heart's congenitally weak. With all the pressure, no wonder it gave out."

The baby started crying again, loudly. Tamaki just ignored her.

"I respect you for what you've done. You had a terrible experience, but you managed to put your life back together. You're my big sister, and I've always looked up to you.

Everyone always praised you; you were tall, good-looking, good at sports, could get the gist of a textbook just by looking at it. Me, I was never like that. The only time people ever paid any attention to me was when they found out I was your sister. That was the only way I got any respect."

Reiko's mind drifted back to when they were teenagers together.

"As girls, we were very close. I looked up to you — but at the same time I resented you. With everybody comparing us all the time, I ended up convinced I was worthless. When that thing happened to you, a little part of me felt, 'serves you damn right.' I kind of hoped it would bring you down to my level. . . . But oh no, not you. You bounced right back. You got straight into college without needing an extra year to retake your exams. You got into the Tokyo Metropolitan Police, and then you made lieutenant before thirty. You're amazing. Nobody else could have pulled it off."

Reiko's jaw clenched as she struggled to keep her dark memories at bay.

"Can you guess what the first thing to go through my mind after I had Haruka was? I thought, maybe now I can outshine my big sister for once. I was proud to give Mom and Dad their first grandchild. They traipsed all the way to the other side of Tokyo to see Haruka." Tamaki choked up. "But I could see from their faces what they were thinking when they saw her. They wanted to be holding *your* baby, not mine. *My* granddaughter wasn't good enough. They won't be truly happy until their Reiko finds herself a husband and produces an authentic Himekawa grandchild."

Haruka's little hand let go of Tamaki, and her arm dangled helplessly down.

"Anyway, how come you didn't notice that Mom was in a bad way? There's no way she was right as rain right up until the attack. There must have been some signs. Why didn't you spot them? That's not the big sister I used to know. You used to be the first to pick up on it when someone was sick or anxious. Where's that sister gone? When did you change? The big sister I heroworshipped, hated, and adored wasn't the sort of person to ignore her own mother's phone calls and hang her out to dry."

Oddly enough, Tamaki was now the one crying. Reiko just stood there, looking at the little round belly of the baby as it went up and down. She must have cried herself to sleep. The tears sliding down Tamaki's cheeks and onto her chin plopped down onto Haruka's face. The baby's mouth twitched, but her eyes stayed shut.

After a shower, Reiko had a light dinner prepared by Tamaki. She was all apologies as she chopped the vegetables at a painfully slow pace. "I'm sorry about what I said. I crossed the line." Reiko wasn't so sure she deserved an apology. In the end they ate their rice and vegetables in silence, then went up to their rooms.

Reiko went straight to bed. She wasn't in the mood to sleep, but she didn't feel like doing anything else. She was shattered, exhausted. She lay down, switched off the bedside light, and closed her eyes.

So much of what Tamaki said came as a shock to her. They were sisters. They had known each other forever. Reiko had known that Tamaki was jealous of her. She had noticed how much more lively Tamaki became after the incident. She had sensed it was about something more than showing sympathy to her traumatized sister, but she had never expected Tamaki to be so forthright about how she really felt. It was her own selfishness that had driven her sister to it, though. She had no right to fight back. None whatsoever.

The biggest shock was the discovery that her mother was only pressuring her to find a husband because she blamed herself for what had happened that day. It was when the dates didn't pan out and her sister — their auntie — started giving her a hard time that she'd been carted off to the hospital.

Reiko had to admit that she wasn't the only person to have suffered. Still, she'd suffered *more* than anyone else. No one could deny that. She had worked hard to find a way of living life that made sense to her, and she wanted the rest of her family to respect the choices she had made. So maybe what made her happy was different than other women. She had joined the police, become a detective, made lieutenant in Homicide. And because of that, she felt fully and completely alive. Was it selfish of her to want them to try to understand that? Did she need to painstakingly spell out all the whys and wherefores before they would accept the life choices she had made?

On the day it happened, her mom had been out. That much was true. She'd gone to Shinjuku for a school reunion. Knowing that her mom would be back late, Reiko decided to go for a night out in central Tokyo with some friends. *That* was the root cause of it all. Her mom not being at home had nothing to do with it. Responsibility lay with the seventeen-year-old Reiko and her insouciance in deciding that getting home late was okay, since both her father and mother were out for the evening.

That night, Reiko made it back to Minami Urawa station at 8:30 p.m. Although her parents were not there to scold her, she still felt she should hurry. She decided to cut across the park. She had no idea it could be dangerous.

As she was crossing the park, she caught sight of a male figure. Had he been lurking behind a tree? They would bump into one another if she stayed on the path. She made a spur-of-the-moment decision to cut across the grass — but before she could do so, the man had flung himself at her and was crushing her in his arms.

"Don't fight me."

A deep, rasping masculine whisper.

Reiko was dragged into a patch of darkness behind the public toilets. There were shrubs on one side and, behind a fence, a water tank on the other. She was shoved to the ground. She felt the cold damp hard earth against her back. The acrid stink of the toilets. The bestial panting of the man. The still air. The suffocating humidity. The heavy darkness of a summer night.

The man was far stronger. Even without the muttered threats and the knife he pressed against her throat, she couldn't have gotten away.

She was unable to put up any meaningful resistance as her panties were ripped off, her legs forced open, and her body penetrated. He had a hand over her mouth. She screamed wildly but no sound came. She felt terror at the violence being done to her. She felt desperately alone: no one was coming to save her although she was so close to home. She felt despair at the thought of the future she was losing.

And it got worse. Without any preamble, the man stabbed Reiko in the ribs. He raped her again, this time with the knife stuck inside her. Drifting in and out of consciousness, Reiko prayed for the nightmare to end. *Don't stab me anymore. Don't rape me anymore. I don't want to die.*

Then. "Hey, what's going on over there?"

A beam of white light sliced through the darkness. She caught a glimpse of the rapist's face. *He was smiling.* He wrenched his head away, jumped to his feet, leaped over the hedge, and ran off in the opposite direction.

"Are you all right, miss?"

A pair of legs came to a halt nearby. There

257

was the clinking of metal against metal. Strong arms picked her up. She smelt sweat on a shirt. Overwhelmed with relief and with shame, Reiko passed out.

When she came to in the hospital, Reiko was told that she had fallen victim to a serial rapist active in the area. She'd also seen the man's face. That was significant. A number of detectives came to her room to ask her about what had happened. Reiko didn't reply. *She couldn't say anything.* It wasn't just the detectives; she couldn't bring herself to speak to the doctors, the nurses — not even her own family.

She didn't yet see herself as a rape victim. She was gripped by a crushing sense of despair. She felt irremediably soiled. The life she had pictured for herself would never be hers.

Waking from her shallow sleep, for a brief moment she hoped that the whole thing was nothing more than a bad dream. But the wound on her left side, the white walls of the hospital room, and the endless parade of visiting detectives brought home the fact that her private nightmare was a public crime. No one was going to let her gloss over the incident. They weren't going to let her cry herself to sleep and pretend that nothing had happened while her physical wounds, at least, slowly healed. She couldn't deceive herself or anyone else with a nice comforting story about being attacked by a stray dog. Reiko had been raped and stabbed. She was the victim of a full-fledged crime. She found herself hating the policeman who had rescued her. If he hadn't shown up, she could have reported the incident as just a simple stabbing. . . .

After a few days, the number of detectives coming by suddenly dropped off. Only one kept coming: a short, pudgy, and — even the teenage Reiko had to admit it — rather cute woman detective. She had been there before, but hadn't yet spoken to Reiko.

The woman's name was Michiko Sata. She was an officer in the Saitama Prefectural Police Criminal Investigation Bureau. She brought Reiko flowers and her favorite kind of candy, as well as music CDs, fashion magazines, comics, and a portable game device.

Reiko was surprised to find that Detective Sata avoided any mention of the rape. She treated Reiko like a friend or like a sister, just chatting about normal, everyday stuff — snafus at work, her obnoxious bosses, her favorite movie stars, books, TV shows, whatever.

Reiko's first response was puzzled silence.

She gazed abstractedly out of the window. Eventually one of Sata's anecdotes got to her, though, and she burst into laughter. The story was about how Sata had accidentally put the handcuffs on herself instead of the perp she'd just collared. After that, Reiko began talking to Detective Sata. She didn't say much, but slowly began to open up, though she still refused to speak to anyone else.

After a few days, Sata asked Reiko if she could perhaps "help them with their inquiries." It was the first time she'd referred to the rape. She wanted Reiko to take a look at the facial composites the police had created based on the other victims' statements to see if Reiko could identify her attacker.

Reiko refused. To see that face — the grinning face of the man who had violated her looming out of the darkness — was the last thing she wanted to do. The thought was enough to unleash a swarm of buzzing flies around her head.

"If it's going to be difficult, we can forget about it. The most important thing is for you to get better."

Detective Sata left it there and went home.

She continued to drop in on Reiko at different times every day. She generally steered clear of the rape, but every second or third day she would gently ask if Reiko felt up to looking at the composites.

"I can't. I'm too frightened."

"All right. Not to worry then."

Every time she came, Detective Sata brought Reiko a little gift: home-baked cookies one day, a favorite book of hers or an ice cream on another.

While Sata tactfully kept her references to the rape to a minimum, Reiko's attitude was undergoing a gradual change. *I want to face up to what happened to me. I want to help Detective Sata, and I want her to help me so I can face this rape full on.* But on the day she finally made up her mind to look through the mug shots, Sata, for some reason, failed to come. Nor did she come the next day either. On the third day, a burly, middle-aged male detective she recognized as the first person to try to interview her came into her room. He brought with him an older woman.

"You're looking a whole lot better," he said by way of greeting. There was something strange and forced about his smile.

Reiko said nothing. She examined the faces of both her visitors then looked away.

"Miss Himekawa, I have some news for you. One is a very good piece of news: three days ago we made an arrest in the incident that we're investigating here."

The incident that we're investigating here. The detective had to speak in these nebulous terms because Reiko had yet to provide any details about what had happened to her. She hadn't admitted to being raped, so he couldn't come out and say, "We arrested the man who raped you." But they thought they'd got him. They'd caught that man with the grinning face in the darkness.

"Unfortunately . . . I have another piece of very distressing news."

The words stuck in the detective's throat. While he struggled to keep his emotions in check, the woman beside him stared vacantly into space.

"Detective Sata . . . lost her life in the line of duty." Getting the words out cost him a huge effort. Reiko's brain froze in shock.

"The suspect resisted arrest. Detective Sata was stabbed as she grappled with him. She was taken to the hospital as fast as possible, but she'd lost too much blood. They couldn't save her."

The detective gestured at the woman. "This is Detective Sata's mother. She has something that she very much wants to show you. Mrs. Sata?"

The woman gave Reiko a formal bow, then pulled a book out from her battered cloth handbag. The book had a dark green leather cover with a strap and buckle.

"I'd like you to look at this, Reiko. It's my daughter's journal. She kept it up right up to the night before she . . . was killed." The woman broke down. The tears poured out of her as if a dam had burst. The male detective tried to comfort her with a hug. Reiko timidly picked up the diary and opened it.

She flipped through it until she found the day after she'd been raped and started reading the entry. Along with a description of the overall incident, there was a great deal about Reiko personally.

Reiko's face is a complete blank. You can tell that she'd be very pretty if she smiled, but at the moment she isn't even able to register sorrow or pain. I know she's doing her best to process what happened to her. It's not an easy thing to watch. The doctor in charge of her case says she'll need to stay in the hospital for a couple of weeks because of the internal damage she sustained.

Reiko played one of the computer games I brought in. She isn't reading the fashion magazines or comics though. I think she likes flowers. I went for something colorful and brought her some freesias. She looked at them for a while. That's a good reaction. She won't eat while anyone else is with her. I don't want to force her to do anything, but perhaps candy would do the trick.

The next entry was about a day Reiko remembered very well.

Reiko laughed! She laughed at my little story, the old chestnut about silly me putting the cuffs on myself by accident. God, I'm so thrilled. She looked so cute. She has such a lovely smile. Today was a good day.

Reiko suddenly realized that her cheeks were wet with tears. Since the rape, she'd been emotionally numb and not cried even once. Now warm tears were streaming from her eyes.

Today for the first time Reiko tried to open up to me about what had happened. It didn't work out. I'm pretty sure that I mishandled the situation. Something I said made her clam up and look sad. Reiko, I'm so sorry. I know that the worst thing I can do is try to hurry you. God knows, you've suffered enough already without me coming in to make things worse. I'll back off a while. I wonder if Reiko likes cookies. I may not have much time to sleep if I start baking this late at night.

I've got quite a few books on sex crime and just finished another one today. Regardless of how many I read, my basic philosophy remains the same: we've got to get Reiko to confront what happened to her head on. Burying it inside and pretending like it didn't happen is the worst thing to do. She needs to draw a line under it. That's how she can beat this thing. And she's got to beat it. Her whole life is ahead of her. We can't let this single awful incident wreck it. We must beat it together. We're going to fight and we're going to win. Work with me on this one, Reiko. Let's fight it together. You can help me, Reiko. . . .

Today Reiko told me "she just needed a bit more time." It's a major step forward. Her attitude is definitely changing. She's starting to confront the reality of what happened to her. The lieutenant in charge keeps banging on about how we need to make a quick arrest. As far as I'm concerned, rushing things would be a mistake. I don't want anyone else interfering with Reiko. They should leave her to me. I'm not saying that just because I'm a cop and I'm handling her case. I feel that way because I like her. I'm her friend, and I'm a woman. She's got to confront what happened to her. She's going to have to fight to get her life back. That's what I want for her. Reiko, I want you to get back on your feet, and live facing forward. Come on, Reiko. Let's work together on this. Fight to live. Fight to get your life back.

The next entry was the last one. It was from four days ago.

I decided not to mention the rape today. I'm not worried. Any minute now, Reiko is going to come back and agree to work with me on beating this thing. Her eyes have changed. They're brighter now. The will to live is there again. I'm going to step back and leave the rest up to her. Her emotional state is all-important. It's her life. You've been an inspiration to me, Reiko. You've given me so much positive energy. Thanks, Reiko. I'm ready to go to bat for you.

Tomorrow it's my turn to be on stakeout in the park. Based on the time cycle we've identified, the perpetrator should be straining at the bit by now. Bring it on, you bastard! Try me! I'm not facing you alone. Reiko will be with me, and we won't let you win. I don't care how dark it is or how cunning you are. I'm going to find you, and I'm going to take you down. Bring it on, you pervert! You're going down.

Reiko closed the journal and sat quite still. For a while, she said nothing. She couldn't speak until she had brought her breathing back under control. Sata's mother and the detective waited quietly.

The cicadas were singing shrilly. Reiko looked out of the window. The leaves of the trees were black against the white rays of the sun. It was a quiet and windless afternoon.

"I will fight."

Reiko looked up at the expanse of cloudless azure sky. Looked up at Michiko Sata, who was now watching over her. And she made a vow: she would fight side by side with Sata.

It was the start of a long battle.

The police interviewed her and took her statement. They checked her statement against the crime scene. Then came the lineup: five men on the far side of a small plate-glass window. One glimpse of the face of the second man from the left, and Reiko felt as though an army of filthy caterpillars were crawling all over her. She wanted to scratch herself, dash her head against the wall, knock herself out. Instead, she closed her eyes, pictured detective Sata's smiling face, and recalled the words of the journal.

Work with me on this one, Reiko. Let's fight it together.

Reiko inhaled deeply and forced herself to look through the window for a second time.

"Could you get that guy — the second from the left — to smile?"

"Huh?" The detectives were mystified.

"Please could you ask him to smile?"

One of the detectives went around into the next room and pulled the supervising officer out for a quick word. Then four of the men in the lineup filed out. Only the man who'd been second from the left remained behind. The officer said something to him. The man tilted his head quizzically, shook it, then said something back. The thick glass made his voice inaudible. A smile flickered across his lips as he was speaking.

Oh my God!

Reiko knew that face.

It was the face of the man who had held her down, stabbed her, violated her. A man whose existence she didn't even want to acknowledge.

"That's him."

"Nice work," chorused the detectives.

Reiko, to the departed Detective Sata, thought, *I tried to do what you wanted. I took him on.*

Unfortunately, that was only the first stage of her struggle. The police were all very much on her side, but once the case went to court, it was a different story. Standing in the same room as the perpetrator, in front of crowd of strangers, she had to publicly admit that she'd been raped.

The lawyer for the defense did his best to minimize his client's guilt. Was Reiko sure she wasn't at least a little bit responsible for what happened? Perhaps she'd been . . . a little heedless? He produced a medical certificate showing that Reiko, except for the stab wound, barely had a scratch on her. Was Reiko seriously claiming that she tried to fight him off? Wasn't the sex actually consensual? Was she really a virgin at the time? The lawyer fired these questions at her at machine gun speed. Reiko began to flag.

"I contend that there are very real reasons

to believe that you were not raped by my client," continued the lawyer smugly. "He propositioned you, and you consented. I earlier touched on the sexual proclivities of my client. There is a side of him that derives pleasure from forcing himself on women who resist him. This courtroom is not the place to debate the normality or abnormality of that, so let's leave that for another day. What I can say with confidence is that the defendant only stabbed you, Miss Himekawa, *because you put up no resistance.* In other words, the defendant only stabbed you to goad you into fighting back. This is proved by the fact that none of the other victims — all of whom fought him off aggressively — were stabbed. So, while my client is prepared to accept the charge of bodily injury, we contend that the charge of rape lacks all plausibility."

Are you serious? You're trying to argue that it was consensual? That I was happy to give myself up to a complete stranger in the dirt in a park at night? How can you? How can you even suggest such a thing?

While Reiko furiously rejected his insinuations, she also began to lose her sure grip on the actual facts of the case. She was convinced that everyone in the courtroom now saw her as a slut who'd willingly had sex with the man. The weight of their imagined disapproval bore down on her. She couldn't hold her own.

The girl's a slut. A lowdown, dirty slut.
The girl's a slut. A lowdown, dirty slut.
The girl's a slut. A lowdown, dirty slut.

The libelous voices multiplied, tearing at her flesh like so many knives, ripping her open and replacing her true self with the sluttish version that the lawyer had invented — the sluttish self that had given herself to the man. *She was a slut. A lowdown, dirty slut.*

You know that's not true.

Reiko heard a voice in her head.

That's not true. You're going to beat this thing. You're going to fight, and you're going to win.

It was Detective Sata! Detective Sata had come back to support her.

You're going to fight, and you're going to get your life back.

Reiko imagined herself holding hands with Sata.

You're right, detective. That is not who I am. I would never consent to anything like that.

Reiko now had her confidence back. She glared scornfully at the defense lawyer.

"The fact that I had no scratch marks does not mean that the sex was consensual.

The man was holding a knife to my throat. His other hand was over my mouth. I *chose* not to resist because I was afraid of being brutalized even more and of the knife cutting me. Submitting is not the same thing as consenting. Why don't we apply your logic to Detective Sata? Detective Sata was prepared to put her life on the line to arrest that man. According to your reasoning, the fact she was ready to risk her life meant that she was happy to be killed — and that her murder was therefore consensual. You can't seriously think that."

Reiko was vaguely aware that the judge was telling her off. Nothing he said got through to her, though, and she went right on haranguing the defense lawyer.

"That flies in the face of common sense. Are you married? Maybe you have a girlfriend? A sister? Don't try and tell me that if they were the victim in this case, you'd still be standing there arguing that it was a consensual act? Can you look me in the eye and tell me that because Detective Sata was willing to risk her life she actively *wanted* to be killed? Are you going to stand there and tell her family and the whole police force that she *wanted* to die? Well, are you?"

A couple of court clerks darted out from either side of the room, to pull Reiko off the witness stand and off to silence. They made it halfway, then stopped in their tracks. They were looking not at Reiko but at the people in the gallery behind her.

What was going on? Reiko turned to look.

Reiko's parents and Detective Sata's parents and the other rape victims and their families were all sitting in the front row. They remained seated. All the other spectators, however, had risen to their feet and had their hands to their foreheads, saluting Reiko.

The uniformed cop who had rescued Reiko in the park was there. The detective who had first tried to interview Reiko was there. There were men and women, people in suits and people in uniforms, faces that she knew and faces she didn't know. But all of them were cops. The gallery was crammed with cops, and they were all standing and saluting Reiko. Some had clenched jaws, some were weeping, some were squaring their shoulders in indignation. But all of them were saluting her.

Reiko felt something thick and warm flood in toward her like a wave. It encircled her and rose up like a thick wall to protect her.

That's the police for you.

They had that fierce sense of solidarity. On a daily basis, they might squabble and undercut one another to notch up more arrests, but whenever one of their number was in danger, they would unite and come to that person's aid. Reiko suddenly realized what being a cop was all about and how their world was different from everyone else's.

Reiko chose to believe that they were saluting not her but the spirit of Michiko Sata that had expressed itself through her. The comradeship and unity of the police force astounded her. She began to tremble.

That was the moment when Reiko made up her mind to join the police.

Simply joining the force wasn't her only goal. She wanted to become a detective, get assigned to Homicide, and achieve the rank of lieutenant. Just like Sata, who had received a posthumous promotion, elevating her two ranks to lieutenant.

Reiko had achieved her goals. She was fighting the good fight side by side with Michiko Sata. She'd made lieutenant, shaken off the curse of her own past, and felt that she was living life to the fullest. The spirit of Detective Michiko Sata was watching over her.

Mom, I know I made the right choices.

As dawn started to break outside, Reiko finally felt sleepy.

I'll come and see you in hospital tomorrow, Mom.

By then "tomorrow" was already today.

7

Reiko got to the hospital at two in the afternoon. She gave her name at reception and took the stairs to the third floor, room number 312. When Reiko quietly slid open the door, she saw her mother lying in bed. She had her eyes shut, possibly sleeping. She had a drip in her arm but wasn't wearing an oxygen mask.

Reiko slipped in, closing the door gently. She walked over to the side of her mother's bed but was too anxious about making noise to sit down.

"I'm so sorry, Mom."

A faint smile flickered across her mother's lips, and she opened her eyes a little way.

"I thought you were asleep." Reiko pulled out a stool and sat down. "I'm not here to give you grief. I was shocked. I'm worried about you."

"That's nice. . . . The good news is I don't need to have bypass surgery."

Reiko got up and put the flowers she'd brought into a vase, then asked her mother for details about her condition. Things weren't as bad as they could have been, but she still needed to be very careful.

I'll avoid bringing up any sensitive topics today, Reiko thought to herself. However, it was her mother who steered the conversation onto difficult ground.

"It's *me* who should be saying sorry to *you.*"

"What do you mean?" Reiko hated herself for asking. She knew what was coming.

"I'm sorry for trying to stampede you into getting married. I can't help it. I want you to leave the police, get married, live a normal life. And you only joined the police because . . ."

"What are you talking about, Mom? I was only apologizing for not picking up when you rang yesterday. That's got nothing to do with all that stuff from the past."

"You can't say that. I mean, if I —"

"Not another word," said Reiko, cutting her off. "What happened to me and my not getting married — the two things have nothing to do with one another. The reason I'm not married is because I haven't found anyone I *want* to marry."

"You should have gone to meet the nice

men I found for you, then."

For a moment Reiko felt herself flailing. "To be completely honest, perhaps I just don't feel like getting married."

"I knew it." Her mother looked away. There was sadness in her eyes.

I've put my foot in it again. It looked as though she was going to have to tackle the elephant in the room after all. Reiko sighed and squeezed her mother's hand. It was desiccated and frail.

"Listen, Mom. Right now, being a cop is the only way of life that's right for me. Being a cop is what keeps me going. That thing that happened to me — it wasn't easy. Still, I managed to beat it and put it behind me. I stood in the witness box, and I helped close the case. I've got my issues with the verdict, sure, but in my mind it was still a win for me. I went out there, and I did everything that I had to do. That gave me the right to start my life over. Does starting over mean that I've forgotten about what happened? No way. Thinking about it makes me sick to my stomach. Sometimes I still wake up screaming. That doesn't mean I have to despise myself and give up on life. I've been there, done that. Now look at me. I joined the police, made lieutenant, have a squad working under me. The police value me for who I am."

Reiko pictured the faces of her team: Yuda, Kikuta, Otsuka, and Ishikura. Eventually Ioka's grinning countenance pushed its way in.

"I am willing to think about marriage, but only if I meet a man who can accept me as I am — can accept what happened to me, my being a cop, *a lieutenant,* all of it. I'm not a complete freak, you know. I have my own ideas about what will make me happy. Right now, your ideas and my ideas on that subject are not quite the same. I just need you to step back and give me some space."

She paused a moment before going on. "Tamaki was giving me a hard time yesterday. She told me that I'd changed. It's true. I have changed, and you're all just going to have to deal with it. Maybe I'm a disappointment as an eldest daughter. You may think I'm shirking my family responsibilities. As an individual, though, I don't believe I'm a total write-off. I just want you to wait and see."

Her mother's eyes were shut. She gave a little nod.

"One more thing, Mom. I don't want you thinking that you had anything to with what happened to me. It wasn't your fault, and it wasn't my fault. The only person who's

279

guilty of anything is my attacker. That's it. End of story. I was the victim, so if I decide it's over, I don't need to hear anyone else's opinion on the matter. Okay, that's it. I've had my say. But I shouldn't have gone into it when you're in the hospital and so tired."

Reiko patted the back of her mother's hand. She felt an answering pressure as a smile spread over her mother's face.

It wasn't an easy thing to talk about. Still, clearing the air like that might have done her mother some good. Reiko had no idea what sort of progress her mother would make. Still, the smile on her face was one of unclouded joy. That was good enough for the time being.

The minute you get back on your feet, I bet you'll be trying to set me up with more damn men.

Reiko put her mother's hand under the covers. Her mother took hold of her hand and wouldn't let go. With their fingers intertwined, Reiko looked out of the window at the lofty blue summer sky.

What gorgeous weather.

As soon as she was out of the hospital, she switched her cell phone back on. There was a message.

"Hi, Otsuka here. I know we're off today,

but have you got time to chat this afternoon? I've got this strange lead I'm following up on."

The time stamp of the message was 2:51 p.m. Only fifteen minutes ago. Reiko called Otsuka right back.

"Hi, it's me."

"Hey, Lieutenant, thanks for getting in touch. You're not busy?"

"No, I'm fine. What's up?"

"There's something I want to show you. Can we meet?"

"Sure. Ikebukuro in, say, an hour and a half?"

"Okay. You've been to the Countess Café, haven't you? Let's meet there."

"Okay. See you at 4:30."

Something he wants to show me? What?

Reiko made it to Ikebukuro just after 4:20, after changing trains once.

The Countess Café was just by the north exit. The décor was on the traditional side, as typified by the suit of European armor that stood just inside the front door. Reiko looked around and spotted Otsuka waving at her from a table at the far end of the room.

"Sorry to keep you waiting."

When Reiko sat across from Otsuka his

281

eyes briefly widened.

"Wow, Lieutenant," he stammered. "You look good outside of work."

She was wearing white pants and a pale blue summer sweater of thin wool. Since she often got called in on short notice, she tended to dress with a certain sober formality even on weekends. Today, however, they'd been granted an official day off. Intending to do some shopping on her way back from the hospital, she'd dressed down. Otsuka, on the other hand, was in his normal work suit.

"Don't be silly."

Otsuka's eyes were glued to her breasts.

"I never figured you for a dirty old man, Otsuka."

"Hey, I'm just ordinary flesh and blood, Lieutenant. . . . It's my first time with you, though."

"That's not very nice."

Otsuka sniggered. "Kikuta will beat me up if I go too far."

"Oh, *puh-lease.*"

Lately, Otsuka had been dropping all sorts of heavy hints about Reiko and Kikuta. Reiko simply wasn't in the mood to play along right now. She wanted to get down to business.

"So, what is it you wanted to show me?"

Otsuka gave a sulky pout. "Oh, Miss Un-congeniality. Indulge me, won't you?"

"Nope, I'm not going to feed the rumor mill."

"I think it's pretty well fed as it is."

Reiko snorted, and Otsuka left it at that. The waitress came over to take their order. Reiko ordered an iced coffee and Otsuka a second cup of the hot stuff.

"At the evening meeting on the nine-teenth, I reported that I'd interviewed a university pal of Namekawa's, a guy called Tashiro. Do you remember?"

"I remember. Didn't you say you'd drawn a blank with him?"

"That was true at the time. But later that same night, Tashiro called me and told me something intriguing."

"Hang on a minute." Reiko frowned. "Why didn't you tell me about this sooner?"

Otsuka scratched his head in embarrass-ment. "Sometimes I just want to follow up my own leads, I guess."

He had a point. Suck-ups who used the meetings to divulge everything they'd learned seldom made good detectives. Of course, overindependence had its down-sides, too. When freelancing led to slip-ups, someone had to take the fall. When it led to the bad guys getting away with it, it brought the whole force into disrepute. Detectives had to inform their direct superior about all the leads they were pursuing at some point. Until then, though, keeping what you knew between yourself and your partner was fine. Leads were like eggs. They needed to be sat on a while before they hatched. Every detective knew that.

The most important thing was that you got to follow through on your own leads. That's how you were able to crack cases and get the credit for solving them.

However, if you had people working under you, like Reiko did, then having a handle on what your subordinates were doing was crucial. Leads that they were following on their own undermined the whole purpose of a multiman team. Reiko needed to keep sounding out her guys to find out what they were doing.

"Okay, hit me. Tell me what's so intriguing."

"Tashiro told me to go online and check out something called 'Strawberry Night.' Namekawa mentioned it to him, apparently. At the time, Tashiro wasn't very interested and didn't pay much attention. Have you heard of it, Lieutenant?"

"What?"

"Strawberry Night."

"Never heard of it," said Reiko. "What the hell is it?"

Otsuka looked serious. "I scoured the Internet, but I couldn't find a Strawberry Night homepage. What I did find were people discussing it on underground message boards, the kind where people hero-worship bizarre serial killers and upload gory crime-scene photographs. All in all, I found seven message boards that contained references to Strawberry Night."

"So what the hell is it?"

Otsuka refused to be rushed. "Well, as far as I can judge," he said, slowly nodding his head. "It's a murder show."

"A murder show?"

The phrase was simple enough, but Reiko had trouble wrapping her head around the concept.

"These are printouts from the message boards." Otsuka extracted several sheets of paper from a large manila envelope. "See for yourself."

Driller killer 08/08/16:45:20
Anyone actually seen the real Strawberry Night page?

Decapitator 08/08/22:01:02
Good question, bro. If anyone had seen

the site, they'd have posted about it here. My guess is that no one has. The comments are all hearsay — *a friend of mine told me* BS. Hard to know what's true.

Entrail epicure 08/09/00:12:36
Guess you guys will think I'm a dick, but "someone I know" (LOL) really managed to access the homepage. He's a friend in the offline world. There's this streaming video of someone being, like, *seriously fucking killed.* Afterward, the words "Strawberry Night" appear in this bloody-drippy gothic-style font on the screen. They fade out and then "Do you want to see this live?" comes up. My buddy was too scared to click the "yes" button.

Decapitator 08/09/00.15.02
Click it, you pussy! (LOL). Wonder what happens?

"I'm not sure I understand what this all means," said Reiko, putting the printouts down on the table.

"I'm not surprised." Otsuka leaned forward confidently. "The people on the message boards all say more or less the same thing. I searched for the Strawberry Night site they refer to, but nothing came up. It must be hidden somewhere in the deep Web. The rumor is that on the homepage there's streaming video of people actually being killed, followed by the message, 'Do you want to see this live?' You can choose to click 'yes' or 'no.' If you choose yes, then you'll get an e-mail inviting you to the murder show. The e-mail doesn't come straightaway, but some while later, when you've forgotten all about it. Some of the posts claim that the invitation comes in the form of a letter mailed to your house. Either way, the invitation always shows up without anyone revealing their real name, or inputting their mail address or home address. That spooks people out."

"Did you find anyone who'd seen the actual homepage or been to the actual event?"

"Not exactly, but there's one contributor who takes an 'I know a whole lot more than the rest of you morons' tone. I don't know how much credibility his postings have, but they include some interesting details."

Otsuka pushed another sheet of paper across to Reiko. He'd highlighted one of the entries with a magic marker.

Wicked Wizard 08/15/01:32:55
You don't know shit. The victim is one of

the spectators who was chosen at random. And the 13th is wrong. The show is held on the second Sunday of the month.

"Tha-that means —" Reiko said, her voice trailing off.

Otsuka, clearly delighted with her response, nodded his head vigorously.

PART III

I loaded the body into the young guy's car.

He was weird. I'd killed his friend, but he was happy to have me there in his car along with the corpse, while he thought about the best way to get rid of it. He could have ditched his dead friend, run away, and reported me to the police. But he didn't. Instead, there he was, racking his brains for a solution to the problem. He wasn't panicky; in fact, he seemed to be enjoying the challenge.

I reached out to someone who could help us. He showed up in no time.

He looked at me with sad eyes. "You've killed someone else?" Then he glared at the young guy with me. "Who's this?" he asked.

I just shook my head. What else could I do? All I knew about him was that he was friends with the dead guy.

"Shall we burn him too?"

At the sound of my voice, the young guy

looked amazed. He didn't know that the person who'd come to help me was the only person in the world I could actually speak to.

"Burning's no good. It doesn't do the job properly."

"That's right. Burning's not a good way to get rid of a body," the young guy chimed in.

"What shall we do?"

"Let me think."

I had done the killing, but now I was sidelined as the other two discussed how to dispose of the body. I was cool with it. I didn't care either way.

"What about chopping it up and throwing away the pieces?"

"Too much hassle," replied the young guy. "We need a quick, easy method."

"Fire's no good? How about dumping it in a lake or something?"

"It'll just float back up to the surface."

"What about a weight?"

"Easier said than done," the young guy said. "Partially encasing him in cement before dumping him in would work, but if we went cement shopping right now, we'd just leave a trail for the cops. And without cement, the body would float up to the surface like a balloon when gas builds up in the belly."

"Gas in the belly?"

"Yes, from decomposition. The bacteria in the gut makes the intestines rot, which turns the whole body into a big buoy or float."

The young guy really seemed to know his stuff.

"What if we slit the belly open?"

"What do you mean?"

"If we slit the gut, then the gas won't build up — the body won't inflate in the first place, right?"

The guy young liked the suggestion. Everybody was happy.

That, I guess, was the start of our strange partnership of crime.

"You're fucking amazing. You blew my mind. What you did, it was like performance art. You're a genius — an artist of murder. I can't get the image out of my head."

The young guy was even more of a weirdo than I thought. I didn't understand half of what he was saying. It felt quite nice, though. Fact is, I'd realized the same thing about myself. And I wanted to kill again.

I killed my parents. After that, I got the nickname F and used violence as a way to feel alive. I was like a trader, and life was the wares I dealt in. Live or die? Kill or be killed? Those were the only times when I felt even slightly alive. Usually, the people I was hanging with stopped me before I actually murdered anyone. No one wanted to trigger a cycle of killing. Not even my friends in the Gang lusted for full-on slaughter.

This young guy, however, was something else.

"I want to provide you with a platform," he said. "A theater of murder, a stage where you can kill all the people you want. You get me?"

I got him. I liked the idea. But could he really do it? It sounded like a shortcut to the inside of a jail cell to me. The "all the people you want" part was hard to swallow.

Amazingly, the young guy seemed to be in earnest.

One night, he came to pick me up. "We've got our first performance, so come with me now." I thought he was bullshitting me, but I felt a little bit excited anyway. I went with him.

He took me to a boarded-up building. It used to be a strip joint. There was a warren of passages, a dressing room, an auditorium, a stage. In the dressing room, I changed into my leather bodysuit, a new one, not the one

I'd gotten from the old homeless fellow. Then I put on a mask, a black mask like the ones that professional wrestlers sometimes wore. It had holes only for the eyes and had mesh to cover the nose and mouth. I looked in the mirror. A real killer was looking back at me.

Cool!

I waited by myself in the dressing room for ages. The spectators came in, and the place gradually filled up. The atmosphere was electric. The spectators knew that something incredible was about to take place. They were going to see a murder show. I was going to kill somebody live on stage. But who?

"F, you're up soon."

The person who came to fetch me onstage was the young guy's buddy — the one who had run off as fast as his legs could carry him the day I killed their friend. Today, though, we were all on the same side. Funny old world, huh?

I left the green room, walked down a narrow passage, and went to the wings of the stage. We hadn't discussed what I was meant to do out there. All I had with me was my pink box cutter, like a lucky charm. Everyone I'd killed, I'd killed with it.

"Get out there and do your thing," said

Mr. Quick Exit.

I went out onto the stage.

A spotlight went on with a thunk and bathed the stage in a beam of blinding white light. The rest of the room was in complete darkness. It was like there was nothing left in the world except the stage and me. It was a nice, simple world split cleanly between black and white. In the middle of the stage there was a bed. A woman lay on the bed. Duct tape covered her eyes, her mouth, her wrists, and her ankles. Her arms were pulled apart and her upper body was naked. Of course, I could see her titties. It was embarrassing, uncomfortable.

In a neat row at the foot the bed there was a saw, a carving knife, a sickle, a bat studded with nails, a broken beer bottle, and a whip. Had to be the tools the young guy wanted me to use on the woman. I'd never seen her before. I had no special reason to hate her. Killing her seemed a bit pointless.

I took a good look. She was slim and her skin was pale. Erect nipples on firm breasts, which rose and fell. Her hair was stylishly cut and dyed an elegant gray. She must have been excited because her breathing was fast and ragged. She was a looker.

You look like one of those normal people —

one of those goddamned happy people.

Suddenly I felt that killing her was okay.

When I picked up the studded bat, she must have heard something. She turned toward me, trying to get a sense of what was happening. Her lips were writhing beneath the duct tape. She twisted and thrashed, trying to move. No chance. She was tied down good and proper.

I hadn't played much baseball, but I knew the basics. I imagined that one of her breasts was a ball and took my best swing.

There was a tremendous clattering of metal. The woman was squirming wildly, rocking the whole bed. Was it going to tip over? I heard sounds coming from the darkness of the auditorium. Scream-like sounds.

I held the bat up. Red blood was dripping from the bat. I looked back at her. As I watched, the red of the blood spread out, covering her whole torso. It was beautiful.

The spectators were making a lot of noise now. Must be enjoying themselves! They think I'm great, like the young guy who organized this murder show. "Make the bitch suffer! Kill her as cruelly as you can!" That was my interpretation of their whooping and yelling.

The applause. The tang of blood. And red, the most beautiful color in the world. I was feeling good now. I was feeling truly alive.

I took another swing. Then another. And another.

I forgot all about the spectators. I was delirious. I was obsessed with making this woman bright red — like a moist ripe strawberry.

Sweet! I grinned behind my mask.

Perhaps it was time for something special to send her over the edge?

Yes, it is time.

I took the pink box cutter out of my pocket.

Saturday, August 23, 8:00 A.M.

Reiko and Otsuka loitered in front of the counter on the ground floor of Kameari police station. They were hoping to catch Captain Imaizumi and Director Hashizume en route to the morning meeting, fill them in on what Otsuka had discovered, and get his findings incorporated into the investigation. Reiko and Otsuka were all but certain that Kanebara and Namekawa were regulars at the Strawberry Night murder show — and had been killed as a result.

Other members of the task force, some from the local precinct, some from the TMPD, strolled by. Ishikura turned up with a morning newspaper stuffed under his arm.

"Morning, Lieutenant. What's up?"

"Just the man I wanted to meet. Could you reserve one of the smaller meeting rooms for us?"

"Sure, no problem. Planning on blindsiding the top brass again?"

Ishikura was sharp.

"Not me," said Himekawa. "Otsuka."

Ishikura grinned at Otsuka. Reiko knew that Ishikura had a soft spot for the younger man. As detectives, the two of them had a great deal in common.

"Nice work, kid."

Ishikura gave Otsuka a playful punch on the chest.

"Just got lucky," Otsuka said.

"Sure you did. Nice work, son."

Instead of heading up the stairs, Ishikura headed down the passage to the admin offices. Reiko thought she detected a spring in his step.

Reiko and her squad gathered in one of the smaller meeting rooms along with Captain Imaizumi. Yuda was waiting out in the lobby with orders to bring Director Hashizume in the minute he showed up.

Several minutes later the door swung open. It was neither Yuda nor Hashizume.

"What's going on here? First thing in the morning, and already doing things behind my back!"

Stubby!

It was Lieutenant Katsumata with his four goons in tow, come to crash the party. Reiko wasn't surprised. He was hardly the type to sit passively in the main meeting room when Reiko and her whole team were somewhere else. She didn't know how he'd tracked her down, but Katsumata would have looked behind every door in the police station including the supply closet to find them. Reiko had never meant to play hide-and-seek with him. That would be lowering herself to his level.

"No one's doing anything behind your back. There's an issue I need to flag up before the main meeting got started. For the good of the overall investigation."

"Yeah? Well, you won't mind if we join you then?"

"Feel free."

Katsumata sauntered in and threw himself into the chair next to Captain Imaizumi. His squad members stood in a neat row behind him. Katsumata leaned over to Imaizumi.

"Hi, Zoomzoom. Full of yourself as ever, you parakeet?"

Reiko was mystified.

"Hear you've been busy flashing the cash," Captain Imaizumi said.

"Says who?"

"Spreading it around in Shinjuku yesterday, I heard."

"Don't know what you're talking about," Katsumata said, then turned away.

Reiko was at a loss, but her impression was that Imaizumi had got the better of the exchange.

A couple of minutes later, Yuda ushered Hashizume into the room.

"Thanks," said the director. "I'll take it from here."

He did a quick survey of the room. From where people were sitting, he deduced that Reiko had called the meeting.

"You again, eh? What now? You want us to mobilize the army?"

Hashizume sat down in the vacant chair on the other side of Imaizumi.

"Keep it short and sweet. The morning meeting is due to —"

Reiko interrupted him. "I already told the task force coordinator to push the start time back by half an hour."

Hashizume frowned in distaste. He was about to snap at her, but thought better of it.

"You boys want a seat?" Reiko pointed to some vacant places on the other side of the table, and Katsumata's four subordinates sat down.

"Officer Otsuka, will you begin?"

Otsuka passed a sheaf of paper across to

Hashizume and Imaizumi. It was a document that he and Reiko had put together the day before. There were extracts from the printouts Otsuka had shown Reiko in Ikebukuro, with key sections highlighted in marker pen.

Katsumata brazenly looked over Captain Imaizumi's shoulder as he scanned the document.

"What you have there is information I got from an interview with Tomohiko Tashiro on the nineteenth of August," began Otsuka. "Tashiro and Namekawa have been close friends since college. Namekawa had mentioned a Web site called Strawberry Night to his friend. Tashiro didn't think much of it at the time, but when he got the news that Namekawa had been killed, he remembered that Namekawa had said something about a 'murder show.' Suspecting a possible connection to Namekawa's murder, Tashiro brought the matter to my attention.

"If you look at the documentation, you can see that this 'murder show' has been the subject of discussion on several message boards for quite a while now. This is a printout of actual postings on a single specific day. If it's hard to follow, refer to the summary I added at the bottom of the page. You can see that there are several points of overlap between Strawberry Night, which they are discussing, and the case we are currently working on.

"For starters, note that the 'murder show' is held on the second Sunday of the month. The different online communities have different ideas on the date: on one message board, they think it's the thirteenth of the month; somewhere else, they say the tenth. However, the contributor who appears to be by far the best informed states that the show is held on the second Sunday of the month.

"The same contributor says something else very interesting. Turn to the next page, please, the one headed 'Event Format.' Apparently, somebody is murdered on a stage. So far, so straightforward. What's really interesting is that the person who's murdered is actually chosen from that day's audience. The spectators, in other words, can themselves end up as victims at any time. What if Kanebara and Namekawa had both been spectators at the show for months, until one day the tables were turned and they found *themselves* being murdered onstage? That would fit the pattern of unexplained absences of both victims on the second Sunday of the month, and it matches the date of their murders.

"That brings me to my third point. According to the various message boards, the Strawberry Night homepage is not normally accessible. It only shows up occasionally, apparently in response to a online search for it, and then it can only be accessed for a few hours. After that, the URL takes you nowhere. You get a 'server not found' notice, and searching for it turns up nothing. As a result, a very limited number of people have successfully accessed the actual homepage. Their reports circulate mostly as hearsay, which diminishes their credibility, of course. There are, however, multiple accounts that the video on the homepage shows someone having their throat slashed with a box cutter. The knife is put to the victim's throat, then pulled to one side, killing them. . . . Since we're talking about digital images, we can't rule out the possibility that the whole thing is a hoax. Against that, there is the fact that everyone who claims to have seen the page stresses how real the video looks.

"Putting all this together, I think that a valid case can be made that both Kanebara and Namekawa accessed the Strawberry Night homepage and attended the murder show, and that Namekawa was selected as the victim and murdered last month, with the same thing happening to Kanebara this month. The oldest thread I can find about Strawberry Night is from November of last year. That would suggest that the show has been running for at least ten months — which would give us a minimum of ten victims.

"Hang on a minute," Director Hashizume said. "The divers spent five days searching the Mizumoto Park pond, and Namekawa's was the only body they found."

"Are you recommending we go on some more fishing trips?" sneered Katsumata.

Hashizume treated Katsumata to a withering stare, then turned back to Otsuka.

"What you've got here is way too much hearsay for me. Most of your report isn't even secondhand — it's third-hand or worse. *Apparently* this and *what if* that. What are you going to come up with next, man — the hound of the bloody Baskervilles? The whole thing looks like an urban myth to me."

That's pretty much the reaction I expected from you, Director.

Reiko got to her feet. It was time for her to strut her stuff.

"As things currently stand, Director, this is the only hypothesis that can establish a link between the victims' mysterious behavior patterns and their deaths and that can provide a logical explanation for both. The numerous cuts on the victims' torsos, we assume, come from torture. The sadistic infliction of injuries like these makes for a good spectacle. Then there's the cut to the neck. That's the show's grand finale. It is also reputed to be the part that was streamed online. They need to kill the victims in an unambiguous, even spectacular fashion — in a way that draws a clear and explicit line between life and death. That's why they slash the carotid artery. Because it releases the most spectacular fountain of blood. Last of all, there's the cut to the abdomen. We've already solved that particular puzzle and how it enables them to conceal the bodies underwater. I believe that Strawberry Night is not a myth, that Kanebara and Namekawa were involved with it, and that they died as a result.

"Nonetheless, I understand your skepticism, Director. Otsuka's report does indeed lack credibility. The information in it is nothing more than hearsay pulled off the Internet. I can't deny that on the same message boards some of the contributors dismiss Strawberry Night as a silly urban legend.

"That is why I don't think we should

make Strawberry Night the main focus of the task force's investigation. At best, it's just one hypothesis for us to test and perhaps eliminate. There's no need to put the entire task force on it. My squad has enough manpower. Why not let us handle it?"

Katsumata glowered at Reiko with pure hatred in his eyes. She had set up this preliminary meeting knowing full well that Hashizume wouldn't devote all of the task force's resources into investigating what might be a fantasy. She'd played her cards well, and now she got to take personal control of this whole aspect of the investigation. Katsumata, meanwhile, was left no way to muscle in on it. At least, not overtly.

Katsumata scowled and clenched his jaw. Reiko savored his frustration.

Suck it, Stubby! How'd you enjoy my master class on how to hijack an investigation?

"I think Himekawa's entire squad is too much manpower to throw at this," said Director Hashizume to Captain Imaizumi.

"You're probably right," concurred the captain.

"I want two of your guys to stick with interviewing the victims' friends and families."

Reiko shot a glance at Ishikura and Yuda. They nodded their assent.

"All right, Director. Otsuka, Kikuta, and I will investigate this lead."

Hashizume jabbed a finger at her. "How, exactly?"

"Based on the available information, I think it's fair to assume that the murder show is probably held in one of the capital's livelier shopping and entertainment districts. Anywhere quiet, and the locals would get suspicious about unexplained large groups. So we'll start our inquiries in Shinjuku, Shibuya, and Ikebukuro. Specifically, we'll be looking for places with a stage and room for an audience — strip clubs, small theaters, and live music clubs — that aren't in daily use or have closed down. We'll locate them by combing through the relevant local publications for the sex industry; we'll also talk to local real estate agents."

Reiko felt a throb of pleasure as the investigation began to develop real momentum.

We're going to fight, and we're going to win.

Reiko no longer knew whether the voice in her head was Detective Sata speaking to her or if she was simply talking to herself.

"Sounds dangerous to me," growled Katsumata.

2

Otsuka and Kitami were assigned central Ikebukuro.

Ikebukuro was one of Tokyo's top entertainment and nightlife districts. There was a whole cluster of department stores — Tobu, Seibu, Mitsukoshi, Parco, Marui, Sunshine 60 — around ten electronics emporiums, plus every kind of restaurant and bar imaginable, movie theaters, karaoke parlors, amusement arcades, pachinko parlors, sex clubs, love hotels. The whole district was so stuffed with people and businesses that it was a challenge to think of anything that was *not* there.

Otsuka stepped out of the north exit of the station and made a beeline for the first "fashion health" establishment — as blow-job parlors were euphemistically known — that caught his eye. It was in the basement of a rather seedy building that housed an array of business tenants. The staircase was stuffy and humid and reeked of mold. Sweat oozed out of their pores as they walked down. When they pushed open the rickety, gaudily painted door at the foot of the stairs, a blast of cold air rushed over them. It was like walking into a refrigerator.

"Good morning, gentlemen."

A woman, on the wrong side of fifty and caked in makeup, greeted them in a bored voice. She looked like an evil-tempered toad. She was sitting at a narrow counter with the photographs of around fifteen girls displayed on the wall behind her. A long hard look at each of the pictures revealed that none of the girls were that good-looking. Compared to the woman at the front desk, however, they were without exception ravishing.

"These girls are available right now." The woman swiveled around and pointed at a number of the photographs.

"That's not why we're here." Otsuka showed his badge. "We're police."

The woman gulped and her body tensed. She was clearly up to something dodgy that she didn't want the police to find out about. Reluctantly, Otsuka let it go. That wasn't what they were there for. They needed information.

"And we're not from Community Safety

either. We're working on a case, and we'd like to ask you some questions."

"Uh-huh." The woman continued to eye them suspiciously but shifted on her stool to sit a little more upright.

"Have any strip clubs or similar establishments near here gone out of business recently?"

"Strip clubs?"

"Yes, or lap-dancing clubs. That kind of thing."

"And you're interested in places that have closed down?"

"Correct."

"That's a funny question."

The woman tilted her blubber-encircled neck to one side and had a think. Unfortunately, she came up with nothing. *It's the luck of the draw,* thought Otsuka. He hadn't expected much.

"I'd like to ask a small favor."

"Oh yes?"

"Have you got any old sex magazines? Can we have them?"

"Old magazines?"

"Yes, from the last year or so."

"You really are a funny pair."

This time they'd hit the jackpot. The old woman brought out around twenty copies of the sort of sex magazines that you'd see on convenience stores shelves. They stretched back to the end of the previous year. It was a bumper crop.

"They're a bit grubby, sorry. You can have 'em all. Saves me chucking 'em out."

Otsuka thanked her. They left, with Kitami carrying the stash of magazines.

We're going to have to look through this lot, but a good strong bag would be helpful.

The two detectives walked around to the west side of the station and settled down in the upper floor of a well-air-conditioned fast-food joint. They went through all the magazines, comparing the data on Ikebukuro sex clubs month by month. Strip clubs and burlesque clubs that had shut down or had a name change were their main focus.

After a while, Otsuka noticed that a place called the Cherry Strip Club, which had both an advertisement and a write-up in the February issue of a magazine, had vanished by the March issue. He then checked to see if a new establishment had opened at the same address. There was nothing in March, or April, or May. The address was inside the cluster of love hotels near the north exit of the station. Otsuka could vaguely picture the area and even dimly remembered there being a strip club there. He made a note to visit the place.

Kitami was looking through the more recent magazines. In the course of the case, he'd picked up the hang of basic fact checking, and Otsuka couldn't fault his concentration or his ability. Kitami eventually delivered his verdict. Plenty of places seemed to be going out of business, perhaps due to the recession. The vast majority were blowjob parlors. In most cases, they were quickly replaced by another establishment offering the same service in the same location.

Blowjob joints aren't much use, thought Otsuka ruefully.

After lunch they headed out into the field. They located the old Cherry Strip Club, which now lay empty. A sign on the front of the building included the address of a real estate agent, so they went to visit him. Otsuka's hunch was right: the building had been vacant for six months now. With its distinctive layout, finding a new tenant was proving challenging.

"The landlord might well renovate the interior so a different kind of business can move in. As you saw, the place is surrounded by love hotels, so there's no point in opening another one of those. At the same time, no regular, respectable business would want to locate there. Frankly, the property's a bit of a headache."

Otsuka asked the real estate agent for a tour, and he was happy to oblige. The three of them headed back to the narrow lane, wiping the sweat off their faces as they went. Since the front door of the building was an automatic door that wouldn't work until the electricity was switched on, the agent took them in through the back.

The interior was pitch black. The stale dank air was even more humid than outside and clung to their faces like dirty bathwater. The daylight coming through the open door revealed an officelike room with corridors snaking off on either side. The agent turned on the electricity, then led them through the building, switching on lights as he went.

"This is the stage," he explained.

Otsuka was startled at the tiny size of the thing until he realized that most of the action must have taken place on the catwalk that stretched out into the auditorium.

"Have you rented this place to anybody since the strip club closed?"

"No."

"Not even for a short-term rental? A single night, say?"

"No. See how all the fittings have been removed? The curtain's gone, the stage lights don't have bulbs, and the seating's all been removed. The state this place is in, you couldn't use it for anything."

You're wrong there, pal. Looks good enough for a murder show to me.

If anything, thought Otsuka, the bleak dinginess of the place made it an even better setting. He imagined the scene: Kanebara, bound, is carried out onto the catwalk; a sheet of plate glass is placed on his chest; then he's pounded with something big and blunt — a bat, maybe. Drenched in blood and pinned at wrist and ankle, Kanebara tries to crawl away. He is squirming like a caterpillar when the perpetrator grabs him from behind — and slits his throat.

How did the spectators feel as the show unfolded before their eyes? If they enjoyed it, they were simply inhuman. Otsuka would feel nothing for them, even if they ended up as the next victims. But if they felt sorry for Kanebara, then how come none of them had lifted a finger to help? Nobody had intervened when Kanebara *and* Namekawa were up there, being killed right in front of them.

Guess a murder show audience is the wrong place to look for compassion.

"Have you seen what you need?"

Otsuka snapped back to himself.

316

Despite the agent's having told them that he hadn't rented the place, it wasn't hard to imagine someone sneaking in and using it without permission. Provided they could get through the locks, setting things up in an abandoned place like this was probably more convenient. Using the back door was good for the spectators, as it reduced their chances of being seen.

Himekawa had needed nothing more than a few postings on online chat rooms to intuit that they should be looking for a place like this. The woman had a sort of sixth sense. This abandoned strip theater seemed to be crying out to host a murder show. Himekawa had also played her cards pretty smartly to make sure that the top brass gave this lead to her and her alone. She'd led Director Hashizume by the nose and done a great job of sidelining Katsumata too. You didn't learn how to manipulate people that way from hard work or experience. No, it was raw, God-given talent — and a talent that Otsuka didn't have.

I can't change who I am. I'll keep slogging on.

Otsuka took a last look around the little auditorium.

Wonder if it's worth getting Forensics in to give this place the once over?

Otsuka already had something interesting to report on at the evening meeting. He felt a warm glow of self-satisfaction.

They also visited a burlesque club and a transvestite bar, both of which were under new management and trading under different names.

The burlesque club, they discovered, had only been empty for a couple of weeks between mid-March and early April before it secured a new tenant. That two-week window didn't cover the second Sunday of either month so the probability that it was used for Strawberry Night was almost nil.

They learned about the tranny bar from a second real estate agent. It had stood empty between March to May after the previous tenant did a runner. By coincidence, the new tenant opened another tranny bar. When Otsuka asked if the place had been let to anyone during the roughly three months it was unoccupied, the answer — just as with the Cherry Strip Club — was no.

Otsuka got the real estate agent to show him around. It was more about his developing a feel for potential locations than anything else. The bar had been completely renovated, the agent explained, and now looked quite different, with a new floor, walls, and ceiling. Even if the place had hosted Strawberry Night, going over it now would turn up nothing. With all the old fittings gone, Forensics wouldn't find traces of blood. Anyway, it was difficult to make the case for checking an establishment that was in day-to-day operation, based on nothing more than a hunch.

At 4:50 p.m., Otsuka and Kitami were standing at the head of some steps that led down into Ikebukuro Station. Otsuka turned to face the other man. "I am very sorry, but . . ."

"Yes?" Kitami frowned slightly. "What is it?"

Otsuka finally got his courage up. "Uhm . . . How can I put this? I need you to give me an hour. There's something I have to do — alone."

"You mean now?"

"Yes. I'm very sorry to ask this of you."

Kitami's frown deepened.

Otsuka had an appointment, and given who he was going to meet, it was better for a fast-tracker like Kitami not to be involved. Otsuka didn't dislike Kitami. That was why he'd told Kitami up front that this was something he needed take care of on his own.

"Lieutenant Kitami, whenever I'm partnered with a local precinct detective, from time to time I chase down my own leads. It's routine, really. All the detectives in Homicide . . . all the detectives in the Met do it. But you're on the management track and, in the future, we'll probably cross paths again under different circumstances. More importantly, you've treated me fair and square and been a good partner to me. That's why I'm being frank. All I need is one hour. Just give me that."

Otsuka concluded his speech with a bow. Kitami pulled himself to his full height and said nothing. Otsuka couldn't see Kitami's face, but the silence was starting to feel uncomfortably long.

"Officer Otsuka, that's enough bowing."

Otsuka was surprised at the chilliness of Kitami's tone. Was he pissed at being sidelined? Was he shocked to discover that everyone in the TMPD flew solo from time to time? Either way, it was a natural enough reaction, and Otsuka could not resent it.

Sorry, Lieutenant, but the one thing I can't tell you is the truth.

Otsuka was about to launch his own rogue investigation, and Kitami would be better off left in the dark. This way Kitami would have complete deniability if things went

320

pear-shaped.

"I apologize," said Otsuka, raising his head. "I can see you don't like this."

"It's all right. I understand."

The smile on Kitami's face was so clearly forced that Otsuka couldn't help feeling sorry for him.

"I know what I signed up for. The station commander only let me join the task force because I begged him to. When he said yes, I promised I wouldn't slow you guys down. Getting out of your way is the right thing to do."

"Thanks, Lieutenant."

Kitami was busy examining his expensive-looking wristwatch.

"I'll need to kill time until six. Where shall we meet?"

"I'm sorry, but let me call you," Otsuka said, with a small bow. "We can go back to the station together. Will that be all right?"

Kitami silently nodded his assent.

Otsuka's contact, Keiichi Tatsumi, had arranged to meet him in a bar.

The interior of the bar was narrow and deep, with room only for six people at the counter. Although it was the weekend, a customer showing up so early was obviously unusual, and the mama-san eyed him with suspicion.

"Come on in," she said warily.

"I'm meeting someone here."

The woman grinned as the penny dropped.

"Oh, you must be Keiichi's friend."

With an elegant wave of the hand, she indicated a seat at the bar.

Keiichi Tatsumi lived in a different world from Otsuka — the underworld, basically. His business was tailing people, doing stakeouts, wiretapping, photo surveillance, hacking. He dealt in information, and provided someone was footing the bill, he had no scruples about how he got his hands on it.

His most important client was the Yamato-kai, Japan's largest organized crime group. Back when Otsuka was working as a precinct detective, he had busted Tatsumi and got him prosecuted for B&E. The court sentenced Tatsumi to two years' jail time suspended for three years. Tatsumi had the distinction of being the only criminal Otsuka had ever nailed himself. No surprise that he hated Otsuka's guts. Ironically, Otsuka could think of no one better qualified for the job he had in mind.

At five past five, the cowbell suspended on the front door of the bar jingled. A man in a garish Hawaiian shirt came in. It was Tatsumi.

"Hi there, Kei-chan. This gentleman is wait —"

Tatsumi sat down next to Otsuka without so much as a glance in her direction.

"Why in the name of fuck did you get in touch?" Spitting out the words, he peeled off his black-framed sunglasses. A nauseating smell wafted over from the gel smothering his dyed blond hair. When he placed his hands on the counter, Otsuka noticed that the tips of the fingers of his right hand were black with grime.

"I appreciate you taking the trouble."

Otsuka made no move to explain why he was there. He was unsure how to broach the matter. The mama-san broke the silence by asking Otsuka if he'd like a drink. He asked for "anything nonalcoholic," and she poured him out a glass of oolong tea. Tatsumi opted for a beer. He made a show of indifference as he brought the bottle up to his lips but seemed happy enough to drink it. Looking at him out of the corner of his eye, Otsuka seized the moment.

"There's . . . uhm . . . this job I want you to do for me."

Tatsumi choked, spat his beer out, and went into a violent coughing fit. He pounded himself on the chest to get himself back under control, while the mama-san reached over to wipe the beer off the counter.

"What the fuck?"

"I'm serious."

"Really?"

"Really."

Tatsumi put his beer bottle down on the counter. His jaw was tight as he stared at the shelves lined with whiskey bottles behind the bar. The mama-san looked at the two of them inquisitively but was tactful enough to say nothing. A tense, oppressive silence filled the small space. Otsuka was wondering if he should say something, when Tatsumi spoke.

"You've got a heck of a nerve. First you get me banged up, then you come waltzing in and ask me to do a job for you? If a cop is coming to a guy like me, then it's got to be something shady. Is it even legit for a cop to work with someone with priors?"

"I know how you must feel," Otsuka said, after thinking about it for a while. "This is a big request. But you're the only person who can do this. There's no one else."

"This is crazy, man. Totally fucking crazy."

"I know." Otsuka tucked his chin down apologetically. "At least hear me out, okay?

My whole career, I've been a background guy, supporting other cops. Arresting you — that wasn't my usual style. I've got almost no collars to my name. In fact, you were my first and only. Right now, though, I'm working this homicide case, and I've stumbled onto a really major lead — big and seriously weird. The crime was abnormal, unusually brutal and complicated too. We need to investigate the lead. It's a good lead, but as regular cops, we can't do anything with it."

"What are you talking about?" sneered Tatsumi. "You're not making any sense."

Otsuka understood where the man was coming from, but he was in a bind. He couldn't give away too much in case Tatsumi refused to take the job, and he certainly wasn't going to explain the dynamics of his relationship with Himekawa.

That leaves me no choice . . .

Otsuka looked over at Tatsumi quickly, briefly meeting his eyes. He ducked his head and climbed off his bar stool. Otsuka squeezed himself into the narrow space by the wall and prostrated himself at Tatsumi's feet.

"Tatsumi, I'm begging you. Don't ask any questions. Just take the job. Please."

"You're wasting your time," Tatsumi

sneered.

Otsuka stayed flat on the floor.

"That's enough of that," said the mama-san, coming out from behind the bar.

Otsuka refused to get up. "I'm begging you," he said, grinding his forehead into the worn crimson carpet. "Please take the job."

Otsuka didn't feel that he was making a fool of himself. It was his only option, and if he persisted, he would eventually get what he was after. He was sure of it.

After a while, Tatsumi exhaled heavily.

"What do you want me to do?"

"Huh?" Otsuka gasped and looked up in disbelief.

"I said, what do you want me to do?"

"You mean you'll do it?"

"You need to tell me what it is first."

"So when I tell you what it is, you will do it?"

"Yeah, yeah. Fuck, but you're one bull-headed bastard. You wore me down."

Otsuka couldn't keep the smile off his face.

Tatsumi emitted a derisive snort. "It was the same damn thing when you arrested me. I'd have been fine if I'd just stayed put in my hiding place, but you waited me out, staying in the same damn place for three hours. I blinked first. You're free to think I fell off that wall, if you want, but that isn't what happened. You wore me out until I climbed down out of that building and I gave myself up."

Otsuka got up off the floor and grasped Tatsumi's hands.

"Thank you. Thank you."

Tatsumi tore his hands away.

"Hang on. I don't work for free, you know."

"I know. What's your daily rate?"

"Like I said, I need to know what the job is first."

Otsuka nodded, pulled an envelope out of his briefcase, tipped out several pages of printouts, and pushed them across. Tatsumi flicked through them.

"Looks like a message board?"

"That's right. I need to identify the individuals who are putting up posts. Take this Wicked Wizard guy here. I want you to get his real name and address. Think you can do it?"

"As long as the guy uses the same handle for all his posts."

"Someone told me that people can only be tracked back as far as their proxy server. You think you can identify the individuals?"

Tatsumi gave an impatient jerk of his head. "Whining about proxies is for amateurs. I'm a pro, man. Identifying individual users — piece of fucking cake. There's only one snag: I need to be online at the same time as they are. When they're offline, there's fuck-all I can do. You need time and patience for a job like this."

"That shouldn't be a problem, then. I want you to identify the regular users of the different message boards. They log on nightly."

Tatsumi held up his hand to interrupt.

"Hang on a sec. Did you say regular *users*? You're talking about more than one of them?"

"I was going to ask you to do eight."

"Eight? Okay, but like I said before, I don't come cheap."

"How much will it cost me?"

"For this — fifty thousand yen per person."

"Fifty thousand times eight — you mean four hundred thousand?"

That was impossible. Totally impossible. What he was asking for was illegal, so he wasn't going to get any funds from the department. He was going to have to pay for it himself, and four hundred thousand wasn't feasible. His salary was less than three hundred thousand a month. Four hundred was beyond him.

"Could you see your way to giving me a discount?"

They spent the next half hour haggling over price.

3

Sunday, August 24

Reiko was visiting empty properties in Shibuya. Yesterday had produced nothing, and they'd drawn a blank at the live music club they'd been to that morning.

"Maybe we'd be better off trying a new angle, Lieutenant," suggested Ioka, leading her into an Internet café. "Here's my idea. If we access the online message boards from the police station, people would only have to check the server to see that we're cops. But here, it's a different story. If we use an Internet café, no one will know we're cops."

As far Reiko could tell, Ioka was proposing that they started posting on the bulletin boards. That way, they might be able to establish contact with the regular contributors, some of whom seemed very well informed.

"Not a bad idea. You think they'll bite?"

"No harm in trying."

They went online and accessed one of the message boards. No one was talking about Strawberry Night right then, so the topic had been pushed down to the bottom of the list.

"We'll need a name to log in with. Hmmmm . . . everybody else here has a male handle, so maybe female would be better."

"Does the name really matter much?"

"People talk about 'the scent of a woman,' " said Ioka, snuggling his head into Reiko's shoulder.

"You're telling me I stink."

"No, you smell good. You're fragrant."

"And you're a pervert."

"Oh, please. Abuse me some more."

Reiko slapped Ioka hard. The sound echoed through the quiet room, and everyone turned to stare.

You never learn, do you? It's impressive in its own way.

Reiko responded violently to sexual harassment. On the train, with would-be gropers, she had notched up a tally of seventeen broken fingers and two broken arms. At work, her record was more modest: six broken fingers and zero arms — but she had kneed three guys in the balls and concussed a couple by kicking their legs out from under them. Ioka was lucky — he'd not yet suffered any broken bones.

Reiko wondered briefly if she was starting to like Ioka a little and was unconsciously cutting him slack.

That, I refuse to accept!

Ioka was unusually tough, she told herself, and could take any physical punishment she dished out.

"How about 'Peaches'?" said Ioka, waggling a finger.

"What the hell kind of name is that?"

"It was the name of my pet hamster when I was a kid."

"I don't want to share a name with your stupid hamster."

"How about 'Kasumi,' then?"

Reiko's cell phone buzzed on the edge of the table. She checked the caller ID. It was from task force HQ.

"Himekawa."

"Imaizumi here. I need you to go to Toda Park. Fast."

"Toda Park in Saitama? That Toda?"

"That's it. They've found a body at the Toda Rowing Course, wrapped in a blue plastic sheet. It's in an advanced state of decay, but it looks like it could be one of ours."

"Yes, sir."

Reiko felt a tingling in her spine.

Toda Park was just this side of the Arakawa River, which marked the border between Tokyo and Saitama. Reiko and Ioka got off the train at Toda Park Station and headed for the rowing course. A minivan with sliding doors — probably Forensics — was parked nearby, along with an unmarked car from the Mobile Unit and a black-and-white patrol car of the prefectural police. Twenty or so curious members of the public were milling around.

She showed her badge to the uniform on sentry duty. There was a pause, then a "Good afternoon." He treated her to the usual slightly skeptical look but had the grace to lift up the yellow tape to let her through.

Advancing down the path, they came to a series of low-slung sheds. All the top universities, from Tokyo University on down, had boathouses here. Beyond the boathouses, they emerged beside a long straight stretch of water — the Toda Rowing Course.

The police had closed the park to the general public, so there were no civilians on this side of the river. The road on the far side, however, was a crowd of rubberneckers. It was a noisy, heaving scrum over there.

Not even the blistering heat could keep people away.

The crime scene was indeed out of the ordinary. Bundles of blue plastic sheeting lay on the concrete bank — nine of them, all human-sized. As Reiko approached the cluster of middle-aged men gloomily inspecting the line of corpses, she slipped on a Homicide armband and introduced herself with a crisp bow.

"Reiko Himekawa, TMPD Homicide."

"Good to see you. Fumihito Azuma, Homicide, Prefectural Police."

The geniality of his smile as he presented her with his card took her aback.

"You got here fast. I specifically requested you. So, what do you think? Déjà vu all over again?"

The police forces outside Tokyo seemed to be staffed by people with a major chip on their shoulder with regard to the Metropolitan Police. But the Saitama Prefectural Police appeared to be the exception to the rule. Not only was Azuma friendly, none of the other detectives were eyeballing her either.

Azuma's the same rank as Sata was in the Saitama police.

It felt like good karma to Reiko.

"The plastic sheeting's certainly similar.

Can I have a look inside?"

"Be my guest."

Azuma gestured to end of the line.

"We lined them up in order. Newest to oldest."

"Uh-huh."

So the nine bodies were all in different states of decay, were they? That would make sense if they'd been dumped in the water at the rate of one per month.

"We think this one's the freshest."

Azuma peeled back the sheet. Reiko inspected the body, taking care not to breathe through her nose.

Although the face had disintegrated, it was clear from the body shape that they were looking at a woman. There were two X-shaped cuts where the breasts ought to have been. It looked as if the X had been the leitmotif of her particular torture session; there were around twenty similar-shaped cuts on her upper body. The flesh around them was blanched and puffy, giving her body the appearance of being covered in white flowers. Reiko checked the presence of the incisions to the carotid artery and the abdomen. Assuming this corpse was the one directly before Namekawa, it would be about two and half months old. The state of decomposition looked about right.

Reiko got as close to the body as she could stand. She stared at it, as if willing it to speak to her. But like the previous two bodies, it was silent. Strange. Unable to learn anything new from the corpse, Reiko stood up.

Reiko nodded at Azuma. "Definitely the same MO. Who discovered the bodies?"

Azuma, who had been squatting down beside her, stood back up. "The sheet around this particular body seems to have been tied especially tight. The decomposition gases, which accumulated around the head, couldn't get out. That made the string around the feet snap and the whole thing floated up to the surface like a big balloon."

He jerked a thumb at the row of boat sheds behind him. "Some Tokyo University students found this one during morning rowing practice. They were merrily rowing away, when this thing bobbed up right next to their boat. Must have given them one hell of a shock. It sank straight back down again. That could have been the end of it, but luckily for us one of the boys had been paying attention to the news and knew something about you lot finding bodies wrapped in blue plastic in a pond in Tokyo. He called it in, and the local precinct got

336

HQ to send in a team of divers. Their search turned up these nine. That's about it, really. The divers called it a day when they ran out of oxygen. They'll resume the search tomorrow. It's funny how after you found your bodies in Tokyo, this lot pops up over here. It's almost like they're trying to be found to get back at whoever killed them."

Azuma paused, then flicked to the next page of the report in his hand. The second most recent body was already so far gone, he explained, they couldn't identify its sex. Assuming they'd got the order right, they presumed it dated from three and half months ago. The overall skeletonization process was advanced, and they'd been unable to confirm any wounds to the neck or abdomen.

Azuma showed Reiko the third and then the fourth body. Both were in a state of almost total skeletonization, and she could see little difference between them. Inspecting the others would be a waste of time. Just as the thought crossed her mind, a most unwelcome voice boomed out behind her.

"I'm impressed, Lieutenant Himekawa. Working so hard in this heat."

She spun around. Lieutenant Katsumata was standing directly behind her, his florid face gleaming with sweat. Had the task force

HQ sent him here, or had he sniffed out the crime scene on his own? Whichever it was, Reiko knew that his presence could only make things harder.

"Hi, all. The name's Katsumata, Metropolitan Police, Homicide," he said. "Damn, this heat."

"Hi, I'm Azuma, Prefectural Homicide."

The sight of Azuma handing his business card to Katsumata, as he had just done to her, made Reiko irrationally angry. She cleared her throat loudly to get everyone's attention.

"Lieutenant Katsumata, why are you here?"

"Are you so up your own ass that you think you're the only one to hear about this crime scene? You think a fool like you knows anything I don't? You're too damn arrogant, you dumb hick."

Azuma, who was standing next to Katsumata, looked utterly mystified.

"I'm not arrogant."

"Yes, you fucking are. Anyway, everything's turned out roses for you. This parade of stiffs will give a nice credibility boost to that murder show theory that you and your sidekick floated."

"Hey, wait a —" exclaimed Reiko.

"What are you talking about?" broke in

338

Azuma. "What's this about a murder show?"

Katsumata turned to him, his face beaming. "We've got some unusual information I can't really tell you about, but the fact is —"

"Lieutenant Katsumata!" Reiko grabbed Katsumata's shoulder to make him shut him up. His beady little insect eyes slid back to her, and he glowered furiously. Reiko was past caring. She shoved him off to the side.

"Lieutenant Azuma, we will provide you with a full written report only when this is officially designated as a joint investigation. Katsumata, I need a word with you."

As she dragged Katsumata into the bleachers behind them, his middle-aged cop partner attempted to follow them. Reiko glared at him and he retreated.

"What's going on here? Why're you manhandling me?"

Every word he said only stoked her rage.

"Katsumata." Reiko glared at him. "What the hell do you think you're doing, shooting your mouth off before a joint investigation's been authorized?"

Katsumata raised an eyebrow. "Are you really that stupid? The two crime scenes are almost identical. Of course we're going to join forces with these guys. And since when did you become the poster girl for doing things by the book? I know what this is all about — you wanting to take all the credit and not share your leads with anyone else," Katsumata said. He spat in the direction of Reiko's feet.

Me, a credit hog? That's pretty damn rich, coming from you, Stubby.

Reiko was seething inside. The way he kept needling her like this whenever their paths crossed was unbearable. Reiko decided to have it out with him then and there.

"Lieutenant Katsumata, why are you always barging in and getting in my way? Have I done something to antagonize you?"

"Barging in?" sneered Katsumata. "That's not very nice. You only *think* I get in the way, because you're too much of a slowpoke to know which way this thing is going in the first place. If you were willing to take a back seat, you wouldn't need to throw a hissy fit at me."

"I got here first."

"Bravo, wonder woman. Only because Captain Zoomzoom tipped you off."

"How did you hear about it, Lieutenant?"

"None of your business."

"What about Kasumi Shiratori then? I was supposed to interview her."

"You were assing around doing something else, so I stepped in and dealt with her.

340

Welcome to the big leagues, slowpoke. Things move fast here. You're not in Hicksville anymore."

"What's with this 'hick' crap you keep throwing at me?"

"If Urawa isn't Hicksville, then where the fuck is? I'm a Tokyo man, born and fucking bred. You — you're an ignorant potato-eating slut from the boonies. That's why you like to screw behind park toilets."

"What the —" Before the words were even out of her mouth, Reiko's right hand had reflexively shot back.

I've had it with this filthy bastard! I'm going to punch his lights out!

Someone gently took hold of her wrist. "Probably better not, Lieutenant."

She suddenly noticed Ioka standing right behind her.

"Do it and they'll take you off the investigation."

Good old Ioka. He's right, of course.

Katsumata would have no qualms about presenting himself as a victim. Even if the charges ultimately failed to stick, he could kick up an almighty stink — which would be enough to get Reiko pulled off the case.

Why? Why does he treat me like this?

Reiko gritted her teeth and forced herself back under control. She turned around and began to walk away.

"Your whole approach. It's too damn dangerous."

She knew that Katsumata was still talking to her, but she kept right on going.

4

Otsuka was at the evening meeting.

"The autopsy report and forensic test results for the bodies found at the Toda Rowing Course in Saitama this morning have come in, so I will start there. There were nine bodies in total, all of which were wrapped in plastic sheeting manufactured by Minowa Building Materials — just like the two bodies found earlier. In what is believed to be the most recent of the bodies, there was an incision severing the carotid artery and another large vertical incision slicing open the abdomen. The state of decay of the nine bodies suggests that they were dumped in the water at one-month intervals. This matches the interval between the Namekawa and the Kanebara murders. The evidence leads us to conclude that the same perpetrator is responsible for the bodies found at Toda and Mizumoto. We have therefore decided that we should cooperate fully with the prefectural task force handling the Toda case and investigate the two cases jointly.

"It's not yet an official joint investigation, but I still want you to think of our two task forces as a single unit and act accordingly. The ground rules are as follows. On our side, we share all the information we have unearthed so far with the prefectural police; they, in turn, share anything new they find with us.

"I don't want to see any territorial rivalry about which task force can crack the case first. This isn't about us versus them. Our priority here is to catch this brutal murdering freak. With eleven victims to his credit already, media interest can only grow, and the longer the investigation continues, the worse we — the police — will look. Starting tomorrow, I need you to redouble your efforts. Be tough, be smart, and make me proud."

Is this a progress report or a sermon?

During Chief of Homicide Wada's overlong speech, Otsuka's eyes wandered around the room.

Katsumata was sitting in the front row with his arms crossed and his eyes closed. Was the man smiling? What the heck was there to smile about? Otsuka had a bad feeling. No one in the task force, Katsumata included, was keen on rolling over for the Saitama police.

Let's hope Katsumata isn't cooking up a nasty surprise for our squad.

Himekawa sat biting her lip and sighing loudly from time to time. Otsuka sympathized with her irritation. She'd hit the ground running on this case. She'd solved the riddle of the sliced-open abdomen, figured out that Yasuyuki Fukazawa was in charge of dumping the bodies in the water, and predicted where Namekawa's body would be. Sure, Otsuka tracked down the Strawberry Night lead, but it needed Himekawa to connect the dots and tie it in with everything else. Their searches of empty buildings had yielded zip so far; nonetheless, Otsuka was pretty sure — scrub that, he was one hundred percent certain — that something would turn up soon. The lead he'd gotten hold of was golden. He wanted to follow it up and close this case personally.

Now, the whole case was about to slip out of their hands. While there was no guarantee that the Saitama Prefectural Police would catch the perp, it was looking likely that the Himekawa squad would lose its monopoly on the murder show lead. The bodies found in the Toda Rowing Course all predated Namekawa. Given their state of decay, the autopsies had revealed little, and so much time had passed since the actual dumping of the bodies that the neighborhood canvass wasn't yielding anything either. Nor had Forensics covered themselves in glory. Their failure to identify the bodies was preventing the investigation from moving on to the next stage — interviews with the family, colleagues, and friends of the deceased. All in all, the Saitama Prefectural Police had an investigation but almost nothing to investigate.

That only increased the chances of their wanting to muscle in on the Strawberry Night lead. It looked promising, as leads go. With eleven victims in total, it was pretty clear that they were looking at something far beyond a "normal" murder investigation. When everyone was looking for a way to make sense of the whole freaky case, the concept of a murder show suddenly seemed a great deal more plausible.

So that's why he's got that creepy smirk on his face!

Katsumata was probably desperate to pursue the Strawberry Night lead himself. He probably recognized that it was the key to the entire case. The trouble was, it was *their* lead, and Katsumata had as good as burned his bridges with the Himekawa squad. It would have been too much of a retreat for him to express any interest in their lead.

The discovery of nine more bodies had resulted in a collaborative investigation, which was going to force the Himekawa squad to be open and upfront about everything they knew — and give Katsumata access to all their intel without so much as lifting a finger. Katsumata being Katsumata, he might have some other malicious plot in the oven too. Otsuka knew one thing about Katsumata: you never knew what he was thinking.

Otsuka was feeling nervous about his rendezvous with Tatsumi. The reason was simple: the job he had asked Tatsumi to do for him was illegal.

This was Otsuka's first descent into illegality. He had his reasons, though. Good ones. Strawberry Night was the first major lead he'd dug up himself since his transfer to TMPD Homicide. His squad was under pressure with Katsumata and his goons snapping at their heels. The threat of the joint investigation with the Saitama police only added fuel to the fire. He had to do something soon to drive the investigation forward.

That didn't keep him having cold feet about the meeting with Tatsumi. It was set for five p.m. tomorrow. He would hand over the cash and get the information in return. Otsuka was afraid — but he had to go.

When had the murders been committed? Who had committed them? Why? How?

Otsuka ran through what they knew. It wasn't much: "When" was the second Sunday of the month. "How" was by slicing the carotid artery after public torture. If Otsuka's suspicions were right and one of the eight contributors to the online forum had actually attended the show — and if Tatsumi managed to identify him, then they would finally discover the "who" and the "where." It would be a great leap forward for the investigation.

Otsuka had managed to negotiate Tatsumi's fee down to ¥240,000 for all eight. Although still a hefty sum for Otsuka, it was not unmanageable.

Tatsumi had imposed conditions in return for lowering his price. He would spend two days on the job, and Otsuka would have to pay whether or not he succeeded in identifying all eight people. Otsuka swallowed the terms, despite the risk.

Everyone in the meeting room was delivering their progress reports in turn. The current speaker was Kikuta, who was sitting directly in front of Otsuka.

Otsuka himself had nothing significant to share today. In his head he ran through what he was going to say — the vacant buildings they had visited and what they had found in them. Of course, they had found zero evidence that any of them had been used for the murder show. Getting to your feet to deliver a dud report was tough, but everyone else was in the same boat tonight — the neighborhood canvass, the interviews with next of kin, vacant properties in other parts of the city were all "nothing to reports."

I've got to do it. I've got to go and see what Tatsumi found out.

Otsuka clenched his fists to bolster his courage.

Monday, August 25
Just as he had done two days earlier, Otsuka took Kitami aside to tell him that he needed time alone to take care of something. "This will be the last time I do this," he added with an apologetic little bow.

"Officer Otsuka, I don't want you to feel that you have to treat me any different from anyone else. I'm a total greenhorn as a detective," Kitami replied, with a relaxed smile. "You do what you think needs to be done."

The guy's more on my wavelength than I thought.

They agreed to meet an hour later in front of Rockman, a music club that had gone out of business. Kitami went off in one direction, and Otsuka headed back to the hole-in-the-wall bar where he had met Tatsumi.

It was five fifty-five when he pushed open the front door.

"Oh hello, Officer Otsuka."

The mama-san gave him a friendly smile.

"Tatsumi hasn't arrived yet. Please, have a seat."

"Thanks."

Otsuka sat on the same stool as last time. The mama-san asked him if he was still officially on the job, and when he said he was, she poured him a glass of oolong tea.

"You're probably wondering what sort of relationship me and Tatsumi have . . . ," the mama-san said as she finished pouring.

"No, not really," he replied noncommittally and took a swig of his tea.

There was a brief silence.

"Tatsumi . . . he helped me out when I

was in trouble."

The mama-san was clearly determined to confide in him, with or without his encouragement. She just wanted to enlighten him about the "good side" of his character.

Otsuka never got to hear that particular story. Before she got started, the cowbell on the door jangled.

"Hi, Tatsumi. Officer Otsuka's waiting for you."

"You saying I'm late, woman?" he snapped.

Like last time, he was wearing a garish Hawaiian shirt. He sulkily swung himself up onto the stool beside Otsuka.

"Sorry for putting you to the trouble."

Otsuka had no reason to apologize. Somehow, though, the words seemed to say themselves.

"No worries. Shit, man, the job was tough." Tatsumi sighed wearily. "I estimated what time the contributors were most likely to access the sites, added on an hour either side as a safety buffer, and ran three PCs at full throttle. God knows how many times the site reloaded."

"Ah," gurgled Otsuka.

"Not the sort of job you want to do in two days."

"Thanks a lot. I owe you big-time."

351

Despite being desperate to hear what Tatsumi had found out, Otsuka couldn't bring himself to come out and say so. The mamasan poured Tatsumi a beer. After the usual display of indifference, he drank it down with obvious relish. Otsuka watched and fidgeted, aware that he wasn't any closer to getting answers. Unable to feign patience any longer, he fished a sweaty envelope full of banknotes out of the inside pocket of his suit.

"Here's your money. Count it."

Tatsumi took the envelope in silence, pulled out the wad of notes, and counted them. Twenty-four ten-thousand–yen notes — precisely as promised. Otsuka jammed the notes back into the envelope and set it on the edge of the bar.

"There's something I want to ask you before I hand over the data."

Tatsumi looked at Otsuka searchingly.

Otsuka uttered a silent prayer. *Don't let Tatsumi confess that he failed to identify anyone.* Was that the reason he was being all sullen? A wave of unease roiled Otsuka's chest.

Tatsumi set his jaw. "Are you investigating this Strawberry Night murder show? Seriously, are you?"

His tone was disapproving.

That was hardly a difficult conclusion to reach. The comments posted by the contributors on the list Otsuka had provided would have made that crystal clear. Trying to lie about it would be a waste of time. Still, Otsuka didn't know *why* Tatsumi wanted to know. And the mama-san was a civilian with no involvement in the case. He had to be careful what he said in front of her.

"Maybe I am."

That was as far as he was prepared to go.

Tatsumi leaned toward him and lowered his voice. "My advice to you is to drop it. Don't take it any further."

Now Otsuka was more mystified than ever.

"It's not like I'm doing this for fun. It's part of an investigation. That's why I asked for your help."

"My advice is the same — *Don't take it any further.* The devil's sitting right on your tail."

"Dammit, you lowlife. Just tell me what you damn well found out, okay?" exploded Otsuka. "It's important."

"You go fuck yourself," Tatsumi retorted. He swept his beer bottle off the bar and onto the floor. It landed with a thunk but did not break. White foam dribbled out onto the floor with a gentle gurgling sound.

"Know why I hate you fucking cops?

Because you're all so damn stupid. These days information is a valuable commodity, something that's bought and sold. You guys still think that flashing your badge is enough to get people to roll over and tell you whatever you want to know. You've got your heads up your asses."

Tatsumi pulled a small envelope out of his back pocket and smacked it down on the bar. He then grabbed Otsuka's envelope of cash and headed for the door.

"Tatsumi, wait!" Otsuka yelled at the retreating figure. For some reason his body refused to move off the stool.

Tatsumi's findings were sitting on the bar in front of him. Their deal was done, over. But what was all that stuff about the devil being on his tail? One thing was obvious: getting an answer would cost him. Tatsumi had made his position very clear.

Tatsumi turned around at the door. "Listen, Otsuka. I have a conscience — and occasionally I even listen to it. I'm telling you this for your own good. Drop this case. Drop it right now. That's all I've got to say."

"I have one last thing to ask of you," Otsuka said. "It's clear that this Strawberry Night thing has you worried. And you believe it's dangerous. If anything happens, call my boss, Lieutenant Reiko Himekawa.

You can trust her. You have to promise me. Please."

Tatsumi stared at him with a look of annoyance and then turned away. With a jangle of the cowbell, Tatsumi disappeared without another word into the sweltering backstreets of Ikebukuro.

The mama-san looked upset as she squatted down by Tatsumi's stool and mopped the spilled beer off the floor. Otsuka noticed a small dent in the wall. The bottle must have hit it on its way down.

Otsuka resettled himself on his stool and picked Tatsumi's report up off the counter. It was in an ordinary long thin manila envelope. Inside were two sheets of paper. Otsuka wondered how many people Tatsumi had identified for his ¥240,000.

He ran his eye over the two pages of text. All eight handle names were there! Tatsumi had managed to do the whole damn lot.

Incredible! The guy actually did it!

Otsuka struggled to keep a lid on his excitement as he ran down the list. It turned out that Tatsumi had not just provided the names and addresses of the eight people, but details about their jobs and bank accounts — even domain names and passwords in some cases. The report was a treasure trove of data.

That Tatsumi's quite a guy!

Why then did he get so angry and storm out of the bar? Was it embarrassment at helping the cops? Was it that he didn't want the mama-san to see that he was a good guy at heart? For whatever reason, Tatsumi had urged him to drop the case.

Otsuka shrugged those thoughts off and gave his full attention to the report. He'd reached the sixth name in the list when a single word burst from his lips. "Him!"

The name was a complete shock. At the same time, seeing it there in front of his eyes, in black and white, it made perfect sense. Otsuka had screwed up — badly.

"The bastard!"

The mama-san stared at him, shocked. Otsuka was past caring what she thought.

That fucker! He was making a fool of me!

Otsuka mumbled his thanks, punched the door open, and left.

Otsuka was in a bind. He needed to share his new information with Himekawa as fast as possible. The problem was how. He'd started a rogue investigation without consulting her. At least there was some time before the evening meeting kicked off. That was in his favor. For now, though, he needed to keep his appointment with Kitami. He headed for the music venue where they had agreed to meet.

He went down into the underground concourse of Ikebukuro station and came out again at the east exit where he walked a short distance north, parallel to the railway tracks. The Rockman club, which had shut down two years ago, was located on the edge of a cluster of love hotels and sex clubs. The building's once white walls were caked with grime and smoke stains and laced with cracks. Back in the day, the club had boasted its own colorful neon sign; now all that remained were seven rusting brown letters and a tangle of wiring. The skeletal sign looked as spectral and tragic as a rock star fallen on hard times, thought Otsuka — or was his imagination running away with him?

There were still ten minutes until the rendezvous time, he thought — why not put the time to good use and do a quick reconnaissance?

He noticed a gap between the club and the building to its right. It was an alleyway just wide enough for him to squeeze through. He followed it about ten meters to an open space behind the club. From the smoke and the strong smell of cooking, Otsuka guessed that the building behind it was probably a bar.

There was a door in the back of the empty building. There was also a flight of stairs leading to the basement around the side, but the stairs were blocked by a fence with a locked gate. The back door looked like his best bet for breaking in.

He put his hand on the knob and was startled when it turned easily — too easily, as it turned out. It went around and around without engaging. Probably stripped, he thought. He tried pulling the door toward him. There was an earsplitting metallic grinding noise as the door opened.

That's pretty damn sloppy.

Inside, the club was pitch black.

"Hello, anyone home?" called Otsuka, more out of habit than anything else, as he walked in.

The stale, mold-tinged atmosphere was the same as in the Cherry Strip Club. Abandoned places all seemed to share the same sour smell. How many of them were there in central Tokyo?

What with the long-drawn-out recession, the answer seemed to be: more and more all the time. Even in the bustling shopping and entertainment districts, you didn't need to venture much off the beaten track to encounter a rash of "To Let" signs. These vacant properties gave Otsuka the feeling that he was getting a backstage view of the city. He was privy to a secret that no one in the front of the house knew — that the whole gaudy, glittering metropolis was nothing more than a cheap papier-mâché façade. And out of sight, something incredible was happening — a murder show.

A sharp squeal of metal interrupted Otsuka's train of thought. Behind him, the door shut. He spun around but could see nothing. The little bit of daylight that had peeped through the half-open doorway had disappeared. Otsuka was trapped in the dark.

Suddenly he sensed that someone else was there.

Who?

Before he could ask the question aloud, he was struck on the head by something hard. He felt dazed as strange colors flashed before his eyes.

I'm screwed!

Unable to stay upright, he sagged to his knees. A powerful light was directed at him from above.

Gritting his teeth through the pain, he forced one eye open. His vision was blurred. He thought he could make out two sets of legs, one in jeans, the other in black leather pants.

"Wait."

A young man's voice? It seemed to come from Jeans. Leather Pants then passed Jeans the flashlight. Then — a deluge of blows.

Someone was kicking him in the belly, the chest, the arms. A knee connected with his head. The assailant used his body weight to press him to the floor. Otsuka was unable to offer any resistance as they went though his pockets.

Who the hell are these people?

His personal effects were tossed any which way onto the dusty concrete floor: his police badge, his wallet, his cell phone, his notebook, his handkerchief.

Eventually, the young man found Tatsumi's envelope in the inside pocket of Otsuka's jacket. He pulled it out. Somewhere above his head, Otsuka heard the crackle of paper.

"You'd got this far, huh?"

He heard the thud as a boot went into the back of his head. As he slid into unconsciousness, he felt his arms being twisted behind him and heard a familiar metallic click. They were handcuffing him — him, a policeman.

5

Monday, August 25

As soon as the evening meeting came to an end, Reiko summoned Lieutenant Kitami to the front of the room. He'd come back to the police station without his partner, and she needed to find out what was going on.

"Where's Otsuka? What's happening?"

Kitami's head lolled from side to side like a little boy wilting under a teacher's scolding.

He had fine, delicate features and straight black hair, which he wore slicked back. His muscular torso was at odds with this initial impression of delicacy. Kitami was far more athletic than the usual management fast-trackers, whom Reiko regarded as a bunch of wimps.

However handsome he was, right now Kitami was staring pitifully at the floor, refusing to make eye contact.

"Lieutenant Kitami, I need an answer," she said sharply.

Out of the corner of her eye, Reiko saw the look of alarm that flashed across the faces of the station commander and the local chief of detectives. Kitami's dad was the director of the Third District, and Kitami himself was a Tokyo University grad destined for the upper echelons. However, right now Reiko didn't care even a little bit.

"Where is Officer Otsuka?"

Kitami didn't reply. With his frown and his tightly clamped lips, he seemed to be locked in a struggle with himself. Reiko was at a loss. Why was Kitami refusing to tell her anything? Behind her, Kikuta was calling Otsuka's cell phone, but Otsuka wasn't picking up.

"When did you split up?" Reiko spoke more quietly this time. Kitami still said nothing.

"Why did you come back here alone? Did you think Otsuka was already here?"

Kitami winced.

"Your silence isn't helping me get a handle on things. Stop behaving like a damn child. If you know what the fuck is going on, you need to tell me. Where did you leave Otsuka?"

Kitami set his jaw.

"Lieutenant Kitami, are you even listening?"

Kitami briefly raised his eyes off the floor, then his head lolled down again. He spoke jerkily, hesitantly.

"Officer Otsuka was flying solo."

Reiko groaned. It was a reflexive response. The idea of Otsuka going it alone chilled her to the marrow.

"What was he investigating?"

"I don't know," stammered Kitami. "He wouldn't tell me."

"When did this start?"

"He went off the day before yesterday. Today was the second time. That's all I know."

"All day?"

"No, we split up at five and arranged to meet up again at six. We were only supposed to be apart for an hour. . . . Today I went to a department store café to kill time. At six I went to the place where we'd agreed to meet. He wasn't there. I called his cell but couldn't get through. . . . I waited there until seven. Then I came back here. I couldn't think of anything else to do. . . . I'm sorry."

Otsuka only worked solo for an hour. What could he do in such a short time?

"I'm assuming that Otsuka asked your

permission before going off on his own?"

Kitami clammed up.

"Lieutenant Kitami, I asked you a question."

A pause. "Yes, he did."

"So why did you let him? It's an ironclad rule in homicide investigations: everyone works in pairs. You know that. Otsuka having experience is no excuse. You're a lieutenant. Your giving him permission undermined the whole chain of command in this investigation. Am I right?"

"Yes," he mumbled.

"Forgetting Otsuka, wherever he is, for one minute, you're not going to get away with this. It's a serious breach of protocol."

"I know."

Everyone in the hushed meeting room was listening to them. The top brass were all there, along with Reiko's squad. Only the local detectives and Katsumata and his men had left already.

"I am going to stay here and wait for Otsuka. If you've got any sense of responsibility, you'll wait here with me."

"Yes," Kitami whispered, bowing deeply to Reiko.

Eventually only Himekawa and her squad, together with Ioka and Kitami, remained in the meeting room waiting. They continued calling Otsuka's cell with no luck. It was past eleven when Captain Imaizumi reappeared.

"Himekawa."

"Yes, sir." Reiko rose to her feet as the captain slowly approached the circle of six chairs. When he got up close, he looked at them all gravely, one by one, until his gaze finally settled on Reiko.

Captain Imaizumi paused and swallowed. His angular Adam's apple jerked up and down in his throat. "They found Otsuka's body."

"Otsuka's body?"

"A call just came in from Ikebukuro. They found him in an empty music venue. I don't know the details, but I'm guessing that's where he'd arranged to meet Lieutenant Kitami. Otsuka was shot —"

Reiko didn't wait to hear any more. She broke into a run. Imaizumi stepped forward, blocked her, enfolded her in his arms, immobilized her.

"Himekawa, no. You can't."

"Let me go," she raved. "I've got to go."

"You can't. Ikebukuro is getting Kusaka to handle things. Just because Otsuka's a cop doesn't mean that procedure can go out the window. Even if you went, they wouldn't let you do anything."

Reiko shook herself free of Imaizumi's grip.

"Otsuka was my man. Why bring Kusaka in?"

Reiko tried to push past Imaizumi. She closed with him, and they grappled. She was like a rebellious daughter fighting with her father to leave home. It was only when Kikuta and Ioka joined in and got Reiko in a shoulder lock that she began to calm down.

"Lieutenant, I know how you feel, but you've got to get a grip."

"The captain's right. You've got to stand back and let Kusaka handle this one."

Reiko, who was unable to move, could only moan feebly. "Why Otsuka? Why him?"

She couldn't imagine why Otsuka would have been killed, let alone shot. It was simply incredible. She'd said good-bye to him on the train that morning. Otsuka, who was with Kitami, got out onto the rush-hour platform and disappeared into the surging crowd without looking back. Was that the last time she'd ever see him?

Otsuka had joined Homicide after Reiko, which made him the only person on the squad who was incontestably her junior.

It was like Otsuka was her kid brother. She only had a sister; she had gone to a women's college; her subordinates at Traffic had all been women. A male subordinate younger than she was a novelty. In her mind, her squad was a family, with Ishikura as the father, Kikuta as the big brother, and Otsuka and Yuda the baby brothers. Otsuka was only her junior by a whisker, and as they'd gotten to know each other better, he'd started teasing her a little — still, she knew that he was as rock-solid and reliable as if he were her real brother. If anything, his plodding and methodical approach made him stand out at Homicide where brilliance was in over-supply.

I will not cry.

That was the one thing Reiko would not permit herself to do on the job.

Today turned into tomorrow, and it was half-past midnight when Lieutenant Kusaka came into the meeting room with a "Sorry I took so long to get here." His usual over-bearing, almost aggressive manner was nowhere to be seen, and he was a shadow of his normal self. Normally, he and Hime-kawa were at one another's throats. But a detective from Unit 10 — Kusaka's unit — had been killed. That was all that mattered.

"Thanks for coming," said Captain Imaizumi gloomily.

"Himekawa?"

Reiko did not reply.

She had a pathological dislike of Kusaka. The first thing to turn her off him was his physical resemblance to her rapist. Beneath a receding hairline, he had big bug eyes and thin, cruel-looking lips. The likeness was close enough to revive the dark memories that still festered inside her.

She'd managed to get used to his appearance, but working with him made her dislike him even more. Kusaka sifted through the crime scene, the physical evidence, and the testimony with extreme thoroughness. His investigations were fanatically scrupulous and one hundred percent by the book. He marched around Tokyo like a martinet on parade, sucked up information like a robot vacuum cleaner, and typed up his reports like a data-entry professional. Reiko despised his whole mechanical approach.

As a person, Kusaka wasn't devoid of feeling. Reiko's prickly attitude had irked him once too often, and he started to provoke her deliberately. They were always at loggerheads.

Today, though, was an exception.

"I'm really sorry about Otsuka," Kusaka said sympathetically. "I always thought he

368

was the most promising member of your squad."

His words did not register. Nothing felt real to Reiko anymore. She had the strangest sensation, as if she were floating off into the sky — or drowning.

She'd broken into a cold sweat when she got the news of her mother's heart attack the other day, but this was a thousand times worse. For the first time, one of her direct colleagues had been killed. The rest of her squad might well be in danger; she might be in danger. It brought it home that being a detective was a dangerous job, with death always lurking around the next corner.

She felt quite helpless. The everyday volume of work and her smugness at making lieutenant had deprived her of a basic sense of danger. Tamaki had said something about her having changed as a person. Was she a failure not just as a daughter, but as a cop too?

"Tell us what happened," said Captain Imaizumi.

Kusaka gave a curt nod. "We found Otsuka's body in an empty building that used to house a live music venue called Rockman. The bullet was a 9mm Parabellum. A single shot. It entered the left eye and exited through the middle of the back of the head.

As far as we can tell, the perpetrator left nothing behind. Ishii of Unit 6 is setting up a task force to work on this. They will need to interview you, Captain, and you, Lieutenant Kitami, tomorrow morning." He paused. "Anyway, Otsuka seems to have crawled about thirty meters across a dark room and pushed the back door of the building open. It's incredible. His hands were cuffed behind his back and his head half blown off, yet he managed to squeeze halfway through the door before he died. Someone from the pub opposite spotted him and called it in. If he'd not made it to the outside, there's no way we would have found him."

Kusaka glanced at Reiko. "The guy had guts. He was a true cop."

Reiko pictured Otsuka crawling through the darkness with his hands cuffed, his left eye gone, and his head covered in blood. It was too horrible. She shook her head to drive the image from her head.

"Nothing else?" asked Imaizumi.

Kusaka grimaced. "One odd thing. We found Otsuka's badge and all the other stuff you'd expect him to have on him at the crime scene. Among his effects, though, there was an ATM transaction slip. At lunchtime yesterday — one p.m., to be precise — Otsuka withdrew two hundred and forty thousand yen from his Police Credit Union account, but his wallet only contained thirty-six thousand yen in notes, plus a little change. We couldn't find a receipt to help account for the missing two hundred grand."

Imaizumi looked at Kitami meaningfully. The young man inhaled sharply. "Otsuka did go to an ATM after lunch, and he didn't spend any money between then and five o'clock, when we separated."

Captain Imaizumi crossed his arms.

"Two hundred and forty thousand yen, eh," he grunted. "What would he need that kind of money for?"

Kusaka cocked his head. "It's a decent sum, but not a huge one."

"I think it's fair to assume that the money had some connection to whatever he went off to do by himself."

"Agreed. But the money might have had nothing to do with the investigation. Is there any chance that Otsuka was being black-mailed?"

Reiko got the impression that Kusaka's question was directed at her.

"I . . . uh . . . really don't . . ."

She was disgusted at her own incoherence. Even Kitami was keeping it together better than she was.

"Otsuka went off on his own to pay that money to someone. . . ." said Captain Imaizumi, looking around the circle for suggestions. No one said anything.

"Himekawa." Kusaka's tone was almost creepy in its gentleness. "No decision's yet been made as to whether I'll help the Ikebukuro task force or come here to reinforce you and your squad. I'm at your disposal. Whichever assignment I get, I'll coordinate with you. I need you to pull yourself together and catch this perpetrator with your usual speed. We don't know if Otsuka's shooter is connected to your ongoing investigation here, but catching him is the best tribute you can pay your dead comrade. Are you listening, Himekawa?"

Reiko couldn't bring herself even to nod in reply.

I know all that. Spare me your stupid lectures.

Why Otsuka, of all people?

She couldn't bring herself to think about tomorrow, about the investigation and the task force that was being set up in Ikebukuro. The only thing she could feel was the awful reality of Otsuka's death: the fact that she had to go on living in a world where a man on her squad had been killed. The thought of it spread slowly through her like aching poison in her veins.

Kusaka picked up his briefcase, then turned back to Reiko as though he'd just remembered something.

"Be careful about Stubby. A dead copper means no more to him than a dead cat. The state you're in now — he'll wipe the floor with you."

Reiko still said nothing. Eventually, with a nod at Captain Imaizumi, Kusaka stalked out of the room.

6

Tuesday, August 26, 11:30 A.M.

Katsumata sat alone in the sauna, deep in thought. Word of Otsuka's death had reached him the night before. Someone at the morning meeting had suggested that perhaps his murder had nothing to do with the Kanebara-Namekawa case. Katsumata wasn't buying it. His take was that Otsuka had found out something connected to the case that he wasn't supposed to find out — and had paid with his life. The ¥240,000 he'd withdrawn from the PCA Bank was obviously significant.

What was that Otsuka kid up to?

Someone had floated the possibility of blackmail. That was downright silly. Otsuka wasn't blackmail material — and that wasn't a compliment. The guy wasn't into anything big enough to blow back and hurt him.

For a detective, having enemies came with the job. Nobody *liked* being investigated.

And the people you arrested and sent to jail were all going to get out eventually, even the murderers — at least, the ones who didn't get the death penalty. It was a thankless task: the better you did your job, the more dangerous enemies you ended up with.

Katsumata had consulted Otsuka's file. The man had never put a hardcore villain or murderer behind bars. Maybe someone from a whole other part of his life was extorting him, but no, the whole thing — the idea of his being blackmailed and then withdrawing money and going AWOL to pay someone off when he was still on the job — didn't fit with his character. Besides, ¥240,000 was an unconvincing, half-assed amount of dough.

Still, the guy must have been killed for something. . . .

It had been a long time since Katsumata felt sorry or angry about fellow cops who were killed in the line of duty; his main concern was to avoid the same fate himself.

That's why I'm taking this little break.

The whole sauna — the benches, walls, ceiling — was made of Japanese cypress. Since it was a weekday morning, Katsumata had the whole place to himself.

Katsumata's personal responsibility was

the investigation of Yukio Namekawa, the adman, but so far all their interviews had led nowhere.

At one recent task force meeting, another investigator reported finding a pattern of monthly withdrawals from Taiichi Kanebara's bank account: ¥100,000 on the Friday immediately preceding the second Sunday of the month. The logical conclusion was that it was the price of a seat at the murder show. The whole Strawberry Night murder show theory was getting more credible all the time.

Regrettably, his guys hadn't been able to find a similar pattern in Namekawa's accounts. Since the man lived large, it was much harder to pinpoint the movement of a modest sum like ¥100,000. Katsumata felt that of the two cases, he'd got the shit end of the stick.

Well, I've planted the seeds. There's no point in worrying.

The proverb about "all things come to him who waits" flashed into his mind. He decided to lie down and do some serious sweating.

He had swung one leg up onto the bench, when he noticed someone peering at him through the little window in the wooden door. Another person coming in wasn't going to stop him having a nice lie-down. The door swung open just as Katsumata lowered his back onto the hot dry bench, and a man came in accompanied by a draft of cool air.

If this is the same guy who whacked Otsuka, I'll be in trouble.

Katsumata quickly swung himself back upright.

"Oh, Lieutenant, fancy bumping into you here!"

The voice caught him in the stomach. And the fellow hadn't even bothered to cover himself with a towel.

"You!"

"As God made me."

Ioka stood before him, stark naked.

Katsumata's designated partner changed every day. Today his partner was this Ioka character. Ioka had been Reiko Himekawa's partner until the day before. Why he'd been saddled with him today was one of life's mysteries. Captain Imaizumi had brought Ioka over after the morning meeting and announced, "You'll be working with Senior Officer Ioka today." All the senior officers were particularly grim at this morning's meeting. Director Hashizume ordered that, after Otsuka's murder, everyone on the team would start carrying a gun while on the job. Right now, there weren't enough at precinct headquarters to issue them to the TMPD detectives, but the precinct officers they were partnered with were required to check out a sidearm. When Imaizumi declared Ioka would be his partner, his tone didn't invite discussion. Katsumata wasn't much bothered by who his partner was; he just didn't like it when they managed to track him down when he thought he'd shaken them off.

"You sly bastard, how'd you know I was here?" said Katsumata, scowling. Ioka sat nonchalantly down on the bench opposite.

"Oh, just a wild guess. Thought you'd be in the mood for a nice long soak, Lieutenant, so I decided to pop into a few saunas before looking for you at the beach."

That was bullshit. From the whole of Tokyo, how on earth had Ioka tracked him to this sauna, miles away?

I mustn't underestimate this fellow.

All the other local partners Katsumata had had at Kameari had been spineless losers. He'd got rid of them with ease, either by sneaking off the train as the doors were closing or bribing them with a note or two.

I'll show you, you smartass.

It'd been a while since he'd gone on the warpath, but Katsumata was determined to teach Ioka a lesson.

■ ■ ■ ■

Katsumata caught the train from Okubo and went as far as Yoyogi, where he got off. Threading his way between several buildings, he reached the main road, where he leaped into a taxi heading for Shinjuku. Getting out at a traffic light by the railway station, he weaved his way through the crowds in the station and then walked out into a department store. He took the down escalator, slipped through a restaurant kitchen, and emerged into a back street.

Finally, he went out onto a long, straight street with very few pedestrians, where he turned around every few seconds to make sure no one was on his tail. It was okay. There was no one after him.

If he could keep up with me after all that, I'd have to admit defeat.

To be completely sure he was safe, Katsumata slipped into a nearby antique shop owned by a friend of his to kill half an hour.

"What are you so nervous about, Mr. Katsumata?" asked the owner, peering out the window as he poured his guest a cup of tea.

"Incredible as it may sound, I'm being followed. *Me!*"

The owner grinned meaningfully.

"Oh, so the higher-ups found out about your links with the yakuza?"

Katsumata grabbed the old man by his cotton-wool-like hair.

"Listen, old timer, you know what they say about walls having ears. If you want to stay alive, you'll keep your trap shut."

Far from being cowed by Katsumata's threats, the old man beamed merrily. This sort of overheated banter was a playful ritual they both enjoyed.

"So I'd better keep what I know about your gangster buddies at the Yamato-kai and those dodgy new religions to myself?"

"Listen, why don't you pick up that plate there — yes, the one with two extra zeroes on the price tag — and do some plate-spinning practice?"

"You looking to spend some of that 'pocket money' you're so good at earning?"

"Like hell I am."

Katsumata's cell phone rang loudly in his pocket. The caller ID said it was the desk sergeant from Kameari police station.

"Yep."

"Lieutenant Katsumata? Suyama here."

Suyama was the sergeant who handled the administration and documentation for the case. Katsumata had slipped him ¥100,000 the day he had joined the task force, to keep him sweet. The stage whisper Suyama was speaking in was a good omen.

"What is it? Something come up?"

"A moment ago someone called Tatsumi called for Lieutenant Himekawa."

"Tatsumi what? I need more than that."

"I'm sorry, that's the only name I got."

"Fat lot of use you are. Time to give me my money back."

"Hang on, sir. Lieutenant Himekawa was out, so I asked Tatsumi if he wanted to leave a message. He was pretty insistent about wanting to speak to her directly, but when I pushed him, he finally agreed to leave a message for her."

"Nice work. And may I assume that you have yet to pass this message on to the good lady lieutenant?"

"No, I haven't."

"Attaboy. So what did this Tatsumi guy have to say?"

"He wanted the lieutenant to call him back, and he gave me the number of his cell. Ready?"

"Fire away."

Katsumata wrote the number down on his hand.

"Got it. More like this, and you'll soon be in line for a bonus."

"Thanks." Suyama paused. "What should

I do about Lieutenant Himekawa?"

"Don't give her that number *under any circumstances*. Play dumb."

"Will I be okay?"

"You'll be fine. Just trust me."

Katsumata ended the call.

Tatsumi . . .

He'd come across the name somewhere very recently, either heard it or seen it in print.

Tatsumi.

That was it! Heck, it was about as recent as you could get. The name had been in Otsuka's file. The guy was the only collar Otsuka had ever made himself: a sleazy PI based in Ikebukuro — Keiichi Tatsumi, the notorious trader in stolen information.

Why the hell was Tatsumi trying to contact Himekawa?

Given their history, he could see why the guy might get in touch with Otsuka — but Otsuka was dead. Was he trying to contact Otsuka's immediate superior? No, that wasn't it. Otsuka's murder had made the morning papers, and Tatsumi had seen the news. He was trying to get in touch with Himekawa *because* Otsuka was dead.

But what business could a lowlife like him have with Himekawa?

Katsumata gulped down his lukewarm

green tea.

Katsumata called up some of his old buddies and asked them what they knew about Keiichi Tatsumi. They all had him pegged as harmless. In that case, why had Otsuka even bothered arresting the fellow? Whatever he was guilty of was just a youthful indiscretion — a healthy display of natural high spirits, in Katsumata's book. The best thing to do with people like him was to turn a blind eye and let them get on with their lives — until you needed them. Then you threatened them and smacked them around until they did what you wanted.

Hang on, that made sense.

What if Otsuka had asked Tatsumi to look into something for him? Perhaps when he'd headed out on his own, he'd gone to meet Tatsumi. That was the sort of thing one should always do outside of normal work hours, though. Otsuka had ignored that simple rule, and things had, predictably enough, gone south. The man was a fool or worse.

Katsumata decided to get the proprietor's tarty young daughter to call Tatsumi on his behalf. Her main job was with a repertory company, so her acting skills were good. Katsumata promised her fifteen thousand yen for her pains and gave her some background on Reiko Himekawa. "You're a twenty-nine-year-old lieutenant, tall, good-looking — and well aware of the fact. Oh, and you and the person you're calling have never met." That was enough for the girl to put in a fine performance.

"Okay. I'll see you at three."

The girl put down the phone and handed Katsumata a scrawled note. "Fountain Square, Sunshine 60 Building, Basement Level 1," it said. Sunshine 60 was one of Tokyo's oldest skyscrapers and was in Ikebukuro.

"You did good."

Katsumata handed the girl a couple of ten thousand–yen notes.

"Anytime," she said as she stuffed them into her pocket.

"Hey." Katsumata stretched out his hand. "I need my change: five thousand yen."

She clasped his hand in both of hers. "Don't be stingy. I'll keep it for pocket money. Hey, maybe I'll let you spend the night with me."

Katsumata shuddered and wrenched his hand away. "Don't kid yourself. I wouldn't even pay five hundred for a dog like you. Give me back the five thou."

He gave her a smack on the head, but she

kept stonewalling him. He finally got his change from the storeowner, who was laughing so hard he could barely stay on his feet. Hardly a model father.

Katsumata got out of a taxi at the entrance to Sunshine 60. He checked his watch. Seven minutes to go. He hurried down the stairs and headed for the rendezvous point in Fountain Square.

The broad underground promenade was lined with shops selling clothes for teenagers. It was summer vacation, and the place was heaving even though it was early afternoon on a weekday. Katsumata could have done without the crowds. The color and movement made staying focused harder.

After a short walk, he came to a plaza with a fountain on his right. Luckily, the stage in front of the fountain wasn't being used for a special event. Instead, young couples sat wolfing down crepes and burgers, and there were gaggles of teenage girls here and there.

That must be him.

A man in a loud Hawaiian shirt was sitting to one side of the steps that led up to the fountain. Katsumata checked the photo he'd had sent to his cell phone. The Tatsumi in the photo had black hair; Mr.

Hawaiian Shirt was blond. The face was the same, though.

Katsumata made a beeline for him. The man must have sensed something, as he looked over and eyed him with suspicion.

"You must be Tatsumi?"

"And who the fuck are you?"

"Katsumata, Homicide."

Tatsumi scowled. "I made an appointment with a Reiko Himekawa, a female lieutenant from Homicide. If she can't make it, then I'm out of here."

Tatsumi tried to get to his feet. Katsumata grabbed his shoulder and pushed him back down.

"Cool it, brother. Himekawa couldn't get away. There's a lot of shit happening right now. Officer Otsuka, the cop who collared you, was shot, and Himekawa's dealing with the fallout from that. Her plate's full. That's why I'm here. I'm a lieutenant from Homicide, same as her."

Tatsumi was unmollified.

"Not interested. 'If anything happens, contact Lieutenant Himekawa. You can trust her.' That's what Otsuka said to me."

That set alarm bells ringing.

"Something happened?"

"Someone ransacked my apartment," said Tatsumi, through clenched teeth. "Last

386

night, a bit after eleven. They smashed my hard drives and infected all five of my PCs with a virus. Professional job. Lucky I always keep a backup with me, so it's not that big a deal."

Tatsumi spread his arms, palms upward.

"It's Himekawa, or nothing. A sly old fox like you — no, thank you very much."

Concealing his irritation, Katsumata sat down on the steps beside Tatsumi.

"No need to get nasty. We know that Otsuka asked you to investigate something for him before he died. Otsuka was a serious cop, so I'm guessing that 'something' was connected to the case we at Homicide are working on right now — Strawberry Night. Am I right? Someone went through your place, and you heard the news about Otsuka being bumped off, so you called the station to talk to Himekawa. Here I am instead. Perhaps I gave you a shock, but perhaps we can make it work to your advantage. Look, we know you gave Otsuka a report and that he paid you two hundred and forty thousand yen for it. How 'bout you sell the same information to me? You get a double payday for one job. It's better than a kick in the teeth."

Katsumata did his best to sound friendly. He thought he was offering a good deal.

Why was Tatsumi glaring at him with undisguised contempt?

"Don't dick around with me. My original price was four hundred thousand."

"Well, take my deal, and you'll clear four eighty. It's pretty good."

"It's pretty shitty. You want the same again, you'll pay me five hundred grand."

What's this guy on? Is he kidding me?

Katsumata raised a skeptical eyebrow. "Hold your horses, friend. What's with the price gouging? Two forty's a good deal."

"Otsuka asked me to look into something specific. He had the data. You don't even know what you want me to look into — that's why it'll cost you."

"I get you, but come on, be reasonable. I mean, you said you've got a backup, right? You don't need to redo your research. You can double your income without lifting a finger. Life doesn't get much sweeter than that."

"Wrong. When I contacted the police, moneymaking was the last thing on my mind."

"So why not take the two hundred and forty thousand?"

"You really don't get it, do you? I'm not here to do business. That's why I've named a price that's out of your range. You want to bankrupt yourself, go ahead. It's no skin off my nose."

The bastard! Unbelievable.

Katsumata tried to recall how much money there was in the account he had set up under his daughter's name. It was a little under three million yen, so it wasn't like he didn't have enough. Still, the idea of forking over five hundred grand to this sleazeball investigator got his back up. On the other hand, someone thought the information was worth killing for. If it cracked the case, half a million was a bargain-basement price. Since they broke into Tatsumi's place to destroy the data, it had to be important.

Katsumata's made up his mind. "Okay, I'll do the deal. Five hundred grand it is." He was expecting Tatsumi to be pleased. Instead, the man squinted at him suspiciously.

"You've got a lot of dough for a regular cop."

Tatsumi ran his eyes over Katsumata, as if sizing him up, then looked up at the roof of the atrium. Suddenly he smacked a fist into his palm, as if he had remembering something. "Katsumata of Homicide! I know all about you. You're that crooked cop they kicked out of the Public Security Bureau. You line your pockets by auctioning off sensitive information. People call you Stubby."

Katsumata emitted an appreciative grunt. He wasn't wild about the "crooked cop" part, but everything else was on the money. "I'm impressed. So I'm a celeb in your world?"

"Dream on," Tatsumi sneered, but his expression was less hostile now. "You and I, we're two of a kind. Ah, fuck it. I don't care who you are or what department you're in — you accept my terms, then a deal's a deal. I need cash, though. In advance."

I like this guy, thought Katsumata. *He's nice and easy to understand. People who get tied up in knots about their precious feelings and principles are such a pain in the ass. I like dealing man-to-man with people who believe in one thing only: cold hard cash. You always know where you stand with them. Tatsumi was right — they were two of a kind.*

Katsumata cranked out a smile. "Fine. I'll get you the money right now. You want to wait here or come with me?"

"Come with you," replied Tatsumi, after a moment's thought.

They walked back to the area with all the shops. As Katsumata entered the ATM booth, Tatsumi squeezed in after him.

"Get the fuck out!"

"Old timers like you probably can't operate a cash machine right. I'll keep an eye on things for you."

"You calling me old?"

"Oh, knock it off. Just get the money."

Katsumata turned to the cash dispenser. He felt rather self-conscious.

"Don't look."

"I won't. Hey, it's not like I need to watch to find out your PIN number anyway."

Katsumata slid his card into the slot and punched in his PIN. It was his daughter's weight at birth.

"Oh yeah? So why don't you earn your living that way?"

Katsumata carefully entered a five followed by five zeroes.

"PIN fraud's small-time and risky. Not my thing. Buying and selling information's a far safer business model."

"Here we go. Five hundred thousand yen."

He slipped the notes into one of the envelopes provided and handed it over.

Tatsumi grunted his thanks and crammed the money straight into his back pocket.

"Aren't you going to count it?"

"Can't be bothered. Your dirty money is my easy money. I won't throw a fit if it's a note or two short. Relax."

Tatsumi pulled out another envelope from his other back pocket and held it out. Katsumata plucked at it, but Tatsumi refused to let go. Each of them was holding a corner of the sweat-dampened rectangle.

"What are you playing at? Give it to me."

"There's something I need to ask you first," Tatsumi growled.

Katsumata had been starting to like Tatsumi. Now he lost his temper.

"You dirty rat. I did my part. I paid you the five hundred grand."

"Cool it. I'm not backing out of the deal. I'm asking this because I've got a conscience. You don't want to answer, that's fine."

That PI sleazeball had a conscience? Yeah, sure he did. Katsumata hated it when people got all moral on him. Morality was so much wishy-washy bullshit.

Katsumata looked directly at Tatsumi and jerked his chin. "Keep it short, then."

"Truth is, I warned Otsuka to stay away from this case. And look what happened to him. Was there an envelope like this on Otsuka's body?"

"No. We didn't find any envelope."

"As I thought," sighed Tatsumi. "His estimated time of death was in the newspapers. If the papers were right about it,

Otsuka was murdered almost straight after I handed him the information. Someone must have been sitting close on his tail."

Katsumata gave his corner of the envelope a tug and Tatsumi let him have it. He wanted to hear what Tatsumi had to say.

"Why did you warn Otsuka to drop the case? You knew something?"

Tatsumi took a deep breath then exhaled loudly through his nose. "It's just something I heard," he began. "I heard from a pal in the same line as me that some yakuza gang asked him to take a look and find out what this Strawberry Night was all about. Whatever he found, it wasn't what anyone was expecting. He reported back to his yakuza clients, and they decided just to step away. It was nothing to do with them being frightened, the guy said. The yakuza thought it would be more 'interesting' to let Strawberry Night go on." Tatsumi paused. "You know what that means? Their deciding not to interfere with the show has to mean that the organizer was someone they wanted to get into trouble, that they didn't care if he got found out. Get my drift?"

Katsumata said nothing. He got Tatsumi's drift all right. He just didn't want to believe it. Tatsumi plunged ahead.

"I don't know the full story. My guess,

though, is that the yakuza stood back because the organizer has some connection to the police. That's why I warned Otsuka off. 'There's a devil on your tail,' I told him. You'd better be careful too. You've got the same information. You don't want to end up dead."

Katsumata looked at the envelope in his hand, then stuffed it into an inside pocket of his jacket.

"What about you? You know too much as well."

"Whatever. I can take care of myself."

Tatsumi made to leave the booth.

Katsumata hastily reached out and grabbed his wrist. "Not so fast. Are you telling me that you knew someone was targeting Otsuka?"

Tatsumi shook off Katsumata's grip angrily.

"Course I fucking didn't," he snarled, glaring at Katsumata.

Katsumata turned back to the machine.

"Just stay there one second. I need you to do another job. How much will you need to identify the people behind the show?"

Katsumata shoved his card back into the ATM.

"How much is it going to cost me?"

Tatsumi hesitated. Was he afraid to go

394

after a cop killer? Was he unsure if he was up to the job? Or was he simply having trouble pricing his services?

"I said, how much?"

Katsumata had already entered his PIN number. Now he was waiting to input the money figure.

Tatsumi swallowed. "Two million." His voiced trembled slightly. "Then I can do the job properly."

Fuck! That was serious wage inflation.

Katsumata, however, didn't intend to haggle about the price. He punched in a two followed by six zeroes.

Gonna have to shake down more than a few people down to get that back.

He pressed the "Enter" button tenderly. The flapping sound of the machine counting the ten-thousand-yen notes seemed to last forever.

7

Reiko's former partner, Ioka, had been taken away from her and paired with Katsumata. In his place she now had Lieutenant Kitami. Reiko felt as though the people she cared for were being torn away from her, one by one.

She decided to put Shibuya on hold and go to Ikebukuro instead. She felt a physical pain in her chest at the thought that Otsuka had walked these same streets for the last three days of his life. What had he seen, heard, and thought there? Why had they killed him? Reiko had no idea, she didn't even know what he'd been investigating when he decided to fly solo. Everything was gray and unclear.

Like the weather. The day was cloudy. The bustling pedestrians, the flashing neon signs, and the colorful billboards all seemed to be leached of color.

Otsuka . . .

Reiko's heart felt like a lead weight in her chest, dragging her down. Staying upright cost her an effort; moving around was worse.

Otsuka, are you really dead?

Reiko hadn't yet seen Otsuka's body, but his absence alone made his death all too crushingly real. Was death always so hard to deal with? So painful?

What about all those other deaths?

It dawned on Reiko that she hadn't been treating the dead people she encountered on the job with the respect they deserved. "I channel the victims' rage and use it to power my investigations" — that's what she'd always told herself. Now, however, she was forced to acknowledge that her empathy was superficial. She'd been heartless and shallow — not a recipe for a good detective.

Her sister had complained about her having changed. This was another problem altogether.

Detective Michiko Sata's death in the line of duty was what had shaped Reiko's whole approach to her job. Sata's death had inspired her not just to become a detective but to try to put herself in the victim's shoes. At least, that had been her original goal.

But Reiko had also set out to make lieutenant, the rank Sata had achieved through her posthumous promotion. She'd worked hard and achieved that rank relatively young. Had success made her arrogant? Yes, that it had. The moment she'd fulfilled her dream, she lost touch with her better self and unconsciously betrayed everything that Detective Sata stood for.

She tried to analyze the attitude with which she approached the cases she worked on. It wasn't comfortable. Her strongest emotions, she decided, were probably excitement at being on a task force and relief at not having to go home — something she never passed up an opportunity to joke about. And where had that got her? She'd failed to notice her mother's deteriorating health. If things had gone worse for her mother, she might have even failed to make it to her mother's deathbed.

It was all too much. Otsuka's death, her mother's heart attack, the stalled investigation, the pressures of the job. So many weighty things, all crushing the heart in her chest.

"Here you go, Lieutenant."

Reiko was sitting at a long counter by the window in the upper floor of a fast-food joint. The window overlooked Meiji Boulevard, one of Tokyo's major thoroughfares. Kitami stood there holding two trays, one for him and one for her.

"Oh, thanks."

Reiko left her food untouched until she noticed that Kitami was reluctant to start without her.

"Dig in. Don't you worry about me."

"Okay, sorry."

Kitami began nibbling his French fries one at a time. She could see the tension in his bunched-up shoulders.

Most cops ate like vikings and could polish off a burger in two mouthfuls. Kitami, though, was a shadow of his normal self. Otsuka's death seemed to be have shrunk him physically.

"Don't apologize all the time," she snapped. "And stop blaming yourself for Otsuka's death."

"Yes, sorry."

"There you go again."

Kitami mumbled something.

Reiko tried to give him an encouraging smile but was unsure that she managed one. The two of them had spent the morning wandering vaguely around Ikebukuro. Nothing that deserved to be called an investigation.

Reiko sighed softly and helped herself to a

French fry.

The music venue where Otsuka had been murdered wasn't far away. Since Otsuka's death was being handled by the Ikebukuro precinct, showing up at the crime scene would only be a distraction for the officers working the case. Captain Imaizumi had provided a statement on behalf of the unit. Kitami had given a statement first thing this morning. Reiko didn't know what he'd said; frankly, she was afraid to ask. Sitting right there in Ikebukuro beside Kitami, the idea of hearing about the last few days of Otsuka's life terrified her. She was sure she would go to pieces.

"Tell me something funny."

She wasn't surprised when Kitami looked put out.

"I can't just . . ."

She was being unreasonable, and she knew it. That didn't change the fact that she wanted to hear him talk about anything except Otsuka and their investigation.

"Anything . . . You graduated from the Tokyo University law department, didn't you?"

Reiko closed her lips around the straw in her drink. Kitami nodded stiffly.

"Suppose so."

"You *suppose* so? Come on, it's great. You

should be proud of yourself."

"Sorry."

"There you go, apologizing again."

"That wasn't what I meant . . ."

Reiko was struck by Kitami's good looks. He had to be wildly popular with women his own age. What did he think of someone like her?

He probably thinks I'm way past my sell-by date.

A question flashed into her mind. What had Otsuka thought of his partner? This Tokyo University law grad, young, handsome, a lieutenant from day one — classic fast-track material.

Was he jealous?

She'd never be able to ask Otsuka to his face. They wouldn't be going to any more meetings or to any drinking sessions together — ever. She felt a sharp tingling behind her eyes. She forced herself to speak in an exaggeratedly cheerful tone to keep control.

"You're quite a strapping lad. Did you do sports in college?"

"Huh? Well . . . you know, I . . ."

Her crackbrained question seemed to have thrown Kitami. She went blithely on, ignoring his discomfiture.

"You're tall. Was it basketball, maybe? Or

401

volleyball?"

"Neither." He sheepishly shook his head.

"Karate, then?"

"Never done martial arts in my life."

"Tennis?"

"Nor ball sports."

"What then? Horse riding?"

"No. Look, can't we talk about something else? I'm not really the sporty type."

Kitami was just being modest, thought Reiko. It was obvious that he was fit. The brisk way he'd marched around the vacant properties that morning bespoke an unusual level of athleticism.

"There's something else, Lieutenant Himekawa."

From his tone, she could tell he was serious about wanting to change the subject.

"When Otsuka was doing his own thing, I wandered around and came across this building nearby. The firm that built it must have gone bust just before completing it. The building's almost finished, but it's never been occupied, and the fence around the site is riddled with holes. It's easy to get in. Don't you think we should check it?"

"Doing his own thing"?

Kitami was trying to be tactful. He was deliberately avoiding the phrase "solo investigation," out of respect for Otsuka — or

402

possibly out of pity for the frazzled woman lieutenant.

Normally Reiko would have bristled at being mollycoddled by this fast-track golden boy, but now her primary emotion was gratitude.

Reiko, you're turning soft.

She broke into a self-mocking laugh. It felt good. Perhaps bottling up her feelings had been a mistake.

"Good idea. Let's go there after we've visited all the other places on our list."

"Oh, okay."

Reiko looked at her watch. It was already past three o'clock.

8

The envelope Tatsumi gave Katsumata contained two sheets of paper and three photographs.

"These are grabs from the infrared camera in my apartment," Tatsumi explained. "I retrieved the cameras and went to an Internet café to extract the data. You can have them. The images are a bit blurry, but they could help with Otsuka's murder."

The green-tinged photographs showed two people: a large, sturdy man in a dark polo shirt and jeans, and a smaller man in a black leather bodysuit. These had to be the people who killed Otsuka.

"You've got an infrared camera in your place? You don't take any chances."

"I'm no amateur. They won't kill me so easily."

"You went back to your place. You're lucky to be alive."

"B&E's one of my specialties."

Katsumata found the two sheets of paper even more interesting. *This must have bowled Otsuka over.* The list included the name of someone Otsuka had interviewed.

Tomohiko Tashiro was the one who had posted under the handle "Wicked Wizard." He was the thirty-nine-year-old salesman for an electronics firm who'd belonged to the Haseda University hiking club with Yukio Namekawa. Tashiro had alerted Otsuka to Strawberry Night. His claim that Namekawa had told him about it was clearly an out-and-out lie. Tashiro's postings gave the unmistakable impression that Tashiro had attended the shows himself. His comments included descriptions — almost eyewitness accounts — that matched exactly how Kanebara had been killed. Tashiro was trying to play a double game: dropping hints to nudge the investigation in the right direction while trying his best to conceal his own participation.

Scumbag! You went to the show, your own friend was butchered, and now to top it off, you're a snitch as well.

Katsumata felt an uncharacteristic surge of moral indignation.

"This is valuable stuff, Tatsumi. Now I need you to identify the guy behind the show, pronto."

The two men separated. Katsumata immediately put in a call to Suyama at the task force coordination desk, got Tashiro's number from him, and called it.

"Good afternoon. Matsumoto Electronic Industries' sales division." A young woman answered the phone. That was enough to get Katsumata's back up.

"Is Tomohiko Tashiro there? This is Lieutenant Katsumata of the Tokyo Metropolitan Police Department."

He thought he did a good job of sounding polite. Much good it did him.

"I'm sorry, sir. Mr. Tashiro is out of the office right now."

"I need to get in touch with him urgently. Have you got the number of his cell phone?"

"Yes, but I would need to know what this is about."

Something inside Katsumata snapped.

"Oh no, you don't. Your job, little lady, is to answer the phone, make the tea — and fuck all else. Tell me the number. If you don't want to do that, then call Tashiro and get his permission to tell me. Somehow I don't think he's going to refuse to cooperate with the police. Okay, which is it — tell me or ask him? If the latter, I'll call you back in five. Make sure you pick up. Okay?"

Silence.

"I asked you a question. Can't you do *anything* right?"

That final shouted insult seemed to do the trick. Between sniffles, the woman gave him Tashiro's cell number.

"So the last four digits are seven-oh-nine-two? Got it. And next time a policeman asks you to do something, jump to it. Don't try using that thick head of yours for thinking. That's not what it was designed for."

He felt pleasantly refreshed after ending the call.

Tashiro was in Shinjuku when he took Katsumata's call. "I'll be there as soon as I can," said the detective. "Make the time to see me." Four thirty was the earliest Tashiro said he could manage. "That's fine for me," answered Katsumata. "But I need you to show up without fail." Not wanting to make Tashiro nervous, Katsumata did his best to sound friendly.

They'd agreed to meet at a diner. Katsumata got there at four twenty-five. Not knowing what Tashiro looked like, Katsumata called his cell. A man sitting on the bench for patrons waiting to be seated pulled out his phone.

Katsumata walked over to him. "Are you Mr. Tomohiko Tashiro?" he inquired mildly.

"I am. You must be Lieutenant Katsumata. I —"

Before the man could even finish his sentence, Katsumata had grabbed his tie and yanked him onto his feet.

"You sewer rat, you're coming with me. Hey, waitress, this gent won't be needing a table after all."

Katsumata dragged Tashiro out of the diner and down to the parking lot. A couple getting out of their car looked at them with openmouthed suspicion. Katsumata ignored them and hauled Tashiro right to the back.

"Wha-what's this about?" Tashiro sputtered.

He looked ready to burst into tears. Dragged along by Katsumata, he stumbled, fell, and scrambled back to his feet repeatedly.

Katsumata only let go of his tie when they reached the back wall of the parking lot.

"Listen, buddy, I'm not here for Tomohiko Tashiro. I've got some questions for the Wicked Wizard of Oz — or whatever you fucking call yourself in computerland — and I need answers."

Grabbing the lapels of Tashiro's jacket, he threw him against the wall. The man's face was contorted with terror, his whole body was rigid, and his eyes stared vacantly into the distance.

"Did you attend the Strawberry Night murder show?"

Tashiro's face crumpled as he began to cry.

"Did you?"

Tashiro gulped and sputtered.

"You're making a big mistake if you think that keeping quiet is going to make all this go away and that your life will go back to normal. You did some magnificent aiding and abetting, my friend. You're an accessory to murder. You're looking at serious jail time, I can promise you that. But for now at least, I have the power to keep your name out of this. So, what'll it be? Come clean with me here, or do the strong, silent act and go to the slammer? Your choice."

Tashiro spasmed to his full height then collapsed in on himself and slid slowly down the wall. He curled up into a ball on the ground and promptly pissed himself.

"Goddammit. You filthy bastard."

Katsumata took a brisk step backward to avoid the dark puddle that was spreading across the cement toward him. What the fuck was a pathetic jerk like him doing, going to see a murder show?

"Come on, talk to me. Then I'll buy you

some new underpants. I'm a nice guy, you know."

Katsumata lit a cigarette and waited for the whimpering to stop. He'd almost smoked it to the filter when Tashiro began to speak in short bursts.

"It just kind of happened. . . ."

He had stumbled on the Strawberry Night homepage by accident last September and first attended the event in October. Curiosity was his main motivation. Intrigued by the online video of what looked like a real murder, he had clicked the "Yes" button that popped up with the "Do you want to see this live?" text. He hadn't really been serious about it. When nothing happened, he'd written the whole thing off as a joke. Until . . .

"It was about two weeks later. This black envelope came to the house. There was no stamp or postmark. It said, 'Confidential. Mr. Tomohiko Tashiro' on the front in white ink. On the back there was the red Strawberry Night logo I'd seen on the Internet.

"It gave me a big shock. All I'd done was view a homepage and click a button. That was enough for them to figure out where I lived. I was terrified. I was worried they might kill me too.

"Things only got worse when I opened

the envelope. There was a headshot of me — God knows where it had been taken. Then there was this page listing my birthday, my current address — they obviously knew that — my job, even the names of my wife and children! At the bottom it said, 'Please check that all the above information is full and correct. If it is, your identity as Tomohiko Tashiro has been confirmed and the registration process is complete.' It didn't say anything about how to contact them if the data was incorrect. It looked like a threat to me. 'We know everything about you. You cannot escape us.' That was the real message."

Katsumata agreed. The basic technique had a lot in common with loan sharking: pile on the psychological pressure until people lost the ability to think rationally. The approach was effective — on amateurs, at least.

"Go on," said Katsumata encouragingly.

"The invitation proper arrived two or three days later. The date of the show was November the tenth, the second Sunday of the month; the place was Kabukicho in Shinjuku; the time was six fifteen p.m., and the entrance fee was one hundred thousand yen.

"By that stage, I was convinced that I'd

end up being murdered like the person in the video if I failed to show up. I made up my mind to go. My idea was to just go the one time and ask the people behind it to let me walk away if I promised not to contact the police and never breathe a word to anyone.

"I felt a whole lot better after making that decision. 'It's not like *you're* going to kill anyone,' I kept telling myself. 'You're only going to be a spectator.' Gradually, I started feeling more positive. Perhaps there was nothing to it after all. Perhaps the elaborate video and the nasty threats were just a tasteless prank.

"When I went to the venue on the day specified, the thing that really spooked me was the meticulous organization. There was this derelict building, with no sign or anything outside, and all these people milling around. They would check their watches, then one would go in, then another. . . . I realized that there was a reason why my invitation said six fifteen. They were managing the inflow, getting people to come in one by one."

Was there anyone stationed outside for crowd control? Katsumata asked. Tashiro said no. You just went on in when your time came.

"So when it was my turn, I went in. There was this passageway with a black curtain at the far end. It was the only way in, so I pushed through the curtain. Behind, it was like a tunnel with black curtains on either side. I was going along it until suddenly this voice commanded me to stop. A man in a black mask with a flashlight was inspecting me from between two curtains. It's the same drill every time. You give your name, and they check that the name and face match. That's also when you pay the entrance fee. When that's all taken care of, you keep on going until you emerge into this auditoriumlike space.

"It was bigger and a bit brighter. There was a stage. Nothing else. By the time I went in, there must have been about ten people there already. With the others who came after me, there must have been about twenty of us in total.

"Then I heard this loud bang behind me. 'They've shut the door,' I thought. It didn't occur to me to leave. Might as well stick it out and see what was going to happen. There were twenty of us. They couldn't very well murder all of us!"

Katsumata noticed a moist glint in Tashiro's bloodshot eyes. Crybabies were another of his pet hates.

"The show eventually started. The first time I went, there was this guy nailed to a cross. Two men in black masks carried him out onto the stage. He had trousers on, but was bare above the waist. There were these strips of cloth over his eyes and his mouth. Next, the two men carried out this brazier full of charcoal. . . . We soon discovered why.

"Just one of the masked men came back out. There were these long metal chopsticks sticking out of the burning charcoal. He pulled one of them out, then held it up against the man's stomach in an almost playful way. There was smoke and a sizzling sound, and the man on the cross moaned into his gag. The chopstick left this long thin purple welt on his stomach. Then the man in the mask began skipping around the stage, pressing the hot chopsticks into the man's flesh over and over and over again.

"There were plenty of chopsticks in the brazier. When one of them cooled down, he would just help himself to another. He stuck one up the guy's nose — all the way up. People screamed. He gave his ears and mouth the same treatment, straight through the gag. Next he went for the eyes . . . he was relentless. He poked and jabbed until the eyeballs popped out. There was a lot of blood and smoke. The smell wafted over to where I was standing. . . . It was like roasted meat.

"Eventually, the guy on the cross stopped moving. He'd passed out. The masked fellow slapped him. No reaction. Doused him with water. Again, nothing. That was when he whipped out this knife, an ordinary cheap box cutter thing. He drew it across the guy's throat like this."

Tashiro mimed a slashing motion. "He was so offhand about it, but, oh my God, the blood — it just exploded out like water spurting from a fountain. Some of the audience got spattered. It was thrilling, beautiful. . . .

"It was like art. It blew me away. Your take on life changes when you see death close up. This person is beaten to a pulp and murdered right in front of you, there's no space between you and them. And all that separates life and death is the flimsy little blade of a box cutter."

A confusing jumble of expressions scudded across Tashiro's face. He smiled, then cringed; his eyes shone with elation, then brimmed with tears.

It's like watching a speeded-up film of someone losing their marbles.

"It took me a while to figure out that the person who got murdered was always one

415

of the people who'd come to see the show. This one time I noticed that the woman up on stage was wearing the same skirt as a woman I'd seen waiting outside in the street before. I guess that the passageway that led to the auditorium, that dark tunnel, was where our fates were decided. The person they grabbed ended up on stage, while the rest of us were the audience.

"The realization terrified me — but I still wanted to go. Maybe more than ever. Even though I knew I could end up on the stage myself, I felt this compulsion. God, the relief I felt when I made it safely through the tunnel to the theater! You saw the victim torn to pieces, each month a completely different method, each time brutal and horrible. They were reduced to a bloody mess, killed. *And you knew it could have been you.* You got this incredible sense of superiority, of being special. 'I survived today, and I've got another whole month of life ahead of me.' It was pure, unadulterated joy. Knowing — really feeling in your bones — that your life exists as the flip side of death, of death of the nastiest and most degrading kind. It's wonderful. The whole world seems to open up before you."

Katsumata gaped in mute astonishment.

Sense of superiority? Pure unadulterated joy?

Tashiro began giggling.

A forty-year-old man who still peed his pants was raving about a murder show with a look of pure ecstasy on his face. There was no way to put a positive spin on it, thought Katsumata. The man's mind must have given way.

Katsumata flicked the stub of his umpteenth cigarette into the half-dried puddle of Tashiro's urine.

"How did Namekawa end up going? Did you introduce him?"

"Yes, I did. Though *introduced* is the wrong word. I just chatted to him about the show and recommended it to him. The guy was in a slump and had lost all his inspiration. He was jaded. The show, I told him, would help him rediscover his sense of what it really meant to be alive. He found the homepage for himself and showed up on his own. That was the way it worked."

"Okay. Listen, I've had about all I can take of your blow-by-blow reportage. I'm going to ask you a serious question, and I need a serious answer. Who organizes the event?"

"No idea." Tashiro shook his head, the ecstatic glow on his face quite undimmed.

"Okay then. How many people are involved in running it?"

"I don't know. Maybe five . . ."

"You sure?"

"No, that's why I said 'maybe.' Could be fewer, could be more." Tashiro gave a start and looked directly up at Katsumata. Apparently he was lucid again. "Oh, I just remembered something. There was this time when I was standing near the side of the stage and I heard people talking in the wings. Someone said, 'Go and fetch F.' Yeah, I remember that."

"F? Like the letter f?"

"It's just something I overheard. . . . Still, the show got under way very soon after. Perhaps the psycho killer's name was F."

Psycho killer F?

"Let's rewind a bit. There was the guy who said, 'Fetch F'; the guy who did the fetching; and then F himself. That gives us at least three people."

"Sounds about right."

The most obvious way to interpret *F* was as the first letter in the anglicized version of a Japanese name. The only person Katsumata could think of whose name fit was Yasuyuki Fukazawa.

There was a problem, though. If Fukazawa was the perpetrator, he could have killed the ten victims up to and including Namekawa. But he couldn't have killed the most recent victim, Kanebara. Could somebody else have stepped in to take his place as a one-off? Another member of the group could have copied Fukazawa's method of killing.

"You were away on a business trip when Namekawa was murdered, right?"

Tashiro smiled creepily. "Not really. I finished my business in Osaka early and hurried back for the show. When I realized that Namekawa was the victim that night, I was horrified — but felt a whole new level of excitement too. My old friend was being killed right in front of me. There was the usual sense of superiority but with added complexity. The joy of having survived had an intensity, a potency —"

"Aw, shut it Tashiro. . . . There's something else I need to ask you. At the most recent show, was it the same killer as before? Were Kanebara's killer in August and Namekawa's killer last month one and the same person?

Tashiro cocked his head. "Hmm. Difficult to say. They all wear these black masks, so it's hard to tell them apart. I *think* it was the same person. He's a scrawny guy, not very tall, always wears a black leather body suit."

A black leather body suit? That's it! That's the link!

Katsumata tore Tatsumi's envelope out of his pocket and showed the photographs to Tashiro.

"So this fellow is F?"

Tashiro's head bobbed frantically up and down.

"Yes, that's him. That's F."

"So who's the other one? The guy who processes you on the way in?"

"I'm not sure. . . . No, he looks different. I don't know."

At the same time he was providing valuable testimony, Tashiro was also demolishing one of Katsumata's pet theories.

Katsumata knew of one more person whose name began with *f* — Yasuyuki's little sister, Yukari Fukazawa. However, the person in the black leather body suit in the photographs was quite clearly a man.

What the fuck's going on here?

Katsumata felt jittery, uneasy. Like that feeling you got when you wore a shirt with the buttons done up wrong.

I've got to go see that Yukari girl.

"Okay," Katsumata muttered to himself, as he stuffed the photos back into his inside jacket pocket. "I'm going to need a formal statement from you tomorrow, Tashiro. Wait

420

for my call — and don't forget to put on a fresh pair of underpants."

Katsumata turned and walked away. Behind him, Tashiro continued jabbering to himself. Paying no attention, Katsuma raised a hand and hailed himself a cab.

PART IV

1

After going to take a look at a burlesque club that had recently changed hands, Reiko and Kitami dropped in on a couple of real estate agents. They learned nothing helpful.

This is a complete waste of time.

As they walked around Ikebukuro, they occasionally caught sight of investigators from the other task force based in the local precinct. They were busy doing the canvass in connection with Otsuka's murder. Reiko recognized several of the guys from the Mobile Unit and from Homicide. Normally she would have said hi, but today, without being fully aware of it, she was doing her best not to be noticed.

She felt partly responsible for Otsuka's death. She had no idea why he'd embarked on his solo investigation, and her ignorance was proof enough that she was doing a poor job managing her squad. In her emotionally fragile state, she was haunted by the sense of having failed one of her subordinates.

She was so focused on avoiding the other detectives that she found it difficult to concentrate on the interviews. Despite hearing the words that came out of people's mouths, she couldn't process the information. Allowing meaningless jabber to wash over her hardly counted as investigating anything. It certainly wasn't going to lead to any arrests. Pathetic. She was being pathetic, and she knew it; but sloughing off her powerful feeling of self-loathing was easier said than done. Still, she knew that by wallowing in her own emotions, she was only letting time go to waste.

She looked at her watch. After 6:30 already. She could legitimately pack in the investigation for the day. She felt too low to show her face at the evening meeting. Kitami mentioned something about finding a vacant building. It sounded as good a way as any other to kill time.

"Shall we go and take a look at that place you found?"

Kitami was enthusiastic, and they set off through the twilight streets of Ikebukuro.

The outdoor air-conditioning units spewed heat. The street noise was like a solid wall. The faces of the people they passed glistened with sweat. All around them flowed crowds of people, crowds that intermeshed, unraveled, and dispersed. To Reiko, the normal, everyday bustle of the city was no more than a pantomime, devoid of reality.

They went south down Meiji Boulevard, past the Seibu department store. The overwhelming mass of people was heading in the opposite direction — toward the train station rather than away from it.

Gradually their numbers thinned out.

"I think it was this way," said Kitami doubtfully as he turned into a street on the right. "Pretty sure it was around here. The building's nearly finished. The windows have been installed, but it doesn't yet have a front door. Perhaps I should have double-checked with the real estate guys. They'd have known the place."

They were only two or three minutes' walk away from Meiji Boulevard and not that far from the train station. It was good location if you were looking to draw a crowd.

Kitami eventually found what he was looking for. "That's the place," he said, pointing to a building. Reiko felt a sense of letdown: it hardly looked like Strawberry Night material to her.

"Seems like an ordinary apartment building to me."

"I guess. But the second and third floors have an open-plan layout for business tenants."

"So? What about all those? You can see straight in."

"Maybe it's different around the other side."

"Maybe . . ."

"The location isn't bad at all."

"Yeah, maybe you're right."

"There's a gap here."

Kitami gave a shove to the corrugated iron fence that ran around the site.

"See? You can easily slip through here."

"Guess so," said Reiko tepidly.

This is a total waste of time.

She couldn't see any point in inspecting the building. On the other hand, she didn't want to say as much to Kitami, who was unusually fired up. The boy thought he was to blame for Otsuka's death and was doing his best to contribute to the investigation. No harm in indulging him.

Reiko smiled. "All right. Let's take a quick look."

Kitami nodded brightly.

He was right about the fence. Anyone could get in. The still doorless entrance of the building was a gaping concrete rectangle. They stepped inside. Sacks of cement and other building materials lay scattered around the floor.

You couldn't host a murder show in a dump like this.

The daytime heat still radiated off the walls of the entranceway. No air seemed to penetrate the building, and it was even more humid than the outside. At the far end of the passageway was the elevator shaft, with a bare concrete staircase just to the right of it.

"Shall we take a look at the upper floors?"

Reiko followed Kitami upstairs, wondering what he was so excited about. After turning back on themselves once, they emerged onto the second floor. As Kitami had said, it consisted of two large open-plan rooms. The third floor was a single, even bigger room. Reiko wondered what sort of business would do well there. A hairdresser? A restaurant? A boutique? She walked inside and peered out of a window.

The building was set much further back from the street than she expected. Looking around, she realized that there were no other normal buildings nearby that overlooked that side of the building. Immediately opposite was the back of an automated parking tower, with an ordinary parking lot next to it. The bright lights of the train station and its environs looked very far away. The place was much more isolated than she'd thought.

Otsuka was checking an empty building just like this when he was killed.

He had been inspecting a live music venue that had closed down. His killers sneaked up on him in the dark, hit him with a blunt instrument, handcuffed him, and then blew his head off.

Perhaps Otsuka's rogue investigation had unearthed something — something major. If the boys in the Ikebukuro task force figured out what it was, they would get all the credit for solving Otsuka's murder — and the murder-show thing too.

Reiko simply didn't care anymore. Normally, she would have been obsessed with catching the culprits herself. Now, as long as they did it fast, she didn't care who took down Otsuka's killer.

So this is how things feel when you're on the victim end of things.

It came home to her again just how much she'd been treating homicide investigations as entertainment. It hurt her to acknowledge it, but she'd seen the homicides as so many trump cards in the promotion game. Kusaka had urged her to get out there and catch the perpetrator herself. She was no longer up to the job. Why didn't someone else step up and solve Otsuka's murder, find the Strawberry Night killers, and just bring the whole fucked-up case to an end?

I wonder how the Saitama prefectural police are getting on.

An image of the nine bundles neatly lined up on the bank of the Toda Rowing Course flashed into Reiko's mind. Nine corpses, all wrapped in blue plastic sheeting. Nine victims, all of whom had been killed before Kanebara and Namekawa.

Kanebara, Namekawa, plus nine more. Nine more before Kanebara and Namekawa.

A question suddenly popped into her head. Why had Kanebara and Namekawa been dumped in the Mizumoto pond when all the others had been dumped in the Toda Rowing Course? Why had the perpetrator switched from the rowing course to the fishing pond last month?

Why didn't I think of this before?

She remembered something Ioka had said to her: "I was moved here last month."

Last month. That means Ioka started at Kameari police station in July. Ioka said he'd moved from Oji police station. Then she went back to the bodies. Where the bodies had been dumped had also moved in July. But the dumping ground had been moved from the Toda Rowing Course to the Mizumoto Pond in Kameari. From Toda to Kameari. Suddenly her mind put the pieces together.

She felt the blood draining from her head. Her body seemed to disintegrate like a crumbling pillar of sand. She welcomed the sensation, because she knew what it meant. She embraced the fear that was making the hairs on the back of her neck stand up.

You gift them to me, don't you, Detective Sata? These insights that seem to come from nowhere.

"Hey, Kitami," she said. He was behind her, but she did not turn to face him. "My guess is that you were in the rowing club at university."

"What — ?"

There was a hysterical note in his voice. Then a few seconds of silence.

"Where the fuck did that come from?"

His voice was an oafish snarl.

"You're a real fucking handful."

She sensed that he was reaching for something. There was the swish of metal on cloth. She turned. The muzzle of a gun was in her face.

Kitami used his left hand to unlock the safety.

Got to move.

Reiko jerked her head to one side.

A burst of flame. A bang. Hot smoke.

The shot was piercingly loud. A great balloon of numbness suddenly inflated around the right side of her head. She could hear nothing from that side.

"Careful with those sudden movements. Startle me and I shoot."

A few seconds earlier, Reiko had perceived the truth, but incredulity was still uppermost in her mind.

You're the killer, Kitami!

She was too disoriented to speak. She crumpled to her knees with a hand clutching at her injured ear.

Kitami still held his firing posture. He had a .38 automatic in his hand. *The bullet that blew Otsuka's head off was a 9mm Parabellum. That was a match. Except that Kitami had been in a coffee shop at the time of the attack . . . or so he claimed.*

An icy smile spread over his face. It suited him all too well.

"When you came up with that idea at the meeting about the perpetrator rummaging around inside Kanebara's stomach? It was so idiotic, I wanted to burst out laughing. But then you came up with the idea that the bodies were being dumped in the pond. . . . That one blindsided me. And then what do you do but go and find out about

433

Fukazawa, who'd popped his socks three weeks before. Awesome detective work."

Kitami kicked her in the stomach.

"Ugh!"

Her gorge rose. Her face flushed hot and cold. Her throat seemed to be clogged with stones. Her breathing . . .

"I know I made a few mistakes, but I've got to hand it to you, you and your boys pulled some unexpected moves on me. I never thought I'd have to go this far."

As Kitami spoke, he slid a pair of hand-cuffs out of his pocket.

Katsumata got out of the elevator on the sixth floor of the hospital.

During his previous visit, he'd managed to win over one of the nurses, a woman called Akiko Kurihara. Having first asked her for directions to the medical office, he had bumped into her for a second time after his meeting with Dr. Omuro. Something about her face told him that she'd be open to earning a little on the side.

"Hey, you seen Nurse Kurihara?" he asked random people as he wandered around. Eventually he tracked her down.

"There you are!"

They stared at each other for a moment, then the nurse took Katsumata's hand and pulled him into a deserted stairwell. She took him to the next landing down, then stopped, checked that no one was coming up, and turned to Katsumata.

"Glad you're here. I was about to call you."

"Something happened?"

She nodded. Her eyes were grave.

"Yukari Fukazawa ran away two nights ago."

"What?!"

That means Yukari was on the loose at the time of Otsuka's murder!

Why hadn't the woman alerted him two days ago? What the hell did she think he was paying her for? He struggled to keep his anger under wraps. If he flew off the handle now, he'd only regret it later.

"You've got to try and tell me these things a little more promptly."

"I can't believe you said that!" The nurse pouted in annoyance. "I don't do night shifts, and yesterday was my day off. Plus Yukari's not even one of my patients. I heard the news literally two minutes ago. What did you expect me to do?"

Uh-oh. She was one of those broads who lost her rag at the slightest hint of criticism. "Okay, I'm sorry. I didn't know." After a cursory effort at soothing her ruffled feathers, Katsumata asked her for the details.

"Turns out that Yukari Fukazawa has run away several times before, but she always came back by morning. This time, it's been

436

a day and a half, and she's still not back. The doctors and the administrators have had several meetings to discuss the problem. They haven't yet reported it to the police though. They want to give it a bit more time. As you can imagine, they're not wild about bringing in the police. This could be your chance, Lieutenant. Turn the screws on Dr. Omuro, and he'll probably tell you everything you need to know about the girl."

The sense of unease Katsumata was feeling in his chest expanded through his entire body.

"Where is Omuro?"

"Consulting Room 3. I'll go with you. If he's got a patient with him, I'll need to deal with them."

Nurse Kurihara was proving quite an ally after all.

Sure enough, the doctor had a patient in his consulting room.

"Mrs. Yoshimura, could you step outside a moment?" Nurse Kurihara shot a meaningful glance at Katsumata and led a middle-aged woman, who could only shuffle at a snail's pace, out of the room. Katsumata telegraphed his thanks with his eyes and shut the door behind them.

Omuro sat facing him just as at their last

meeting. He looked every bit as uncooperative too, though Katsumata did detect a shadow of anxiety.

"Heard you're in a bit of trouble, Dr. Omuro. Interested in my take?"

Katsumata flung himself into the chair for patients and lit himself a cigarette, fully aware that smoking was prohibited.

"When a severely troubled mental patient does a runner, is doing jack shit the normal response of this hospital? Looks to me like you've got a serious problem on your hands." Katsumata took out his portable ashtray, placed it on the desk, and tapped the ash from his cigarette into it. The doctor's eyes tracked his every movement.

"What if Yukari's raising hell outside? What'll you do about that?"

The doctor inhaled sharply.

"Let's say — just for the sake of argument — that she kills somebody. How exactly would you deal with that little eventuality?"

Omuro shot a furtive glance at Katsumata, released his breath with a hiss, and gazed into the middle distance. It was not the body language of someone who saw Katsumata's suggestions as ridiculous.

"Listen, doc. That, or something like it, is what's already happened. There's a whole lot of things I can't make head or tail of.

438

Things I need to sort out before I can make any headway. I'm not here to tell you how to do your job, and I'm not here to frame Yukari for crimes she didn't commit just because the poor girl's a head case. If Yukari is innocent, or if you're serious about wanting to help her, you're better off working with me. It will be good for her and probably for you too."

Omuro slowly tilted back his head back and stared up at the ceiling. Then he closed his eyes and exhaled deeply as though he'd come to a decision about something. It was a pattern Katsumata was familiar with from suspects about to confess. He said nothing, deliberately leaving space for the doctor to fill.

"We think Yukari suffered terrible abuse at her father's hands," began Omuro, his voice hoarse with fatigue. "He was an ex-yakuza and a drug addict. He wasn't just violent toward Yukari, he was sexually abusive too. That's what drove her over the edge."

Katsumata had taken the precaution of doing a little advance study after his last visit.

"Are you implying that she suffered from multiple personality disorder?"

"No, I'm not implying that."

The offhandness with which the doctor

contradicted him was a humiliation Katsumata could have done without.

*Guess acting like he knew something about
this wasn't such a good idea after all.*

"Then what is wrong with her?" he asked,
crushing out his cigarette with his fingers.

"Yukari's mother was remarried, so her
abuser was her stepfather. Yukari hated the
fact that she was female, and the thing she
hated most fiercely of all was her own body
— the body that her stepfather had polluted
and contaminated. Can you imagine how
she dealt with that?"

Katsumata decided not to even try and
just shook his head. The doctor exhaled
violently, as if in physical pain.

"Yukari's first visit to this hospital was not
to the psychiatry department. She was
brought to the ER from the orphanage
where she was then. She was admitted after
using a box cutter to slice off her right
breast."

Even Katsumata was shaken. His face was
a mask of horror.

"At that point, she had already cut up her
own left arm so badly that it was just a lump
of hardened scar tissue. You see, with the
condition she has, the sight of her own
blood acted as an emotional tranquilizer or
sedative. The media calls it wrist-cutting

440

syndrome.

"On the one hand, she saw herself as worthless, as irredeemably vile, filthy — subhuman, basically. On the other hand, she was also resistant to that notion and was looking for a way to confirm her worth as a human being in her own mind. She needed to do something that proved to her that she was alive, that she had the same blood running through her veins as the rest of us. She needed demonstrable proof of things that anyone normal would just take for granted.

"The psychological pressure was so intense that all she could do was scream. Metaphorically, I mean. With nowhere left on her arm to cut, she resorted to slicing off her breast — which symbolized her femininity.

"She has an abnormality — I'll spare you the medical terminology here — that causes her blood to coagulate fast, so she stopped bleeding relatively quickly. That's what kept her alive. From her perspective, that just meant more suffering. While she was in the hospital, she sliced off her other breast. Then she slipped out of the hospital and went back out onto the streets of Shinjuku. She was found stark naked in the middle of the day, gouging at the flesh on her buttocks and her belly."

So the young girl had eliminated every trace of womanliness from her body. Katsumata could imagine how she must have looked after that. There was no doubt: *Yukari was F.*

"Doctor, I need you to take a look at these photos."

Katsumata laid the three photographs he had got from Tatsumi on the desk. The expression on the doctor's face was all the answer he needed.

"Can you see Yukari Fukazawa in these pictures?"

Omuro nodded despondently.

"It certainly looks like her."

"How about the other man? Have you seen him before?"

Omuro shook his head, then craned forward for a closer look at the photograph in the middle, where the man's face was relatively clear.

"There was this young man who occasionally came to see her. He claimed to be her cousin. This could be him."

"You sure about that?"

"No. It was a while ago, so I don't remember him clearly. I think there's a resemblance, though."

"Know his name?"

"The hospital administration keeps a visitor log. They should know, provided they haven't thrown the old logs out."

"Tell them to check ASAP."

Omuro obediently reached for the telephone.

Katsumata put another cigarette in his mouth and lit up.

After relaying Katsumata's request, Dr. Omuro returned the receiver to its cradle. His attitude was one of complete resignation, as if he, not Yukari, were the suspect.

"I hear that Yukari ran away several times before?"

Omuro nodded feebly.

"Did that tend to coincide with the second Sunday of the month?"

Omuro tilted his head quizzically.

"I need you to check that for me too. I'm pretty sure that's what you'll find."

Omuro gave a dazed nod.

The sky outside the window was dark with clouds threatening rain. Katsumata stared at them as they ground their way toward him. He knew it made no sense, but somehow the sight unnerved him.

He was wondering how long the administration people would take to review their visitor logs when Omuro began to speak.

"If anything, Yukari's symptoms seemed

to have abated a bit over the last year. In mid-July, her brother died. He was the only surviving member of her immediate family, so we couldn't very well keep the news from her. We knew it would be a big shock, but she took it even harder than we feared.

"We already know about her tendency toward profound depression, depersonalization, and self-harm. After her brother's death, it became all too clear that she also wanted to harm other people. There was this incident where she grabbed one of the nurses and held a box cutter — God knows how she'd got hold of the thing — to her throat. I managed to talk her down and resolve the situation safely, but what she said then made my blood run cold. 'If I kill her, my brother will help me sort it out.' "

Katsumata's smoldering suspicions burst into flame.

"When did that happen?"

"About the end of last July."

That was after the visit of the officer from the Nishiarai precinct.

"Listen, you're a doctor. I know you've got a professional duty to protect your patients' rights, and I respect that, but if you'd told Officer Todoroki some of what you've told me, a man by the name of Taiichi Kanebara would probably still be alive.

And if you'd given me the lowdown on Yukari's abnormalities when I came to see you, then a young cop called Otsuka wouldn't have been murdered."

His cell phone buzzed in his breast pocket.

"Katsumata here."

"This is Tatsumi," said a gruff voice. "I know who's organizing Strawberry Night."

Katsumata felt as though a hole had been punched in his chest.

"Damn! That was quick."

"Because I'm a pro. I threw everything at the problem. Anyway, forget that. The answer blew me away. The guy behind it all is Noboru Kitami, the son of the TMPD director of Tokyo's Third District. He's just a kid. He's doing his training at Kameari police station, where your task force is based."

"I'll be back," yelled Katsumata to the doctor as he made a dash for the door.

3

Kitami was on the phone, yelling at some-one.

"Don't go there. I shot the bitch and I can't undo it, so just haul ass over here. Yeah, that empty building in Ikebukuro. And tell F. Yeah, yeah. Quit riding me and get a move on."

He snapped the phone shut and spat on the floor where Reiko lay with her hands cuffed behind her back. The floor was bare concrete — just like the place where Otsuka was murdered.

"Lieutenant Himekawa, your time of death will fall between eight thirty and nine p.m. — or precisely when I'm attending the evening meeting."

Kitami was going to get his buddy to kill her so he could craft a watertight alibi. He must have used the same trick to put himself in a café at the time of Otsuka's murder.

Kitami squatted down beside Reiko's head

446

with his knees wide apart. If he wanted to shoot her now, there was nothing she could do about it.

"When I was at college, I committed every crime in the book, and then some. I took every drug I could get my hands on — dope, speed, LSD, coke, heroin, you name it. I'd get stoned, race my car down Route 466, and help myself to a nice piece of pussy along the way. I'd bundle some skirt I fancied into my car, lock her up, and then share her with my mates. I usually videoed the fun and posted it online — not for money, you know, just for a laugh. We'd go to Shibuya and Shinjuku and beat the shit out of the cocky little twats there who strut around like they own the place, then we'd tie them up and dump them on the runway at Tokyo Airport.

"Eventually I got bored with it. Enough was enough — plus, I was destined for the upper echelons of the police. I had to be discreet. I stepped back from the rapes, the fights, the drugs. If I ever got into trouble, I bought my way out. That was when I met F."

"F?" echoed Reiko. Kitami had said the name on the phone just now.

"Uh-huh. Should be here any minute now."

A few minutes later a silhouette appeared in the doorway of the room.

"Aha, here's our headliner. We were all waiting for you."

The shadowy figure did not move.

"Couldn't find the place?"

No reply.

"It's all good." Kitami looked down at Reiko with a genial expression on his face. "Lieutenant Himekawa, allow me to introduce you. This is F, an *artiste* of murder and the leading lady of Strawberry Nights. Her real name is Yukari Fukazawa."

This is the killer? Yukari Fukazawa?

The figure silhouetted in the doorway was about the same height as Reiko but as thin as a rail. Her hair was short but looked more as if it had been torn out than cut. Reiko was reminded of a stray dog with mange.

"F here came after me and my buddies when one of our pranks had gotten a bit out of hand. I thought I could buy her off in the usual way. She wasn't remotely interested. Then, out of the blue, she slits my buddy's throat with a single deft movement. It was brilliant, beautiful. Her finesse, the way the blood came bursting out of him, her stage presence — art is the only word that does her justice.

"The guy she killed, my buddy, he was all

set to take up a job in one of the government ministries. His life had followed
exactly the same course as mine. But in a
tiny fraction of a second, he was reduced to
a bloody rag doll, twitching and squirming
— and then the fellow was dead. She
snuffed out his life just like that, with that
hundred-yen box cutter of hers.

"The sight made me realize that I had
something inside me that no amount of
routine hell-raising could ever satisfy. The
thought that all the crazy shit I'd done in
my youth was going to fade into the back
mirror as I rose up the smooth escalator of
the police bureaucracy made my blood run
cold. There had to be more to life, I
thought."

Kitami looked at Reiko with rapture in his
eyes. "Know who put me on the right path?
It was F here. She showed me that death is
always with us — close, accessible, *real*. A
death more real and vivid than anything
you'll see on TV is there right in front of
you.

"Since I was a kid, my parents raised me
to focus on success. I was so obsessed with
aiming higher, looking higher all my life,
that my damn neck ached! I lost any sense
of what was below me, of where I stood in
relation to other people. This girl showed

449

me what was really what. That I could stand at the apex of the thousands of people who just spend their lives crawling miserably over the face of the earth. She showed me that people who live their lives without clarity of purpose will end up like my dead buddy — a ripe rotten strawberry of a corpse.

"She's an artist of death, and I am her self-appointed patron. I supported her because I was desperate to see her perform the act of killing live on stage. I knew that she would have the same effect on other people that she'd had on me. Directly confronting the reality of death would teach them how precious its opposite, life, is and help them reconnect with who they really are."

Reiko wondered if Kitami was recalling a moment from an actual show. His eyes were shut, his arms spread, and there was an expression of elation on his face, as if a tide of orchestral music were washing over him.

"Think about it. People nowadays are born in a hospital, and they die in a hospital. No one gets the chance to *feel* death as a reality anymore. But we all want to. Everyone wants to see and feel the reality of death. I make that happen for them. I show them real death — and its opposite, real life. The name 'Strawberry Night' was my idea, but F liked it. She never says a word aloud, but she gave the nod on it."

Reiko was only pretending to listen. She was busy looking for a way to escape before the third member of the gang turned up. Kitami, despite appearing to be swept up in his own eloquence, was keeping a careful eye on her. She had to work her cuffed hands around to the front of her body to even stand a chance.

"Your guess was right. Originally we were dumping the bodies at the Toda Rowing Course. I only discovered the pond at Mizumoto Park after being posted to Kameari, and we started using it in July. Dammit, though, I never expected Fukazawa to go and die on us, let alone from some brain-eating amoeba! I've got to tip my hat to that intuition of yours. No idea *how* you figured it out, but you were right. Life suddenly became complicated. Really, we should have finished you off before dealing with Otsuka."

For some reason Kitami was no longer pointing the gun at Reiko. He jerked his chin to signal for her to get up. Reiko slowly dragged herself up off the floor.

"It's a shame. I quite like your type."

With his left hand Kitami reached for Reiko's breasts and began to fondle them through her sweat-stained blouse. Kitami's roving fingers crawling over her, trespassing on her body, made rational thought impossible. His fingers touched the skin at her throat, slid down inside her bra, found a nipple, and pinched it painfully hard.

"I think you of all people can understand me. I'm right, aren't I? Because you're the same as me. In your job, you see people who've been murdered in the most horrible way, day in, day out. And what does that make you feel? *'I don't want to end up like that myself!'* I bet you've thought that."

Kitami had the gun pressed to her temple again. He was behind her now. He slid one hand around her waist.

"You thought to yourself, 'I'm alive. Thank God, I'm alive.' You felt superior, special."

No, no! That's not what I felt.

"Yeah, you're the same as the rest of them. Or maybe worse. Fuck, you get paid for looking at dead bodies. On the outside you're pretending to take your job oh-so-seriously, but in your heart of hearts you're thinking, 'Only losers end up dead. God be thanked that I'm a fucking cop.' "

To Reiko, it felt as if the whole thing was happening to someone else far, far away. She seemed to be sinking powerlessly into the blackness of that summer night.

A soft, timid voice suddenly interrupted her thoughts.

"No."

Reiko could not figure out who had spoken. Kitami stepped away from Reiko.

"No. . . . You . . . and . . . me . . . we're . . . not . . . the . . . same."

It was Yukari. The clear girlish voice and her ghoulish appearance made for a jarring contrast.

"How can you say that, F?" asked Kitami, in a tone of extraordinary tenderness.

"I never . . . looked high . . . expected success. Just wanted . . . to feel . . . alive. Know that . . . the blood in my veins . . . was the same . . . as the rest of you. Just wanted . . . to be normal."

The ghostly whisper of a voice had an extraordinary hypnotic power.

Kitami left Reiko and walked unsteadily toward Yukari.

Now! This is it!

Reiko lowered herself into a squatting position, moving slowly to avoid attention.

"What do you mean, F? You and I are the same. We're one of a kind. We feel fully alive by feeling the reality of death. That's why we do what we do."

"Not . . . true."

The silhouette shook its head.

Reiko stepped over her handcuffed wrists. Her arms were now in front of her.

"I . . . only ever . . . felt . . . death. Never . . . believed . . . that I was . . . alive. You . . . just . . . take life . . . for granted. You and me . . . we're not . . . the same."

"What the fuck are you saying? I mean, *What the fuck?*"

Reiko could see the despair in Kitami's sagging shoulders.

This is my last chance.

Keeping her center of gravity low, she launched herself at Kitami's back.

He swung around, one knee raised. She doubled herself up to minimize the impact.

"Think I'm that stupid?"

He kicked her in the solar plexus. Once. Then again. Reiko managed to cover herself. At his third kick, she grabbed Kitami's ankle with her cuffed hands and heaved.

He lost his footing and staggered to the side. She took the opportunity. She started running as fast as she could across the room. She had to get to the front door and shout for help.

Behind her, shots rang out. Reiko crashed forward as if her legs had been knocked out from under her. But it wasn't the floor that was coming up to meet her: she was tum-

bling into a smooth gaping square hole —
the elevator shaft!

I'm going to fall!

In a panic, she twisted in midair and managed to land at the edge of the shaft. Half
her body landed in front of the hole, while
the other half dangled over a three-floor
drop. With the fingertips of one hand, she
grabbed at the edge of the floor. Her legs
began to slide toward the darkness. She
managed to get half a grip with her other
hand at the moment her legs tumbled over
the edge. She began to tremble. She felt the
individual grains of sand sliding between
her fingers and the concrete of the floor.
Her body started sliding further into the
shaft. She could only manage to hold on for
a few more seconds.

Despair was a crushing weight.

Kitami's face loomed toward her. He held
the gun, and its black muzzle was pointed
at her.

"Argh!" Kitami cried out. "What the
fu— ?" He spun around and away from the
elevator shaft.

Then came the sound of several shots.

A familiar voice cried out from across the
darkened room, "Kitami, stop!"

"Freeze, or I'll fire," another voice yelled.

Several more shots.

Grunts and groans.

"Kitamiiiii!"

Barely suspended in the shaft, Reiko had no idea who had fired, who had been hit, or who had screamed Kitami's name. What was going on?

All of sudden Yukari's bloodstained face appeared. Down on all fours, she leaned forward and grasped Reiko's wrists and tried to pull her up. She was extraordinarily strong.

"Mako . . . you came to help me," was all that Yukari said before Reiko's eyes closed.

4

Katsumata was heading for Ikebukuro by taxi. He frantically called Himekawa's cell phone but got the same "no signal" message every time.

I can't believe this. What's the damn woman using for a phone — a Coke can and a piece of string?

Katsumata knew that Kitami was with Himekawa, checking vacant properties in Ikebukuro. He needed to find them, swoop in, and arrest that bastard Kitami with all necessary force. It would be a slam dunk, a hole in one, the mother of all wins. Forking over the two and half million had hurt a bit, but, hey, money comes and money goes. Katsumata had no regrets.

Katsumata looked across the hustle and bustle outside the east exit of Ikebukuro Station. Were Reiko and Kitami inspecting actual empty properties or just talking to real estate agents? It didn't matter much.

Tracking down a pair of detectives in an area this big would be like finding the proverbial needle in a haystack. Plus, he was going to have to do it all by himself.

By myself? Come to think of it . . .

Katsumata suddenly remembered his partner, whom he'd shaken him off earlier in the day. Where had Ioka got to? What was he doing? If he was anywhere nearby, they could join forces.

With two of us on the job, the odds of finding Kitami and Himekawa will get a little better.

He called Ioka's cell. It was picked up after a single ring.

"Hello. This is Hiromitsu Ioka, a.k.a. the king of Kameari police station."

"Where are you, you fucking clown? I'm in Ikebukuro and I need you here right now," bellowed Katsumata, oblivious to the other people at the intersection where he stood.

"Golly, what a coincidence! I'm in Ikebukuro too."

A rivulet of warm sweat trickled down Katsumata's back.

Don't tell me Ioka's been sitting on my tail all this time.

He looked around. There was no sign of the man.

"What the hell are you doing in Ikebu-kuro?"

"Me? It's a bit embarrassing for a bashful boy like me . . ."

"Get a frigging move on, will you!"

"Okay, cool it. It's Reiko. I'm worried about her. Very worried."

Ioka worried about Himekawa? Katsumata felt a spasm of fear. Had Ioka worked out what was really going on?

"Today she's been paired up with the fast-track golden boy. The fellow's so damn handsome on top of everything else. What if Reiko's fallen for him? And they're checking vacant properties together. The thought of them making out in some disused building's driving me crazy."

Katsumata pictured Ioka biting his nails with theatrical anxiety.

"Yeah, yeah, yeah. And what exactly are you doing with yourself in this crazy state of yours?"

"You'll think I was behaving like a lovesick teenager, but I went to find Reiko in Ikebu-kuro. And I found her. I'm ashamed to say I've been tailing them all afternoon."

Katsumata swallowed. He couldn't believe his luck.

"Senior Officer Ioka." He was stuttering with excitement. "Can you confirm that you have a lock on Kitami and Himekawa's location?"

"I can. They're inside an uncompleted building on the edge of central Ikebukuro. If Kitami has made his carnal passions known and moved on Reiko, then my life's as good as over."

Good job, Ioka! You're the man!

Keeping his excitement in check, Katsumata asked Ioka to give him the address and directions from the station.

Ioka launched into an explanation. "Take the second turn along, then go straight. At the third left you need —"

Suddenly Ioka broke off.

"Hey! I take the third left, and then?"

". . . I'm not sure, but I think I heard a bang . . ."

"What!"

It had to be a gunshot. Katsumata didn't know for a fact that Kitami was responsible for Otsuka's murder, but the idea of someone finishing Himekawa off in another empty building was too easy to believe.

This is so fucked up!

Katsumata ordered Ioka to keep watching and not to move from his current position under any circumstances, then hung up.

Katsumata dashed into one of the electronics megastores nearby. He charged up the escalator, pushing people aside. He knew that these sorts of places had recently started selling toys on the higher floors.

Please, God!

He was panting by the time he got to the seventh floor. Sure enough, the toy selection was as extensive as any department store.

Katsumata beckoned over a passing clerk and asked for the replica firearms. The man eyed him a little suspiciously, but Katsumata stayed calm. Right now he didn't have the time to explain his reasons or to yell at the guy either.

"Where? Show me."

"This way, sir."

The clerk led him a couple of aisles down and gestured at the shelves. Katsumata carefully examined the guns on display. His first instinct was to look for a New Nambu M60, the standard issue revolver of the Japanese police, but he almost immediately realized that it was too minor a make to be popular — besides, revolvers were regarded as old-fashioned anyway. The shelf was full of automatics.

Walther P88. Smith and Wesson M3906. Beretta M92F. SIG Sauer P228. A selection to bring joy to a man's heart!

This looks like a safe choice. The thing's just a prop anyway.

"I'll take this one."

Katsumata pointed at the SIG Sauer P228.

"Does it make the right noise when you fire it?"

"Yes. And it takes thirteen rounds in the magazine plus one in the chamber, just like the real thing."

"The rounds come with it?"

"Yes, a full magazine with fourteen rounds."

"Sure it won't misfire on me?"

"I don't think so, sir. If you're worried, I recommend these."

The clerk held out another box of bullets.

"Quite the salesman, aren't you! Okay, I'll take 'em. Load it up."

Katsumata paid cash, then dashed down the stairs out of the store.

He didn't stop running when he got out to the street.

All this exercise is wearing me out.

Katsumata felt bushed, but now wasn't the time to start feeling sorry for himself. Should he contact the local precinct for backup? No. It would too hard to explain himself. He was following a lead he'd picked up from an illegal investigation.

He was still debating the issue when he reached the apartment building.

"Over here, Lieutenant," Ioka hissed. He was standing at the corner ahead, waving him forward. "This way."

"What've we got?" Katsumata panted.

Ioka bit his lip and looked up at the building.

"No one's come out, but some weird skinny kid went inside."

A weird skinny kid!

Katsumata grabbed Ioka by the collar. "Was he wearing a black leather body suit?" he asked under his breath.

"He was, he was. A chum of yours, Lieutenant?"

By way of an answer, Katsumata drove his fist into Ioka's face.

"It's our perp. The person in black is Yukari Fukazawa. She's the killer. The person behind the whole thing is Kitami."

"What the hell are you talking about?" sneered Ioka.

Katsumata paid no attention and rummaged in his paper bag.

"I didn't have time to call for backup. We're gonna have to go in alone."

Ioka sneered again when he saw the P228 in Katsumata's hand. "That thing's a toy."

"So what, provided it sounds right? Kitami is definitely armed. It'll be dark in there, and this thing will look the part."

All the investigators on the case were supposed to have been issued a sidearm that morning in response to Otsuka's murder. Due to an unfortunate administrative mix-up, there were only enough for the precinct officers. The rest of the weapons were supposed to be ready that afternoon.

In the end, here he was, armed only with a toy. What with playing hide-and-seek with Ioka, the whole sidearm business had slipped his mind.

"You carrying, Ioka?"

"Carrying what?"

"A sidearm. We're under orders to."

"Uhm . . . no. After the morning meeting, I suddenly noticed you weren't at the station, Lieutenant. I thought, 'Heck, he's gone and left me' and dashed out after you. So, no, I didn't stick around to get one."

You damn clown!

Basically, the man was no use at all.

"Enough time wasting. Let's go in."

Katsumata moved toward the building. Ioka followed. They slipped through the fence, taking care to make no noise. Straining their ears, they could hear voices coming from an upper floor, though they

464

couldn't make out what was being said.

A passage led from the entrance to an empty elevator shaft. Next to the shaft was a bare concrete staircase. They padded up as quietly as they could. There was no one on the second floor, but they heard movement one floor up.

Suddenly there was the sound of angry voices.

"Hurry!"

Now wasn't the time to worry about stealth. Wringing the last ounce of strength from his body, Katsumata charged up, two steps at a time. The moment they reached the third floor, there were more gunshots. Himekawa came careening toward them — and then seemed to vanish into the wall.

Isn't that the elevator shaft? Has she fallen in?

Kitami stood in front of them. He had a gun.

Katsumata was about to give Kitami the "freeze or I fire" order, until he realized the futility of it. His gun was only a replica. If he shot first and Kitami returned fire, he'd be in real trouble.

Katsumata was desperately reviewing his options when Yukari, with a shriek, flung herself on Kitami from behind. Katsumata noticed that she had something in her hand.

"What the fu— !" Kitami spun around and pumped two shots into the girl.

"Kitami, stop!"

"Freeze or I fire."

Katsumata fired multiple rounds from his replica gun.

Kitami turned and took aim at him.

Yukari pulled herself back to her feet and swept her hand across Kitami's throat.

Did she get him? Yes, direct hit.

Kitami pressed a hand to his throat and made a gurgling sound. He pointed the gun at Yukari again.

"Kitamiiiii," the girl screamed.

A burst of gunfire.

As he fired, Kitami sank to the ground. Katsumata was firing his toy at Kitami. Yukari was knocked sideways by the impact of Kitami's shots, but even as she fell to the floor, she was trying to reach Reiko in the elevator shaft.

"Kitami," bellowed Katsumata.

"Reiko," Ioka yelled.

Katsumata sprang over Yukari to Kitami, kicked the gun out of his hand, and dropped a knee into his solar plexus. He stuck the P228 under Kitami's jaw to prevent him from seeing that it was a replica.

"Your little game's over, boy wonder."

Katsumata snapped the cuffs on the wrist

of the hand Kitami was pressing to the wound in his throat. He turned out not to be bleeding badly after all. Despite having killed more than ten times, Yukari's knack for locating the carotid artery apparently left her when her victim wasn't strapped down and she was under pressure.

"Let go of her. Let go, creep."

Ioka had pulled Himekawa out of the shaft and now held her in his arms. Yukari still had her hands clasped around Reiko's wrists. Ioka tried to wrench her fingers off, but the girl was strong and wouldn't let go. Ioka was shocked to see that beneath the girl's fingers, Himekawa was handcuffed.

"I'm okay, Ioka."

Himekawa sounded calmer than she had any right to be. Yukari was lying facedown on the floor. Himekawa turned her over and lay her across her lap. She stroked the thin fingers that still clutched at her wrists.

Yukari appeared to have taken shots in the stomach and the legs. One bullet had also grazed her cheek, which was bleeding. Her breathing was rasping and uneven. She probably wasn't going to make it.

"Thank you, Yukari. You saved me. You've had a tough life, but you're going to be all right now."

Himekawa began to cry. Ioka, who was

standing next to her, got out his phone and called for an ambulance. Himekawa was now wailing so loudly that Ioka had trouble making himself heard.

"Don't die on me, Yukari. You can't die. You mustn't."

Katsumata looked at her with something verging on disgust.

Birds of a feather . . .

Katsumata hastily consulted his watch, as if he'd just remembered something. "Oh, I forgot — Noboru Kitami, you are under arrest. What's the date? Oh yes, August twenty-sixth . . . at . . . uh . . . seven ten p.m. The charges — for now, at least — are attempted murder and unlawful possession of a firearm. Got it?"

Katsumata heaved a sigh and looked out through the dust-grimed windows. The clouds looked like spilled ink on a sheet of paper. The world was a dreary gray place.

Far off in the west, Katsumata spotted a tiny glimmer of red sun.

PART V

Tuesday, August 26
Sometime After 7:00 P.M.

The series of incidents that began with the Mizumoto Park Dumped Bodies Case were brought to a conclusion with the arrest of Noboru Kitami, Yukari Fukazawa, and a third person.

Noboru Kitami's injuries proved non-life-threatening. He was taken to the Tokyo Metropolitan Hospital and is cooperating with the inquiry. His accomplice, Yukari Fukazawa, is currently being held in a different hospital. She is in critical condition, having sustained two bullet wounds in the chest, one in the face, one in the stomach, and another in the left thigh. The doctors managed to save her life, but she's not able to answer questions. Much about her history remains unclear. Her past will likely be one focus of the investigation.

The third member of the group,

471

Harunobu Ogawa, was also arrested today. After receiving a phone call from Kitami, Ogawa drove to the crime scene in his own vehicle. Patrol cars from the Ikebukuro Station and an ambulance arrived immediately afterward. More by accident than anything, Ogawa found himself surrounded. One officer, who was suspicious about Ogawa's car being parked directly in front of the crime scene, went to ask him some routine questions. Ogawa responded by ramming his way through the paramedics and police with his vehicle, but he soon crashed into a nearby electricity pole. The Ikebukuro police arrested him on the spot and charged him with interfering with government officials in the performance of their duties and with bodily harm.

Ogawa, a fourth-year science major at Tokyo University, is believed to have handled the information technology aspects of the gang's work. His interrogation is ongoing.

Inquiries have show n that the sidearm that Ogawa had in his possession was the revolver checked out by Senior Officer Otsuka on the morning of his death. Noboru Kitami and Harunobu Ogawa have been charged with multiple offenses, including murder, attempted murder, instigation of murder, accessory to murder, unlawful disposal of bodies, and violations of the sword and firearms law. Their chances of avoiding the death penalty are low. A joint task force is about to be established to investigate both the case of the bodies found in the Toda Rowing Course (currently being handled by the Saitama Prefectural Police) and the shooting of Senior Officer Otsuka (currently being handled by Ikebukuro precinct).

Wednesday, August 27

Reiko was convalescing in one of Tokyo's university-affiliated hospitals. She'd been convinced that Kitami had shot her right ear clean off. In fact, his bullet had only grazed her. Although there was tearing of the tympanic membrane, the prognosis was that she would eventually recover her hearing in that ear.

"Bullets revolve at extremely high speed. That alone was enough to make you feel that your whole ear had been ripped off when the bullet had only grazed it. Add in the hearing loss on that side, and it's no surprise you thought the whole ear was gone."

Reiko was relieved at the news that her ear was still intact. She also felt embarrassed to have kicked up such a fuss about nothing.

That was her only gunshot wound. For

the rest, she had bruises and abrasions, including an all-too-noticeable graze on her forehead. The doctor assured her that she would be left with no visible scarring.

If no one shot me, why did I crash to the floor like that?

Reiko probed her memories of the moments before she tumbled down into the elevator shaft.

Kitami had fired at her — that much was certain — but apparently he'd missed. Reiko nonetheless remembered feeling an excruciating burst of pain in her leg before she went down. What was that about?

She rolled up the trouser leg of her pajamas and uncovered a horrendous bruise on her left calf just above the ankle.

Was it Yukari?

Yukari had been standing to the left of Reiko as she made her attempt to get out of the room. Yukari must have tried to help by kicking Reiko's feet out from under her when she saw that Kitami was about to shoot.

What was it Yukari had said to her? "Mako, you came to help me."

Reiko had no idea who this "Mako" was. Her best guess was that there must have been a physical resemblance and that Yukari, in her confused state, had mistaken

Reiko for some friend from her past and so tried to help her.

Yukari was a remarkable young woman, thought Reiko. Her ghoulish appearance and innocent, girlish voice. Her scarecrow-like thinness and that iron grip. Reiko had only seen Yukari's face spattered with blood. What did she look like underneath? What sort of history was the girl dragging behind her to throw herself so enthusiastically into the Strawberry Night show?

I'm going to find out.

As the Strawberry Night murderer, Yukari Fukazawa was guilty of multiple grave crimes. When Reiko inquired about her age, she learned that she was eighteen — old enough for the death penalty. Apparently, Yukari had spent her whole life in and out of psychiatric hospitals. A successful plea of diminished mental capacity could dramatically reduce her sentence. Reiko wasn't sure which would be better.

Reiko was reluctant to believe that Yukari was intrinsically evil. A handful of random impressions formed during the chaos of yesterday were hardly grounds for her to declare an eleven-time murderer "not a bad person," but she could feel her heart tugging her in that direction.

What's got into me? Siding with the perpe-

trator like this!

Reiko had breakfast. The nurses took her temperature and changed her bandages. With that out of the way, she was alone in her private room with nothing to do. Tamaki, her sister, showed up as soon as visiting hours started.

"I can't look after both you and Mom, you know," was all she said. She deposited a bag with some clothes in it and bustled off.

Outside it was raining. The air conditioning was on high, and the chilliness of the room conjured a wintry bleakness. The weather was just too depressing. If it brightened up, so would she, thought Reiko.

Otsuka was dead. Kitami had gotten the drop on her. She'd failed to make an arrest. And — this was the icing on the cake — one of the perpetrators had saved her life, and she was now starting to pity the poor girl.

God, I hate myself!

She felt as miserable as if she were stuck outside in the rain, buried up to her neck in cold mud.

Then, just after eleven o'clock:

"How are you, Himekawa?"

"Hey, Lieutenant. You look healthy as a horse."

"Yeah, you've got good color."

477

"Reiko, it was me! I pulled you to safety!"
It was Captain Imaizumi and her squad.

"Captain, you didn't need to come. I know you're busy," Reiko protested. Inside, she was ready to burst into tears of joy. They must have come straight over from the morning meeting. The figures loitering in the corridor outside must be their partners from the precinct.

Ioka was his usual self and Ishikura's face the usual imperturbable mask. Only Kikuta was different. There was something stiff and awkward about him. He said nothing and avoided eye contact.

Come on, Kikuta. Talk to me.

Reiko had a pretty good idea what was going on with the man. No doubt he was beating himself up for not having swung in and rescued her when she was in danger. The fact that Ioka and Katsumata had been the ones to do so must have been salt in the wound, because Kikuta disliked them both.

It's over now. There's nothing you can do about it.

Reiko glanced at him from time to time, but he stubbornly refused to catch her eye.

There's really nothing I can do. Best thing is to give him some space.

Yuda was unusually hyper. Reiko suspected he was trying to fill the gap left by

478

Otsuka. His strained efforts at jollity back-fired; she found herself thinking of Otsuka more than ever. There was a hole between Kikuta and Yuda, a gap that no one else could fill. Their visit only reinforced what she already knew: Otsuka was gone. Forever.

I'm sorry, boys. I'm a crap lieutenant.

There was a short silence. Sensing that things were getting a little awkward, Ishikura called time on the visit.

"We need to be moving. Eh, Kikuta?"

Kikuta nodded. He looked as miserable as a freshly pinched suspect.

"Thanks for coming when you've got so much on your plates. I'll be fine. No need to come back."

"No fear of that, Lieutenant," shot back Yuda. "Get a move on and come back to work."

Yuda's rejoinder made her injured ear sting.

Ishikura poked the younger man in the ribs to keep him in line.

"I'll be back," chirped Ioka.

Kikuta said nothing.

The guy's hopeless.

"No more visits," reiterated Reiko firmly.

In her heart, though, she hoped they would be back — though perhaps without Ioka.

"Captain, we'll be going now," said Ishi-kura.

Imaizumi nodded, and Ishikura bowed at him.

"Good luck."

"Thanks for coming. I know you'll all do a great job."

"Good-bye."

"Bye. Get well soon."

Ishikura and Yuda left the room. Kikuta, who still hadn't said a word, followed them out.

"Get well soon. It's lonely without you. So lonely."

"Oh, piss off, Ioka."

"Parting is such sweet sorrow."

"I'll slam the door on you."

"Oh, Reiko."

Ioka finally left too. Their partners, who'd been waiting in the corridor, went with them. Now there were just the two of them left in the room — herself and Captain Imaizumi. There was a moment of silence as Imaizumi planted his hands on his hips and gazed out of the window.

"Director Kitami of Third District re-signed his position. It seems his son used his father's influence to be assigned to the task force and then again later to be as-signed as your partner. Then he hanged

480

himself."

Reiko's mind served up an image of a middle-aged man dangling by a kimono sash from the wooden lintel of a traditional Japanese room.

"He was found at five this morning. Taking responsibility for the scandal his kid caused, I guess. Leaves a nasty taste in the mouth."

Captain Imaizumi grimaced as though he had bitten into a lemon. He looked up at the sky and took a deep breath.

"Stubby really wiped the floor with us this time," he said, darting a glance at Reiko. "It's a grand slam for him."

"I know. Still, God only knows what would have happened if Stubby and Ioka hadn't turned up."

Kusaka's warning had come true in the worst possible way. Still, Reiko refused to let herself wallow. No sour grapes. No grudges.

She still loathed Katsumata, but she was quite prepared to acknowledge that he was a cut above her as a detective. She also knew that he would make a good job of preparing the charge papers for the public prosecutor's office. What did she have to bellyache about?

"There's something I've been wanting to ask you, Captain. Where did Katsumata get his 'Stubby' nickname?"

Uncharacteristically, Captain Imaizumi's face betrayed surprise.

"You don't know?"

"No."

Imaizumi sighed and went back to staring out of the window.

"When he was young, he was a real stickler for procedure. His stubbornness was legendary."

"And 'stubborn' got shortened to 'stubby'?"

"Yeah. Is it so hard to believe?"

"No, it's not that. . . ."

Imaizumi nodded and went on. "You see, when Katsumata was young, he wasn't the outlaw he is now. He was very by-the-book, visiting crime scenes over and over again. He believed in the old-fashioned shoe leather approach. If you'd known him then, you'd get where the whole 'stubby' thing came from. Working in Public Security changed the guy. I don't really know what happened to him in the years he was away from regular police investigations, though I've got one or two ideas. . . .

"When he rejoined us, he'd hardened into what you see now. Did you know that he earns pocket money by selling off intel about the police department? The top brass know what he's doing, and they more or less tolerate it. You know why? Because he has the dirt on them too.

"In one sense, though, the guy hasn't changed at all. All the money he gets from selling information, he recycles into bribes and payments to further the investigations he's assigned to. It's like a rainy day fund. It's not for him; he'd never spend a cent on himself, as far as anyone can tell, anyway. He acts like a one-man Public Security Bureau. In a way, it's just another expression of his stubborn, all-in personality."

Imaizumi smiled sheepishly and went back to discussing the ongoing investigation.

That evening, just as the official visiting hours were coming to an end, she had an unexpected visitor: Katsumata.

"I'm looking for the detective who kicked up a storm about losing her ear and didn't have the decency to croak when it was a false alarm."

"Hey, hey. No need to tell the whole world."

"What's with the private room? Bit fancy for a hick like you." He snorted contemptuously, then, without being asked, plunked himself in a chair.

Katsumata handed her a rolled-up weekly

magazine as a gift. Reiko assumed he'd already read whatever he wanted in it and was just using her as a dustbin. "No thanks," she said, handing it back.

"No damn manners," said Katsumata in mock horror. The man didn't hold back. He ridiculed the pajamas Tamaki had brought her — "You're not a little girl. What's a woman of thirty doing in floral fucking pajamas!" — told her she looked awful without makeup; complained about the smell of the room, and offered to wash out her bedpan.

Reiko waited until the abuse had run its course before saying what she felt she had to.

"I have to thank you," she stammered. "If it weren't for you, I'd be dead."

Katsumata looked away, a confused welter of emotions on his face.

"Where's the damn sick bag? Nicely brought up girls don't come right out and say stuff like that. You're such a hopeless hick."

But the acrimony was missing from his voice. A heavy silence hung over the room. Clearly uncomfortable, Katsumata started hunting for something in his jacket pockets. Not finding whatever he was looking for, he briefly put his hands on his knees before getting out a cigarette. He was about to light it, when he remembered where he was.

Now's my chance.

"Lieutenant Katsumata?"

He only jerked his chin vaguely by way of response. He didn't look at her but sighed. Reiko caught a glimpse of the very real exhaustion in his face. He was human after all.

It's a good time to ask him.

"Lieutenant, what did you mean those times you told me that I was 'dangerous'?"

Katsumata snorted. "I'll tell you, but there's something I want to ask you first."

He was going to string her along a while. She didn't mind.

"Okay. Fire away."

Katsumata scowled and eyed her suspiciously. "Oh, Little Miss Cooperative all of a sudden, are we?" He straightened himself in his chair and leaned in. "It's about yesterday. Ioka was the one who told me where you and Kitami were. He was right outside the apartment building. I was on the phone with him when the first shots were fired, so how come you got out with nothing more than a scrape on the ear?"

"Oh, that's what you want to know."

Reiko talked Katsumata through what happened. How she speculated about Ki-

485

tami having been in the rowing club as a student. How that would explain the bodies being dumped in the Mizumoto Park pond in place of the Toda Rowing Course. How she had realized that the switch — which coincided with the freshly graduated Kitami arriving at Kameari police station as a trainee — was simply too much of a coincidence.

"I asked Kitami, 'You were a rower when you were at college, weren't you?' and he tried to shoot me. I got out of the way — mostly."

Something like disappointment scudded across Katsumata's face.

"I can't tell if you're smart or stupid."

"Come on. My instincts are razor sharp."

"They are. Except that Kitami wasn't the rower. It was Harunobu Ogawa, his accomplice."

Reiko wiped the cold beads of sweat from her forehead.

"The real reason they switched to the Mizumoto pond was that Kitami thought it was easier to get up close to in a car. So you were right about the bigger picture and wrong about the details. In my report, I was having a hard time explaining why I tailed you and Kitami. Think I'll borrow your pet theory."

Katsumata produced a ballpoint pen from his inside jacket pocket.

"What do you mean about 'having a hard time'?"

"Forget about it."

"Oh, okay. I'll forget about it. It and everything else. Go ahead and use the rowing angle. Just don't forget, when you write your report, to give the credit that's due to Officer Otsuka."

Startled, Katsumata stared at her for a moment. He wondered how much she knew. Did she really know anything, or was she just guessing again? Either way, she'd offered him a deal, and she'd named her price. He could respect that. Maybe she wasn't such a dumb hick after all.

He silently nodded his agreement as he jotted down a note on the back of his hand.

"What happened after that? It took us a while to get there. Don't tell me that you, Kitami, and Yukari had a threesome."

Gross!

Katsumata, sharp though he was, had no way of knowing what had happened during that time. Reiko omitted any mention of how Kitami had physically abused her. She simply explained that Kitami had been boasting about his criminal exploits as they waited for Ogawa to turn up.

"He went on about how he had lived his life 'looking higher' and how that had made him want to look down into the depths — at death, basically — to give him a sense of how far he'd risen. Yukari was the complete opposite: she knew only the dregs of life. Maiming and killing was the only way she knew to make herself feel human like the rest of us. By making people bleed, she could show herself that her blood was red like everybody else's. Kitami and Yukari were the co-organizers of Strawberry Night, but their motives couldn't have been more different. That was the essence of their revelations."

"So by the time Ioka and I rolled up, those two were in the middle of a messy breakup."

"Correct." Reiko paused and sighed. "Kitami said something about me being the same as him. That I came across dead bodies every day of the week at Homicide, and that he knew what they made me feel. *Thank God I'm a detective and not one of those dead losers.* He went on about what a rush it is to see death up close — about the intense sense of being alive and warm glow of superiority it gives you. . . . You know what shocked me? Kitami was right."

Katsumata spread his arms palm upward as if to say, "I told you so."

"That's exactly what I meant when I said you were dangerous. Your instincts are incredibly sharp. You've got a real genius for profiling. That's a fact, and it's why you've collared so many perps. I'm happy to give you that.

"But your approach and proper profiling are not the same thing at all. You don't identify the perpetrators by extrapolating from a small amount of hard data. No, what you do — and you may not be aware of it yourself — is tune directly into their minds. The reason you can identify perps and figure out why they act the way they do through little more than guesswork is because your brain is wired the same way as theirs.

"You were horrified when Kitami said basically the same thing to you at the crime scene. And then what do you go and do? You burst into tears and start cuddling the wounded Yukari. Same thing when I asked you why the gang had put the body on the hedge by the pond when Yasuyuki Fukazawa was already dead. It happened because of a communication slipup by Ogawa. In other words, you were right about that too. That's what I meant about your way of thinking being dangerous."

My brain . . . is wired like theirs.

Reiko had never thought of herself in those terms. To have someone come out and say it to her face was a shock, but she couldn't very well protest. It was true. She acknowledged that.

Reiko had done the whole weeping and hugging act before: there was that young repeat offender who had killed himself just as they moved in to arrest him. No one else had him down for the crime; only Reiko believed him to be guilty, and she took the initiative to bring him in. Casting her mind back, she could think of any number of cases where her empathy with the perp had made her break down in tears.

Of course, it wasn't always like that. She was not a random crybaby who wept over any old scumbag. Plenty of murderers deserved no sympathy at all. Nonetheless, there were times when she felt sorrier for the murderer than for the victim. Murder was an exceptionally heinous crime — and sometimes people had exceptional reasons that justified committing it. On those occasions, empathy got the better of Reiko, and she would cry, oblivious to her position as a detective and the dictates of the law.

She was not sure which of the two categories Yukari fell into. She suspected the latter. Captain Imaizumi had given her an update on Yukari's status before he left.

"Her heart, her lungs, and even her immune system are all in a critically weakened state, and she's barely conscious. Despite that, the minute the nurse leaves the room, she rips the drip out of her arm. It's a miracle that she's alive, but it's obvious that she actively wants to die."

Sounds like Yukari probably won't make it, thought Reiko. She knew that Yukari's death would make closing the case a whole lot harder, but on a human level she just wanted to let her go. She couldn't explain why. That was just how she felt.

Maybe I'm not cut out to be a cop.

Reiko sighed. Katsumata gave another impatient snort. Had her face given her away? She had a pretty good idea of what Katsumata must think of her — a loser, a pitiful washout. Although the open distaste with which he was contemplating her was uncomfortable, she felt duty-bound to grin and bear it.

"Hey, you," growled Katsumata after a while.

"Yes?"

"What's with the long face?"

She'd been right. Her face was an open book.

"Sorry."

Might as well apologize, she thought, *though I don't know what for.*

Katsumata rose languidly to his feet. He sauntered over to the window and opened it all the way, despite the air conditioning being on full blast.

"Don't let nonsense spouted by some nasty little murdering crook get you down. 'I was always looking up, so I wanted to look down.' 'I could only look down, so I wanted to look up.' What the fuck's that about? You can look up, down, left, or right for all I care. The only thing that matters is to focus on the important things."

Katsumata swiveled around from the window and looked Reiko straight in the eye.

"There's only one way to live your life: *facing forward.*"

Reiko gulped involuntarily.

Live facing forward? He's not the first person to tell me that. Detective Sata had used the same phrase in her journal. "Reiko, I want you to get back on your feet, and live facing forward."

After all these years, she finally understood what the words meant.

"Right, got to go. Shitloads to do."

Reiko was in a daze when Katsumata left. The chilled air was sucked out of the open window. The muggy outdoor heat rolled in and took its place. It was summer — summer, the season that Reiko hated so. Or did she? Now she felt as though the summer heat was going to thaw the frozen numbness of her heart.

Yes. Live facing forward.

Reiko looked up at the sky. It was a solid blanket of gray clouds without a glimmer of sunshine. But Reiko knew that it wouldn't stay that way forever. At some point, the sky would brighten. And then it would get cloudy; then it would rain; then it would snow — and then, at some point, it would brighten up again. *It always did.* The banal insight filled her with unreasonable joy.

"Detective Sata," murmured Reiko, looking up at the sky. "I'm ready to fight again."

Soon the sky would be the same pure expanse of blue that it had been on that hot summer day, all those years ago.

For the first time in ages, Reiko wanted to walk through a park on a warm summer night.

ABOUT THE AUTHOR

Tetsuya Honda is one of Japan's best-selling authors with the ongoing crime series featuring Reiko Himekawa, a Homicide Detective with the Tokyo Metropolitan Police. The series has sold roughly 4 million copies in Japan, and is the basis for two TV mini-series, a TV special, and a major theatrical motion picture. Honda lives in Tokyo.